WAINSCOT ON THE HELOISE

J. TERRY ADDINGTON

ILLUSTRATED BY

J. TERRY ADDINGTON

GenZ
The Future of Publishing

To my wife, Tobey, for always being by my side, making sure I don't stumble, and supporting me through all the ups and downs of life. I'd be nothing without you.

HMS HELOISE
Longitudinal Section

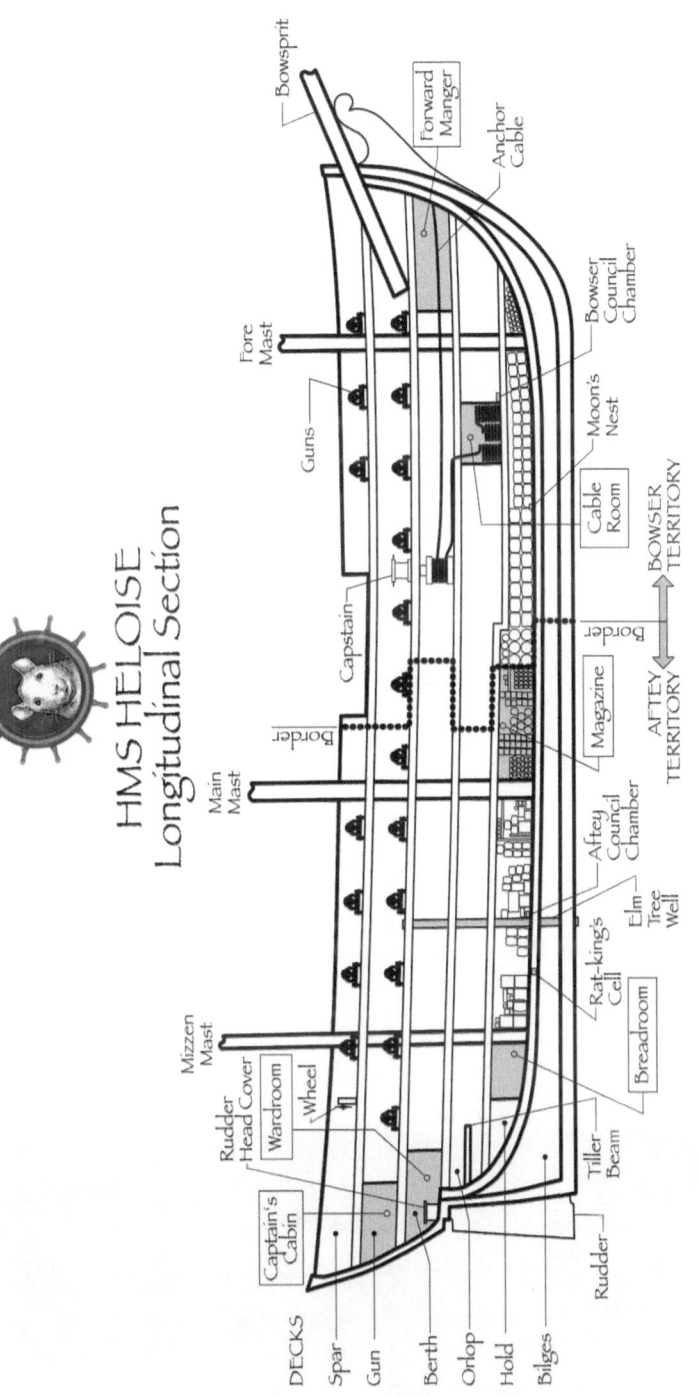

Bowsprit

Forward Manger

Anchor Cable

Bowser Council Chamber

Fore Mast

Guns

Moon's Nest

Cable Room

BOWSER TERRITORY

Captain

Border

Magazine

AFTER TERRITORY

Main Mast

Border

After Council Chamber

Elm Tree Well

Rat-king's Cell

Breadroom

Mizzen Mast

Rudder Head Cover

Wardroom

Wheel

Captain's Cabin

Tiller Beam

Rudder

DECKS

Spar

Gun

Berth

Orlop

Hold

Bilges

CHAPTER 1

HIDER

He was a rat. A skulking, crawling, dirty rat. A thief and a sneak. Vermin.

These are not reflections on his character, but merely a description of what he was. Like his father, and his father's father, he was a scurrier in hidden places and a gnawer in the dark; one of the skin-tailed brotherhood who crept in the shadowy fringes of Man's world, leaving behind droppings, like Morse-code clues to their existence. He skulked, crawled, thieved, and sneaked because those were the ways of the rat, but he was vermin only in the eyes of Man, which were blind to the rat's many admirable qualities.

This particular bundle of ratty traits, both good and bad, was named Wainscot.

Although he was a rat from the tip of his pointed snout to the end of his hairless tail, Wainscot bore little resemblance to the sharp-toothed, yellow-eyed creatures that haunted the pages of gothic novels and skittered in the cobwebbed gloom of children's nightmares. Small and slight, he was a rat who normally kept himself clean and well groomed, but now he appeared ragged and underfed, and his coat was matted and damp. His white-rimmed eyes flicked nervously back and forth in search of something that was not there, the fur on his flanks dancing to the rapid rhythm of his breath.

He crouched, shivering, within a jumble of lumber stacked at the landward end of a weather-worn pier. The weathered planks of the pier, slick from the damp night air, pointed into a mist-shrouded sea like an accusing finger.

Peering out through a narrow gap in the timber pile, Wainscot tried to pierce the gloom with squinted eyes. He strained to see if anything moved in the space between his refuge and the row of buildings that faced the pier, but the shifting blanket of mist did not give up its secrets willingly. The moon, full and fat, did its best to illuminate the night, but succeeded only in casting a ghostly glow through the fog. The cool light painted the scene in subtle variations of grey and white, yet this did little to reveal what might be lurking in that darkness. Wainscot tested the air with his quivering nose. Nothing. The pitchy smell of the planks masked any telltale odours the damp air might have carried.

There—was that a flicker of movement? he wondered. *Had they caught up to him?* He thought he saw a thickening of the shadows in the shape of many dark bodies gliding close to the ground, but he quickly dismissed it. It was too soon – but it was only a matter of time.

He might have wriggled farther into the tangle of timber, but it offered no lasting refuge; only a postponement of the inevitable. They would find him, and when they did, they would drag him from his feeble sanctuary to—

To what? To kill him? Wainscot knew that the penalty for his crime was death, but a small voice in his mind tried to convince him that they would not carry out such an extreme sentence. *They wouldn't actually kill him,* it said. *He was still a member of the clan after all.*

However, another voice insisted that it was the only possible outcome, and he knew that this second, louder voice spoke the truth. His pursuers had not chased him so far, and so tirelessly, to mete out a lesser punishment. They were the C'law, ruthless in their execution of the Clan Council's will, and they had already killed Scuffle, after all. The C'law, short for 'Clanlaw', though no rat used the full name, were the clan's army, police, and executioners. They always carried out their duties with loyal ferocity.

They killed my sister, he thought, and a twist of almost physical pain flashed deep in his chest. He was sure they had—or as sure as he could be without having actually seen her body.

He felt a welling of grief at the thought of her. She had protected him his entire life, but in the end he had been unable to do the same for her. He knew that it was only by blind chance that it had been he who had hurtled through the exit hole first and she who had been dragged back into the darkness, but that knowledge did nothing to ease his growing sense of guilt. He forced down his turbulent emotions, and squirreled them away for re-visiting at a safer time. Wainscot could not afford to let them hinder him now—he would need all of his wits about him if he hoped to live to see another sunrise.

He told himself that he would mourn Scuffle later—if there were to be a later for him—but, try as he might, he could not stop his thoughts from wandering back to the beginning of that day; a day that had started so peacefully, but had ended with the loss of everything he had ever loved.

Chapter 2

Rat-king

"It's a rat-king," said Scuffle. There was no doubt in her voice. "They've had one in there for generations now. Old Lupu says they had it even when her mother was young, and that must have been many seasons ago."

"A rat-king," Wainscot repeated. They had been in the feed bins moments before, and were now settled in the safety of their nest for some comfortable after-breakfast conversation. Neither had any inkling that the day would take Scuffle to her probable death, and Wainscot well beyond the only world he had ever known.

Scuffle and Wainscot were from a litter of twelve. It had been a robust litter, and nine of the twelve had survived the early rigors of childhood, though Scuffle and Wainscot had very little contact with the others. Most rats naturally drifted away from the rest of their siblings. Wainscot and Scuffle staying together was an exception.

Now at the intersection of youth and adulthood, the two had almost reached their full weight. They shared a common colouration —a rich, deep brown, so dark that it was almost black along their backs and flanks, fading to creamy chocolate on their bellies and under their chins. However, Scuffle was a solid, well-muscled rat who demonstrated a remarkable ability to put on weight, while Wainscot hardly seemed to grow at all. Scuffle's fur had the rich sheen of robust health; Wainscot's was dull and lank.

What set them apart from each other even more than their size or the relative glossiness of their fur, however, was the odd discoloured patch that ran along one side of Wainscot's body. A streak of pure white began just behind his right eye and travelled the length of his body, tapering to a point at the base of his tail. It was this strange abnormality —along with his scrawniness and general lack of fighting ability—that had firmly established Wainscot at the bottom of the rigidly maintained pecking order among the young rats of the Nest. All of his would-be playmates had found his stripe endlessly amusing, had devoted considerable energy and imagination to dreaming up cruel nicknames for him, and would, if not for the constant burly presence of Scuffle at his side, have mauled him mercilessly, just for the sport of it. But Wainscot's sister was a fearsome adversary when roused, and nothing affected her more than an assault upon her brother. It was a foolish rat who persisted in troubling Wainscot when Scuffle was within earshot, and since she was never far from him, he was spared the worst of it.

"A rat-king," Wainscot said again, turning the word over in his mind, savouring it. Wainscot valued words, and this was one he had not heard before. "A rat-king. What's a rat-king?"

"It's... um... it's a thing of great wisdom," Scuffle said. "The

Council relies on it. It guides them when they make important decisions. It's as wise as it is because it's been around for so long. You know what Lupu's always saying about age and wisdom—of course she says that, though, being so old and all." Scuffle laughed. "Not that she seems to have any great store of the stuff herself. Always going on about how the C'law of older times used to feed only on the milk of nursing brood-mothers, which made them stronger by keeping their 'ratness' pure, whatever that means. Mad stuff like that. She says that because of this the brood-mothers–"

"You don't know, do you?" said Wainscot.

"What?"

"You don't know what a rat-king is."

"Of course I do," said Scuffle, her voice swollen with mock indignation. "Unlike some rats I could name, I don't make things up. When I say something, it's a fact, not a lie."

"I don't lie," said Wainscot, "I weave."

Wainscot was a storyteller—he loved to build tales from the stuff of his imagination. True, the Council had not named him a clan storyteller yet, but he had a natural gift, and if the rapt attention of his audiences was anything to go by then it was only a matter of time.

"And don't try to change the subject," he said. "Answer my question. What's a rat-king?"

Scuffle rolled her eyes. "I told you—it's very old and very wise."

"That's what it is, but not what it *is*," said Wainscot. "What does it look like?"

"No one really knows."

"You mean *you* don't really know."

"*No one* really knows." Scuffle took a deep breath, and spoke slowly. "They keep it hidden away in the back of the Council chamber and no one sees it, even when they feed it. They just push food to it through a small hole."

"Feed it? You mean it's alive?"

For some reason this made Wainscot uneasy. He had been picturing some sort of totem or talisman that inspired the Council to wiser decisions, but the thought of a breathing, thinking... some-

6

thing… squatting in the darkness and dispensing wisdom was much more frightening.

"Well, I'm not sure if 'alive' is the right word," Scuffle furrowed her brow, considering. "But, it does eat."

"If it eats, then it's alive," said Wainscot firmly.

"Not necessarily. Fire eats wood. Water eats stone. Time eats everything. Are they alive?"

"Well, aren't you the philosopher?" said Wainscot. "But I assume it isn't made of fire or water."

"Probably not," said Scuffle. "But never mind what it isn't, the rat-king *is* old, and it *is* wise."

"Really," said Wainscot, the single word crisply conveying his disbelief.

"Of course. Why else would the Council go to it for advice?"

"I don't know that they do."

"Well there must be some reason why the Law says that it's death for anyone but councilrats or C'law to enter the Council chambers." Scuffle sniffed. "What about that?"

Wainscot looked at his sister for a moment. "And the only explanation of those rules that you can think of is that they have some sort of mysterious beast tucked away in there? And that it secretly runs the clan for them? Sometimes you worry me."

"We could find out." There was a hint of laughter in Scuffle's voice.

"How…" Wainscot began, but stopped when he saw the twinkle in her eye. "Oh no. Definitely not."

Scuffle continued, despite her brother's apprehension. "The Council will be inspecting the new run to the grain bins tonight."

"I said no."

"You know how seldom they leave the chamber. We might not get a chance like this for some time, if ever. It'll be perfectly safe: the chamber will be empty."

"But not unguarded." Wainscot thought that the reasons for not going anywhere near the Council's chamber were painfully obvious, but Scuffle apparently needed to hear them. "The C'law will be outside. They always are."

"I'm not afraid of the C'law. They're just rats."

As far as Wainscot knew, every clan had Clanlaw, and every rat lived in fear of them. He shook his head.

"Why not?" asked Scuffle.

"You said it yourself: the penalty is death."

"Only if we're caught."

In the end it was not any argument of Scuffle's, but Wainscot's very nature that convinced him. Had he been a mouse or a shrew he would have been perfectly content to let the Council continue to govern his affairs as it always had, happy in his ignorance. However, he was not a mouse or a shrew; he was a rat, and curiosity was as much a part of his constitution as the need to eat or mate. So, when night fell he found himself slinking along toward the Council chamber with his sister, all the while quietly cursing his own stupidity.

He and Scuffle had never been in the Council chamber, of course, but he knew that it was the largest single space in the Nest. The Nest was a huge warren of passageways spreading out under the floorboards of a livestock warehouse in a city of the Men. That the Men called the city Halifax, Nova Scotia was unknown to the rats, but they did know that the city spread for unimaginable distances beyond the borders of their little world. They had all heard the stories about daring rats who had ventured out into the wider world, although how many of these were true Wainscot could only guess.

The Council chamber, walled on all four sides by wooden joists that supported the warehouse floor above, was the inner sanctum of the ruling Council, and the heart of Wainscot and Scuffle's clan. The Council, a group of seven rats who each had been selected by the existing members to replace a former councilrat who had died, were the lawmakers and leaders of the clan.

As he and Scuffle manoeuvred their way toward the chamber, he thought about the darker stories that he had heard about the Council. He knew that its members were selected by their fellow councilrats for their demonstrated wisdom—or their ability to survive long enough to *seem* wise—and political cunning, and that, once in place, each councilrat remained in the position until he died. Since the councilrats spent almost all of their time together, discussing clan business, sleeping, and even eating in isolation from the the rest of the Nest, they almost always died within the chamber. Most succumbed to the ailments and infirmities that accompany old age, but dark rumours regularly drifted through the Nest, whispered quietly to avoid the always-listening ears of the C'law. The whisperers told stories about the Council—how the councilrats engaged in various unnatural activities that were never quite described, and how differences of opinion sometimes ended in blood. No clan rat had ever seen a dead councilrat being removed from the chamber, which added fuel to the rumours, and led to speculation about what exactly it was that the councilrats ate, late at night when their sessions ran long. These disturbing tales, along with the ever-vigilant and deadly C'law, usually kept intruders far from the chamber.

"I must be an idiot," Wainscot said quietly to himself as he pattered along behind Scuffle.

Carefully choosing their pathway through the many passageways around the chamber, they skirted the C'law sentry at the entrance without being seen. Scuffle was large, but she could move in absolute silence when necessary; she was particularly light on her feet as they scurried up the passage along one of the outer wall-joists of the chamber. Just over their heads, the boards squeaked and bowed downwards as something heavy walked across the floor above. Light and dust filtered down through the thin gaps between the floorboards.

"Here," said Scuffle, pointing with her nose at a seam between two planks of the joist. She put her forepaws against one of the boards and pushed, using her full weight and thrusting with her hind legs. It bent inward, opening a narrow gap. "There," she said, "You should just be able to squeeze through."

"Me?" Wainscot stared at her, his eyes wide. "Hang on a tick. You never said anything about me going in there alone."

"Well, obviously I can't hold the wall for myself, and you don't have the weight to do it. Anyway, I'm far too big to get through that crack," said Scuffle. She gave Wainscot what he could only assume was supposed to be a comforting lift of her brows. "Don't worry; I'll be here to let you out after you've had a look around."

9

"I'm not worried about getting out; I'm worried about being in there by myself."

"Mouse," said Scuffle.

"Mouse yourself." Fear made Wainscot's response harsher than he intended. "I don't see you volunteering to go in."

"I told you –"

"Yes, yes." Wainscot crouched down, collecting his thoughts and steeling himself for what he now recognised as inevitable; he would be going into the chamber. Wanting to postpone it for a few moments more, he asked, "How did you discover that the board was loose?"

"Actually, I got the idea the other day when I was giving that rascal Chinhair a thrashing," said Scuffle. "Remember?"

Wainscot laughed. "If ever a rat deserved a good walloping, it's Chinhair."

Scuffle joined Wainscot in laughing at the memory. "He tried to take a piece out of your bum," she said, "and I had to toss him around a little. Well, I slammed him into the wall—we were in the Water Run, if you recall—and the plank shifted. In fact it moved enough for Chinhair to bolt through."

"That's how he got away," said Wainscot. "I remember."

Scuffle nodded her head. "Well, that got me to thinking. So when you were asleep I came down here to do some investigating, and sure enough there is a way in; but only one. As soon as I saw the size of the gap I knew you were the rat for the job. You're always telling your little tales of adventure and derring-do, so this should be your sort of thing entirely."

Wainscot snorted. He was still afraid, but a pinch of excitement now seasoned his trepidation. Scuffle had a point—none of the heroes of his stories would have shied away from such a tempting adventure. Still, this was the real world, where foolish decisions often led to dire consequences.

"So," Scuffle tilted her head at Wainscot, "are you ready? I'm getting tired of holding this."

Wainscot snorted again, but took a breath and squeezed through. The gap closed with a faint creak behind him.

He tested the air with his nose, letting the myriad scents tell him what they could about the layout and contents of this secret domain of the Council. There were the odours he expected—cattle waste; Man's sweat, tobacco, leather and damp wool; the resinous smell of the building itself; rat fur, feces and urine—but laying over these, like a pox-riddled blanket, was another that made him uneasy. It reminded him of the lingering stench of death, but there was something odd about it: something rat, and yet not rat. He suspected that it might be the stink of madness.

All he knew with certainty was that there was something in the chamber with him, and that it was simply... wrong.

"Can you see it?" Scuffle's whispered words squeezed through the hair-thin crack.

Wainscot was so startled that he almost loosed a dribble of urine. A single drop would have left a potent signature and would have told the Council who had been in the chambers as clearly as if he had been caught red-pawed.

"Shut up!" he whispered back. "Have you no sense?"

He heard Scuffle draw breath to reply, but she said nothing more.

Wainscot looked around. The entrance to the chamber lay some six or seven rat-lengths away, but there was no sign of any C'law guard. The floor was littered with the remnants of past meals—grain husks, insect carapaces, and the bones of small mammals and birds. Rat bones were scattered about. Ribs, long-bones, and skulls with staring hollow eyes and wicked chisel incisors gleamed yellow in the dim light. Some, Wainscot noticed with a chill, bore signs of having been gnawed.

Shuddering, he stepped further into the space. There was a shad-owed opening at the rear, leading to a chamber within the chamber. He approached it cautiously.

The stink was strong from within.

He eased into the inner chamber. It was almost too dark to see, but he could make out something—a thickening of shadow deep in the gloom. It looked like a nest, but was larger than a rat's nest should be. Wainscot's tail dragged across a loose piece of bone with a small rattle, and something in the nest stirred. He froze, his heartbeat and shallow breathing seeming unnaturally loud in the darkness. Whether it could hear him or not, whatever it was that lurked in the shadows continued to move.

After a moment, Wainscot saw a dark shape slowly rise from the tangle of the nest. He stared in horror at a large mass, lumpy and shifting, that seemed to be made up of the usual rat parts—but far too many of them. He saw the delicate petals of ears, a tracery of whiskers like cobwebs in the gloom, and the gleam of eyes. Many eyes.

Fascinated, despite his fear, Wainscot took another step forward. He was certain that he made no sound, but the eyes shifted, seeming to fix on him through the darkness.

The thing screamed.

It was a hideous sound, raw with fury, pain and writhing madness barreling out of many throats at once. Starting low and gravely, it rose quickly in both pitch and volume until it filled Wainscot's head and rasped painfully across his nerves.

Horrified, he scrambled out of the inner chamber and bolted to where Scuffle waited, scattering bones and detritus in his wake. She held the crack open for him. How she had the strength of will to stay at her post when every instinct must have been driving her to run, he could not guess, but he knew he would be grateful to her until the end of his days.

Together they ran back up the passage down which they had so recently crept in silence, but this time, spurred on by unreasoning fear, they made no effort to conceal their passing. Before their blind panic could take them too far, however, Scuffle managed to rein in enough of her scattered wits to slide to a halt.

"Hold up, Wainscot," she hissed. "Stop."

He stopped and stood nose-to-nose with her, quivering with the need to keep running.

"What? What?" he said, his voice drawn taught. "Let's go. Come on. We can't... What about the C'law? We've got to leave." The words tumbled out of him. His eyes darted back and forth in a frenzy, and every hair on his body stood erect.

"Think for a moment. Think," said Scuffle, holding his eyes with hers. "We can't just run blindly. They don't know who we are. If we can make it to the nesting chambers we'll be all right. The C'law haven't even started to come after us yet."

A sudden clatter of clawed feet behind them proved her words wrong.

They took off again, careening through the dark maze of the Nest. Passage followed passage, and the sound of pursuit grew behind them.

We still might make it, thought Wainscot, trying to clear the fog of panic from his mind. No one but the many-eyed shape in the Council chamber seen them. They just had to remain unseen until they could lose themselves in the crowded anonymity of the nesting chambers.

A dark shape emerged from a side passage ahead, and he knew that all was lost. It was Chinhair, and he had seen them. Worse still, he had recognised Wainscot. Chinhair opened his mouth to speak, but before he could utter a sound he was thrust aside by the two large rats who emerged from the passage behind him. They were C'law.

Wainscot's claws gouged curls from the wooden floor as he scrabbled to change direction and run down another side passage, Scuffle close on his heels.

They angled away from the safety of the nesting chambers and headed into an unfamiliar part of the Nest. Wainscot knew that if they kept running they would eventually reach one of the many ratholes that exited onto the vast open space of the outdoor stock pens, and he was aware that their life in the Nest had come to an end. Whatever the future held for them, they would find it beyond the walls of the only world they had ever known. His heart sank at the thought, but he also felt a pulse of excitement. He was afraid of the unknown, and the dangers it might offer, but he was a rat, and rats are curious creatures, drawn to adventure.

Wainscot could both hear and feel the weight of the pursuit as the floor beneath him reverberated with the rhythm of the C'law's pounding feet. He could not tell if they were gaining, but knew that he could not maintain this frantic pace for much longer. *If they did not find an exit from the Nest soon...*

There—was that a flash of moonlight through a narrow opening a few strides ahead?

He threw himself through the small hole and into the open air.

He was out. In the world. In Man's world.

The fresh bite of the night air urged him to keep running, but he stopped and turned to wait for his sister.

Where was she? Wasn't she right behind him?

He took a step back toward the hole, horribly aware of how exposed he was in the bright moonlight. His long shadow stretched away from him across the hard-packed earth, like an arrow identifying him to any predators that might be prowling the night. Before he could take a second step there was a resounding thump against the other side of the wall, as though a large body had slammed into it at high speed.

Scuffle's face appeared in the hole for a fleeting moment. Her eyes, wide and white-rimmed, held his for a heartbeat, and then she was gone, pulled back into the darkness. She screamed in pain or fear—to Wainscot it was a far more horrible sound than the shriek of the thing in the Council chamber. Then, as suddenly as it had begun, the scream stopped.

Wainscot stood in place, shifting rapidly from foot to foot as warring instincts fought for control of his body. Love and duty were telling him to rush back through the hole to help his sister, but he could not move. Fear and common sense insisted that he should continue running away, because there was little he could do for Scuffle if he did go back. Still, he did not move.

There was a rustle of movement from inside the hole, and rat's face appeared at the opening.

It was not Scuffle.

Wainscot turned tail and fled into the night.

CHAPTER 3

A ROPE IN THE MIST

From his refuge in the timbers, Wainscot peered out across the quay at the ramshackle row of buildings lined up along its edge. Night and mist rendered the structures grey and indistinct.

He was waiting for the C'law. It had taken him some time to muster the courage for the dash across the exposed expanse of the pier towards his current hiding space, but he knew that his pursuers, confident in their numbers, would not hesitate. Like flame running over oily water, they would stream unchecked across the open space, and into his fragile sanctuary.

When he escaped from the Nest he had hoped that the C'law would not take the chase out into the open world; but almost as soon as he had begun to run again, he had heard them pattering from the hole behind him. They had not lingered over Scuffle, but had poured out into the night, seemingly unafraid of its dangers. They had run without any word, silent but for the rumble of their feet on the hard dirt. It had sounded as though every rat in the Nest had joined the hunt, though he had not risked slowing to look back.

His desperate flight had taken him along alleys, across wide roads all but empty in the night, and through the crumbling foundations of many buildings. A mist had risen while he had been running, but it had not been thick enough to mask his trail; although he had lost his pursuers several times, they had always found his scent again. He had rested for a precious few breaths when he could, flopping panting to the ground, but the knowledge that the C'law were close behind drove him back to his feet again and again.

While running, he had begun to pick up an unfamiliar scent. Faint at first, it had grown stronger by the heartbeat. It was an alien smell—a sharp tang seasoned with the stink of rot—and its very strangeness had spoken to him of unknown worlds that lay beyond the reach of the C'law. It was the smell of the sea, and in his ignorance Wainscot had rushed toward it as though it might offer some sanctuary.

And now he was trapped. Trapped between the teeth of the C'law and the unknown, unknowable vastness of the sea. One look told him that there was nowhere left to run; a huge, impassable... something... lay beyond the edge of the pier. It was water, he knew, but he had never imagined that water could be so... big. He had no experience of the sea—no perception of its depth or breadth or ferocity—but he knew that he could not cross it. His nose had led him to his death.

So he waited, hidden amongst the timber, unsure of what he would do when his pursuers arrived. He thought of Scuffle. *Had she turned on the C'law? Had she sacrificed herself so that he might escape?* If so, it had been in vain, for he was now out of running room.

He tried to keep alive a faint hope that Scuffle had survived. She was a tough, capable rat. She might have fought their pursuers. She might have escaped. He could not simply accept that she was dead. However, when he remembered the two C'law he had seen emerging from behind Chinhair, almost all of his hope died. He had recognised one of them—a formidable rat named Dayrunner, with a reputation for brutal enforcement of the council's rule—and knew that there was little chance that the C'Law had shown Scuffle any mercy.

Wainscot was almost certain that he would never be able to ask Scuffle why she had not followed him through the exit hole, but for the present he did not care. All that mattered was that she was gone. Even if she were still alive - and he clung desperately to the small chance that she was - he would have to face his new life without her strong, cheerful presence by his side; no more good-natured ribbing, no more roughhousing, no more midnight raids on the clan food-stores, and no warm, comforting body nestled close to his through cold winter nights. He was alone, and it was almost enough to make him crawl out into the light, expose his throat, and wait for the C'law.

However, when the black tide of the pursuit finally appeared and fanned out across the pier toward him, Wainscot broke cover, and ran again.

He skittered away from the land, making his way out along the pier on a path that led nowhere. He felt slightly safer hugging the edge of the pier, and ran with his heaving left side actually overhanging the drop. Far below, the water lapped quietly under its covering blanket of mist.

The rushing C'law wave followed him onto the pier. There seemed to be hundreds of them. *How could there be so many? Why were they so concerned about him, one insignificant little rat?*

Wainscot passed between the edge of the pier and a large black bollard that loomed over him like an iron mushroom, streaked red and white with rust and seabird dung. A thick rope, frayed and black from use, ran up and away from the bollard, and disappeared into the mist.

Wainscot had no way of understanding what he was seeing, but the rope was a mooring line that tied a ship to the pier. He did not know what a ship was, nor did he have a word for it. All he saw was an avenue of escape.

A quick jump was all it took for Wainscot to cling onto the rope and scurry away from the pier. The rope was heavy and stretched iron-taught by the weight of the ship, which made for an easy climb. He scrambled up as quickly as he could, spurred on by the knowledge that the leading C'law were only a few tail-lengths behind.

Something appeared out of the murk ahead, and Wainscot's heart fell—a large metal disk, pitted by rust, blocked his way. The rope passed through a hole in its centre. Wainscot could not know it, but Men had placed the tin disk there for the very purpose of stopping rats like him from boarding the ship. It was an impassable barrier. Once again, he was trapped.

He did not hesitate, instead launching himself toward the top of the disk. Astoundingly, his front claws hooked over the disk's rim, and he pulled forward. The sharp edge of the metal sliced into the thin skin over his ribcage as he balanced precariously on the top, his back feet scrabbling uselessly for purchase. For a couple of remarkable heartbeats he maintained equilibrium, but then the disk began to rotate sideways, pivoting around the axis of the rope. He rode the accelerating arc down, horribly aware that it would drop him into the sea when it passed the horizontal.

The knife-edge of the disk cut deeper into his chest as he slid toward the sea. Then, just as he fell, one of his front claws hooked onto a pinhole rusted through the thin metal, and he swung down below the disk. Pain streaked down his foreleg from the outraged claw, but he maintained his fragile hold, dangling above the void.

Staring back down the rope he saw that the first of his pursuers had reached the disk—Dayrunner was amongst them. Lined up on the rope, they looked down at him, startled and uncertain, but Wain-scot knew that it would only be a moment before one of them leapt at him to drag him down into the darkness. It would mean death for both of them, but many of the C'law would not hesitate to sacrifice themselves for the good of the clan.

Fuelled by panic, Wainscot swung his tail for momentum, twisting his body back up on itself. With the rasp of claws on metal, he pressed both back feet against the shipward side of the disk, preparing to jump. His only hope was that he could reach the bottom of the rope above him and hook his claws into it, but it was a slim hope at best. If he missed he would tumble into the cold sea below.

He pushed off with a spasm of energy.

And missed the cable by a tail's width, his front claws brushing through the loose strands poking like whiskers from beneath the rope. Wainscot dropped into the gloom with a squeal.

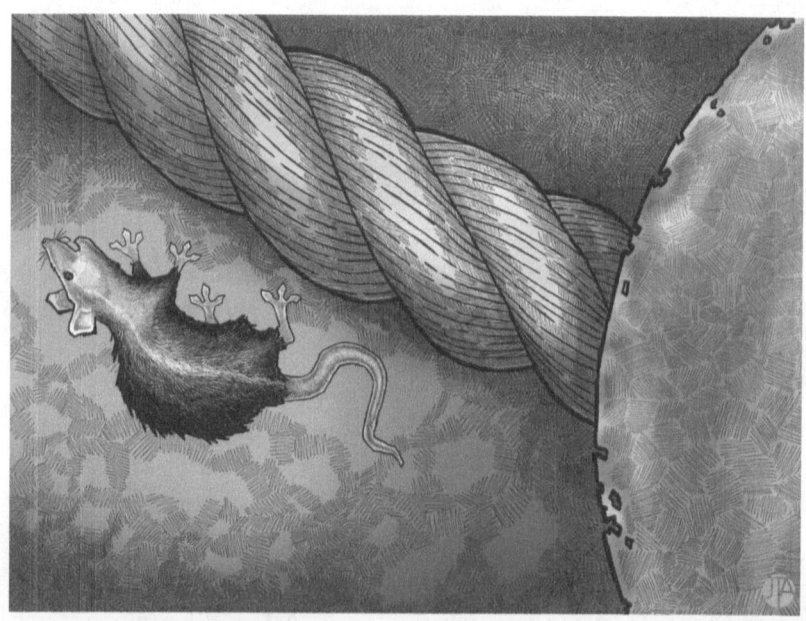

CHAPTER 4

AN INNOCENT ABOARD

S he was the *HMS Heloise*, a thirty-eight-gun frigate of His
Majesty's Royal Navy, stationed in the Americas to remind the
fledgling—but ambitious and increasingly effective—US Navy that
Britannia still ruled the seas.

It was May of 1813, and war was raging between Britain and her
troublesome cousin, the United States of America.

The *Heloise* was lying in Halifax harbour on a well-earned respite
from her martial duties along the coast, where she had been plying her

trade in the cold Atlantic waters, fulfilling her duty to remind the upstart Americans that they ventured from the safety of their harbours at their peril.

One hundred fifty-two feet from bow to stern, not including the length of her bowsprit, the *Heloise* had a draft of thirteen and a half feet. The tallest of her three masts towered one hundred thirty feet above her deck, and her gundeck bristled with 18-pounders. Since she was a frigate, that flexible jack-of-all-trades of the fleet, she was possessed of a fine balance of speed, agility and firepower. Sleek and fast, she could, under a skilled captain, run with the best of them, and no vessel short of a massive ship-of-the-line could stand toe-to-toe with her when she ran out her guns and loosed her broadsides.

Sailing the *Heloise*, manning her guns, and carrying out the myriad activities needed to keep a large number of Men alive at sea was a complement of three hundred and eleven crew, officers and marines. Some of these were unwilling landsmen or merchant sailors forced into service at the point of a bayonet, some were cleaned-faced boys just beginning their careers as officers, and some were seasoned hands who had spent many more years at sea than on land. But all of them—green and weathered alike—were subject to the absolute authority of her lordly captain, pacing his quarterdeck.

The *Heloise* was also home to a surprising number of non-Human passengers. Cattle, sheep, goats and pigs—fresh meat for the crew on their long ocean voyages—were crammed below decks, and chickens clucked and fretted in their wooden coops on her main deck. There were pets too: dogs, cats, and more exotic creatures from far-flung ports. During her service the ship had housed various parrots, cockatoos, parakeets and birds of paradise; monkeys that had swung nimbly through her rigging, shaming even the most agile of topmen; and lizards that had lived in wicker baskets tucked into corners of her holds. Most remarkably, in a brief and disastrous episode, a misguided midshipman had even managed to keep a half-grown Nile crocodile hidden in her bilges.

And, despite the ongoing efforts of her crew to keep her free of unwelcome passengers, the *Heloise* was also home to hundreds upon hundreds of uninvited tenants: the rats.

W ainscot lay stunned and winded. It took a moment for him to realise that he was not dead. He lifted his head, throbbing and fuzzy, and tried to look about, but the effort almost made him sick. Everything within sight was hazy and indistinct; he found it difficult to focus on anything. He pulled himself shakily to his feet and almost toppled from his perch—a narrow wooden shelf that ran along the hull of the ship some twenty lengths above the surface of the water.

When he had made his futile leap to reach the rope, Wainscot had fallen to bounce against the ship's side, delivering himself a stunning crack to the head in the process. His senseless body had then flopped bonelessly down the slope of the hull, but instead of dropping into the sea, it had, by blind luck, fetched up against the narrow timber toehold called the 'chains'.

Because of the drifting mist, he could no longer see the rope. He also could not see the C'law, which meant, he hoped, that he was hidden from them as well. *Did they watch me fall and wait for a splash that never came?* he wondered, *and are they even now steeling themselves to jump after me?* He did not know how long he had lain unconscious, but he was certain the C'law would soon be attempting the leap, if they had not done so already.

Wainscot cocked his head to one side, listening for some sound from above, but all that he could hear were the squeaks and groans made by the ship and the wooden pier as they muttered to each other across the short stretch of water. He could hear nothing of the C'law.

He took a wobbling couple of steps along the chains. As he did so he heard a thump and a splash from behind. There was another thump, another splash, and then two more in quick succession. The C'law were leaping at the ship and bouncing off its side, dropping into the water. Wainscot was aware that if one of them were lucky enough to land on the chains, it would mean a quick end for him.

Wainscot ran carefully along the platform, looking for some path up and away from his precarious perch. The C'law were relentless; he knew that he had to put more than the space of a single leap between

23

them if he hoped to live to see the morning. As he approached the end of the chains a heavy rope appeared through the mist ahead. It was within easy jumping distance, and he was soon climbing quickly up the anchor cable, through the hawsehole, and into the darkness of the ship's interior.

Once inside, he crouched under the heavy bulk of the cable, sniffing the air and peering into the gloom. Oddly, the scents and sounds that greeted him were comfortingly familiar. He was in the forward manger of the ship, and the night noises of the livestock and the tang of straw, dung, and urine transported him for a moment back to the safety of the Nest. The soft lowing of cattle, a constant part of his old life, soothed and lulled him.

Wainscot knew that this was not the place to sleep, but exhaustion, exacerbated by the effects of the recent blow to his head, threatened to overwhelm him. Only moments before he had been in full flight—fear keeping him in motion despite his fatigue. Now he was incapable of any movement. Wainscot mustered the last of his strength to curl himself into a tight ball, his tail across his eyes.

If the Claw find me I hope they kill me without waking me, he thought as he spiralled down into sleep.

He dreamt of Scuffle.

"If you stay there, one of the cats'll have you for breakfast, no error."

What an odd thing for Scuffle to say, he thought. They were curled together in their nest, happy and comfortable after a good meal. It was the best time for stories, and Wainscot was telling one of Scuffle's favourites: the one about Chewtooth and the Vixen[1]. He had just reached the part where Chewtooth has entered the Vixen's lair, when Scuffle interrupted him. Her voice was strange—higher than usual and oddly accented.

"What?" he said in a bleary mumble.

"The cats," she said again. "They'll find you here."

He started awake, instantly alert and moving. Before taking more than a few steps, he stopped and gathered himself. The noise behind him was not at all threatening—it sounded like soft, pleasant laughter.

He turned, and there, standing before him, was the ugliest rat he had ever seen. She might have been the ugliest *anything* he had ever seen. She was about his age, but even smaller and her fur, what little there was of it, was darker than his, more black than brown. Her skin showed through her fur in scaly patches, drawn so tightly over her skull that her lips pulled back from her teeth in a grin, and her eyes bulged. She looked as though she had just seen something very surprising, and he suspected that she always looked that way. He imagined that her too-large hindquarters and too-bony shoulders would make her clumsy and comical when she moved.

Her laugh, however, was lovely.

"If that's the best you can do, then you're lucky I'm *not* a cat," she said. "I would've had you before you'd gone a step—assuming I'd been considerate enough to wake you 'stead of just gobbling you up while you slept."

Wainscot blinked, saying nothing.

The stranger continued, "Don't they have cats where you come from? Imagine sleeping in the open like that. I swear I've never seen anything so foolish. How you slept through the weighing of the anchor is beyond me."

Her tone was sharp, and her words derisive, but there was a lift to her voice and glint in her goggle-eyes that took some of the sting out of them. Still, Wainscot bristled. He had been through too much to have some spindly lump of a rat have sport at his expense.

"I had a bad night" was all that he could manage to say.

"Well it's daytime now, so let's get a move on," she said. "The cats are most active at night, but that doesn't mean you're safe from them now."

Her self-confidence was unsettling. Surely something so ugly should be skulking in the shadows, not standing boldly before him in broad daylight, giving orders.

With a sudden shock, Wainscot realised that the floor was moving under his feet.

He squealed and skittered out from under the cable, scrambling up on top of it. The action caused a jagged streak of pain across his ribs as the ragged cut opened again.

He then noticed that the cable was also moving, swaying gently back and forth. With another squeal, he jumped back to the floor.

The stranger began to laugh again, much louder this time.

"Well, that was interesting," she said when she managed to regain her breath. Wainscot was hopping from leg-to-leg in agitation.

"What's happening?" he spluttered.

"What do you mean?"

"Is the building falling down?" Wainscot was struggling to control his panic.

"The building falling...?" She furrowed her brow. "Oh, I see... No, we're under sail. The ship's moving across the water. Haven't you ever been on a ship before?"

"No," he said. "And what's a ship?"

"Ah, this should be fun," said the stranger. "Let's get you somewhere safer, and then we can talk. Come with me, but be quiet and move with care. I don't know how things are where you come from, but on the *Heloise* we're always cautious. There are cats, and Men, and... others... to be avoided." She slipped past him and jumped up onto the heavy anchor cable. "Come along, then."

The word '*Heloise*' puzzled Wainscot, but there was so much here he did not understand that he decided to save his questions for later. He followed the strange rat as she scurried nimbly up the rope ahead of him, and realised that he had been entirely mistaken in assuming that she would be ungainly when underway. There was a gracefulness to her movements that was quite beautiful to watch, and she flowed along the cable as though she were a part of it. From that moment on, he decided, he would never think of her as ugly again.

They crouched close together in the stranger's nest beneath several stacked water barrels. It was fortunate that he was only slightly larger than she, as the one entry to the space was tight. The nest, lined with well-chewed wood fibres, was cosy, warm and inviting.

They could hear the heavy footfalls of Men—sailors, she called them—clumping about, but their hiding place was deep within a huge stack of casks, and they were as safe as rats could ever hope to be.

She offered him some of the desiccated fruit rinds that lay in a curling heap at the back of the nest. They were lime, she told him, and they were delicious. As he ate she tended to the cut across his chest. It looked more serious than it was. She worked for long moments with her tongue to clean the rust fragments from it.

Wainscot's thoughts drifted to the countless times he had spent with Scuffle in similar comfortable nests. He felt a deep stab of loss.

"What is this place?" he asked, making an effort to shake off the mantle of melancholy that was settling over him.

"She's called the *Heloise*," said the tatty rat, looking up from her work. She seemed to think he would know who 'she' was.

"Who's called the *Heloise*?"

"Not too bright, are you? The ship's called the *Heloise*."

"So this building is a ship?"

She sighed. "She's not exactly a building," she told him, and explained that a ship was similar to a building, but one that floated on the water and moved from place to place at the whim of the Men who lived on her. Wainscot thought that this was clearly ridiculous, but he did not tell her so.

"It's a she?" he asked, "and you named her?"

"Not us—them."

"Them?"

"Them." The stranger gestured upward with her snout. "The Men, stupid."

Wainscot considered this for a moment.

"How do you know what the Men named her?" he asked. "You can't understand them, can you?"

"Of course not," she said. "What an idea."

She lowered her head and thought for a moment before continuing. "I really don't know how we know her name, but we do. We always have."

"So she's the *Heloise*," said Wainscot, "and you are...?"

"I'm a *Heloise* too." The strange rat spoke slowly, with exaggerated patience. "We call ourselves by the name of our ship, so all of the rats aboard are *Heloise*. It's how we identify each other if we ever meet rats from other ships. I'm a *Heloise*, a rat from the *Shannon*'s a *Shannon*, one from the *Victory*'s a *Victory*. You understand?"

"Yes, but what I meant was –"

"Good. So I'm a *Heloise* and you're a Lander." There was a hard bite to the word. She used it like a tooth.

"A Lander, how nice. But what I meant was: what's your name?"

"Oh, I'm Moonpatch." She lowered her eyes, and spoke quietly. "Most rats call me Scraps, because of the way I look. I don't like it very much." Then, regaining her confidence, she raised her eyes again. They flashed a challenge at him, daring him to call her by the hated name

"I'll call you Moon, then," he said, quickly. "And I'm Wainscot."

Moon brightened. "May your voyages be calm, Wainscot."

After a brief hesitation, Wainscot said, "And yours, Moon." It felt like the correct response.

They both rose, and stood face to face, nose touching nose. She looked at him steadily for a few moments, her eyes holding his, unblinking—she seemed to be weighing him, judging him. Then she released his gaze and looked past him at the curve of the barrel arching

over them. The light was dim in the nest, but it was sufficient to illuminate the beads of fresh water sweating from the wood. She lifted her head and licked at the droplets.

Has she reached some sort of decision about me? Wainscot wondered. He opened his mouth to ask, but she spoke before he could say anything.

"I knew you for a Lander the moment I saw you," she said, speaking rapidly. The poise and brashness she had displayed until this point had suddenly, startlingly, disappeared. The confident, prickly, sarcastic rat of a few moments ago was replaced by a pup, uncertain and anxious to please. "You're built a little differently from ship rats, and your colour is different. You're brown, and we're much darker. And there's that white mark. Does everyone in your clan have it? I think it looks good, makes you stand out. I stand out too, but there's nothing good about that. You also carry the smell of the land in your fur. You smell of earth and green, growing things instead of pitch and salt. I can also smell what you've been eating. You've never had a ship's biscuit in your life, have you? Well you will soon enough, and they're delicious.

"Am I the first Lander you've ever met?" asked Wainscot.

"No, you're not the first Lander I've seen on this ship, but..." She seemed reluctant to continue. "...but they died almost as soon as they came aboard."

Wainscot blinked nervously.

"Anyway, I won't let you die," Moon promised. "I can show you where to go for food and water, how to stay clear of the cats, how to get from one part of the ship to another without being seen by the Men—that sort of thing. There's very little space to spare on a ship, and what little there is we share with the Men. There are also the cats and the monkey. The cats are always dangerous, and the monkey is... well, a monkey."

Wainscot had no idea what a monkey was, but did not interrupt.

The words tumbled out of Moon in a breathless torrent. "When I visit the breadroom I generally travel using the rigging to avoid the others on the way. Sometimes I see the monkey up there. The other Bowser rats mostly have their nests between mine and the galley, so

29

the rigging is the only way to get past them without being seen. I'll wager I know the upper parts of the ship better than any rat who's ever lived. Things are clearer up there—safer too. Neither the Bowsers nor the Afties venture up there, but you always have to watch for the monkey."

As she rambled on, Wainscot stopped trying to follow the sense of her words and considered her. *She's an outcast*, he decided. *She survives on the fringes of rat society and regards everyone with suspicion, avoiding them as she does the cats, the Men, and the... monkey.* He did not think her isolation was self-imposed; the warmth with which she had accepted him spoke of a desire for companionship.

With a flash of insight, Wainscot suddenly realised why Moon's manner had undergone such an odd transformation—she was lonely and wanted a friend, but she was out of practice. She did not know how to talk to a friend, and she was simply nervous. Wainscot was touched. He decided that he liked this strange, shabby little rat very much.

"Shall I tell you a story?" he asked. The question stopped the flow of her words like a cork thrust into the mouth of an overturned bottle.

"I..." Moon was actually shaking with the effort of talking. She seemed bewildered by the question. "Yes, I suppose..."

"I like to think I'm rather good at it—storytelling I mean, "Wainscot said. "I'd always intended to be a clan storyteller, though I doubt I will now. I'd like to tell you one of the tales of Chewtooth. Do you know about Chewtooth on the *Heloise*?"

"I... I haven't really heard a story for a very long time," she said, "I remember something about a rat named Sure-not-truth. He was called the Liar. He might be the same."

"That's him—Chewtooth the Liar. Or Chewtooth One-ear. I'd heard that all rats tell stories about Chewooth. Maybe it's true. In any case, long before Chewtooth settled with the Underwalk Clan, he found himself in a difficult situation, and it took all of his cunning to save himself—but his cunning alone wasn't enough, as you'll soon hear."

They lay down, side by side, and Wainscot began the tale of Chewtooth and the Ginger Twins.

CHAPTER 5

CHEWTOOTH AND THE GINGER TWINS

In his early days, Chewtooth was a traveller without a destination. He wasn't going anywhere; he was just going. He would have many adventures in his long life, but this was the first of them.

On one occasion, he followed his wandering paws until they led him to the nest of a clan that lived in an abandoned mill perched above a small but swift-moving river. As he neared, he saw ratways through the long grass around the mill, but they appeared to be unused. Creeping vegetation was reclaiming them, and it was with some difficulty that he forced his way through, seeking the shelter of the mill for the night.

The mill stood on a small island that had once been reached by a stone bridge. The bridge had given up its battle against the elements long ago, and had partially collapsed, so now the only way to the island—short of swimming—was by the two wooden planks laid across the gap. The planks ended directly before the huge oak horse-doors, now closed, that were the only way into the old building. Sealed, barred and windowless, the stone mill was accessible only to those animals small enough to slip beneath the great doors. Rats were the largest of the creatures that could squeeze through the narrow gap.

An ancient fir tree, which must have been just a sapling when the mill was in operation, had grown up next to the building, near the doors. As it had grown, its great trunk had forced its way through the wall. The living bark of the tree now bulged over the stone, and held it firmly between lips of wood, completely sealing the crack it had made.

Chewtooth arrived at the gap in the bridge and started across one of the planks. They were each a little wider than a single rat, and separated by a distance of about six lengths. He'd reached the halfway point when a pair of voices hissed as one from behind him, "Tasty, tasty. Look what we have here."

Chewtooth knew the sibilant tone of a cat when he heard it, and without risking a look back, he bolted for the far end of the narrow bridge. The plank bounced as heavy bodies bounded onto it behind him. In a heartbeat he was across the gap, and as he flashed under the door he heard the scrabble of claws on the gravel outside.

There was an angry growl. The two voices from beyond the door said, "Come outside, rat. Come out and play. We'll be gentle, we promise."

A paw—ginger, scarred, and very large—thrust through the space beneath the door and slashed the air with hooked yellow claws. Chewtooth leapt forward and sank his teeth into the paw, jumping clear before the raking claws could find him. The cat howled, and the paw withdrew.

"You're very brave, with all that wood between us," said the twin voices. "Come outside and we'll show you how to play properly. We'll have all sorts of fun."

Looking around, Chewtooth found that he was not alone in the large, dimly lit room. Two rats cowered in a far corner. He licked cat blood from his lips, and approached them. They were both painfully thin, the emaciation of their bodies reflected in their eyes. They were terrified – but whether of him or the cats he wasn't sure.

"Cats can be very annoying, can't they?" he said, trying his best to sound nonthreatening.

One of them, emboldened by Chewtooth's friendly tone, said shakily, "I don't think anyone's ever managed to get a tooth into one of them before. No one who's lived to talk about it, at any rate."

"They're a problem, are they? How many are there?" Chewtooth asked.

The two millrats were too frightened of the fit, healthy Chewtooth to answer his questions. Instead they volunteered to take him to their Council.

As they led him into the gloom of the mill, one of them summoned the courage to ask him about his ear. Now, Chewtooth had only one ear. He hadn't lost it in a fight or by some accident – he'd just never had it. There was only a smooth unbroken curve of fur where his left ear should have been

"Never had it, and never missed it," said Chewtooth.

His new companions led him to the heart of the mill and summoned their Council, who arrived, hesitant and bemused. There were six of them, and they were easily as thin as his two guides. Other rats began to slip into the room, until he found himself surrounded on all sides by skeletal creatures who regarded him with dull, hopeless eyes. It took but a few moments for Chewtooth to learn that the cats —there were two of them—relentlessly kept the clan trapped in the mill.

"They arrived at the end of the cold season, and they've been patrolling the bridge ever since," explained the oldest of the councilrats. "They're twins. Horrible great ginger beasts. Identical in every way, even down to the fact that they've each lost an eye—the only difference between them is the side they lost the eye on. They stay out near the bridge. There's always at least one of them, but usually both."

Since the bridge offered the only way to leave the island, it was a simple matter for the cats to keep the millrats from venturing out to forage for food. At first the rats had tried tricking the cats, or attempting to sneak past them during the day when they were the least wary. However, after losing several of their number, they had given up. They had been forced to rely on whatever food they could find within the mill, but there were too many of them, and the building was soon stripped of everything edible. They were now living solely on the few insects that made their way into the mill, and were on the verge of starvation.

"Since there are many of you, and only two of them, couldn't you rush them and bring them down under the weight of your numbers?" asked Chewtooth. "Some of you would die, sure – but as it stands right now, all of you will."

"We might have once," said the oldest council rat, "but now we're too weak to try. We're beaten and we know it. We're merely waiting to die."

"I might be able to help you," said Chewtooth, "But I won't be able to do it alone. I'll need one of you with me, and it'll have to be someone who not only has the nerve to face the cats in the open, but also looks enough like me to pass as my twin—at least to a cat."

The millrats said nothing, continuing to stare at him with lustre-less eyes. Then a voice from the back of the crowd spoke up.

"I'll join you."

A rat shouldered his way forward to stand by Chewtooth's side. The newcomer did indeed resemble Chewtooth. He must once have been massive, but hunger had carved away at him until he was roughly the same size as Chewtooth, and his fur was exactly the same rich brown, lacking only its healthy sheen. The only difference between the two that would have been obvious to a cat was that the millrat had two ears, and Chewtooth only one.

Chewtooth walked a circle around the other rat, appraising him. "You'll do," he said. "What's your name?"

"Barge," said the large millrat.

"We'll have to do something about that ear, Barge. Come with me."

He led the other rat to where the massive bole of the fir thrust into the building. The trunk of the aged tree was armoured with thick, creviced bark, rough and scaly, and here and there sluggish streams of resin oozed across its surface like amber blood. Using his forepaws, Chewtooth pushed the side of Barge's head against the gummy discharge.

The larger rat started to pull back, but then relaxed and allowed Chewtooth to move his head against the thick sap until the area around his right ear was sticky and matted. Chewtooth released him and examined the ear. He pressed it flat against Barge's skull with one paw. It stayed down, flat and smooth, glued in place by the resin. Then he rubbed his shoulder vigorously against the side of Barge's head. Soon hairs from Chewtooth's shoulder completely covered the area, stuck fast in the resin, and Barge's pink ear had disappeared under a layer of brown fur. He was now as one-eared as Chewtooth. The two rats were now as close to twins as was possible, with Chewtooth having only a right ear, and Barge only a left.

Leaning close to Barge, Chewtooth quietly explained his plan. Barge looked at Chewtooth, plainly worried, but said nothing. When Chewtooth was finished speaking, both rats moved to the base of the huge horse-doors.

They peered out through the opening. The two cats were still waiting outside. A tickle of anxiety crawled up Chewtooth's spine at his first clear view of them. They were huge, russet monsters with hard, battle-scarred bodies. The left-eyed one was on the left plank, the right-eyed on the right one.

"And now we wait," said Chewtooth. He settled into a comfortable position, still looking out beneath the door.

Countless heartbeats passed as he stared at the cats. As the sun moved across the sky, the cat-shadows slowly stretched over the doorstep toward him.

The feline sisters yawned in unison, stood, stretched with forelegs out before them and haunches high, and turned to walk back along the planks. They had almost reached the far bank when Chewtooth said, "Now," and squeezed through the opening, followed closely by Barge. He took the left plank and Barge took the right.

"Oi, cats!" he called.

The two ginger giants stopped and turned back, spinning nimbly in place with a grace that only cats can manage. "Well, well," they said with one voice, "Dinner comes to us. What do you want, Dinner? Do you want to play? Dinner has come out to play."

They began to walk back along the planks toward the rats. Chewtooth and Barge continued forward. When they were a cat's leap apart, the rats stopped and so did the cats. They stared at each other—the cats hungrily, the rats oddly calm.

"Well, Dinner," the cats asked, "What do you want?"

"We're here for you," said Chewtooth. "We're here to make a deal. You can have us if you agree to let the millrats out once a day to find food."

"And why would we want to do that?" the cats hissed. "Why would we settle for only the two of you when we can just wait? Eventually you'll all get hungry enough to come out, and then we'll have the lot of you."

Chewtooth gestured toward Barge with a shift of his head. "Because we're special," he said. "Look at us. We're twins, like you, and like you we're both marked. I'm for you." He lifted his nose toward the cat who shared his plank. "A left ear for a left eye. And my brother is for your sister. A right ear for a right eye. Does that appeal to you?"

He could see by the glint in their eyes and the twitching of their tails that it did. He knew something of cats and their great love of all things whimsical. He was certain that they would find the poetic symmetry of his offer irresistible.

He continued, "We're yours. We're willing to sacrifice ourselves for the good of our clan, if you agree to let our nestmates out once a day. The rest of the day and night is yours."

"You're ours, anyway," said the cats. "We can eat you before you leave these planks. We don't bargain with dinner."

They tensed, preparing to spring.

"We'd jump into the river before you could reach us," said Chewtooth, "We're both dead anyway, and personally I'd rather let the river take me than end up in your gullet."

The cats relaxed a little, sheathing their claws. The offer was very tempting. It wasn't often that dinner came in such a delightful package.

"Very well," they said. The fire rekindled in their eyes. Neither cat moved for several breaths—even the flicking of their tail-tips ceased—but the muscles beneath their ragged ginger fur bunched. Their mighty shoulders dipped and their front paws splayed, their claws re-emerging from fleshy sheaths.

"Now!" shouted Chewtooth, and both the rats leapt sideways. They had planned the jump carefully, and Barge sprang slightly higher so that he passed over Chewtooth's back. They each landed on the opposite plank in the exact space from which the other had just leapt.

The two cats had jumped at the same instant, and they instinctively adjusted their leap to follow the rats as they changed planks. So intent was each on her prize that she failed to watch for her sister. They met in mid-air over the gap between the planks, crashing head-long into each other. With twin howls they dropped between the boards and into the swift-flowing millrace below. Chewtooth and Barge had a momentary glimpse of them as they surfaced, yowling and paddling furiously, before they disappeared around the first bend in the river.

Chewtooth and Barge scrambled off the planks on the mill side of the bridge. The millrats were already pouring from beneath the door, blinking and squinting, unaccustomed to the direct sunlight.

The old councilrat stepped to the front of the rapidly growing crowd. "We owe you the life of our nest," he said. "We would offer you a feast of thanks, but as you know we have no food, and it will take a while for us to gather enough to begin rebuilding our strength. Is there anything we can give that you'd accept as a token of our gratitude? You're welcome to stay with us, if you choose, but I sense that you're seeking something that you do not find here."

"I'm looking for nothing but open fields, unexplored ratways, and whatever adventures might lie ahead," said Chewtooth. "But there is something I would like from you. I'm happy to wander, but there is one thing about a clan that I miss dearly. My home nest is now gone, but I still crave the company of other rats. If you consent, and he's willing, I'd like Barge to accompany me on my travels. He's proven himself a capable rat, and I think he would be a good friend."

Barge was more than willing to join Chewtooth on his travels, for he too dreamed of life beyond the safety of the nest. The two rats remained companions for the rest of their days.

Chewtooth was able to outwit the cats, but his wits alone weren't enough. He needed the help of a friend, and in the adventures that followed, he and Barge came to be as close as two claws on one paw.

As for the Ginger twins: no one knew whether they perished in the fast-moving water, or managed to reach the safety of shore somewhere downstream. They never returned, and no rat of the mill ever heard of them again.

CHAPTER 6

TELLING TALES

M oon was silent for a few moments as she absorbed the story. "Does that work on the pups of your old nest?" she asked.

"What do you mean?" asked Wainscot. He was confused by the question. Did she not like the story?

"That friend stuff at the end. It's a little heavy-pawed, don't you think? Shouldn't you be teaching them to look after themselves, think for themselves? You'd have to be pretty stupid to think you can rely on anyone else in this world." Her voice was sharp and bitter. The prickly rat was back.

"It's not supposed to teach them, " he said, hurt. "It's... Look, I just thought you... Never mind." He had simply wanted her know that he valued friendship, and was offering her his. He might just as well not have bothered.

"I'm sorry," said Moon after a few heartbeats. "I didn't mean anything by it. I don't often talk to other rats, and when I do, I tend to be aggressive. It's armour. I lash out before anyone has a chance to hurt me. I think I know what you were saying, what you meant by the story, and I do appreciate it. I have to remember that you're not one of the ship's rats." She seemed embarrassed by this admission and looked away from him.

"Your family, your clan –" Wainscot began, but she interrupted him.

"And you?" she asked. "What's your story? You're not a black rat; you're a brown—a Lander. You don't belong on a ship and yet here you are. You said you had a bad night. I'll wager you have quite a tale to tell."

He did, and unlike her he was not reluctant to talk about himself. He did love to tell a story.

So he told her of his days with Scuffle, and their boisterous life in the crowded warren of the Nest. Thought of her brought his sadness at her loss back to the surface, but he found that talking about her helped to ease the pain. He painted a portrait of a generally happy life. It was not idyllic, but its harshness was balanced by the love of a sister, ample food, and the genial camaraderie of a bustling community.

Moon watched him wistfully as he spoke. His suspicion that she was an outcast grew firmer with every melancholy look she gave him as he described some mundane aspect of the Nest's communal life.

When he reached the part of his story about the desperate flight through the warren and his final glimpse of Scuffle, Moon began to cry. Wainscot was surprised. He had found the telling easier than he had expected, as though by facing it he had begun to heal, but there was a fragility to Moon that she hid behind her brittle mask.

He was touching an exposed nerve, he knew, and did not want to jeopardise the fragile friendship that was beginning to form between them.

He changed the subject quickly. "Why do you think it screamed?" he asked, hoping to distract her from her sadness.

Moon, startled by the unexpected question, said, "What? Why did what scream?"

"The rat-king. It screamed at me, but I don't know why. And I don't know how any living thing could make a sound like that."

Moon considered for a moment, her head cocked to one side. Then she said, "I don't know what a rat-king is. For all I know, screaming is how a rat-king says "good morning". Maybe it was just being friendly." She laughed—a low, odd sound. "No," she said, more soberly. "What I really think is that what sounded like madness and rage was exactly that. I'm pretty sure that being kept hidden away in the darkness isn't natural for it. You said you thought it had been in there for some time, maybe even many seasons. I doubt if any rat could stand that without going at least a little loopy. I've heard horrible stories about what can happen if rats are confined, or too crowded – cannibalism, and other stuff I'd rather not think about. I guess being too close to other rats can sometimes be even worse than being alone."

"I really don't think it was a rat," Wainscot said quickly. He had to be mentally nimble if he hoped to keep Moon from slipping into melancholy. "At least not a rat as we normally think of one. It smelled like one, and had rat ears and rat eyes, but far too many of them. And that scream—I've never heard a rat make a noise like that."

Moon shivered. "My guess is that it was once a rat—or several rats," she said, "but whatever it was, I think you're well off to be as far from it as possible."

And as far away from Dayrunner and the other C'law of the nest too, thought Wainscot. He had not not mentioned Dayrunner's name to Moon. He was not sure why. Perhaps refusing to name his pursuers was another step in healing the wound left by his loss of Scuffle.

"Tell me more about what you've seen and what you've done," said Moon. "I've never been off the ship."

. . .

S o they talked the day away. Or rather Wainscot talked and Moon listened, partly because of Moon's reluctance, but mostly because Wainscot simply loved to spin a yarn. As he spoke, she sat gnawing contentedly on shards of discarded barrel-stave.

He spoke first of his own experiences and then moved on to his favourite stories; some traditional, and some built from the stuff of his own imagination. He travelled through field and forest, alley and attic, and on into the realm of heroes and ghosts; Moon travelled with him, laughing and gasping by turns. She seemed most taken with the stories that Wainscot had invented himself, and he liked her all the more for it.

Occasionally, Wainscot would rest and lick condensation, eat a lime peel, or chew on a piece of stave. This last was done to keep the growth of his incisors in check. He was not sure that he believed the rumours that if a rat's teeth were not worn down by constant gnawing, they would grow long enough to pierce the skull, but he was not about to risk it.

At first Moon was silent during these respites, but eventually she began to do some talking of her own. She managed to resist the urge to babble incoherently, or make barbed comments about Wainscot's character or intelligence, but she would only speak of practical aspects of life aboard the *Heloise* – nothing about herself, and nothing about her clan. If she ever mentioned other rats, it was only in terms of how to avoid them. They were like a silent army, clustered at the edges of her narrative, but held at bay by her refusal to acknowledge them.

Soon they both began to wind down, and sleep beckoned.

"When it's dark we'll make our way out," Moon said with a yawn. "I'll start showing you what you need to know. It's better at night. Everything topside is very exposed, but I usually prefer to travel there than through the holds. Men are easier to avoid."

Easier than what? Wainscot wondered. *Her clanmates? The cats? The 'monkey'?* He did not ask. She would tell him more when she was ready.

Wainscot settled further into the soft nest, and let the unfamiliar sounds and smells of the ship wash over him. He would eventually come to recognise them for what they were: the groaning of the timbers of the hull holding back the weight of the sea, the stink of the bilges, the hot smell of fresh pitch, the heavy thump and scrape of sailors holystoning the decks above, the ringing of bells, the shouting of orders, and the clean fresh scent of the sea air. For the present they only emphasised that he was a stranger here. A stranger, but one who was no longer alone.

He slept.

CHAPTER 7

OUTSIDER

P lank considered the rat sitting in front of him. Calm and seemingly self-possessed, the outsider was neither frightened nor intimidated. This was unusual, and somewhat disconcerting.

The stranger sat alone in the centre of a circle of ship's rats who regarded him with a hostility that was but a hair's width from killing-rage, but he held his head high.

Does he know that his life teeters in precarious balance, Plank wondered, *and that, at a single word from me, these rats will close in on him and rip him to pieces?*

But Plank did not give the word. Instead, he said, "After I've killed you, I'm going to eat you." He gestured to the surrounding rats with his head. "They can have some too. I'm nothing if not generous."

Still the outsider stared calmly ahead. He did not even blink.

"Well," said Plank, "have you no answer? Nothing to say?"

"I hadn't realised you'd asked a question," said the stranger. There was no insolence in the words; just a statement of fact.

Plank stepped forward until he was muzzle-to-muzzle with the stranger. This outsider was very large. Not as massive as himself of course, but substantial enough to give even an experienced fighter pause. The brown fur, heavy build, and relatively small ears marked the stranger as a Lander. Landers were almost always bigger than ship rats, but they were soft, and fared badly against a ship rat's wire-hardness. This one, however, did not look soft; the interlaced scars along his flanks told of past battles fought, and probably won.

"I am Plank," he said. "Captain Plank. You will call me Captain, or Sir. You are a Lander, and you were dead the moment you boarded my ship."

Plank's first instinct had been to kill the newcomer. He had decided not to, however, because the stranger looked as though he might prove useful; as an enforcer, perhaps, or even a lieutenant. Although he did not admit it to himself, he was a little afraid of the strange rat, and was not at all sure that killing him would be an easy matter. Plank was a seasoned bully, having clawed his way to the top of the Aft Clan over the bodies of many hard-fighting competitors, but there was something about this rat that unnerved him.

"Look around you," Plank said. "I don't know what stinking city sewer you come from, but you're in my world now. You may have been a rat of consequence back on dry land, but no longer. You're not of my clan—not even of this ship—so you're not even a proper rat, and the moment that you dared to enter my territory you became mine to do with as I wish. You are now a possession, genderless and nameless. I'll likely kill you, but I may decide to let you live if I think you might be of some value to the clan."

He paused to allow the intruder a moment to absorb his words, but the strange rat seemed unaffected by them.

"And if you are of some use," he continued, "then maybe I'll let you live out a full life. I might even let you join the Afties one day. But if you prove difficult, I'll tear your throat out. You'll only have one chance to —"

He did not finish. The stranger hit him fast and hard without warning. There was no lowering of the head, no shifting of weight to the hindquarters, and no baring of teeth—none of the usual warning signs of imminent attack that had kept Plank alive for so long—just a blur of movement. The Captain found himself on his back, legs clawing uselessly for purchase in the air. He tried to carry through with the roll to throw himself clear of the attack, but he was too late. The stranger followed the blow with his teeth, and his wicked incisors, with the weight of his considerable body behind them, sliced a deep arcing path across Plank's shoulder before snapping shut on the Captain's exposed throat.

Plank died, more surprised than he had ever been in his life.

Dayrunner lifted his muzzle, red and dripping, from Plank's throat.

The Aftey rats were so surprised by the suddenness and ferocity of the attack that they did not react at all, but simply stood, stupidly staring. The utter impossibility of the mighty Plank being cut down so easily robbed them of the ability to act, so they waited, stunned into immobility.

The moment was one of delicate balance, and Dayrunner was aware that once the watchers shook their minds clear of the numbing fog, they would either fall on him or slip away into the shadows. In either case, the fragile advantage that he now held would disappear. He would have to act quickly and decisively to put into action the plan that was still forming in his mind.

Dayrunner drew himself up, thrusting out his chest and baring his crimson-smeared teeth. Keeping one forepaw on Plank's now still body, he leaned toward the frozen watchers, and growled menacingly.

"I am neither nameless nor genderless," he said. "I am called Dayrunner, and you will remember that. I'm a stranger here, yes, but not new to the world. I'm not old, but I have learned much, and have seen much, and have much to offer you. This," he gestured at the dead rat beneath his feet, "was not a leader. If he had been, you would not have let him die. I am everything he was not. I *am* a leader. Your leader. Your... Captain." He was unfamiliar with the word, but it felt right to him. "I will be your father and your guide. I will take care of you."

He paused and met the eyes of the gathered rats, his gaze moving from face to face until he settled on a large individual in the front of the rank.

"But," he continued, "If any of you cross me, if any of you disobey me, or if any of you fail to do as I bid, it will not go well for you."

He lunged, and his teeth closed around the throat of the large rat. He did not clamp down, however, and after a few moments, he released his grip.

"I hold your lives between my teeth," Dayrunner said, pleased with his demonstration. "All of your lives. Remember that, and we'll get along just fine."

With that, the Afties had a new Captain.

The timbers of the *Heloise* groaned as if in pain. Theirs was a ceaseless battle against the pressures of the sea—a constant struggle to hold at bay the countless tons of water that strove to crush the fragile vessel in its frothing fist. But the ship had been well built, and the curving planks of her sides held back the deluge in fair weather and foul, though not without complaint. The symphony of squeaks, squeals, chuckles, and pops was the voice of the *Heloise*, and it told her residents—whether Man or rat—of her moods. Despite the moaning of her hull's timbers, she was happy this day. The sun shone, the sea was smooth, and the breeze that sent her clipping along was light but steady, offering no threat to spar or canvas.

Far belowdecks, away from the sun and wind, Dayrunner was oblivious to what the ship had to say. He did not yet know the language. Perhaps one day he would become as attuned to the nuances of the *Heloise*'s speech as the ship-born rats, but for now he had little attention to spare.

He had killed Plank, but complete mastery of this new clan was still just beyond his reach, and he had to move quickly. The heart of a clan was always its Council, and he would—by word or claw—have to bend this one to his will. He would eventually have to dispose of them, as there was no room in his plans for a Council that was not of his own choosing, but that was not as easy as it sounded. The simplest way to deal with them would be to kill them, but the murder of a Council was not to be undertaken lightly. The killing of any councilrat was forbidden by the law and custom of all rats, but he would find a way to rid himself of them.

The Aftey Council sat before him in a single curving line, with their C'law arranged on either side. They were gathered in an open space between stacked barrels deep in the lower hold, shielded from the eyes of Man.

The councilrats were seven in number, and very old. Most of them would not survive another winter, but their great age gave them the wisdom they needed to guide the clan. Dayrunner could not read their eyes, though he saw no fear in them. They were nearing the ends of their long lives; they were not impressed by the threat of violent death. They were also confident in the laws that protected them.

It was vitally important that he win the support of these old rats. Captains came and went, but a Council was constant, and a leader could not truly rule without its support. The councilrats made the laws and guided the clan through the stormy seas it sailed every day, and without them a rat, no matter how strong, could never be Captain. The clan knew this, and even if Dayrunner were to kill half of their number, they would not follow him unless the Council supported him.

So, satisfying as it might be, brutality was not the answer if he were to win this Council. He would have to seduce it.

"You don't know me," he started, in a reasonable tone. "You don't know me, and you don't know my clan. You don't know why I'm here. All you know is that I'm a stranger who has come amongst you, and my first act was to deprive you of your Captain. That's a reasonable reaction. He was your Captain, and I'm... Well, I'm an unknown. You need a Captain. You need a leader. That is undeniable. However, I maintain you did not have one in Plank. A leader who is so easily dealt with was not up to the task, and you're better off without him. If he were a true Captain I wouldn't be standing before you now."

Dayrunner moved slowly along the line of councilrats as he spoke, holding the eyes of each as he passed.

"You know as well as I do that a leader needs strength to rule, but there are different kinds of strength. A Captain must be strong in tooth and claw, certainly, but he needs more. He needs strength of mind as well. If he relies solely on his teeth he'll soon fall to an equally brutal but slightly smarter rat – but if he uses his mind well he'll retain his power. There's always a role for brutality, but it's the mind and not the tooth that rules a clan. Your former leader—your Captain Plank—did not know this simple truth."

He paused for a few heartbeats, waiting for some indication from the Council that he was approaching them on the correct tack, but they remained stoic and silent. "I know this," he continued, "because I'm still alive. Had he been a good leader, a wise leader, he would have had the loyalty of his followers, and they would have killed me the moment he fell. If he had trained them properly, they would have reacted instantly instead of gawping at me like frightened mice."

There was a low, angry muttering from the C'law.

"Plank was nothing but a thug," Dayrunner said, "and now he's gone. I, however, am more than just muscle and claw. I am your future." He gave his audience a few heartbeats to absorb his words. "I look around me and I see rats. Nothing more than that. Just rats who live and die as they always have, struggling in a world that conspires against them. I see traps and poison. I see hunger and sickness. I see death at the hands of Men and the claws of cats—and, yes, at the teeth of other rats. But although I see nothing more than rats before me, I also see nothing less."

As he spoke, he shifted his attention away from the Council toward the crowd of rats, C'law and others, watching from the sides. He now faced and addressed them squarely, his eyes moving from rat to rat, holding the gaze of each for a moment before moving on, as he done moments before with the councilrats.

"You are rats, not mice or moles, or even cats or Men. You are more than just skulkers in the dark. You should be lords of all that you see. And why not? You have teeth and claws and cunning, and, most importantly, you have numbers. You," he gestured with a lift of his snout to a rat in the front rank of the onlookers. The chosen rat flinched, and pulled his head back into his shoulders, terrified by Dayrunner's attention. "You've had personal experience with cats, yes?"

The rat stammered, "yes."

"And could you take one in fight?"

"No."

"How about with five friends?"

"Probably not."

"Well then, what about with fifty, or a hundred?"

The other rat considered, "I guess so. Yes."

"Yes, you could," said Dayrunner. "So you see, you have your teeth, and you have your claws, and you have your cunning, and you have your numbers, but you still don't rule. You still hide and sneak. And why is this? I'll tell you: it's because you lack leadership, and you lack organization. Well I can give you those. Your Council knows this. They know what you can achieve with a Captain who's more than just a bully-boy."

He turned back to the Council and spoke to them directly, "who are your enemies? Aside from the Men and the cats, I mean."

"The Bowsers," replied one of the Council. It was the first time any of them had spoken, and Dayrunner knew that he was reaching them. "The other clan on the *Heloise*. They have the front of the ship."

Dayrunner was unfamiliar with both of the words "*Heloise*" and "ship", but he did not ask their meaning. "So we'll destroy the Bowsers first," he said. "Then the cats."

There was considerable noise from the onlookers at this. The councilrat who had spoken gestured for silence, and the din subsided. He took a step forward. He was very old and frail. Dayrunner suspected that the opinion of this aged councilrat held great weight with the other Council members.

"Tell us how," said the old rat.

Hearing those words, Dayrunner knew that the clan was his.

D ayrunner had assembled the C'law—*his* C'law.

They were the strongest and hardest of the Afties, and as such were the most likely to resist him. The brightest of them would realise that their future lay with Dayrunner, but there was always the possibility that some of them were still loyal to Plank. And some, particularly the more senior, might be considering their own ambitions, and eying the captainship for themselves. One more lesson in brutality was required.

"We need to talk," he said. "Who speaks for you?"

Without hesitation, a rat stepped forward and said, "Me, sir."

The speaker was at the fine point of balance where he would soon leave his fighting strength behind and begin the swift slide toward old age—soon, but not quite yet. Like Dayrunner's, his flesh was tattooed with the scars of a lifetime of fighting.

Here's an old warrior, Dayrunner thought. *He'll do quite nicely.* "What's your name?" he asked.

"Mizzen," the scarred rat responded.

"Well, Mizzen, you're going to help me make a point. But first, what were you to your erstwhile Captain?"

Mizzen cocked his head, looking puzzled. "Sir?" he said.

"Did you hold some position of authority when Plank was leader?" asked Dayrunner.

"First lieutenant, sir."

"I see. And was there a second lieutenant?"

"Yes sir," Mizzen gestured over his shoulder to his left. "Cuddy was."

"Cuddy, step forward," Dayrunner said. Cuddy, another large battle-worn veteran, took his place beside Mizzen.

"Cuddy," said Dayrunner. "Do you want to be first lieutenant?" Cuddy looked puzzled, but said nothing.

"I said, do you want to be first lieutenant?"

"I um... I... Yes sir."

"Then kill Mizzen. And know, Cuddy, that if you don't kill him, you'll have to answer to me."

Cuddy blinked twice, astounded. "Sir? he said. "I don't understand. He's my—"

Dayrunner took a step forward, growling low in his throat. "So you'd rather deal with me?"

Cuddy blinked again, then he collected himself and attacked. He snapped his head sideways, his mouth open and teeth bared, aiming to catch Mizzen under the chin. He was very quick, but Mizzen was a whisker quicker, and he was already slashing with his own teeth when Cuddy moved.

Cuddy did not connect with Mizzen's throat, but his jaw collided with the top of the older rat's skull. The impact caused Mizzen to miss his intended target, and instead of fastening on the other rat's neck, his teeth sank deep into the hard bulge of muscle at Cuddy's shoulder. With a squeal of pain and rage, Cuddy recovered and twisted his upper body away. He tore free of Mizzen's grip and brought his front legs around in a sweeping arc, claws rigid. Rather than meet the blow, Mizzen ducked low, and sidestepped. Before Cuddy could correct his aim, Mizzen hit him again, gouging a long gash along the other rat's ribcage with his incisors. Cuddy staggered away a few steps, then turned to face his opponent. He stood panting in place for a moment, spatters of blood stippling the deck beneath him. With a shriek of rage and pain, he lunged forward again, but Mizzen did not wait for the attack. The older rat spun about and broke for an open space between two large crates. He was into the gap in a flash, and his long tail disappeared just as Cuddy arrived behind him.

"Stop!" bellowed Dayrunner, and Cuddy caught himself before

entering. He turned to face his new Captain, and reared back as he saw Dayrunner bearing down on him, teeth flashing. Dayrunner drove into Cuddy and knocked him onto his side. Before Cuddy could regain his feet, Dayrunner pinned him down. Cuddy twisted his head to look up at the larger rat. His black pebble eyes showed white at the edges, and his lips pulled back in a grin of fear.

"I told you what would happen if you didn't kill Mizzen," said Dayrunner.

The Captain lowered his head. There was a snap and a crunch. Cuddy twitched once and then lay still.

That didn't go exactly as planned, thought Dayrunner. *What kind of C'law runs instead of fighting? I'll have to knock some iron into these rats.*

Still he had made his point, though not quite as he had intended. Mizzen was a loose end, but he would send a party out to hunt for the coward later.

"Right," he said to the remaining C'law. "Who wants to be first lieutenant?"

CHAPTER 8

IN THE BREADROOM

"There it is again," said Moon, "I told you I wasn't imagining it."

Wainscot tilted his head in an effort to hear what Moon was hearing. When she noticed something, he knew it was in his best interest to pay attention. They were in the shadows of the empty wardroom, on one of the many foraging expeditions that occupied the bulk of their days.

"I didn't hear anything that time either," he said. He lifted his nose from the damp patch on the leg of the stool under which he was crouched. One of the sailors had evidently spilled something on the leg. He could not identify it, which was not particularly surprising; even after several days aboard the *Heloise* he was still almost continuously bumping his snout against the unfamiliar. However, it was delicious. He looked into the dark in the direction in which Moon was staring.

"I suppose you don't smell it either," she asked.

"I smell rat," he said, "but all you ship rats smell alike to me. I can't tell a Bowser from an Aftey—not that I've ever smelled an Aftey, or really know what an Aftey is. Or a Bowser, for that matter."

"This is definitely Aftey." Moon's tone was affectionately mocking. "Honestly, I don't know how you managed to survive puphood with that nose."

"There's nothing wrong with my nose. In fact, I—"

"Shh! He's moving." She pushed him further into the shadow. "It's the same rat who's been watching us for the past few days."

She took several tentative steps toward the still-unseen stranger. Wainscot had not heard anything, but was more than willing to trust Moon's senses.

Moon lifted her snout to sniff the air, muttering something that sounded like "at least it's not spume".

"What?" Wainscot whispered.

She ignored him and continued to creep cautiously forward. He followed, ready to bolt. He had developed a degree of awe at Moon's ability to make her way about the ship without encountering other rats. The fact that a rat had managed to watch them without being seen in turn hinted at something not quite natural. Several of Wainscot's stories featured the shades of rats who had died, or things that seemed like rats but were actually something quite different. While he did not really believe in such nonsense, there was something about this unseen watcher that caused the hair on his back to stir.

"Whoever it was," said Moon, "he's not there now. I don't understand why he doesn't approach us. If he were a Bowser, he'd likely just ignore us and go on his way. Of course there are some Bowsers..." She paused, reconsidering what she had been about to say, "...but an Aftey shouldn't be here; not alone. It doesn't make any sense."

Wainscot did not ask her to explain. He had learnt not to bother. Moon was more than willing to tell him where to find food and water, or how to avoid Men and other rats, but she remained close-mouthed about her clan, as well as to why she was no longer a part of it. All he had managed to winkle out of her was that there were two groups of rats aboard the *Heloise*—the Afties and her old clan, the Bowsers — and that she was afraid of both of them.

Wainscot's first few days on the *Heloise* had been uneventful, or at least as uneventful as a rat could ever expect, but they had been full and satisfying. He was a stranger to the sea, and a danger to himself and anyone who happened to be with him, but Moon was giving him the tools he needed to survive aboard ship. She was a good teacher. As she grew to know him over those several days she became less snippy in her manner; she was no longer the sharp, sarcastic rat he had first met, but rather a thoughtful and caring companion, though still somewhat reserved. She patiently guided him through the ratways of his new world and seemed willing to share almost all of her hard-earned secrets with him.

One of the still-kept secrets was the breadroom. Laughing, she would dangle the wonders of the breadroom before him like bait before a fish, only to pull it back when he showed interest.

"Of course, this doesn't compare to the food in the breadroom," she would say as they fed on a spray of spilled grain or potato peel. When he asked where that might be, she would chuckle and tell him that he was not ready yet.

Although she taught him the geography of the *Heloise*, and how to use it to avoid danger, there seemed to be some sort of invisible line through the middle of the ship that she would not pass, and he suspected that the breadroom lay on the other side of it. If she approached it, she would become increasingly nervous and find reasons to turn back. If Wainscot asked why, she would sidestep his questions.

She also never took him aloft. He was not exactly sure what 'aloft' meant, but Moon assured him they could use it to move from one end of the ship to the other without once setting foot on deck. She used words like 'rigging', 'sails', 'sheets', 'canvas', 'masts', and 'spars', but would not explain their meaning, only repeating that he was not ready. He did not have his sea legs yet, she said, and he might fall. If he hit the deck, that would be bad enough, but if he landed in the water it would be much worse. Rats who fell overboard did not come back.

Ever.

She held nothing back when she taught him how to listen. Listening on a ship was very different from listening on dry land, she said, because the ship and its Men spoke a language that no Lander knew. The Men communicated through a hodgepodge of whistles, bells, and shouts, and an experienced rat could predict their behaviour by the noises they made. The voice of the ship was the creak and groan of timber, the moan of wind through rigging, and the rumble of rope through block; to those who could understand her, she talked of such things as a coming storm, imminent battle, or arrival in port.

It was by these newly acquired skills that Wainscot learnt of the rumours of change that were percolating through the ship like bedbugs through an old mattress. Even he and Moon, living as pariahs at the fringes of the ship's ratty society, heard the whispers. They overheard other rats talking, picking up words here and there, listening around corners or through cracks in the planking.

There's something up with the Afties. Something's changed. Something's different. Something's wrong. The voices were usually muted, as though the speakers were afraid to talk too loudly. *He's killed more'n a dozen of them. Eats them up if they get in his way. There'll be trouble for us 'fore long, you mark my words.*

However, trouble for the other rats of the *Heloise* was not necessarily trouble for Wainscot's new two-rat clan. It might pass them by without noticing them, although he had enough experience of the world to know that it was unlikely that any threat would be that selective. He wondered briefly if Moon might be feeling some spiteful pleasure at the knowledge that her old clan was in danger, but he discarded the idea as uncharitable. She was better than that.

Despite the fog of unease that was creeping over Moon's former clan, Wainscot was contented. In just a few days he and Moon had settled into a comfortable life. They had sufficient food and water, their nest was secure and isolated, and, most importantly, neither of them was alone any longer.

But now they were being watched.

Wainscot did not know if there was any connection between the rumours and their shadowy observer, but he and Moon were now going about their activities with even more caution than usual. This made him all the more surprised when Moon said, "We need some biscuits. It's time I introduced you to the breadroom."

Crouched together in the shadowed lee of a coil of rope, they looked out across the main deck of the ship. The night was dark, but the blackness of the deck was broken by islands of light cast by hanging lanterns. Moon had told Wainscot that there were generally fewer Men about the ship at night, but it still looked to him to be a very crowded place.

They had made their careful way up from belowdecks along a series of ratways through gaps and cracks in deck and beam. Thanks to Moon's skills, they had avoided other rats, though they had seen plenty of evidence of them. Droppings littered the ratways, clumps of hair hung snagged on exposed nails, and the edges of narrow places were dark and polished from the passage of many bodies. They had heard them too, chewing and scuttling close by.

"This is the most dangerous part," said Moon, watching the Men as they moved about on the deck. "Once we're in the rigging, they won't notice us. Too busy concentrating on what they're doing to pay us any mind. Down here, though, they'll stomp us if they see us. Then it's either over the side, or into the pot."

"Into the pot?" Wainscot wondered if he had heard her correctly.

"They'll eat us."

Men eating rats? He thought she might be teasing him, but her tone said otherwise.

"Are you serious?" he asked.

"Probably not this early into the cruise, but when the fresh meat starts to run out, that's another story. Come on, let's go."

She burst from the shelter of the rope, skirting a puddle of light, and clambered up the bulwark and onto the ratlines; the wide rope-ladder structure that angled up from the edge of the deck to meet the mast, far above. She turned to watch Wainscot; he hesitated, then followed her.

"Up we go," she said, and flowed up the ropes. Wainscot followed, less nimble but sure-footed enough.

Once on the rope, Wainscot felt his apprehension crawl across his skin like an invading army of fleas. Never before in his life had he felt so exposed. There was nothing around him but open space—nowhere to run, nowhere to hide. He felt as if every eye on the ship—rat, Human and cat—must be on him.

Moon pressed on despite the exposure, thoroughly at ease in this airy world of swinging ropes. Her confidence gave him courage. He supposed that with practice he might come close to matching her agility on the ropes, but knew that he would always feel like a trespasser in these upper reaches of the ship. Moon had been born to the open spaces, while he was a rat of the tunnel.

Soon Moon reached the first of the wooden platforms that clung like barnacles to the bole of the mast, and peered back down at him through an opening in the floor—the 'lubbers' hole', as Wainscot would eventually come to know it.

Suddenly, a jolt of uneven vibration shook the rope. Wainscot looked back over his shoulder, alarmed. A dark form, indistinct in the night, was moving up the ratlines toward him. It was large, but moved with surprising speed, and its weight made the ropes buck and shiver. With a thrill of horror, Wainscot realised that it was a sailor climbing up to the mast. The Man would overtake him before he could reach the platform. He looked up at Moon, his eyes beseeching.

"Don't move," she called, her voice a hissing squeak. Her face disappeared from the opening in the platform.

Wainscot blinked in surprise. He obeyed and froze to the rope. The huge mass of the Man reached him and rushed past, clambering around the platform and into the rigging above. The Man's face had passed so close that Wainscot had smelled the ripe tang of tobacco on his breath, but the seaman had not even glanced at him. His eyes had not strayed to either side.

Shaken, Wainscot quickly covered the remaining distance to the platform. Moon was waiting for him, crouched beside the huge bole of the mast. She grinned when she saw the expression on his face.

"I told you they don't see us when we're up here," she said.

Wainscot shivered. "But he was so close. He almost touched me."

"They aren't expecting to see a rat up here, so they don't. You'll soon get used to them. I hardly notice them any more. On the decks or in the holds, however, it's a different story. Always watch out for them there."

Wainscot doubted that he would ever be comfortable in this alien world of swinging ropes and impossibly large skies. Everything here was strange and dangerous. The dry, earthbound world of his old nest had also been perilous, but there at least he knew what death looked like, and therefore how to avoid it. Here he might die not because he had been unwary or made a mistake, but simply because he did not recognise danger when it came sweeping down on him.

"Come along now," said Moon. "We can't stop every time you have a little scare."

She moved out onto another rope that curved away from the platform, and, reluctantly, Wainscot followed. They travelled a complicated path of line and spar that wove through a strange landscape of thrumming rope, creaking timber, and huge expanses of canvas that bulged, creamy and taut, like great gravid bellies all around them. Wainscot was both exhilarated and terrified by the dizzying drop and the vastness of the moonlit sea and sky. Although he longed to be down where a rat had something solid beneath his feet, he knew he would spend many a night revisiting this windy, wonderful place in his dreams. When they reached the third mast and descended once more to the deck, he was surprised that his relief was tinged with a shading of regret.

As soon as her feet touched the smooth planking again, Moon's demeanour changed. The confident grace and sinuous agility that had made her seem a part of the living ship had disappeared. She hunched at the edge of the open deck, exposed and easily visible to the Men who bustled about the ship's business. She twitched visibly when Wainscot dropped down beside her. The dark mouth of a rathole beckoned from only a few lengths away, inviting them into its safe embrace. However, Moon did not move. She shifted from foot to foot as though her body were resisting her commands.

"Shouldn't we move?" asked Wainscot, trying to keep the anxiety from his voice. This was Moon's world, and she knew its dangers better than he, but it would not be long before one of the seamen spied them.

"Yes," she said, and then in a sudden rush, hurled herself forward into the opening.

Wainscot, followed, but more cautiously. It was a foolish rat who entered a strange ratway without pausing to sniff and listen, and although he knew that Moon was no fool, she seemed to have left her common sense in the rigging. Wainscot thought of the old rhyme that he had been taught in his puphood: *Wide eyes and no-one dies, open ears and no-one fears, sniffing nose with safety goes, but enter fast and breathe your last*

When he entered the hole he found Moon just inside, wide-eyed and shivering.

"Well, we're in," she said.

A reflex sniff told Wainscot that they were not in any immediate danger, but something was frightening her. He brought his head close to hers and asked in a whisper, "What's wrong?"

She said nothing.

"Look," said Wainscot, "don't you think you'd better tell me a little bit about what's going on? Let's go to the breadroom, you said. Biscuits, you said. Fine, we're going to get biscuits. I didn't mind the trip through the rigging—well, I did, actually, but I've got to learn my way around some time—but now we're back on level ground. I haven't seen any biscuits yet, and all of a sudden you're too scared to move. If you're afraid of something, I want to know what it is so I can be afraid too."

He pressed his body against hers, and after a moment's hesitation she leaned against him. Her quivering eased slightly.

"You're right," she said. "You need to know. It's just that I have trouble talking about what frightens me. I've been alone for too long. But I'm not alone now and I have to change the way I think. Please be patient with me."

Wainscot nodded, waiting for her to continue.

"We're between Aftey decks now," Moon said. "In their territory. They'll know us for what we are, or at least what they think we are—Bowsers—and they'll kill us, or worse. I'll explain when we're safe in the breadroom. But for now just make as little sound as possible and keep close."

With that, still shivering but regaining her courage with every step, she led him deeper into Aftey territory.

Only once did they encounter another rat. Moon stopped short and hissed to Wainscot to freeze. They crouched, utterly still but for Moon's quivering. Wainscot slowly lifted his head and laid it against her flank, but this time the contact did nothing to ease her shaking. A rat, just a silhouette in the dim light of the ratway ahead, made its way slowly toward them, its head moving from side to side as it tested the air. They could hear the short sniffs quite clearly, even over the ubiquitous creaking of the ship. Before it reached them, the strange rat turned into a side passage, apparently having neither seen nor smelled them. Many heartbeats passed before Moon's shivering subsided enough for them to continue on their way.

They travelled on, descending deck by deck through ratways bearing evidence of heavy traffic, until they squeezed through a narrow gap between two poorly cut planks. As soon as they were through, the pervasive smell of rat faded, and Wainscot suspected that few rats other than Moon ever travelled the path they were now taking.

"Don't pass droppings, or urinate," she said, "and try not to leave any hair behind on splinters. We want to leave as few signs as possible that we were here."

They ran along the top of a broad wooden beam just beneath the planking of the deck overhead. On either side a long drop fell to the floor of an open space filled with row upon row of stacked barrels. A bulkhead with a Man-sized door stood at the end of this storage room, and they could see, by lamplight spilling down from a grate in the ceiling, that both the door and bulkhead were covered with overlapping sheets of tin. The beam along which they were crawling passed through the bulkhead above the closed door, and the metal sheeting fit tightly around it, leaving no exposed wood through which a rat might gnaw an opening. Wainscot was puzzled. Moon had led them to a dead-end.

He was about to ask her what they were going to do now, when she said, "Do you see there, up near the underside of the deck, where the metal's bent away from the wood?"

He peered into the shadows and saw that a corner of one sheet of tin did indeed bend down near the top of the bulkhead a few lengths above them and to their right. It formed a small triangular shelf. He could not see whether the exposed wood of the bulkhead was intact because the shadows were too deep.

"When you jump, aim beyond the tin," said Moon. "If you land on the metal you won't find any purchase—you'll fall."

"Jump? Beyond the—?" started Wainscot, but before he could finish his question, Moon launched herself out into open space. Her jump carried her smoothly into the wedge of shadow above the corner of the tin, and she disappeared into the darkness. Wainscot waited for a moment for her face to appear from the shadow, but there was no sign of movement.

It's all very well for her, he thought. *She's used to all this leaping about, but I'm a land rat, and we like to keep our feet firmly on the ground.*

It was much farther than he was comfortable jumping, but Moon had done it, and probably many times before as well. *Well,* he decided, *I'm doing all sorts of things I never expected, so I might as well learn to fly too.*

With that he threw himself toward the patch of shadow. He struck the flat upper surface of the tin shelf before sliding through a rat-sized hole in the exposed wood of the bulkhead. Then he was out into open air again, and falling. He opened his mouth to squeal his panic, but he landed on a hard wooden surface before he could make a sound.

He was on top of one of the many wooden barrels packed into the room. Moon squatted on an adjacent barrel. A wonderful smell, rich and yeasty, filled the room.

"What—?" he began.

"Biscuits," said Moon. "You're going to love this. Don't pass any droppings while we're in here, either."

She led him down to the deck. The room was full of over-stuffed jute sacks, and wooden barrels of various sizes. They were stacked many layers deep on either side of a central aisle that was just wide enough for a Man to walk.

"The voyage has just begun, so the room's still full," said Moon.

She stopped beside a small barrel that had fallen and spilled its contents. Flat, dry bricks of hardtack biscuit lay scattered on the deck. Wainscot lifted one in his front paws and had an exploratory nibble. It was delicious. He took larger bites, revealing a pleasant surprise. The biscuit contained small wriggling beetles that crunched juicily when he bit down on them.

"They're weevils," said Moon, seeing the look of pleasure on Wainscot's face. "After a while, these'll be more bug than biscuit, but I prefer them at the beginning of the voyage."

"These are wonderful," said Wainscot, around a mouthful of crumbly biscuit and half a weevil.

"Aren't they?" said Moon. "And a little further into the trip, the maggots will start to appear, and they're even tastier than weevils. Sweeter." She took a bite. "And the maggots bring something even better—fish. The Men put dead fish on the open sacks. The maggots prefer the fish, and crawl out of the biscuits to eat it. When the fish is covered with maggots, the Men throw it overboard. But if we get to the fish first, it's feast time."

"I've never eaten fish," said Wainscot.

"There's so much food to be had on the *Heloise*," said Moon enthusiastically. "Aside from the breadroom, there's fruit and salted meat in the holds, and dried vegetables—mostly peas. If nothing else is at paw, sometimes we get lucky and find eggs in the poultry coops. If things go badly, we can always find a good piece of leather to gnaw, or even eat the droppings of the livestock." She then looked at him wide-eyed, licking her lips." And then there's cheese."

"I've heard of cheese, "Wainscot said. "My mother had it once and told her pups about it many times. *If rats go anywhere after their time in this world is done,* she always said, *it's sure to be full of cheese.* I've always hoped to try it some day."

"Just what *did* you eat on land?" asked Moon. "No fish, no biscuits, no cheese. Your life must have been almost unbearable. I've eaten cheese many times, and so will you. It's fairly easy to find, and nothing in the world compares to it. I'm actually surprised we haven't come across any yet. It's usually only available fresh at the beginning of the cruise. The sailors don't like it when it starts to get mouldy, so they tend to eat it quickly. When the fresh stuff is gone, we'll have to raid the sailors' personal stores, or eat the buttons on their jackets while they're asleep."

"Buttons?"

"Part of their clothing."

"Clothing?" asked Wainscot.

Moon laughed. "You really don't know anything, do you?" she said. "Clothing is the stuff that they wrap around themselves because they don't have any proper fur. Anyway, when the cheese gets old and hard, the Men carve it like wood. They attach it to their clothes. Cheese buttons may be hard, but they still taste marvellous. Risky to get, though, because you have to climb onto the sleeping sailors."

"Carve?" Wainscot was a little annoyed that there were so many words that he, a storyteller, did not know.

"It's sort of like gnawing it into a shape that they want. I don't really understand how they do it."

Wainscot, like any rat, had an endless appetite for conversation about food. He would normally have been content to sit and listen to Moon for as long as she was willing to talk, but she had promised him explanations, and he was not about to let the opportunity pass. "You were going to tell me more about what you're scared of," he prompted.

"Yes," she said, but sat silent for a moment, gathering her thoughts. "It's difficult for me to talk about myself and my clan, but if you're to survive, you need to know about the Afties and the Bowsers, and all the rest of it. Things are changing. Even you sense that something's in the air, and I have a feeling that we'll soon be needing each other for more than just companionship."

She took a bite of biscuit, and thought for a moment more, composing the tale in her mind.

"I'm a Bowser," she said. "Or rather, I was. That is, I was born a Bowser, but I haven't actually been one for some time now."

Wainscot nodded. He had gathered as much.

"Bowsers," she said, "are the clan that live at the front of the ship; the bow. Afties are the other clan. They live at the back."

"The aft," Wainscot said.

"Yes—well, sort of. The back of the ship is actually the stern, but you're close enough. There's an invisible line through the middle of the ship that separates Bowser territory from Aftey, and we don't trespass. I think we were originally all one clan—at least that's what my Mum used to say." Wainscot thought he heard a catch in her voice when she mentioned her mother. She continued, "Anyway, she told me that there had always been some division between the rats in the fore and aft of the ship. Nests were scattered throughout the *Heloise*, but rats in a ship always regard their neighbours more warmly than they do others from farther aship."

"It's the same on land," said Wainscot. "There wasn't much tolerance for strangers in the Nest."

"That doesn't surprise me," said Moon. "I think all rats are a suspicious bunch. Here on the ship there were eventually some fights about rights to the breadroom—this very breadroom we're in now. Apparently it didn't used to be lined with tin: the Men did that only a few generations ago. Rats from all over the ship would visit it. At any rate, the rats who lived nearest to the breadroom began to feel that they had a greater claim to it, since they paid a higher price for their biscuits. You see, the Men hunted them more aggressively. So the breadroom rats began to drive away strangers from other parts of the ship. Soon they turned to killing. Antagonism between the rats at the front of the ship and those at the rear grew until they separated into two clans, and now their only contact is skirmishes between patrols along the border."

"But we're in the breadroom now," said Wainscot, "and I didn't see any patrols. We didn't have much trouble getting here all the way from the front of the ship."

"True," said Moon, "but remember, no one can get into the breadroom now that it's sealed with tin—well, no one except for us. No one comes in any more—no rats at any rate. I've never seen any sign of another rat in here. The Afties don't even bother to guard it anymore. Most of the patrols are concentrated along the border, and I get past them by going up in the rigging. I'm really the only one who goes up there, so I can travel the ship by routes that no one expects."

Wainscot nodded, recalling their exhilarating journey.

"I know the *Heloise* better than any other rat," she said proudly. When the Men lined the breadroom with tin it meant the end of biscuits for all the rats on the ship."

"Except for you," said Wainscot.

"Except for us," replied Moon.

Wainscot was suddenly struck by the significance of Moon's sharing this precious secret with him. She had been living isolated from the company of other rats for most of her short life, had developed an unmatched knowledge of the ship's byways, and had done so for the sole purpose of avoiding other rats. In sharing her knowledge with him, Moon had offered him the precious gift of her trust, and she had done so unconditionally. She did not demand anything in exchange for her help. He was still completely dependent upon her, but by teaching him her secrets she was giving away the tender with which she might have purchased his companionship. With a shock Wainscot realised that by blind luck he had stumbled upon possibly the only rat on the *Heloise* capable of filling the aching hole left in his life by the loss of Scuffle. He felt the warm flush of something he had not expected to find again—happiness.

Moon was still speaking, so Wainscot marshalled his wandering thoughts to focus on her words. "...and the nature of the killings began to change," she continued. "They were still over territory, I suppose, but they were different. More cruel. There were stories of rats doing horrible things to each other, and not just in battle. I don't know the truth about what happened to rats who were captured by the enemy, but the stories made me cry. And the worst of it was that it wasn't only the Afties doing these things. To the eternal shame of my clan, we also treated our enemies terribly—and took pleasure in it."

She stopped, and stared at Wainscot from beneath half-lowered lids, as if begging forgiveness for the sins of her tribe.

"This began," she continued, "long before I was born, but the situation is the same today. Of course the Bowsers always claim that we're just defending ourselves, but we do so with such savagery that I don't think it's just about protecting our territory anymore. I'm sure the Afties justify themselves in the same way. At first they were just establishing ownership of 'their' breadroom, and then they were defending against Bowser raiders, but it's really just about hatred now. They hate us and we hate them. The reasons no longer really matter."

"You don't hate them," said Wainscot. "You keep saying 'we', but I know you don't really feel that way. You're not a Bowser any more. Their enemies aren't yours."

"No. No, I don't hate them. I never did," she said. "The whole sorry mess always made me sad rather than angry." She sighed. "As time passed, each clan began to raid the other's territory, and soon it was very dangerous for rats of either clan to wander near the border. Midship is always deserted now. Normal rats leave it to the patrols."

"Have you known anyone who was taken by the Afties?" asked Wainscot.

"No," she said, "but there were always stories."

"And let me guess: we came down from the rigging near the border."

"Yes. That's why I was so nervous-"

"Nervous? You were scared scatless," said Wainscot. "But you're not a Bowser. Not now, at any rate."

"I'm not, as far as the Bowsers are concerned," she said, "but to the Afties I am. I smell like a Bowser—I always will. But it just means that I have to watch for both Aftey *and* Bowser patrols. Either would make quick work of me if they caught me." She ran a pink tongue across her incisors. "Which leads me to a little story that you need to know to understand our situation here. It's about my banishment from the Bowser Clan."

Wainscot was silent, allowing her to take her time. He knew how difficult this was for her, how hard it was for her to gnaw through the walls she had built up to protect herself from the world around her.

"I was born," she said, "on an inauspicious day."

CHAPTER 9

MOON'S TALE

When the day of Moon's birth began, no one knew that it would be different from any other. Certainly not her mother. She only found out when things began to go wrong, and they were looking for someone to blame.

It might seem that her mother was either blind or stupid not to have noticed what was painfully obvious to everyone else, but she was never a stupid rat. A little blind, perhaps, but a mother's love for her pup will often have that effect.

She saw right away that Moon was different from her brothers and sisters: how could she not? Even when they were all hairless and blind, Moon stood out from her siblings like a sardine among bluefish. She was small, but it was not only her size that marked her. While her brothers and sisters were a healthy, normal pink, she was white—well, grey, really. "Like a mackerel that's bin lyin' in the sun for a couple'a days too long," as one of her uncles put it.

Then there was her face. Everything was just a little too tight. As an adult, most rats found her face startling, if not alarming, and as a pup—with closed eyes and no hair—it was even more so.

Everyone but her mother was put off by Moon's appearance. Even the rest of her litter seemed to sense that there was something different about her, and abandoned her to her own corner of the birthing nest.

Word of the strange little rat began to spread around the clan. Nothing particularly bad—just the sort of things one would expect about something so unusual. That probably would have been the extent of it, had it not been for what else that happened on the same day. She would have been teased and abused, and her chances of mating would probably have been slim—but she would have stayed in the clan.

Moon was born when the *Heloise* was in port. Whenever the ship was in port the sailors often went ashore, and when they went ashore they sometimes bought things back aboard with them. On the day of Moon's birth, three of them came back with cats. Not one—three. One was only a kitten, granted, but kittens eventually grow up, and the other two were already experienced hunters. Why they brought the older cats aboard was a mystery—sailors usually prefer kittens—but they did. Perhaps they wanted ratters.

There had always been creatures other than rats and Men on the ship. Dogs, generally. There was one on board now, but it was not a terrier, so it never bothered the rats. And then there was the monkey, which *was* dangerous, mostly because it was so unpredictable, but it usually left the rats alone.

Cats were a different matter entirely. Cats were bad news, and three cats were a disaster; a typhoon; a shipwreck.

There had not been any cats on the *Heloise* for a very long time, and then suddenly there were three. The rats were not even aware that they were aboard until they struck. Not the kitten, but the other two. They were not working together—cats seldom did—and they hit at two different places and at two different times, but the effect swept through the Bowsers like a plague.

The first attack tore the very heart out of the clan. The Bowser Council was holding one of its regular meetings in an open space between two feed bins in the forward stock pen, and they had no warning. The cat—the Bowsers now called him 'Charger'—came over the top of a manger and landed right on top of them. Charger was not a large cat, but he was tough, mean, and very experienced. There was no telling how many rats he had killed before coming aboard, and he had since added many more to the count. Cats generally kill once and then drag their prey away to eat at leisure, but Charger was like a terrier, killing as quickly and as many as he could. It was terrifying. Even the C'law ran. It would be different today, because the ship's rats were more familiar with cats now—but on that day they ran.

When Charger left, he took two councilrats with him and left the bodies of three others on the deck. Only two had run in time to survive. In one bloody moment, the Council was all but destroyed.

Later that same day, the cat that the Bowsers called 'Glide' struck near the border. She took on a patrol of eight. They were alert and ready for a fight, but Glide still managed to kill three of them, including the C'law sergeant.

So on the first day of Moon's life, the Council was devastated and the Bowser Clan was changed forever. Naturally, everyone began to look for someone to blame.

Ship's rats are a superstitious lot. Most believe that nothing ever happens that is not the result of luck, either fair or foul, and luck is never random. Almost everything is a portent of some sort. If the wind changes when a mother is giving birth, all of her offspring will be female; if a rat sees a flying fish on a cloudless day, they are destined to fall overboard—that sort of thing. So who better to blame for the disaster of the cats than a sad, pale, ugly little pup? After all, the cats had not arrived until she had.

Her mother fought for her, of course. She was given a chance to offer an explanation for the events that did not lay the blame at Moon's little white feet, but how could anyone defend against such an arbitrary charge? It was a testament to her mother's character that they let Moon live, because she managed to convince them that her daughter was no further threat to the clan. Her mother had argued that her daughter's death would only invite further catastrophe; that some other event had brought the cats aboard, and it was only the strange birth that had prevented them from destroying the whole Council. It had been enough to convince the Council not to kill the sad little pup. They let her live, but she was branded a Jonah. A Jonah is a rat who brings bad luck. The name might have come from an old story told by sailors, but no rat knew if this was true. However, the label was something that Moon could never escape. In the eyes of the Bowser clan she would be a Jonah until the day she died.

S o she was allowed to live, but almost every rat in the clan either hated or feared her. As far as she knew, they all wished her dead.

When she reflected on it, Moon was surprised that not only was she not killed, she was not exiled either. Her mother must have been *very* persuasive.

Moon was still allowed to use the clan's runs, feed from the stores, and speak to anyone she chose. Not that anyone would talk to her, but at least they were not actually barred from doing so. However, that was soon to change.

As she began to grow, Moon kept to herself—mostly by choice, but also because most of the clan ignored her. She did get some attention, but it was almost all the kind of attention that she could have done without. There were some rats who were not happy unless they were hurting someone else. They seemed to feed on the misery of others, just as most rats feed on grain, and they preyed on the weak or the defenceless. Moon was weak, defenceless, and ugly to boot.

There was one particularly nasty character named Spume. He was many seasons older than Moon; definitely old enough to know better. At some point he decided to devote himself to making her life as miserable as possible. Why he treated her the way he did was a mystery; perhaps he was just plain mean. Some rats were born that way. He was not well liked—most of the clan could tell there was something not quite right about him—so maybe it made him feel slightly better about himself to pick on a rat who was even more unpopular than he was. Whatever the reason, he would taunt her and call her names, and whenever he and his cronies found her alone, they would attack her. They never went too far, as she was still a member of the clan and protected by its laws, but they would claw and bite and beat her. She lived in terror of them.

It eventually became clear that these petty cruelties were not enough for Spume. He wanted more. He began to devote considerable energy to Moon's undoing. He started whispering spiteful things about her into any receptive ear that he could find. He said that she hated the clan, and had actively tried to bring it bad fortune. She was bitter, he said, about the way she had been treated, and she wanted to hurt the Bowsers. It was ridiculous, of course, and no doubt most of those who heard the whispers recognised them as Spume's usual bilious nonsense. Unfortunately, some of his nasty seeds fell on fertile ground. There are always some who are willing to think the worst of their fellows. A rat named Drogue was one of them.

Drogue was a councilrat, and he was as nasty a specimen as anyone could ever hope to meet. Very old and shrivelled, he was a wizened husk of a rat, who seemed to have shed all of those parts of himself that were not mean and spiteful. He was one of the two councilrats who had survived the cat attack, and he had rebuilt the Council with others who shared his twisted, bitter view of the world. The other survivor, Currach, was a decent, reasonable rat, but he was too meek to have much of an impact on the Council. So, under Drogue's paws, the Bowser Council regrew into something harsh and cruel.

The evil old creature must have become aware of Spume's poisonous whisperings, and apparently intrigued by what he heard, had Spume brought to him. Drogue must have liked what Spume had to say, because he kept listening. So Spume, against all reason, had the ear of the most powerful rat in the clan. It was only a matter of time before they came for Moon.

The first inkling Moon had that her world was about to unravel was when the C'law arrived at her nest. There were three of them. Two she did not know, but one she did—their leader, a rat named Marlinspike. He was an important lieutenant in the C'law, and he had a reputation as a hard rat and a formidable fighter. He was known to place great store in the value of discipline, and everyone in the clan was at least a little afraid of him.

The other C'law wanted to be rough with her, but Marlinspike kept them in line. "Easy there," he said. "She's not going to resist."

They offered no word of explanation. In fact Marlinspike was the only one who said anything at all to Moon, and that was just five words. When the two other C'law took up station behind her, he positioned himself in front, and said over his shoulder, "Come along then, young one."

They marched in silence through the ratways to the place where the Council held their public meetings. All along the way, rats peered out of cracks and holes at them, whispering to each other. It seemed that everyone but her knew what was happening.

When the little party arrived, the Council was already arranged in its customary half circle. Moon was deposited inside the mouth of the arc. Marlinspike and his companions placed themselves behind her, where they could block any attempt she might make to escape.

No one said a word. They sat quietly as the space around them began to fill with rats. It appeared that all of the clan wanted to witness what was about to happen. When Moon saw Spume sitting behind the councilrats, her blood froze.

Drogue waited patiently for the gathered rats to settle, and when all was quiet save for some furtive whispering, he lifted his head and spoke. His voice was thin and cold, and it stabbed into Moon like a claw.

"You all know why we're here," he said.

Moon did not, but was too frightened to say anything.

The crowd murmured, but no one asked any questions. It seemed that they *did* all know why they were there.

"We're here to rectify a problem," Drogue said. "It's one we should have dealt with some time ago, but for a variety of reasons *we* decided to do nothing." He emphasised the word 'we' to suggest that the decision had been made against his better judgment. He continued, "We have a curse aboard this ship. We all know this. We all know this, just as we all know what we must do about it. We must rid ourselves of it before it destroys us all."

He took a deep, quavering breath, as if weakened by the weight of what he had to say, and then his voice softened slightly, though it lost none of its frost. "We're rats. Our lives always have been and always will be hard. Cats, Men, Afties, disease, storms, traps—these are the perils we face every day. We accept them. We revel in them, for they make us harder and stronger. They temper us. We're rats, and that is the lot of our kind.

"But just because we accept danger, does it mean that we should welcome it? That we should nurture it? That we should raise a kitten in our midst, knowing full well that it will grow into a cat? No, of course not. Why then should we allow something far worse than a kitten to share our food and sleep beside us?

"The answer, of course, is that this thing in our midst, this thing that we harbour under the protection of our clan, seems to be one of us. It acts like us and it smells like us. It even looks like us—" he cast a long glance at Moon, and added, "—after a fashion."

There came a snickering from the crowd.

"But it—she—is not one of us. This rat here before us is not a Bowser. Her name is Moonpatch, and all of you know of her, but she is not a Bowser. She is a Jonah."

He paused as if waiting for the import of the name to register with the crowd. They already thought of Moon as a Jonah, but his bald use of the word charged it with fresh menace. It was as though she was growing more dangerous as they watched.

After calculating the length of his dramatic pause to perfection, Drogue continued his speech. "On the day she was born, three cats came aboard the ship. They almost destroyed us on that same day. This very Council was shattered. We knew why then and we know why now. One look at her makes it plain—she does not belong.

"But we were merciful on that day. Foolish, I say, but merciful. We let her live, and not only did we let her live, we let her stay within the clan. Many, many days have passed since then, and our fortunes have not improved. Our battles with the Afties go poorly—we've lost two patrols in the last two days alone—storms are becoming more frequent, and the Men are using tin-lined boxes and barrels more and more. All these are things you know. What you *don't* know is that earlier today several rats fell ill with the Red Tear."

It was lie, of course, but Drogue knew his audience. All muttering ceased at the mention of the dreaded disease. All ears pricked forward, and all eyes fixed on his with fierce attention. Drogue paused, and let the silence stretch until it was brittle thin.

"It has not spread yet, and it may not," he said at last, once again perfectly judging the length of his pause. As he warmed to his role, his voice became even more coldly persuasive. "But we have to take steps to protect ourselves. We have to destroy the source of the sickness."

He stared significantly at Moon. She did not know what he meant. How could she have possibly caused the Red Tear?

"This," he said, "this Jonah, this curse, is responsible for all our troubles. She threatens us all."

Drogue gestured, and Spume came to his side within the circle.

"One look at her should be enough to convince any reasonable rat that she cannot possibly mean anything but trouble for the clan," said Drogue, "but there is further evidence against her—evidence that she is not just a Jonah, but is actively working to harm us."

Moon could not imagine what he meant. She had never deliberately done anything to hurt the clan.

"This rat," he said, indicating Spume, "has come to me with evidence against her. The evidence is of his own eyes. Spume, tell them all what you told me. Tell them what you saw."

Spume drew himself up to speak. He looked nervous, but exultant.

"I have known Moonpatch all her life," he said, "and from the moment she was born, I recognised her for what she was." He spoke in the same grandiose, self-important manner as Drogue, adopting the speech patterns and inflections of the older rat. "I saw her grow from pup to adult," he said, "and as she grew I watched the hatred eating away at her; consuming her. Knowing what she is, I watched her. I have been vigilant for the sake of the clan, and I have seen her on several occasions eating corn kernels in the direct rays of the Sun. I have also seen her aloft in the rigging when the wind is up."

This would sound like nonsense to many rats, but Moon knew what Spume was implying. She was aware that many aboard the ship believed that corn belonged to the Sun, and that the Sun got angry at Men for stealing it. They thought that it sent storms as punishment if it saw anyone—rat or Man—eating corn. As for going aloft; the breeze was supposed to blow bad luck from the ship like a noxious odour; if a rat went into the rigging on a windy day they risked catching it in their fur and bringing it back to their clan. Moon was skeptical of these superstitions, but knew that most Bowsers believed them implicitly.

"But there is worse, much worse," Spume continued.

He paused for effect, and the crowd, still silent, leaned forward expectantly.

"Just the other day, I saw her on the taffrail. She was looking down into the water, and she had something in her mouth. I could not see what it was, so I crept closer. To my horror, I saw that she had two pups by the scruffs of their necks, and was dangling them over the water. Before I could say or do anything, she dropped them over-board. Then she leaned over the rail and began to sing; she was calling sharks."

The watching crowd of rats hissed, outraged.

Moon started to protest, but a guard silenced her with a nip to her flank. None of what Spume had said was true, but she knew the signif-icance of the accusation. Sharks follow the ship to feed on garbage thrown overboard by sailors, and they would eat any rat clumsy or unlucky enough to find themselves in the sea. Bowsers commonly believed that sharks brought the Red Tear sickness to a ship. Moon did not know whether or not this was true, but the fish certainly bene-fited when the disease struck. If the Red Tear took hold, rats died by the score; the Men then dumped the bodies overboard in heaps, and the sharks feasted. By saying that Moon had called the sharks, Spume was accusing her of bringing the sickness to the *Heloise*.

"There you have it," said Drogue. "She's a Jonah, and not only a Jonah, but also an enemy of the clan. There can be no doubt. The only question is what we do about her, and I say there can be no doubt about that either. We all know there's only one way to deal with a Jonah and a traitor. She must die, as she should have died on the day she was born."

The crowd murmured its agreement.

"I—or rather we—have decided," continued Drogue, "that she is to be taken from here by the C'law, and—"

Marlinspike stepped from behind Moon, and into the half-circle. His tail draped across hers, and the touch gave her more comfort than she would have thought possible. He said, "Her fate was decided by the Council when she was first brought before you. You decided she was to live. Are you now saying your decision was wrong?"

To this day Moon did not know why Marlinspike spoke for her as he did. She doubted that he had even been aware of her existence prior to that day. Yet there he was, standing up for her before the most powerful rat in the clan.

Drogue was evidently taken by surprise as well. It took him a few breaths to respond, though his expression did not change. "Lieutenant Marlinspike, you forget yourself," he said. "You were not given leave to speak."

"No sir, I wasn't, and I ask your pardon," Marlinspike said levelly. "I'll wait until you ask to hear from those who wish to speak about the matter, as is customary."

If Drogue was angry, he disguised it well. "Very well," he said, "Let's hear what you have to say."

Marlinspike stepped toward Spume, who backed up a pace.

"I know this rat," he said, gesturing toward Spume with a contemptuous flip of his nose. "This Bilgemuck here. I know him well enough that I don't believe a single word he says. He's a maggot, and he feeds on the misery of others." He took another step and Spume backed away again. "Well Bilgemuck? Did you really see her do any of those things? You're lying aren't you?"

Spume did not respond. He did not meet Marlinspike's eyes.

"Of course you are," Marlinspike growled. "You aren't capable of anything else. I'm going to thump you 'til your—"

"That will be enough Lieutenant," said Drogue. "Whether or not you believe him is irrelevant. The Council does, and it's the Council that decides these matters, not you. Does anyone else have anything to say?"

No one said a word.

"Well then, there's nothing more to do except pass sentence." Drogue looked pleased. "I think I've made my position clear on that count. Lieutenant Marlinspike, since you've taken such an interest in this matter, we'll leave it to you to carry out. The sentence is death. There will be no further discussion."

Hearing this, Moon gave up all hope. She had not even been allowed to speak in her own defence, and now she was to die for something that she did not do.

However, Marlinspike was not finished. "Sir," he said, "There is something else."

"That's enough out of you, Marlinspike," said Drogue, irritation finally cracking the coolness of his voice. "You stand at risk of angering this Council, and that is something you do not want to do. I said there will be no more discussion."

"You know as well as I that we have to follow the custom, sir," said Marlinspike. "You can't pass a sentence of death unless there is unanimous agreement by the Council. We haven't heard the vote."

Fury burned icy hot in Drogue's eyes, but he controlled himself. "Very well," he said. "You are, of course, correct. We will hold the vote." He turned to his fellow councilrats and asked each in turn.

"Death," said the first.

"Death," said the second, and so on down the line, until he came to Currach.

"Banishment," said the old rat.

Drogue was livid, but Currach stood his ground. Moon suspected that old Currach knew that since he was the lone moderate voice in an increasingly vicious Council, his days were numbered, and he wanted one last chance to make a difference. Whatever his reason, she knew that she owed her life to both him and Marlinspike.

So Moon was allowed to live, but she was no longer a Bowser. She was never again to have any contact with her old clanmates, to sleep in the clan nests, or to feed from the clan stores, and she was subject to execution on the spot if she broke any of these rules.

No one died from the Red Tear, of course. Moon did not think anyone ever had it. She suspected that Drogue said that her banishment was enough to break the run of bad luck, but she doubted if anyone really believed it. When they had had time to think things over, she was sure that all but the stupidest of them knew that Drogue and Spume had concocted the story, but she did not think that anyone really cared enough to do anything about it.

But, when all was said and done, Moon thought it was almost worth the price of banishment just to see the look on Spume's face when she realised that she was going to escape with her life.

CHAPTER 10

GETTING OUT

Wainscot sat in silence for some time after Moon had finished her story. She stared at him, mute appeal in her eyes, as though she were waiting for him to pass judgment.

Is she afraid I'll abandon her? he wondered. *Part of her actually believes the lies they've told about her, and she's accepted the blame for any ill-fortune suffered by her clan. She's afraid that I'll blame her too.*

He realised that, despite his helplessness aboard the ship, Moon needed him as much as he needed her.

He did not know what to say to her. He longed to comfort her, to find a way to ease her pain, but for the first time in his life, words failed him. He was a storyteller; words were his life, but now that he truly needed them, they had abandoned him.

Finally, he said, "You're not alone now. I'm your clan."

It seemed so inadequate, but it was enough.

"Thank you," she said, and moved closer to him. They sat that way for some time, side by side in the breadroom, each lost in thought and saying nothing.

A niggling bubble of worry was nagging at Wainscot. For a while it had lurked in the murky depths of his mind, but now it made its way to the surface and popped.

"Um..." he said, breaking their mutual reverie, "...how do we get out of here?"

"What?" she asked, her face solemn.

"The way we came in... It's too high. We'll never climb back up." He gestured with a lift of his nose. The bottom three quarters of the room was lined with tin. Above, the wood was bare and easily climbable, but too far up to reach by leaping.

"Oh," said Moon, surveying their surroundings. "You're right. There appears to be no way out."

Wainscot waited, but she added nothing else. "Well?" he said.

"Well, I guess we're stuck in here for the rest of our lives," she said casually. "Good thing there's plenty of food. We'll get a little thirsty I suppose. Still, can't be helped."

"This isn't funny," he said, becoming annoyed "If we're trapped..."

Moon laughed. Wainscot had heard her do so many times now, and was surprised to find it just as fresh and appealing as the first time he had heard it. Still, as pleasant as it was, he was a little irritated that she always seemed to be laughing *at* him.

"Sometimes you can be more than a little bit stupid," she said, but the smile in her voice took the sting out of her words. "Of course there's a way out of here. I told you I come here regularly. If there wasn't a way out, I'd still be here."

"You *are* still here."

"Oh shut up. You know what I mean." She began to nibble at a piece of biscuit held between her front paws.

"You're enjoying this, aren't you?" said Wainscot.

"A little bit," she said between bites, and then, "We wait."

"That's it? We wait?"

"Yes."

"You know," said Wainscot, "sometimes the characters in my stories who know something important give enigmatic half-answers because it adds to the drama of the situation. It makes what they're saying seem very, very important. That's why my characters give answers like that. Why are you doing it?"

"Did it ever occur to you that your characters might just be enjoying themselves? That irritating other rats can be fun?"

Wainscot sighed. "Very well, you win. We wait."

"Ah," said Moon, "but it's not quite as simple as that. It's where and when we wait that makes all the difference."

"I place myself entirely in your capable paws. Tell me where and when."

A cook's mate, carrying a lantern before him, wove his steady way through the stacks of cargo toward the padlocked door of the breadroom. Taking a large iron key from a ring at his hip, he unlocked the bulky lock, hooked the key back onto his belt, and pulled the door open. He failed to notice two rats dangling from the length of rope that served as the door's inside handle. Stepping past them into the room, he placed the lantern onto the nearest biscuit barrel, and by the time he turned to pull the door shut behind him, the rats had dropped to the floor and scurried away into the shadows.

S afe in the darkness, Wainscot waited for a moment to allow his racing heartbeat to slow. He turned to Moon, staring at her with admiration. "How many times have you done that?" he asked.

They had waited in the breadroom, eating and chatting, until they heard the Man approaching the door. As he had rattled the lock, they had leapt to the door and clambered up the dangling rope. It had then been a simple matter of riding the door as it swung open. For Wainscot it was only the latest in a series of terrifying, oddly exhilarating, experiences. Life with Moon was anything but dull.

"Often enough," she said. "You get used to that sort of thing. I think you still haven't fully accepted the idea that Men won't see you where they don't expect to. We weren't in any danger."

In the rigging she had told him that they always had to be wary when they were on the decks or in the holds; it was only when they were aloft that they were almost invisible to the sailors. He looked at her, his head cocked slightly to one side.

"Well, not much danger," she said with a smile in her voice.

CHAPTER 11

SPUME

M oon reached the deck and disappeared into the waiting rathole ahead of Wainscot. The journey back from the bread-room through the rigging had been uneventful. All the same, Wainscot breathed a sigh of relief to be safely back home on solid deck. 'Home' was now the front of the ship, dangerous and unwelcoming though it might be. The deck, which moved constantly beneath his feet and would have once sent him bolting in panic, he now considered 'solid'.

Chuckling quietly to himself, he followed Moon into the hole.

As soon as he left the moonlit deck he knew that something was wrong. He had failed again to listen to the instinct that told him to stop, smell and listen. It was a wonder Moon had survived as long as she had, given her tendency to go barreling heedlessly into unchecked openings. Still, she was in her element and he was not, so he had deferred to her greater experience on the ship. Now he regretted it.

His nose gave him warning first. There was a smell of rat—or rather *rats*—that had not been there when they had left that same run earlier in the evening. It took a blink for his eyes to adjust to the gloom. The first thing he saw was Moon backed against one side of the run. Beyond her two rat-shapes loomed in the half light.

Wainscot wheeled about, intending to flee back out onto the open deck, but the bulk of another rat slipped between him and the moon-bright opening.

"I told you she had been along here earlier, Gorp," hissed a voice. It was one of the two rats beyond Moon. "I could smell her. All we had to do was wait until she came back. Who is this then, Scraps? Did you find a friend? Well good for you. It cannot be easy with a mug like yours."

"Biscuits," said the rat blocking the exit. Wainscot could see very little in the dark, but his nose told him that there were three of them: two males and a female. Their odour was aggressive and angry. He did not need to hear their words to know that these were not friends.

"What is that, Gorp?" asked the first rat.

"Biscuits. They've been eating biscuits. I can smell it on them." The voice was slow and low.

The voice of the other male was its exact opposite: high, thin, and razor sharp. "So they have. Well, Pretty, did you find some biscuit crumbs? Were you just lucky, or are the stories true? Do you have some secret hoard that you keep for yourself? It is very selfish of you not to share with the rest of your clan." Wainscot heard him move closer, and caught a glint of eye in the darkness. The rat, evidently the leader, sniffed. "And you have been sharing your biscuits with this Lander. Now is that any way to behave? Surely, your friends should come first."

Moon had been silent, but now she spoke. Her voice was calm, but had that sharp, biting edge that Wainscot had heard when she had first spoken to him under the anchor cable. It was the weapon she used to protect herself from attack, he knew, but beneath the steel there was a slight quaver. She was afraid.

"You were never my friend, Spume," she said. "In fact, I don't think you have any friends. We can hardly count these two—they'd

89

turn on you in an instant if they thought there was any profit in it. Or rather, Keckle would. Gorp's a little too thick to make a decision on his own."

The rat between Wainscot and the opening—Gorp—growled low in his throat. The third rat—Keckle—made not a sound.

"You still have a tongue, Scraps," said Spume. "We may have to do something about that."

Although very little light could slip past the bulk of Gorp's body blocking the passage, Wainscot's eyes had adjusted enough for him to make out something of the strangers. Gorp was large, about Scuffle's size, and still young enough that he had not reached his full adult weight. He would be a hulking creature in a very short time. His voice was slow and ponderous, but his eyes, which Wainscot could see dimly shining in the gloom, held a surprising spark of intelligence. Moon, it seemed, took the big rat for nothing but bone-skulled muscle; Wainscot was not sure.

The other rat, apparently Moon's old enemy Spume, was another matter entirely. He wore his intelligence openly on his sharp-featured face. There was cruelty there too, alongside what Wainscot thought might be hunger. Although only of average size, Spume was still considerably larger than either Moon or Wainscot, and he was also older: an experienced rat of many seasons. Nervous, twitchy energy thrummed though his body, keeping him shifting from foot to foot, his head moving in odd little jerks.

Wainscot could make out very little of Keckle. Not only was she was beyond Spume and further into the darkness of the run, but also her cold, hooded eyes gave away nothing about her. Of the three, she frightened Wainscot the most.

"What do you want?" asked Moon. "You know that when the Council cast me out, they ordered that no clan member was to talk to me, to have any contact with me. You were there, weren't you? And you must also remember that the penalty for disobeying is death. You're not a brave rat, Spume. We both know that, don't we? Keckle certainly does."

She cast her gaze toward the quiet rat behind Spume. "Don't you, Keckle? How can you stomach him, knowing what he is?"

Keckle stared implacably back at Moon. She did not react. She did not blink or change her expression in any manner. Wainscot shuddered.

Seeing that her thrusts were not striking home, Moon shifted her attention back to Spume. "Well, I must say I'm very impressed. I didn't think you'd have the courage to risk the wrath of the Council. You must be developing a spine. I hope the C'law are as impressed as I am when they come to ask you why you chose to disobey the Council."

Spume laughed; a thin, grating sound that made the hairs on Wainscot's shoulders rise. "Oh, Pretty," he said. "It is always such a treat to talk with you. The games you play. Keckle, do you hear what she is doing? Such a clever thing."

He had a precise, fussy way of speaking. He seemed to weigh each word carefully before he spoke it, savouring it as it rolled across his tongue. This contrasted oddly with his quick, jumpy body movements.

He continued, "I *was* there when the Council cast you out, and I *did* hear what they said. If I remember correctly, and I am sure that I do, the penalty of death was laid against you and you alone. If you talked to any of the clan, if you tried to make your way back into the nest, if you ate from our larder, if you attempted to re-enter the clan in any way, then *you* were to be killed. There was never any suggestion that any of us, the upstanding members of the clan, were subject to any punishment. I think that you and your little friend are the only ones who are in any danger here."

"You're sure then, are you?" asked Moon, "Sure enough to wager your life on it? Would you be as willing to play fast and loose if Lieutenant Marlinspike were standing behind you?"

Spume's eyes narrowed at the name, and an expression of mingled fear and hatred flickered across his muzzle before he was able to master himself. "I will not be wagering anything on it," he said, but there was a slight quaver in his voice that had not been there a moment before. "I do not have to. Marlinspike is not here, and even if he were, I would not care. I would—" But he did not finish, perhaps realizing that what he had been about to say was too ridiculous, even for him.

From what Moon had said about Marlinspike, Wainscot gathered that everyone was at least little afraid of him. With a short, nervous giggle, Spume seemed to douse the spark of discomfort that mention of Marlinspike had kindled.

"As it is," he said, "there is no one here but us, so what I do or do not do is pretty well up to me. I cannot imagine that you will go whining to the Council about me. You know what their reaction would be. No, please do not worry your pretty little head about me. You have enough problems of your own at the moment. And so does your little blind friend here."

He considered Wainscot for a moment. Wainscot stared back at him wordlessly.

"He is blind is he not?" Spume sneered. "I mean, he would have to be. Surely only a blind rat could appreciate your particular brand of... beauty."

Spume pressed closer to Moon, the tip of his nose a hair's width from hers. As she hunched back up against the wall of the run to avoid his touch, her front paws left the deck. She shuddered with revulsion at his nearness.

"Been eating your own dung again, I see," she said, sniffing at the snout thrust into her face. "Or is that Gorp's? I think the two of you are becoming a little *too* cozy with each other."

Wainscot felt a surge of pride at Moon's courage. She was holding her own with the only weapon she had—her quick tongue—but he was aware that if the confrontation shifted to tooth and claw, she would be defenceless. Still, she had ample experience with the bully, and he supposed that she knew best how to handle him.

With a hiss, Spume bared his teeth and brought his muzzle even closer to hers. Moon turned her head to one side to avoid contact. For a moment Wainscot thought that Spume would lose control and use his teeth; he tensed, preparing for action. He did not know whether he would leap to Moon's defence or flee, and a flush of shame momentarily banished his fear. Behind him, Gorp growled, and Wainscot felt the huge mass of the rat press against him.

Spume did not strike. Instead he brought his mouth close to

Moon's ear and whispered, just loudly enough for all to hear, "It is *you* that I will be eating soon enough, Pretty."

He pulled back enough to allow Moon to drop slowly down onto her front paws. She was trembling.

"It is funny that you should mention food," he said, his tone now conversational, almost friendly, "because that is exactly what we wanted to talk to you about. But first, introductions. What about your Lander friend here? Wherever did you find him? I would have thought that even you would have had better taste. Still, I suppose, given your unique physical *attributes*," he gave the word an unpleasant twist, "you take what you can. Surely, you could have found a larger one. This one hardly seems worth the trouble—not much more than a mouthful for our Gorp over there."

Gorp gave another growl.

"Well, I suppose it does not matter who he is or where he came from," said Spume. "The important thing is that he is here with you. I am going to assume that you have been sharing your little secrets with him."

He paused, as if waiting for an answer from Moon, but she just stared back at him.

"No denial then?" Spume sounded pleased. "Good. Then I want to talk to both of you, so I will need a name for your little buddy, Scraps. Perhaps you could enlighten me."

"His name is for his friends," said Moon. "You've never bothered to use my proper name, so just give him whatever nasty little nickname you want."

Wainscot noticed that Moon winced a little every time Spume called her 'Pretty' or 'Scraps'. He suspected that there was an unpleasant story behind each of the names.

"What a splendid idea. Right then, let us have a look at him." He turned to face Wainscot. "Why, he looks like a Bob. Pleased to meet you, Bob. I am Spume. You *are* an ugly one: good company for our little Scraps here. Wherever did you get that stripe along your side?"

Suddenly, he swung back into Moon. The side of his head caught her a sharp blow under the chin. The shock of it, as much as the impact, knocked her off of her feet. She landed heavily on her side.

Before she could regain her feet, Keckle stepped forward and pinned her beneath sharply clawed forepaws. All of Moon's heroically maintained bravado disappeared immediately and she seemed to shrink, deflated by Keckle's puncturing claws.

Spume bent over, bringing his face close to hers. All the mock camaraderie was gone from his voice, leaving behind only icy menace. "You scrawny, ugly little barnacle. It offends me to look at you. I want to squash you. The *Heloise* would fare better without you. You are a curse, and a ship at sea can ill afford bad luck."

Moon made a small squeaking sound.

"What did you say?" Spume asked. "Do you want to know if I am going to kill you?" He looked upward, as though considering the question that Moon had not asked. "I *should* kill you," he said. "But I have decided to let you live. And do you know why? Because you are going to tell me about the biscuits. They say you have a way of getting as many biscuits as you want, and I believe them."

He lowered his head again, and ran his pale pink tongue slowly along the side of her mouth. She shuddered at its moist contact, and tried to twist away. Keckle's claws pricked deeper.

"In fact," said Spume, "I can taste biscuit on you now. You think you are quite clever, do you not? You sneak about the ship, always avoiding the rest of us, listening, watching, spying, while we go about our business. You think we have forgotten about you, but we know you are there. You are still a Jonah, still a curse to the rest of us. You are careful, but you still leave traces behind; when we come across your trail, there is often a lingering scent of biscuit. Which leads me to conclude that you are getting more than the rest of us, which hardly seems fair. We feel that we are not getting enough biscuit in our diet. Do you not agree, Keckle?"

Keckle did not reply. She was not even looking at Spume. Instead she had locked onto Moon's wide eyes with her dark, fathomless stare.

Wainscot had the distinct impression that although Spume was talking about biscuits, he actually cared very little about them. There was something in his feelings toward Moon that defied reason: something that smacked of madness.

"So you are going to tell me where you have been getting them or

—" Spume paused, as if a new thought had just occurred to him, "—or how to get into the breadroom. You must have found a way into the breadroom."

He chuckled, low and mirthless. There was nothing but malice in the sound.

"Yes, I would dearly like to know a way into the breadroom. So you are going to tell me. If you do not, I will have one of my friends here hurt you. Oh, do not misunderstand me. They will hurt you whether you tell me or not, but they will be much more serious about it if you are uncooperative. Then I will likely have them kill you." His eyes brightened in evident pleasure at the thought. "Perhaps we will start with Bob."

Wainscot tensed again. Before he could move, Gorp's hard-muscled weight bore down on him, pressing him flat to the deck.

"If, however, you tell me how to get into the breadroom, I will only have them hurt you a little, and then you can be on your way. I hate to be so melodramatic, but I do really want to know your little secret, and if you will not tell me... Well, then things will have to get a little unpleasant." He licked his lips, relishing the delectable taste of his words.

Spume stared at Moon for a few seemingly interminable heart-beats, then continued, "Nothing to say? Very well. Gorp, let us get on with it."

Under Gorp's paws, Wainscot felt the large rat shift his weight and begin to breathe a little more quickly. There was a subtle change in the odours emanating from the three Bowsers, the musk of their aggression now spiced by something that smelled very much like lust.

"I want you," said Spume, "to take Bob there and—" He did not finish his sentence.

Moon shouted, "Lieutenant Marlinspike! It's not my fault! I didn't want this!" She was looking between Keckle's forelegs and down the dark tunnel.

Wainscot felt Gorp's weight lift slightly as the big rat raised himself to peer into the gloom. One of his forepaws left Wainscot completely.

Spume flinched, his head twitching involuntarily as he started to turn. Then he caught himself, and his lips parted in an unpleasant grin. "Well, well," he said, "Is that the best you can do? You must think I am—"

"And what do you think you're up to, Laddie?" said a voice, low and menacing, from the darkness behind Keckle.

Lieutenant Marlinspike? The question flickered through Wainscot's mind.

Keckle spun away from Moon with a hiss. It was the first sound she had made. Spume turned too. Without hesitation, Moon twisted to her feet and leaped past Spume, straight into the startled Gorp.

"Go, Wainscot!" she shrieked, panic lending her voice an unnatural shrillness. Wainscot thrust upward as Moon drove into the huge rat, and together they knocked Gorp against the wall of the run. They were past him and out onto the moonlit deck before he could stop them.

They bolted across the open deck and up onto the ratlines in a flash. When they reached the safety of the ropes, Moon stopped and turned to look down. Wainscot kept climbing, relief giving him a new agility. He was anxious to get as high as possible as quickly as possible. He looked back as he climbed and saw the three rats come boiling out of the rathole. It was obvious from the way they moved that they were fleeing rather than pursuing. They ran along the base of the gunwale, and disappeared into another hole.

"Bilgemuck!" Moon shouted at their vanishing tails. She looked around nervously to see if she had attracted any unwanted notice.

Wainscot studied the opening from which the three had just run, but there was no sign of Lieutenant Marlinspike.

He reached the first platform on the mast and turned to wait for her. Wide-eyed and fur standing on end, he peered down through the lubber's hole and watched Moon resume her climb up the ratlines toward him. She joined him on the platform, and they pressed close together, comforting each other with shared body heat while their urge to keep running subsided.

They were silent for many heartbeats before Wainscot finally said, "How did you do that? It was all very impressive, and beautifully timed, but how did you do it?"

"How did I do what?" asked Moon.

"Conjure up Marlinspike like that. You couldn't have seen him, back there in the darkness, so he must have come at your command. How did you do it?"

"I didn't know he was there," she said. "I was bluffing. I know how frightened Spume is of Marlinspike, and I was only hoping to throw them off balance so we could get away. I was as surprised as Spume when Marlinspike spoke." She paused for a moment, remembering and considering. "He did speak, didn't he? I mean, we didn't imagine it? How could he have possibly been there? I was bluffing." She paused again, then said musingly, as if she were trying to untangle some confusing thoughts, "He called him 'Laddie'. Why 'Laddie'? I've never heard him call him anything but 'Bilgemuck'. Strange. Very strange... " She trailed off.

"Well if we imagined it," said Wainscot, "then so did Spume and his cronies. Did you see the look on his face? And the way they ran? I don't think they would have run like that from a figment of *our* imaginations."

"No," she said. "Still, we were lucky in more ways than one. If Marlinspike had caught us, we would have been in a deal more trouble than Spume and his gang. After all, I'm the one who was banished, and Spume was right: the sentence of death applies to me, and me alone. We were just lucky that Spume panicked."

"I'm not sure about that," said Wainscot. "It's clear that Marlinspike feels nothing but contempt for Spume, and from what you've said, he tried to defend you when you were banished by your Council. I think he would've sided with you over Spume. Spume evidently thought so too, judging by the way he fled. It sounds as though Marlinspike might actually be fond of you."

She snorted. "I doubt that. Marlinspike isn't fond of anyone. He's a hard rat. Everyone's scared of him, even the Council. He'd be Captain if we did things that way in the Bowsers. Things usually get done the way he wants."

"Just because he's hard doesn't mean he's unjust," said Wainscot.

She looked at him without blinking for many long heartbeats. "I'm sorry, you know," she said. There were tears in her eyes.

"Sorry? Sorry for what?"

"For pulling you into this. This business with Spume. It has nothing to do with you, and I'm sorry. If you'd met someone other than me you'd be in much better shape now. You're a fugitive and an outcast, and it's not your fault."

Wainscot laughed. He was surprised that he could do so in these circumstances, but it made him feel a little better. Moon laughed too, and he felt even closer to her.

"I was already a fugitive and an outcast when I came aboard, remember?" he said. "And I was alone. I'm still a fugitive and an outcast, true, but at least I have you now."

"Yes, but..."

"Think about it. If I'd met anyone other than you, they'd probably have killed me. You've told me the way the ship's rats, Bowsers and Afties both, treat Landers. At the very least, they wouldn't have helped me. I'm alive because of you."

He nudged her playfully with the side of his head.

She laughed again. "Well," she said, "we'd better find another way back to our nest. I don't fancy trying my luck with Lieutenant Marlinspike lurking about down there. Come on."

Our nest, thought Wainscot. With that, he followed her into the web of rope and sail that harnessed *Heloise* to the wind.

Chapter 12

A Stranger

It was a good expedition. In one of the holds they had discovered a pile of small wooden boxes that gave off the odour of cheese. To Wainscot the smell was wonderful, but he could not identify it until Moon told him what it was.

"These must be part of the Man Captain's personal store," said Moon. "They don't usually keep cheese in this part of the hold. It's generally in large crates. This," she said, salivating so heavily that it slurred her words, "is something special."

After some exploratory gnawing, they discovered that the boxes were lined with tin—the cheese remained tantalizingly close, yet unattainable. Then Wainscot discovered that a small wedge of the pungent yellow stuff had fallen through a hole in the decking and lay nestled between the joists. After a little gnawing they were through.

Wainscot had his first taste of cheese. It was everything that his mother had promised. "If I die today, I'll be happy," he said.

"Don't say that. If you say it, it might happen," said Moon. She professed not to hold with the superstitions of her clan, but Wainscot knew that puphood beliefs were hard to abandon.

"Biscuits yesterday, and now this," he said. The cheese went a long way toward helping him forget the unpleasantness of their recent encounter with Spume.

They sat for a time in contented silence, munching happily in the safety of their hiding place beneath the decking. Several Men came and went, their heavy footfalls bending the boards overhead, but Moon and Wainscot ate on. When one of the Men opened a crate, a wonderful cheesy odour wafted down to them; Wainscot regretted that he and Moon would soon finish their meagre piece. By the scent, he could tell that what was in the box was of a different variety. He ached to sample it.

How can anything possibly smell so good? he wondered.

"Do you think he might have dropped another bit?" he asked.

Moon did not reply, but as soon as the sailor had left the hold, she gobbled up her last remaining crumb and squeezed back out through the hole. Wainscot followed, and they were soon nosing about between the stacked crates. There was nothing to be found, but the disappointment did not dull Wainscot's acute pleasure.

"That was wonderful," he said, "but I don't think there's any more here, and I'm a little tired, so what do you say we go back to the nest so I can sleep and dream of cheese."

"And biscuits," Moon added.

"And biscuits."

They made their way back to the nest with a renewed caution born of their encounter with Spume. Before they entered, Moon stopped to sniff for danger. She no longer hurried through unchecked openings.

She froze, and behind her Wainscot held his breath.

Moon began to back up, forcing Wainscot to retreat. When they had moved some nine or ten lengths from the opening, she turned to him and spoke quietly into his ear, "He's here."

Wainscot did not need to ask who 'he' was. The unseen watcher. The scent of the strange rat hung in the air.

"He must be inside," she said.

They had enlarged the opening so that they could bring bigger pieces of food and bedding into the nest. Visions of whole biscuits and great lumps of cheese had led to the decision, which now seemed somewhat unwise. Before the change, no rat larger than Moon or Wainscot would have fit through the hole, but now Gorp himself could be lurking in there. However, he was not—the odour confirmed that it was the watcher.

From their vantage point behind a rolled-up jute sack, they could clearly see the entrance to the nest. Nothing moved inside, but the shadows were too deep for them to see if it was occupied. Wainscot looked around the hold. The stacked barrels loomed large and threatening in the light cast by the hold's single hanging lantern, and the guttering flame did little more than paint the shadows blacker, and make them twitch and dance, giving the impression of movement where there was none. There were no Men about, and Wainscot could see no rats, but the feeling of tiny insects running along his spine suggested that he and Moon were being watched. It was a feeling that a rat ignored at his peril.

"I'm beginning to grow a little weary of our shy friend," said Moon. "I think I'll go in there and introduce myself."

"No," said Wainscot. "We can find another nest."

"Nonsense. That's our nest. The least we can do is play the gracious hosts and welcome our visitor."

The whiny tone that had crept into Wainscot's voice mortified him, but he could not help himself. "He'll probably kill us," he said. "You said yourself that he's an Aftey. What do Afties do to Bowsers? Kill them. Horribly. That's what you said."

This gave Moon pause. "Yes," she said after several heartbeats, "but he had plenty of chances to attack us over the past few days, and he didn't. I don't think he means us any harm."

"Then what does he want?"

"That's what I'm about to ask him," said Moon, taking a step toward the nest.

Wainscot ached to say, "Stay here and I'll see what he wants." The part of him that had always identified with the heroes of his stories begged him to step forward and bravely be the first through the hole, but his fear was almost paralyzing. Trembling, it was all he could do to follow her as she strode resolutely back to the opening.

With commendable calm, Moon poked her head into the nest and said, "Ahoy. Isn't it time you stopped skulking about and..." She stopped.

To his shame, Wainscot made ready to flee.

"There's no one here," said Moon. She entered the nest and Wainscot, still trembling, followed.

As soon as his tail cleared the opening, there was a thump from behind. Something blocked the thin light entering the nest. He started to turn toward the sound, but was forced to the deck by a solid weight to his hindquarters. He drew breath to squeal, but a calm, authoritative voice spoke from above, so polite that it stilled some of his fear. Wainscot swallowed his squeal.

"Please excuse me," it said. "Very sorry for alarming you, but mean you no harm." The calmness of the voice banished enough of Wainscot's rising panic that he managed to muster up a little indignation. He was tired of being ambushed in the dark. "Then get off me," he said, his voice only slightly more shrill than usual.

"Yes, get off him," said Moon, advancing toward them, every inch of her diminutive frame bristling with menace. Oddly, the sight of tiny, scraggly Moon in full fury was not as amusing as Wainscot would have imagined. It was strangely impressive, and he was glad that he had never been the focus of her anger when her ire was up.

The stranger did not seem particularly alarmed. He lifted his weight from Wainscot slowly, almost casually, but gave no indication that he did so in response to Moon's stiff-legged approach. He did, however, take a few steps back so that he cleared the entrance of the nest and was visible in the feeble light of the hold.

"Mean you no harm," he said again, and Wainscot truly hoped he was telling the truth. Large, solid and battle-scarred, the stranger was a formidable looking rat who made Gorp seem insignificant by comparison.

The newcomer stood motionless for a moment, giving them time to assess him before he spoke again. "I'm an intruder," he said. "From the Aft Clan, as I'm sure you can smell. For that reason alone you have reason to fear me." The large rat's way of speaking was strange—even stranger than Moon's, whose odd inflections and choices of words were now familiar to Wainscot—and he wondered if the newcomer spoke with the accent of the Afties.

"Also, know you're aware I've been watching you for the past couple of days, which makes you even more wary. Not here to hurt you though. Only wish to speak with you. Appreciate it if you'd hear me out."

Moon and Wainscot, now side-by-side, stared out at the stranger. He was larger and more powerful than they, and he stood in front of the only exit from the nest. Neither running nor fighting was likely to end well, so hearing him out seemed the wisest choice.

"Then speak," said Moon. She looked slightly less fierce than she had a moment ago.

"Name is Mizzen."

Moon drew a sharp breath. Mizzen bowed his head slightly as if acknowledging a compliment.

"Heard of me then," he said. "Good, that'll save some explanations."

"I haven't heard of you," said Wainscot. He decided that Mizzen's odd way of speaking was not an Aftey accent, but just the affectation of a bluff and slightly stuffy old soldier.

"No, but you're a Lander, by the smell of you. Wouldn't expect you to know very much. Ask your lady friend—"

"Moon," said Moon.

"Ask Moon to explain who I am some other time. I'm sure she'll tell you."

"He's a killer," said Moon, and Wainscot's blood ran cold at the word. "All of the Bowsers know about Mizzen. He leads raids into Bowser territory, and kills everyone he comes across. He even murders nursing mothers and pups in their nests. He's said to be responsible for the horrors the Afties inflict on captured Bowsers."

"Just a soldier, no more, no less," said Mizzen. "Only do what's necessary to protect my clan. And you, Moon, would do better not to believe every wild tale you're told. I've no more killed pups than you have. A killer, yes, but no murderer. Raided your territory—many a time, in fact—and true, I've killed your clanmates, but never except in a straight-up fight. Sometimes we've outnumbered you and the killing was easy, I must admit, but at others we've fought hard just to escape with our lives." He let his words sit for a moment, then continued stoically, "Those are the chances of war, but never call it murder. As for captured Bowsers: I've killed them, yes, but nothing more. Don't keep prisoners—no reason to. Don't release them so they can return to attack again, but I've always killed quickly and cleanly. Never seen the need to make anyone suffer."

Moon did not say anything, and neither did Wainscot. Fear kept him from speaking; he suspected that Moon was silent because she was digesting what she was hearing, weighing it against the tales she had been told. She was also likely trying to determine why this Aftey felt a need to explain himself. Why did he not just kill them, as Afties were supposed to do? At length she asked, "Why are you here? What do you want of us?"

"I'll tell you, Lassie," said Mizzen. "But first, with your permission, I'd like to enter your nest. You have nothing to fear from me, but that doesn't mean we can afford to set caution aside. Feel much better if we were safely inside."

Moon hesitated. Wainscot could imagine what she was thinking. If Mizzen chose to enter their nest there was very little they could do to stop him, yet he had asked—politely.

"Very well," she said. "Come in."

There was little room to spare as the three rats settled down to talk. Moon and Wainscot were very much aware that they were sharing a small, confined space with a rat who was their avowed enemy. Mizzen stretched out comfortably, taking up even more of the limited room, but Moon and Wainscot both sat with their haunches pressed as far back against the side of the barrel as possible. They were tense and ready for action, but as usual, Wainscot did not know what that action might be. He was more than a little afraid that it would involve running for his life, his trembling tail between his legs.

He rather admired Moon. She, at least, managed to put on a brave face—she had been ready to attack Mizzen. It would have been a foolish thing to do, yet she had been willing to come to Wainscot's aid. He hoped that he possessed similar courage to fight for a friend, but he doubted it. In truth, he had never really had the opportunity to test himself. The attack on Scuffle had happened so quickly that he had not had time to do anything, and he had been pinned immediately in the confrontation with Spume. Still, in both situations, he had only been aware of the need to flee, the feeling so palpable that it was almost a physical thing, possessing his body and urging him to run. When Scuffle had been dragged back into the Nest, he *had* run. He had not gone back to confront her attackers, as she would have done for him, but had turned and fled immediately. He had not deserved a sister like Scuffle, and he did not deserve a friend like Moon. He felt a flush of shame.

"So," said Moon. She held Mizzen's gaze, anger still evident in her eyes. "You've jumped us and scared the wind out of us. And now you want to talk: so talk."

Mizzen was quiet for a few breaths, as if considering how best to approach what he had come to say. "I know something about you," he said. "Didn't know your names. In fact, I still don't know yours, Laddie." His head, silhouetted against the dim half circle of the nest's entrance, nodded to Wainscot.

Laddie, thought Wainscot.

"It's Wainscot," said Moon.

"Wainscot. Definitely a Lander's name. Yes, I know something about you. Been watching you for several days now. Happened on you by chance the first time I saw you. I'd just left Aftey territory when I heard two rats approaching. You move very quietly, I'll give you that. Or rather, you do, Moon. You, Laddie, walk like you don't really understand how your body works. Still getting your sea-legs I'll warrant—you'll need to work on that. I thought for a moment you might be a Cur patrol—"

"Cur?" asked Moon.

"Ah. Curs. What we call Bowsers."

"Oh I see—Bowsers; dogs; curs," said Moon.

"Thought for a moment you might be a *Bowser* patrol," continued Mizzen. "So I let you pass. But you smelled odd. You were Bowsers, that was obvious, yet you were different. Was intrigued."

Mizzen took a deep breath an hesitated for a moment, as though he was reluctant to continue. "Hate to admit it, but I like to be around other rats. *Need* to be around them."

He seemed to struggle with the word "need" as if unfamiliar with its use. Wainscot suspected that Mizzen seldom admitted a need for anything, and to do so to rats he had previously considered enemies must have been particularly galling. That he no longer thought of them as such was evident by the relaxed manner in which he lay in the soft bedding of the nest. On further consideration Wainscot decided that although Mizzen *appeared* at ease, rats of his type were never fully off duty, and he was sure that at the first sign of danger Mizzen would be out of the nest to face it before either he or Moon could move.

"Can't approach anyone of the Bowser Clan for reasons Moon has made perfectly clear," Mizzen continued. "So I followed and watched you. I understand that you're angry—but I had to know more about you. Saw where you made your nest—good location by the way: dry, easy to defend, and out from under the eyes of Man. Needs another exit though. You're easily trapped in here."

Wainscot and Moon cast each other nervous glances, but said nothing.

"Anyway, what interested me most was that it's isolated from the rest of your clan. Followed you closely enough to listen when you talked, and my suspicions were confirmed: you're no longer part of the Bowser Clan. Don't know why yet. Perhaps you'll tell me when you know me a little better."

He paused for a moment, waiting for an explanation. When neither Wainscot nor Moon gave him one, he continued. "I was with you when you went about your daily foraging, and never far away when you returned here to sleep. Was trying to gauge the best opportunity to approach you. Afraid you'd be frightened and would run, or worse, fight, and I might be forced to hurt you. Didn't want to do that."

"You did frighten us," said Moon, "and badly, despite your intentions. What made you think this was the right time to approach us?"

"Because you need me as much as I need you."

Moon was instantly on her feet. "We certainly do not need you." Her tone was icy, and she quivered with indignation. "I've lived all of my life without any help from you, or from anyone else for that matter. I may not look like much, but I can take care of myself quite well, thank you very much. I don't need you. I don't need anyone."

The words stung, but Wainscot knew better than to get in her way. He said nothing.

"In fact," said Moon, "I think I'd be happier if you just picked up that battered body of yours and took it somewhere else. I don't want you in my nest anymore."

My nest, Wainscot noticed.

Mizzen was unaffected by Moon's anger. Apparently unimpressed by the threat of violence written in every erect hair on her body, he continued to lie in the bedding, calm and relaxed. His lack of concern seemed to deflate Moon.

"Easy, Lass," he said, "You may not need me right at this moment, but you certainly did yesterday." Moon did not sit down again, but she allowed him to continue without interruption. "I was tailing you when you left the decks and took to the rigging. Was surprised by that, must admit. Never thought of going aloft. Afties never venture up there. I wasn't aware Bowsers did either. Too dangerous, too exposed. Man's territory. No way to stand and fight if you're dangling from a rope. Decided not to follow you, but waited to see if you'd return the same way. I could always find you back at your nest, if necessary.

"And, do you know, as I was waiting, three other rats came along. Nasty looking creatures they were, curs of the worst kind. Didn't see me—took care not to let them—and they sniffed about a bit. They obviously knew you and could smell that you'd passed by recently.

They decided to wait, and I watched them. Luckily for you. They didn't seem too fond of you."

"Spume and his... I suppose curs is as good a word for them as any," said Moon. She seemed to be shaking off some of her anger. "No they aren't very fond of me, nor me of them. They were going to—" She stopped and stared at Mizzen, her eyes glinting in the near dark. "It was you, wasn't it? It was your voice in the shadows. It wasn't Marlinspike at all."

Mizzen chuckled quietly. It was not a particularly warm laugh, but at the sound of it Moon's remaining animosity melted like winter's last snow.

"So Marlinspike wasn't there. It was just you playing games," she said.

"Hardly a game. Worked though, didn't it? Those curs ran like... well, like curs."

"Do you know Marlinspike?" asked Wainscot.

"Know *of* him," said Mizzen. "We fighters tend to hear about each other, and Marlinspike has a reputation. A reputation not too different from mine, I'm not too humble to say. Might even have faced him in a brawl or two. Wouldn't know him to see him though."

"But you knew his voice." There was wonder in Moon's voice. "I thought it was him speaking. How could you match his voice so perfectly if you've never heard him."

This time, Mizzen's laugh was full-throated and pleasant. "No idea what he sounds like, but I know the voice of authority. Any good officer or sergeant uses the same tone. Trick is to sound like you're shouting without raising your voice. Just said what I would have said to any contrary young rat under my command. Expect your Marlinspike would've said almost exactly the same thing if he'd come across your little party."

Wainscot wondered if Moon was disappointed that it had not been Marlinspike who had rescued them. Despite her assertion that everyone was afraid of the lieutenant, he suspected that she harboured an affection for him. There was something about the way she said his name.

"And what do you think you're up to, Laddie?" said Mizzen, and both he and Moon laughed. Wainscot did not. He noticed that Mizzen, despite his scars, was a fine looking rat. He wondered if Moon had noticed too, and if that had anything to do with the uncharacteristic haste with which she was warming to the Aftey. Surely she did not trust him? Wainscot had worked hard to earn her full trust—he thought of how long it had taken her to share the secret of the breadroom with him—and he was irritated that Mizzen had penetrated her defences so easily.

"I did think it odd that he called Spume 'Laddie'," said Moon. "Marlinspike has always called him 'Bilgemuck'. At least I've never heard him use another name."

"Bilgemuck," said Mizzen. "Have to remember that next time."

"I hope there won't be a next time," she said quietly.

"You haven't told us why you were following us, why you were spying on us," said Wainscot. He had been badly frightened, and now he was annoyed. Neither Moon nor Mizzen seemed to notice.

Mizzen told them the story of Dayrunner's eventful arrival amongst the Afties. At the first mention of Dayrunner's name, Wainscot started, but said nothing. *It must be the same Dayrunner*, he thought. It did not take a great leap of imagination to guess that at least one of his pursuers had managed to clamber onto the *Heloise* that misty night. The C'law were smart and persistent, and they might easily have found another rope or some other method of getting aboard the ship. *Did any more of them make it?* he wondered. He was only slightly relieved that Mizzen made no mention of any other Landers.

Wainscot was a little surprised at how frightened he was. *It was unlikely that Dayrunner would still be concerned about one insignificant little rat from his old clan*, he thought. The Dayrunner that Mizzen described was a rat fighting to win a place for himself in a new clan, a new world. Even if he knew that his quarry was aboard, would he really care enough to continue the hunt? It defied reason. Then Wainscot gave himself a mental shake. Reason had little to do with what drove the C'Law on. Dayrunner was C'Law, and the C'Law, were always single-minded in their fanatical drive to carry out any order given to them by the Council. Wainscot had broken one of the

Clan's prime laws, Dayrunner had been ordered to kill him, and he would succeed, or die in the attempt. It was that simple. Of course Dayrunner would continue the hunt.

Wainscot, against all expectation, had found a new home with Moon. He was coming to love her as he had loved Scuffle, and he hoped that the scruffy little ship rat might someday feel the same way about him. The knowledge that Dayrunner was aboard the *Heloise*, and was a threat to Wainscot's tiny new family, filled him with dread.

When Mizzen reached the end of his story, both Moon and Wainscot sat silent, absorbing what they had heard. Wainscot almost told them of Dayrunner's role in his flight from the Nest, but he hesitated. He had never mentioned Dayrunner's name to Moon, and he was reluctant to do so now, for reasons that he did not fully understand. Perhaps he simply did not want to share any details of his life with this stranger. He chose not to say anything, at least for now.

Eventually Moon said, "So you do need us. You have nowhere else to go. You can't go back to the Afties, and the Bowsers will kill you on sight." She lay down on the soft floor of the nest, with her paws crossed underneath her chin. "What are we going to do with you?"

CHAPTER 13

TRAPPED RATS

A low sound issued from the darkness. It was something between a moan and a whimper, and seemed strangely discordant, as though it came from more than one throat. It grated on Dayrunner's nerves.

He perched on the rim of the well, two of his lieutenants beside him, and gazed down into its inky depths. He could just discern some movement about eight or ten lengths down the shaft. The well, known as an elm tree pump, was a hollowed-out tree trunk that ran down through the decks of the ship and pierced the hull into the sea below. The sailors drew water up the shaft by bucket if they needed to fight a fire. For reasons best known to the men who sailed the *Heloise*, this particular well had been abandoned and sealed with a heavy wooden plug. Whatever was making the piteous sounds sat on top of the plug, part way down the shaft.

The well was on the gun deck, and Dayrunner's lieutenants must have been acutely aware that he was not happy at being brought this far up in the ship. Like all Afties, they lived in terror of their new Captain's mercurial temper—and of the punishments that often accompanied it. He was particularly hard on those who wasted his time.

"There are just some young rats down there," said Dayrunner. He had taken this break from the all-consuming business of running his clan because not just one, but two of his lieutenants had thought it important enough to overcome their fear of displeasing him.

"A patrol came across them, sir," said Spitkid, one of the lieutenants. "They're trapped. They're starving."

Spitkid had been the first of the new lieutenants promoted after Mizzen had fled. The Captain had chosen him for his size, as well as the fact that he moved as though he knew his way around a fight. Also, there was something in his eyes that suggested that he was a follower rather than a leader. He was clever enough, and Dayrunner could rely on him for sensible if unimaginative council, but he lacked ambition. This was just fine with the Captain. Ambition in a subordinate was dangerous. It led to too much thinking. He chose his officers for their size, strength, fighting ability and willingness to follow orders, not their nimbleness of mind. *He* was the thinker.

"I can see they're trapped," said Dayrunner. "What I can't see is a reason why I should care. Let them starve."

"Don't you see anything unusual about them sir?" Spitkid persisted.

Dayrunner turned on him with a snarl. "Don't play games with me, Spitkid. If there's something you want me to see, then out with it."

"Their tails, sir. Look at their tails."

Leaning as far into the opening as he could without toppling in, Dayrunner peered into the gloom. The light was poor, but as he stared he began to make out a few details. There were indeed several rats in the shaft—he counted six. As he had surmised, they were young. They looked up at him with dull, hopeless eyes, as though they had already resigned themselves to death. He tried to see their tails, but could not make out enough detail. Then he saw it. All six rats were in a circle around the inside of the shaft, with their backs to each other and their tails converging in the middle, like the spokes of a ship's wheel. The ends of their tails were all tangled together in a dark lump. No, they were more than tangled: they were fused. Their tails had become entwined, as sometimes happened when rats lived in particularly crowded conditions, or were forced into tight spaces for an extended period. Hair and filth had bonded into a tough, dense mass in which their tails were now inextricably bound.

Dayrunner surveyed them silently for some heartbeats. *How*, he wondered, *had they managed to survive long enough for their tails to become entangled so? How had they found water and food?* He supposed he would ask them at an opportune moment, assuming they were still capable of speech. They continued to stare up at him with expressionless eyes, mute but for their wordless moaning.

"I think they may have gone mad, sir," said Spitkid.

"I don't think it's madness," said Dayrunner. He was thoughtful, and some of the menace left his voice as he pondered. "Not precisely. It's something else."

He hopped down from the edge of the well, and began to walk away across the deck. Over his shoulder he said, "Find a way to get them out of there, and bring them back to the Council chamber. Don't hurt them. Feed them, but not too much."

Spitkid released an audible breath. He had not been berated or beaten, which was as good as a 'well done' from the Captain.

It was usual for a Captain of the Afties to share a nest with his lieutenants; he was expected to spend his resting hours with his closest confederates, who would provide him with companionship, council, and protection. However, Dayrunner chose to sleep alone. He had built a small nest for himself well away from the clan's crowded sleeping areas. He knew that too much familiarity would undermine his authority, and it was vital to his plans that every rat in the clan, including his trusted lieutenants, fear him. If he needed their council, he would seek them out.

As for his requiring their protection... He would have laughed if he had been capable of it. From whom did he need protection? Wasn't he the most dangerous thing in their world? Others needed protection from him. He feared no rat, and his nest was too deep in the structure of the ship for him to worry about either cats or Men.

He curled into the softness of his nest and thought of how much he had accomplished during his short time aboard the *Heloise*. His comfortable bed was the only luxury he allowed himself, and he found that he did his best thinking in it.

It had only been a few days since he and his fellow C'law had pursued the criminal to the water's edge, and now here he was—the Captain of his own clan. He was not a rat inclined to dwell on the past, but he could not help mulling over the chain of events that had brought him to his domination of the Aftey clan. The recollection unfurled in his mind like one of those tales the storytellers of the Nest had loved to tell.

He had been one of the leading rats in the pack of C'law who had followed the fugitive through the twisting alleys of the harbour town. He had not known him or the other one before the pursuit, but one of the other C'law had, and the names had soon made their way through the ranks—Wainscot and Scuffle. They were young rats—he could tell by their scent—and they had done a foolish thing. Dayrunner had not known the details of the crime, only that the youngsters had been in the Council chamber, and that alone was enough to warrant their deaths. The order had been hastily given as the C'law assembled from various parts of the Nest, and then was passed from C'law to C'law as they ran. It was brief and unambiguous: kill the trespassers.

They had taken the first one before she could escape the confines of the Nest, but the second had proven to be more elusive. He had made his way a considerable distance through Man's world before they had closed in on him.

It should have ended then. They had had him trapped with nowhere left to run, but he had not the grace to accept his fate. He had bolted again, this time out onto the pier and up a rope, until his path had been blocked by some sort of large flat disk. They had followed him up the rope only to watch, astonished, as he had tried to claw his way over the obstacle, and, when unsuccessful, had leapt into the mist and vanished.

There had been no sound of a splash. Dayrunner, several rats back from the front of the pack, had thought he might have heard the thump of a body hitting something solid, but he had not been sure.

The C'law had hesitated for only a moment before the first few had followed the fugitive, hurling themselves blindly into the night. This time there had been splashes. When he had found himself at the head of the group, Dayrunner had leapt without hesitation, thrusting off into the thick night air with little hope that he would land on anything other than the sea below. He had splashed into the water, but not before bouncing painfully off the side the ship. The cold water had forced the breath from his body, and when he had surfaced, spluttering and coughing, he had immediately began to paddle about, searching for a way back onto dry land.

The smooth wooden supports for the wharf above had caught his eye first, disappearing into the shadows beneath the pier like an orderly forest. For a short distance above the waterline they had been encrusted with barnacles that provided ample footholds; above these the wood had been polished to a glossy sheen by the lapping of the sea. They had been too smooth to climb.

The ship had loomed huge and dark above him, and he had set off down its length, hoping to find some way up onto it. He had heard other rats splashing about in the water near him, but could see none of them through the mist.

He had found himself beneath the rear of the ship. Fatigue and cold had leached the strength from his sodden body, and he had known that it was only a matter of a few breaths before he succumbed to exhaustion.

Then he had seen, just above him, a stout iron chain looping down the flat face of the stern, almost touching the water before curving back up into the mist. A swell had lifted him high enough that he could clamber onto the chain, and he had clung to the rusted links, unmoving, until some strength had seeped back into his limbs. Then, he had begun the long climb up to the ship.

Once aboard, he had found himself in a bewildering world. It had been crowded with Men, but there had also been evidence of a large rat population. Avoiding both, he had explored the strange new place, gradually moving down to the lower decks where there were fewer Men.

He had intended to continue his hunt for Wainscot. He would eventually make his way back to the Nest, he had known, but he had wanted to complete his mission before doing so. His duty had been clear: he was honour-bound to find and finish the criminal.

But before he could begin his search in earnest he had come across an Aftey patrol. He had seen them before they were aware of him, and recognised them for what they were—C'law. He had made the decision to step from his hiding place to wait patiently as they surrounded him.

They had not tried to kill him immediately, which was surprising. He had not known these C'law, or the rules by which they were governed, but C'law were C'law, and these would not be too different from his hard, merciless comrades back in the Nest. Perhaps something about him had convinced them that killing him might not be all that easy, or perhaps they had sensed that he might prove useful to their clan. In any case, they had not attacked, but had escorted him to their Captain.

As soon as he had laid eyes on Captain Plank, Dayrunner had changed his plans.

If this lout is what passes for a leader in these parts, he had thought, *then I should be able to turn this situation to my advantage without too much trouble.*

So he had acted swiftly and brutally, and had become the Captain of the Afties before the clan could gather what was happening.

Now, as he lay in his nest, he turned his thoughts to where his future would lie.

It was increasingly evident that he would likely never leave the *Heloise*. The ship was now his world. His previously held certainty that he would return to the Nest had faded. He now focussed his formidable will on strengthening and growing his dominance over his new domain.

It will be a fight, he thought, but he was confident in his abilities. *I'm a land rat—and a C'law from the Nest, no less.*

His natural superiority over the waterlogged little sea-rats of the *Heloise* had made his rapid climb to the top of their ranks almost inevitable. But, when he thought about it, he was a little surprised at how easily he had put aside the life of his old Nest. His loyalty to his clan had been so strong that he had been willing to sacrifice himself to enforce the Council's law, but now he thought only of conquering the shipboard rats. He would not have described his past devotion to duty as unquestioning, but he had never looked for any explanation or clarification of his orders; he had merely carried them out as efficiently as possible, and he now conceded that he might have been somewhat blind in his loyalty.

Yet, as he now engaged in a single-minded drive to make this new world his own, he had abandoned his old life almost completely. He had turned his back on his previous duty without a pang of guilt. He cast aside his past life when it became clear that he would likely never return to it, and he attacked his new self-appointed task with the same focussed ferocity as he had his duties as C'law of the Nest.

But, there was one outstanding issue always lurking at the back of his mind, no matter what pressing concern might be competing for his attention: the matter of the transgressor, Wainscot.

It was extremely unlikely that Wainscot was still alive—if the land rat had actually managed to climb aboard the *Heloise*, the chances that he had survived his first encounter with a ship's rat were slim. If he had found his way back to shore, then the C'law from the Nest would certainly have ended him. However, the mere possibility of the fugitive's continuing existence reminded Dayrunner that he had not completed his last mission for the Nest. He was too much of a C'Law to simply decide not to obey an order from his Council, regardless of whether it made sense any more.

This one nagging duty was the last thread that tied Dayrunner to his old life, and it prevented him from applying his undivided attention to his new clan. He would, he knew, probably never have the chance to obey his last order, but if he were ever to find that Wainscot was still alive and aboard the *Heloise*, he would use his new power to crush the criminal. In doing so, he would finally sever this last link to the Nest.

CHAPTER 14

SKIRMISH

N ow they were three. Although they had not discussed it, and they had not actually asked him to join, Mizzen was now one of them—or, to be more accurate, he was a provisional member of their tiny new clan. Wainscot still did not trust him, and he made no effort to disguise the fact. He spoke to the older rat only when necessary and did his best to ensure that neither he nor Moon were ever alone with Mizzen. Not that this actually afforded them any additional safety, as Wainscot was well aware. If Mizzen wished to harm them, he was perfectly capable of it.

When he was being honest with himself, Wainscot wondered why he continued to be suspicious of the Aftey. Mizzen's story was plausible, and he had certainly saved them from Spume. Also, Wainscot could think of no reason why Mizzen would befriend them except for a need for companionship and a lack of anywhere else go. They certainly did not have anything else that he might want.

It nettled him, but Wainscot was candid enough to admit to himself that at least some of his unease stemmed from jealousy. Moon had become the sister he had lost when Scuffle died. In their short time together, he had grown to love her, and had come to cherish the bond that had developed between them. She was his family now, and he was certain that she thought of him in the same light. *The way that she treats me hasn't changed since Mizzen arrived*, he admitted to himself. But now he was forced to share her, and he did not like it. He also did not like the way she looked at Mizzen. There was something of hero-worship about it—or perhaps a touch of romantic infatuation.

The only sign that Moon had not yet unconditionally accepted Mizzen into their little clan was that she had kept the secret of the breadroom from him. By unspoken agreement neither she nor Wainscot had mentioned it, despite Mizzen having been with them for many days now. It gave Wainscot some comfort that she still shared something special only with him, but unfortunately it meant that they went without biscuits. Mizzen obviously knew that Moon had a way into the breadroom—he had heard what Spume had said, after all —but he never broached the subject.

Still, as the days passed, Wainscot was forced to admit that Mizzen was proving to be a very useful addition to their clan. Moon was extremely good at the business of moving about the ship without being seen, but Mizzen's abilities were almost supernatural. He could sense the presence of Bowsers long before he heard or smelled them, and he heard and smelled them long before either Moon or Wainscot did. On one memorable occasion—Wainscot thought it might have been on the third day he was with them—the older rat's uncanny senses had spared them no end of trouble.

They were foraging for food a little closer to the Bowser-Aftey border than they usually dared to go, near to where a portion of the hold was sectioned off to form the main gunpowder storage magazine. Deep in the ship to keep it is as far from enemy gunfire as possible, this room was illuminated only by lanterns shining through windows from adjacent lamp-rooms, so that no flames were ever near the explosive powder. The strong smell of the powder was disorienting, and masked warning odours, so the clans seldom entered the magazine. However, they usually launched their raids into enemy territory through the passages beneath its decking.

Wainscot, Moon and Mizzen were exploring some barrels stacked against the magazine's exterior bulkhead when Mizzen stiffened and told them to stop moving. He stood still for a moment, head cocked to one side, listening. Then he hissed, "Quickly, with me," and scrambled up several tiers into one of the gaps between the barrels. The others followed, and the three of them peered out from their hiding place at the open space of the hold below.

They waited, but Wainscot saw nothing but rows of stacked stores. He heard nothing but the creaking of wood and the chuckle of water against the side of the ship, and smelled nothing but timber, rot and the sneeze-inducing tang of gunpowder.

"What...?" he began, but Mizzen silenced him with a hiss.

They waited some more: still, Wainscot saw, heard, and smelled nothing. Then, just as he was about to speak again, he saw a group of ten or fifteen rats emerge from beneath the magazine.

They were Afties. Even Wainscot recognised them, although their odour had not yet reached him. They did not move like rats comfortable in their own territory. Cautious and furtive, they crept slowly into the open with their snouts swaying back and forth as they tested the air. It was obvious that they were intruders.

An Aftey raiding party, Wainscot thought, and his suspicion was confirmed when their musty scent reached him. The odour was similar to Mizzen's, but laced with excitement and fear.

The raiders passed beneath the watchers and disappeared into one of the many tunnels in the piles of stores. They had not uttered a sound while they had been in sight, and if their scent had not still lingered in the air, Wainscot might have thought them part of a waking dream. After a few moments he started to crawl from the pile of barrels, but Mizzen stopped him, whispering, "Not yet."

Again they waited. Wainscot suppressed his growing impatience, knowing that Mizzen's senses were far sharper than his. He was grateful for the older rat's caution when the Afties reappeared, now scurrying quickly, a dash of panic in their movement.

The party stopped in the middle of the hold, and turned back to face the way they had come. Suddenly, another group of rats emerged onto the open floor. They were Bowsers, and outnumbered the raiding party by some ten or eleven rats. The newcomers looked like seasoned fighters. They did not hesitate before loosing a shrill screech and launching themselves at the Afties.

What followed was a chaos of flying fur, slashing teeth, and raking claws. The outnumbered Afties did not flee for their lives, as Wainscot thought any reasonable rat would do, but answered the Bowsers with a charge of their own. There was no order given, no shouted command to attack, but the smaller group threw themselves into the fray with savage ferocity, all signs of nervousness vanishing at the promise of action. The two parties met in a squealing tangle of bodies that spread from one side of the corridor to the other, scattering and coalescing almost rhythmically as the combatants grappled and separated, only to weigh into each other again.

Slowly the melee moved along the length of the passageway, away from the watchers. Several dark forms—still or moving feebly—lay in its wake.

The hidden observers watched silently until Mizzen decided that it was safe to slip from the hiding place without being seen. They made their way back to their nest as quickly as possible. Only when they were securely ensconced in its safety did they discuss what they had witnessed.

"Did you see them?" asked Mizzen. "They were magnificent."

"Who were?" Wainscot asked. He was genuinely puzzled. He had not seen anything magnificent in the battle. It had been horrifying.

"The Afties. Proud of my boys. They were outnumbered and outweighed, and they stuck into the curs—er, into the Bowsers—without even a heartbeat's hesitation. Course, they should've split the group to take 'em from each side. Mind you, under my command they wouldn't have been taken by surprise in the first place. We would've only fought when we chose to. Wonder who their leader was. Didn't recognise him, but I'm surprised Dayrunner gave him command of a raiding party. Rank amateur, if you want my opinion."

Wainscot kept his comments to himself, but he thought the Afties mad to have thrown themselves into what had looked to him like certain death.

For several days after the battle, Mizzen regaled them with assertions of how he would have handled things better, much to Wainscot's annoyance. Still, he had to admit that if it had not been for the acute senses of the old warrior, they all would have found themselves right in the middle of the fracas. Mizzen was a handy and capable rat, and Wainscot knew that he would want the former Aftey by his side if they ever happened across Spume again.

Despite all this, he could not convince himself to trust, or even like Mizzen. He found him irritatingly pompous and self-satisfied. No matter the situation, Mizzen always knew best what to do, and was not shy about sharing his opinions. Perhaps sensing that his new membership in their little family did not yet give him the right, he never actually gave orders, but he always had suggestions, advice and comments about how he would have done things differently. Wainscot suspected that Mizzen would like nothing better than to assume leadership of their group, and he would not hesitate to do so at some point. Wainscot promised himself that he would not make it easy for Mizzen, although he was not entirely sure what he could do to prevent it.

For his part, Mizzen seemed completely oblivious of Wainscot's feelings toward him. Wainscot knew that he would have to get along with Mizzen if the group were to survive, and he wanted to keep Moon as happy as possible, so he decided to bury his misgivings. He would treat Mizzen with cordiality—actual friendship was out of the question—and do his best to encourage harmony in the nest; he would also watch the old warrior carefully, and keep his suspicions handy.

With this in mind, he decided that although he had few skills, there was one that he could use to strengthen the bonds that held his new clan together— storytelling. He reasoned that the best way to keep Mizzen from doing anything harmful would be to draw him further into the clan, and closer to his clanmates. *And what better way to do that than with shared stories?* he thought. *Even crusty old soldiers like a good tale well told.* It would go a long way toward bringing their little clan together, and besides, he had not spun a tale since the marathon storytelling session all those days ago when he had told Moon the one about the ginger cats. He missed telling tales.

He waited until the next time the three were in the nest, curled together and preparing for sleep, their bellies comfortably full.

He asked, "Have either of you heard the story of the rat who wanted to fly?"

"Probably have," said Mizzen. "Heard a tale or two in my time."

"Is it another one about Chewtooth?" asked Moon.

"Not this time," said Wainscot. "It's about a rat named Crunchbeetle, and some honey, some bees, and some flies."

"No, I haven't heard that one," said Moon.

Mizzen just grunted.

"I'm not too surprised," said Wainscot with a smile, "since it's one of my own stories, and I've only told it to one other rat."

Moon gave him a poke with her snout. "Then stop teasing us, and tell us about the bees and the honey."

So Wainscot told them the story of how Crunchbeetle, a not particularly bright rat living on a large farm, had decided that the only way to make a name for himself in his clan was to steal some forbidden honey from the farmer. His plan was to eat enough live flies that they would fill his stomach and lift him up so that he could get over an unscalable fence and into the enclosure containing the beehives. It had all gone swimmingly well until he discovered that he could not control the flies, and he was last glimpsed by his clanmates sailing away over the treetops, never to be seen again[1].

The story was a favourite of Wainscot's because although things did not go at all well in the end, it illustrated that a rat, even one as dim as Crunchbeetle, could accomplish anything if he put his mind to it—even fly.

Moon nodded her appreciation when he finished the story.

Mizzen seemed less impressed.

"Not a bad story," said Mizzen. "Always loved a tale. Didn't believe a word of that one, mind, but it's a fair story nonetheless. Course, I'd change it a little bit if I were telling it. Not nearly enough fighting in it. And all that about honey: would have made it cheese or treacle or something of that nature. Definitely not honey."

Wainscot ignored him, but Moon said, "You don't know what honey is, do you?"

"Course I do," said Mizzen. "But treacle's a much more respectable food-"

"I don't know what it is either. Or rather, I know what it is, but I've never tasted it," said Moon, "but at least I have the decency to admit it."

Her tone was teasing and affectionate, but Wainscot was thoroughly annoyed by Mizzen's pomposity.

"And I suppose you could tell a better story," said Wainscot. "One with treacle in it."

"Might have one," considered Mizzen. "No treacle, though. Bit of fighting."

Wainscot stared at the older rat with surprise. "You have a story?"

"Might," said Mizzen.

"I wouldn't have pegged you as the story-telling type," said Wainscot, a bit sourly. "Right then—let's hear it."

"Didn't say I was going to tell it."

"I thought as much."

"Very well, since you insist." Mizzen cleared his throat, and stood to assume what he obviously considered a story-telling stance, legs spread wide and chest outthrust.

"Three brothers were known to have fought
each other when tempers ran hot.
One was named Lumpy,
because he was bumpy,
while the others were smooth, and were not.
One morning as all lay abed,
and the sun hadn't riz o'erhead,
Lump said to the others,
"I hate you, my brothers",
and by evening all three were dead.
Their bodies, all mangled and torn,
lay a-rot 'til the following morn.
When their Ma saw them lying,
she bent over them, crying,
"How I wish they had never been born"."

Finished, Mizzen plopped back down with a satisfied grunt.

The other two were silent for a few breaths. Eventually, Moon said, "That was horrible."

"And not a story," said Wainscot. "It was poem, and not a good one."

"Why would you tell us such an awful story—"

"Poem," interrupted Wainscot.

"Poem, then," Moon said. "Why would you tell us such an awful poem?"

"Told you," said Mizzen. "It has fighting in it."

"Barely," said Wainscot, "Although, you were right about one thing—there was definitely no treacle in that poem."

"You know," said Mizzen, unfazed, "Could do with a taste of treacle m'self right now. All of that talk of honey—"

"Which is completely unknown to you," Moon insisted.

Mizzen ignored her. "All of that talk of honey has given me a hunger for something sweet."

"I'll bet you don't even know what a bee is." Moon was enjoying herself thoroughly.

"After we've slept, I think we should venture out and see if we can scare us up some treacle." Mizzen talked right through Moon's teasing. "Smelled a barrel of the stuff down near where we heard the cat moving about yesterday. Don't know if we'll be able to get into the barrel. More and more of them seem to be lined these days—"

Not one to be discouraged, Moon continued, "In fact, I'll wager you wouldn't know a bee if it stung you on the nose. I, however, do. When my mother was a pup one of the sailors tried to keep a small hive on board. The Man Captain wouldn't have any of it, of course, and the sailor had to get rid of it the first time the ship..."

As Wainscot listened to his nestmates chattering on, he began to drift off to sleep. His last thought before slumber took him was that, all things considered, and despite his misgivings about Mizzen, he had managed to fall into a good life aboard the *Heloise*.

CHAPTER 15

A DREAM OF MAN-RATS

For the first time since he had boarded the ship, Wainscot's dream was not of his life back on land. Scuffle did not visit him, and he did not re-live that last terrifying race through the tunnels of the Nest.

This time, Moon made an appearance, accompanied by Mizzen.

The three of them stood side by side on the main deck of the ship. The sun beat down on them, warming their fur and making the wood beneath their feet pleasant to walk across. That they were exposed on the deck in broad daylight did not seem to concern them, and a glance about told Wainscot why. There were no Men to be seen: none in the rigging, none at the rails, and none moving about the decks in pursuit of their inexplicable tasks. There was no sound of them either. No whistles and shouts, no stamping of feet, and no low hum of voices burbling up from the decks below. There was, however, a trace of their smell in the air. A teasing suggestion of it tickled Wainscot's nose as a draught of air wafted up through an open hatch.

Instead of Men there were rats—many rats, dozens of rats—bustling about the decks as if they owned the ship. They were huge, sleek, and positively glowing with glossy good health. By their scent, they were all Afties.

Most of them sat back on their haunches, their forelegs waving in the air. Then Wainscot looked more closely, and shook his head in disbelief. They were not squatting on their hindquarters, he saw: they were standing and walking on their hind legs like Men.

Suddenly Wainscot did not feel warm anymore. The sun still cast its fire across his fur, but a chill blossomed inside him, and fear raised the hairs along his back.

As he watched, more rats came up the ladders from the lower decks, and he was alarmed to see that some them had cloth draped about their bodies. It clung to them tightly, exactly like the second skins worn by Men. These rats were battle-worn and scarred. Some still had open wounds as though they were fresh from a fight, all of them decorated with splashes of bright blood about their muzzles and on their claws. When they grinned, he saw that their great yellow teeth were stained pink.

These newcomers were much larger than the unclothed rats who still walked about the decks, and were growing before his eyes. They became cat-sized, then dog-sized, and kept swelling until they were as tall as Men. As they grew they changed, becoming long of limb and short of trunk, their tails drawing up into their bodies and disappearing, until they were fully Man-shaped. They did not lose their rich, dark fur, however, and their heads were still those of rats—pointed and toothy—though now perched on wide Man-shoulders.

Wainscot took a step back from them. A small squeak escaped him.

The giant rats turned their gazes, flat and lifeless, upon him. Their eyes, no longer the shiny black pebbles of proper rats, now had the pale irises and dull whites of Man-eyes.

The creatures began to advance toward Wainscot.

He turned to flee, and Moon and Mizzen ran with him. They dashed toward one of the many ratholes aligned in a row along the base of the bulwark at the perimeter of the deck. The holes looked like those found in the baseboards of old abandoned buildings, but they offered refuge. The three rats eagerly piled into one of them.

Once inside, they found themselves in a wide tunnel with a sharp downward slope. Wainscot noticed with surprise that the walls and floor were not wood, but damp earth instead. The soil beneath their feet was cool, and the moist darkness pleasant after the baking heat of the deck. The three rats began to walk side-by-side down the passage.

Before they had travelled more than a length or two, however, they found their way blocked by dark figures packed into the space before them. It took a moment for Wainscot's eyes, still dazzled by the bright sunlight, to adjust to the darkness. When they did, he saw that it was not rats who blocked the tunnel, but Men—rat-sized, naked Men. The rank smell of them was almost overpowering in the confines of the tunnel. They began to advance toward the rats, chanting in their strange guttural voices. They carried clubs, which they slapped against their palms in time with their song.

The three had no choice but to return to the deck, and the Man-rats that waited there. They tumbled out into the bright light, blinking and squinting, and the huge Man-dressed rats closed in on them.

"The rigging," said Moon. "We have to get into the rigging."

"They smell like Afties," said Mizzen. "Afties never go aloft."

They turned, seeking a way up onto the rigging, but the Man-rats blocked the way.

"How do we get up there?" asked Wainscot.

"We'll have to fly," said Moon. "Like Crunchbeetle."

"But there are no flies about."

"Or bees," said Mizzen, but this was not true. There were bees everywhere. They flew in shifting waves above the deck and lay in pulsing carpets on the boles of the masts. The drone of their buzzing grew in volume until it overwhelmed the hissing of the sea and the cracking of the sails.

A flicker of light caught Wainscot's eye, and he turned his head to see a fish soar over him and up into the rigging, dipping and weaving between the ropes and sheets, snapping up bees as it went. Bright sunlight played along the blue-green scales of the fish's flanks, and threw sparks off its long supple wings. The bottom fork of its tail was much longer than the top, and it shed diamond droplets of water from the tip as it rose above the watching rats.

That must be a flying fish, thought Wainscot. *I remember Moon talking about them.*

Several more fish followed the first, gambolling through the clean air like pups playing tag.

"Bite onto their tails," said Moon.

She leapt into the air and bit down on a dangling tail. The fish bobbed slightly, then recovered, sweeping up over the heads of the Man-rats and into the maze of rigging, trailing Moon behind it. Both Mizzen and Wainscot followed her, clamping down on fish tails and holding tight as they were carried aloft.

If Moon's intention had been to drop from the fish onto one of the spars or sails, she was disappointed, for her fish was through the rigging and out into the open air beyond before she had a chance. Mizzen and Wainscot were close behind, and in a moment all three rats were flying out across the open sea. Behind them, the *Heloise* shrank until she was nothing but a white smudge on the horizon. It was only a matter of moments before she disappeared completely.

Wainscot's fish climbed ever higher into the sky. He felt his jaws tiring. He had a firm grip on the tail, but it would soon weaken and he would drop into the sea. He wondered whether the fall would kill him, or if he would drown. Then he remembered the sharks, and he decided that he would prefer to be smashed by the hard surface of the water.

Brine ran from the fish's tail into his mouth and throat, making it difficult for him to breath. He wondered how Moon and Mizzen were faring.

Finally his jaws could support him no longer. He released his grip and fell with squeal, his eyes closed. He sensed the surface of the sea rushing up to meet him, and braced himself for the impact.

Wainscot awoke with a start. He stood and shook his body briskly, trying to shed the fear and confusion of the dream.

Strangely, he was alone in the nest. Moon and Mizzen had been curled up beside him when he had fallen asleep, but now there was no sign of either of them. The bedding where they had lain was cool, and their scent was no longer fresh, so they had been gone for some time. He was surprised that their leaving had not wakened him.

Cautiously he stepped from the nest and sniffed. The scents of his nestmates hung in the air, accompanied by something else; a mixture of odours at once familiar, yet strange in the way they were tangled together.

With a rushing patter of feet, two rats bowled into him, knocking him onto his side. He tried to regain his feet and scramble back into the nest, but one of them grabbed him firmly by the scruff of the neck, and the other by the base of the tail. Neither bit down hard enough to hurt, but they held him fast and began to drag him across the deck away from the sheltering stack of barrels. With a shock, Wainscot realised that his attackers were Moon and Mizzen.

"What's going on? What are you doing?" he asked, wondering if he were still dreaming.

Neither answered, their mouths full of Wainscot parts.

He stopped struggling and allowed himself to be carried along. They brought him through the stacked stores to a small clear space where a low wooden bucket sat on the deck. The strange odours emanated from the bucket.

Moon and Mizzen carried him to the bucket, lifted him over the rim and dropped him inside. He landed in the sticky mess that filled the bottom. The two other rats hopped up onto the rim, and pushed him down with their forepaws, rolling him around until his fur was matted with filth.

When at last they were satisfied with their job, they allowed him to stand. They did not stop him when he climbed out of the bucket. His fur was matted and spiked with the stuff, and his feet stuck to the deck when he walked. Neither Moon nor Mizzen had said a word since the beginning of the attack, and now they sat side-by-side, watching him.

Finally, they laughed. "Welcome aboard!" they cheered in unison.

"I don't understand," said Wainscot. He was not amused.

"At last, you're one of us," said Moon.

Wainscot patiently waited for further explanation.

Moon sighed and said, "You're a bit thick, aren't you? Your scent: it marks you as a Lander. You don't smell like a ship's rat. Well, Mizzen and I decided to remedy that. Now you smell like one of us... only worse. Think of it as your initiation into the Tribe of the *Heloise*."

They laughed again, longer and louder this time. Begrudgingly, Wainscot joined them. Soon they were almost helpless with mirth. It took a while for all three to regain their composure.

Mizzen, likely abashed that he had surrendered so completely to the laughter, and thinking that it had not done his dignity any good, shook himself and mumbled something about Wainscot smelling better now that he had lost the Lander stink.

"What was that stuff?" asked Wainscot. "It was horrible."

"Ah, that was the heart of the initiation," said Moon. "We gathered the smells that most represent the... the essence... of the *Heloise*." She began to laugh again.

"Wanted you to smell like an old tar," said Mizzen. "In fact, tar was one of the main ingredients."

"And gunpowder, salt-water, muck from the bilges, straw and manure from the manger, and... what else was in there Mizzen?"

"Ah, can't forget the one ingredient that almost cost me my life: tobacco juice from the spitkids. A sailor actually missed the 'kid and spit on me when I was getting it. Foul stuff, that."

"How did you bring it back here?" asked Wainscot.

"Rather not elaborate," said Mizzen with a grimace. "Let's just say that nothing has tasted quite right since I collected it."

"But it must have taken days to gather it all. Surely you didn't do it just as a prank?"

"No," said Moon. "Although it was a good joke, we had a serious purpose. We meant it when we said you smell like a Lander. It's obvious that you don't belong, and your scent points the way back to our nest. We can do without that sort of attention. I've been cast out, but at least I still smell like a ship's rat. I blend in with the odours of the ship: you stand out."

"But I stink," said Wainscot.

"But at least you don't stink like a Lander," said Moon.

"What about Mizzen? You said yourself that he smells like an Aftey. Even I could tell. Shouldn't we roll him in the stuff too?"

"Well played, Laddie," said Mizzen, "but it won't be happening."

"Mizzen's still a ship's rat," said Moon. "He carried a different odour when he first arrived here, but he's been away from the Afties long enough that he's lost their distinctive smell. It was a good try, but you won't get him into the bucket that easily."

"Well someone's got to. I'm not going to be the only one."

"'Fraid you are, Laddie," said Mizzen. "And there's worse news. Have to keep the stuff on you for at least a couple of days. Have to mask your scent, so the mixture'll need to get into your skin. When we do clean it off, we'll see if your odour's changed at all, and if not, it's back into the bucket with you."

"It shouldn't take too long," said Moon helpfully. "After all, you're eating our food now, and sleeping in our nest. I'm sure you'll be one of us soon enough."

"Have to stay in the nest until you become a little less... pungent," said Mizzen. "Can't risk you wandering around in that state. We'll bring food back for you."

Wainscot surrendered with ill grace. He agreed to stay in the nest until the other two gave him leave to go out again, but he also began planning his revenge. *Initiation indeed*, he thought. *I can play that game too. They won't soon forget what I'll have cooked up for them.* But, as it happened, he would never have his revenge. Events would conspire to rob him of the chance.

A short time after the malodorous bath, the three nestmates lay together, enjoying a special treat—slivers of dried beef that Mizzen had found near where some of the Men slung their hammocks. Moon and Mizzen were pressed up against one wall of the nest, as far away from Wainscot's stink as they could get.

"Come a little closer," said Wainscot. "If I have to live with it, then so do you." Neither Moon nor Mizzen moved, concentrating on their food.

"Very well. Have it your way." He returned his attention to the beef. "I had a dream," he said after a bout of chewing. "Do you want to hear about it?"

Both of the other rats looked up.

"A dream?" said Moon with interest. Wainscot knew that she put great stock in the meaning of dreams, despite her avowed skepticism about the superstitions of the ship's rats. Although she would die before admitting it, he was certain that she secretly believed that dreams foretold the future. Mizzen, on the other hand, had made it abundantly clear that he had no trouble at all with superstitions: he believed in them implicitly. He *knew* that dreams were portents, and it was only interpreting them correctly that was difficult. For his part, Wainscot thought that they were nothing more than the stories a rat told himself in his sleep. They had provided him with many an idea for his own tales.

"Tell us," said Mizzen.

Wainscot began to mumble quietly.

"Speak up, rat," said Mizzen.

"I'm sorry," said Wainscot. "The fumes from this stuff in my fur must be getting into my throat. I can't speak any louder."

Reluctantly, and with wrinkled noses, Moon and Mizzen edged closer.

"Still don't think you'll be able to hear me," said Wainscot.

They shifted a little further, until they were almost touching his matted fur.

Satisfied, Wainscot told them of the Man-rats and flying fish. When he finished, they were silent, each digesting the elements of the dream.

After a moment, Moon said, "It's rather disturbing. I don't know what it means, but I have a feeling it's nothing good."

"Poppycock," said Mizzen with a snort. "The dream speaks of great things for the Afties. They were powerful—so powerful that they lorded it over the ship like Men. Glorious."

"Are you forgetting something?" asked Moon. "You're no longer an Aftey. How could a powerful Aft Clan mean anything but trouble for you—or us, for that matter?"

"There is that. I suppose you're right," said Mizzen. There was an undertone to his voice that made it clear that the prospect of a mighty Aft Clan still excited him. Old loyalties died hard.

Wainscot laughed. "Stuff and nonsense," he said. "It was just a dream. It meant nothing. Telling the story about Crunchbeetle must have put the thought of flying into my head, and that's where the dream came from. The Afties aren't going to turn into Men, and we're not going to fly out to sea hanging from the tails of flying fish. I just told you about it to get you to move closer, and it worked."

"We know that," said Moon. "We're not fools. We just think it's wise not to ignore dreams. They may not come to pass, but they can often tell us important things. This one scares me."

They said no more about the dream, but as they drifted off to sleep, Wainscot was thinking about its significance. He was now sorry he had told them about it. It had originally upset him, but its impact had quickly faded, and he now found it amusing. However, it concerned him that Moon was so bothered by it, and he was suspicious of Mizzen's reaction.

Does the old warrior still think of himself as an Aftey? he wondered, *and what does that say about his feelings toward us?*

CHAPTER 16

TRAINING

Dayrunner saw the smaller rat fall beneath the weight of her larger opponent, and he stepped forward to stop the attack. It took few heartbeats for the larger rat to master his fighting fury and shift himself from on top of the fallen female. The look on Dayrunner's face was more than enough to douse the male's need to keep attacking.

"You think you've done well?" Dayrunner asked him. "You

knocked her down, and now there's nothing between you and her throat, right?"

The larger rat said nothing, but the arrogant tilt of his head conveyed his answer quite clearly. Of course he thought he had done well—he was winning.

They were in a large open space deep in the stores of the hold. Dayrunner had selected the space because it was large enough for twenty or so rats to move about, but was surrounded on all sides by crates and barrels stacked almost to the underside of the deck overhead. Shielded as it was from the prying eyes of the Men, it was ideal as one of his training areas.

"She's smaller than you," said Dayrunner. "I'd be surprised if you couldn't bully her to the deck. But look behind her. See her groupmates?" He gestured with his snout at the nine other rats arrayed in a tight line behind the fallen female, who was now regaining her feet. "They're each smaller than you too, but do you think that if this were an actual battle, they'd just let you get on with mauling their comrade? Why did you attack alone?"

Dayrunner looked at the watching line of rats. "And what's wrong with you?" he asked. "This lout just attacked your group-mate. Take him."

Squealing in unison, the rats charged and buried the large male in a wave of fur, claws and teeth.

Dayrunner then turned on the other group of nine rats who were watching from the other side. "What about you? Are you just going to watch them tear your comrade apart?"

The other group threw themselves at the melee with squeals of their own.

Dayrunner watched the writhing tangle of rats for a few moments before turning to the two sergeants beside him. "Don't let them kill each other," he instructed, "but don't break them up until there's blood."

He made his way to a small gap between two of the crates, on his way to the next training area. Glancing over his shoulder at the fray, he disappeared into the shadows.

Dayrunner wound his way through twisting ratways deep in the piles of stores, making his way to the next open space where another pair of fighting groups were being pitted against each other by their sergeants. As he scurried through the dim passageways, he considered the progress he had made.

The training was going well. He would not admit as much to his lieutenants or sergeants, much less to the troops themselves, but he was pleased with the progress his fighting rats were making. He could now envision them becoming the army he needed.

As soon as he had established control of his new clan, he had set out to forge them into an effective, efficient fighting force, but it had been discouraging in the beginning. He had joined several raids into Bowser territory during the first days of his rule, and he had not been impressed by what he had seen. Individually, the Afties had demonstrated capable martial skills, but they lacked discipline, and were not aware of the advantages of fighting as a group. On each of the raids, his group had been soundly thrashed, and in one case they had actually lost a rat. One-on-one, his rats were better in a fight, but the Bowsers were better organised and used superior tactics.

Dayrunner's first task had been to give his army structure. Every adult rat of fighting age was placed in a fighting patrol group of ten under the leadership of a more experienced sergeant. These patrol groups were gathered into units of four which he called 'packs', each of which was led by a lieutenant who reported directly to Dayrunner.

It was a simple organization, but effective, and combined with regular mock combat drill, was quickly changing his ragged rabble of brawlers into an army.

At first, the idea of teamwork was difficult for his soldiers to fully understand. Rats are fierce fighters, and a group of them can effectively overwhelm a much larger enemy, but in the heat of battle each rat acts blindly on his own. Fighting rats are very difficult to control when consumed by rage, but Dayrunner trained his troops to face each battle with cool detachment and to work with their groupmates as a cohesive unit. His efforts were beginning to show results; he was rapidly building what he considered to be the finest fighting force the rat world had ever seen.

As he emerged into the next training space, Dayrunner saw that the patrol groups here were sparring with each other in a much more disciplined manner, fighting group against group.

He was pleased, but it was not his way to praise. Instead he burst into their midst with a roar, shouting, "Just what do you think you're doing? This isn't playtime for pups."

With a lunge, he knocked the nearest rat to the deck. He pinned the shocked soldier down with his forepaws. All the rats stared at him, suddenly motionless.

"Right," he said. "I'm going to show you how it's done."

CHAPTER 17

NASCENT RAT-KING

A cockroach, all legs and shiny nut-brown shell, appeared from a loose-fitting seam in the timbers. It stopped, its antennae testing the air for telltale odours and vibration. Reflections from the hold's lanterns glinted from its carapace like distant stars. Satisfied that all was well, it continued its questing way down the sloping wall to disappear through a crack in the decking. In the gloom below the planks it stopped again to search for danger, but before it could move on, something large and dark and many-limbed crashed down upon it with a discordant squeal. The insect disappeared into several eager mouths and, after a moment's noisy crunching, was gone.

Dayrunner, who had been watching the little drama with interest, turned away from the entrance to the rat-king's cell. He signalled a guard to resume position before the hole.

Inside, the pathetic collection of young rats, still joined at the tails, huddled in their small prison. They were guarded night and day to ensure that they did not chew their way out, although there seemed to be little need for this; they had done little since their rescue but mutter quietly to themselves and shift around looking for something to eat. Dayrunner had ordered food and water to be brought to them, but he had also instructed the guards that they were never to be given quite enough. He wanted the prisoners to be kept hungry and thirsty.

Dayrunner brought his head close to Spitkid's so they could not be overheard. He said in a low voice, "Do you know what we have here?"

"I believe so, sir," said Spitkid, "but I've never actually seen one before."

"I have. This one's different though. There's something missing."

"I'd heard of them, but to tell you the truth I'd always half believed that they only existed in stories. That they were made-up, if you know what I mean."

"No, they're real," said Dayrunner, and then lapsed into silence.

Spitkid, as if sensing that the little interlude of uncharacteristic chumminess was at an end, took several steps back. Dayrunner was unpredictable at the best of times, and a sensible rat did not linger too long with him.

Dayrunner, however, was no longer even aware of Spitkid's presence. He had dismissed the lieutenant from his mind and was sifting through memories of his days in the C'law of his old clan. He had often been assigned to guard duty at the Council chambers, and he knew what was hidden away in the inner chamber. He had heard it often enough, and even he, who had little fellow-feeling for other rats, had found its cries pitiable. It had moaned, and cried, and laughed hysterically. Although it was capable of using words, he had never been able to make any sense of what it said. He had never seen it of course; no one but the councilrats had been allowed to lay eyes on it, and even the rats who brought it food had only been allowed into the outer chambers. The councilrats themselves had always been the ones to push the food into the inner room.

Even so, he had known what it was. All of the C'law had. It was the rat-king.

Its purpose had been to provide advice—or possibly prophesy—to the Council. How it had done so he could not imagine as he had never heard it utter anything but gibberish. He did know that it was vitally important to the Council, and that it was fragile. It had to be protected from influence by other rats. That was why the punishment for trespassers in the Council chambers was death. That was why he had been sent out in the world in pursuit of the criminal, Wainscot.

The rat-king had once been several individual rats, but they had joined together to become something new. Something different. Something no longer quite rat.

Can this collection of half-starved young rats possibly be a rat-king? he wondered. *They're so... insignificant. The rat-king of the old nest had power.*

He could sense no power in this sad little group. He had heard them speaking to each other, and although he could not make out much of what they said, what he *could* hear was rambling and nonsensical. Perhaps there was an art to interpreting their words, and he simply did not possess the necessary skill. Still, even if they did not eventually prove to have the unnatural gifts of the rat-king of his old nest, Dayrunner knew that he could use them.

Since assuming command of the Afties, he had been required to defer to the advice of the Council. In the eyes of the clan he was granted authority by the Council—without their support his position was unstable at best. His legitimacy was granted by the will of the Council, and it irked him that he had to seek their approval for any changes that he wanted to make.

I'm the Captain, he thought. *Who are they? Did they defeat Plank? Did they stand before the C'law and bend them to their will? Do they know the true destiny of the Aftey clan?*

The Council had offered no serious resistance to his goal of reshaping the clan, but it had been necessary for him to explain his actions at every step. This was something that no leader should have to do.

He was finding it increasingly difficult to keep his temper in check. The busybodies had questions, demands, and conditions about everything he did, and he was constantly forced to waste valuable time talking them around to his way of thinking. It would have been much easier just to kill the lot of them. He imagined how satisfying it would be to snap their scrawny old necks, but knew that he must resist the temptation; if he attacked the Council, the clan would turn on him. However, Dayrunner had grand plans for his new clan that he would not allow his frustration with the Council to undermine.

He took a deep breath, willing his fury to subside. Forcing his thoughts away from the meddlesome Council and their petty resistance, he turned his mind to the principle barrier faced by the Aftey clan on its path to the glory it deserved—the ship itself.

Almost from the moment he had torn the Captaincy from Plank's bloody throat, Dayrunner had seen that the power of the Aft Clan was defined and limited by the physical size of the *Heloise*. On land, there were few elements to limit the growth of a clan. It could become as large as the food supply would allow, and if it outgrew the barn or building that housed it, it could always relocate. Aboard the *Heloise*, however, there was no room for expansion. She was bounded on all sides by water and sky. To make matters worse, half of the ship was occupied by an enemy clan.

The ship was the size that she was, and no amount of scheming could change that. The Bowsers, however, were another matter. He could do something about them.

But there was always the Council—the nagging, irritating, frustrating Council—constantly delaying and complicating matters, nipping and biting at him like fleas. They shared his goals for the Afties, but they did not understand his methods, and met every innovation with scepticism, scorn and resistance. To realise his plans fully he needed absolute and unquestioned authority over his army. He could not be hobbled by the Counsel. They would have to go. The difficulty lay in how to rid himself of them without alienating the rest of the clan.

He had a plan, and to carry it out he needed the rat-king—but not the rat-king that he now had. His rat-king, in its current state, would not serve his purpose. He needed the power of the one from his old clan.

Just as he was building his army, Dayrunner was also building his ideal rat-king. His tools were hunger, thirst, darkness and isolation, and he pounded his pathetic rat-king relentlessly with them. He kept it alone in its lightless prison, giving it just enough food and water to keep it alive, and allowing no one but himself to see or speak to it. If it was half-mad now, he was bent on pushing it over into howling lunacy as quickly as possible.

Dayrunner was sure there was nothing fundamentally wrong with his new rat-king: it just needed time and care to ripen.

CHAPTER 18

UNDER THE GUN

Wainscot tried to make himself as small as possible. He hunched in the shadows, quivering and squealing as the world came apart around him.

It had all begun innocently enough—the thump of running Men's feet and the cacophony of bellowed orders was something to which he had become quite accustomed during his time aboard the Heloise. Quickly, however, it had all gone horribly wrong. The ship was shaking and roaring so violently that he was certain it would fall to pieces, leaving every living thing aboard to perish in the depths of the sea.

The expedition had seemed completely routine as he, Moon and Mizzen had set out on a foray for food earlier that day. This had been the first foraging trip Wainscot had joined in a while—Mizzen had finally determined that he smelled enough like a ship's rat to venture from the nest. They had decided to look a little higher in the ship than usual to see if they could find anything particularly interesting, and then had made their way up to what the ship's rats referred to as the 'gun deck'.

The Men used this deck, Mizzen had explained, for a variety of purposes. Sometimes they slept on it, suspended like pupae in canvas cocoons slung between the massive black objects that ran in lines along either side of the deck. Mizzen had described these black things as the "guns", though the word meant nothing to Wainscot. Whatever they were, they smelled foul: an unappetizing mix of iron, grease, and gunpowder.

The Men used the guns for some purpose that neither Moon nor Mizzen had been able to adequately explain to him.

"They fight them," Mizzen had said.

Wainscot had cocked his head to one side. "Fight them?" he had asked.

"Fight *with* them," Moon had clarified, as though this might shed some light on the matter.

It had not.

"Well, you'll find out soon enough," Mizzen had said. They had left it at that.

Then, as if in demonstration, there had been a flurry of shouted orders from somewhere above. Men had come barrelling down the accommodation ladders and onto the gun deck.

Moon and Mizzen had been some distance from Wainscot, and in their haste to find a hiding place, they had darted beneath a low wooden structure that held cannonballs. He had found shelter beneath one of the guns.

He had looked for his nestmates and seen their bright eyes peering out at him. They gestured to him, but he had not understood what they were trying to tell him.

Some of the Men had run about the deck, dismantling the walls that separated the space into different rooms. Others took station next to the guns and hauled on ropes to trundle them back from the inside of the hull. Wainscot had moved to keep under his gun as it rolled.

The sailors had milled about with a pounding of feet, rattling of equipment, and a constant, overwhelming babble of curses and shouts as they carried out their unfathomable activities around the cannons. Wainscot had moved again as his gun rolled forward to poke through one of the square hatches in the ship's side.

As the Men stepped back from the gun, there had been a moment of relative silence. Then the world had exploded.

With a shattering, numbing roar, the gun had leapt backwards, the sound so great in the enclosed space that it had battered Wainscot down against the deck. He had squealed in terror, but his voice had been lost in the tumult of sound that washed over him.

T he gun charged backwards above the cowering Wainscot, its rumbling wheels narrowly missing him. He suddenly found himself in the open, both exposed and vulnerable, but too dazed to do anything about it. Sparks and bits of flaming debris from the open end of the cannon rained down, singeing his fur. A cloud of stinking yellow smoke rolled over him. After a few rapid heartbeats of choking and sputtering, he regained enough of his shattered senses to scurry back under the gun.

The whole horrifying process happened again, and again, and again, each flurry of activity punctuated by that awful, world-shattering noise.

Wainscot could not escape—the sailors were all around him—so he stayed beneath the gun as it bucked and jumped and roared back and forth across the scarred wood of the deck. He thought he would die if he had to endure one more round.

Then, just as suddenly as it had begun, it stopped.

The Men rolled the gun back into place, fussed about it for some time, and then left the deck, laughing and slapping each other on the back.

When there were few enough sailors still present to risk the dash across the open deck, Wainscot ran with all the speed he could coax from his still-shocked body to where he had last seen Moon and Mizzen, hiding beneath the cannonballs. His nestmates were no longer there.

He took a moment to catch his breath before making his slow, cautious way back to the nest alone.

"I'm sorry Wainscot," said Moon. She and Mizzen had been waiting for him back at the nest. "I truly am, but we couldn't stay where we were. They remove the balls from the rack as they use them, and we'd have been seen."

"It's true, Laddie," said Mizzen. He seemed more amused than sorry, much to Wainscot's irritation.

"We didn't know where to go so you'd find us. The only thing we could think to do was come back here," said Moon.

"I don't blame you," Wainscot said shakily, his eyes still wide. "I thought I was going to die. I don't ever remember being so scared. You must have been terrified too."

Moon cast a glance at Mizzen. "Well no, actually we weren't." She twined her tail around Wainscot's, as though by the contact she might beg his pardon. "Sometimes we forget what you don't know about life on the *Heloise*. We couldn't believe it when you ran under the gun. We tried to get you to find somewhere else to hide, but you didn't understand."

"Would've loved to have seen your face when the thing went off," said Mizzen. He could barely control his need to laugh.

"Stop it Mizzen," scolded Moon. "It was our fault. We should have warned him." She turned to Wainscot and said, "We weren't afraid because we knew what to expect. The noise and smoke can be overwhelming no matter how many times you've experienced them, but we knew we weren't in any danger. You see, when the Men have a battle—"

"That wasn't a battle," interrupted Mizzen. "There was no damage to the ship."

"No, that wasn't a battle. However, when the Men *do* have a battle, they use the guns against other ships. No one really understands how, but ships can somehow actually fight each other. It sounds impossible, I know, but the *Heloise* is even said to have sunk her enemies. As I said, no one understands all of this, but that's the way it is."

Wainscot could not imagine how ships could possibly fight each other, and he said so.

"Nearest I've been able to figure it," said Mizzen, "is the guns are like the teeth of the *Heloise*, but what they actually do is beyond me."

"And what happened today was like the *Heloise* sharpening those teeth," said Moon. "When we're at sea the Men use the guns even though there's no enemy near. Sometimes they do so every day, or even several times a day. I suppose they want to be prepared for battle when it eventually comes."

Wainscot still did not understand, but he was not concerned about the reason for it. He only wanted to know when it was going to happen again.

"I don't think I could stand to go through that again," he said.

"Oh, you'll get used to it," said Moon. "We all do eventually."

"Never heard of a rat who's been silly enough to be *under* a gun when it goes off," laughed Mizzen.

"A real battle is a very different matter," said Moon, glaring at Mizzen.

She seemed to think it acceptable for her to laugh at the Lander's stupidity, but she would not allow anyone else to do so. Wainscot felt warm inside. Moon's protectiveness made him feel as though Scuffle were still watching over him.

"In an actual battle," Moon continued, "the danger is very real. The ship shakes and sometimes flies apart. It's terrifying. I've been through a battle—"

"And I've been through several," said Mizzen. "I hope to never experience one again."

"I don't understand what happened today, or what a battle between ships could possibly be," said Wainscot. "Maybe I will when I've been aboard the *Heloise* longer, but if a battle is anything like what I went through today, I'll gladly go through the rest of my life without knowing anything more about it."

Both Moon and Mizzen nodded their heads.

"Very wise of you," said Moon," and I hope you get your wish."

"He won't," said Mizzen. He settled into the soft bedding of the nest.

Moon curled up next to the older rat. Wainscot, finally having shed enough of his nervous energy to contemplate sleep, lay next to her, his chin on her flank. It took a little while, but he eventually dozed off.

Surprisingly, he did not dream of cannons.

CHAPTER 19

PRESS GANGS

Thus far, it had been a relatively successful cruise for the *Heloise*. While tumultuous events rattled the rat-world skulking in the shadows beneath her decks, the ship had sailed boldly down the east coast of North America. She had been hunting, and had twice taken merchantmen unfortunate enough to cross her path. Both of the ships were valuable captures—the prize-money from their sale would make the Captain of the *Heloise* a rich Man, and it would go a long way toward ensuring comfortable retirements for her crewmen.

However, this meant that now there were three ships in her little flotilla, with a limited number of Men to sail them, and to take the captured prizes back to Halifax. She required fresh muscle to haul her ropes and man her guns, and her Captain knew where to find it. The *Heloise* turned towards Jamaica.

Kingston was a British port, so she would find British merchantmen anchored there. As a Royal Navy warship, she had the legal right to take Men to supplement her crew; she would be sending press gangs ashore to round up healthy, if unwilling, prospects. Those gangs would start by scouring the seedy haunts of the dockside—the dives and gin-mills—for experienced seamen, then shift their attention to unskilled landsmen if nothing better came to hand. In the end muscle was muscle—the ship could ill afford to be too discriminating.

As the *Heloise* sailed into Kingston harbour and slid to a rest at one of the massive piers that thrust out above the warm Caribbean Sea, her rats revelled in the ripe, rich smells that filtered down through the decks. Wainscot stirred from sleep in his nest, and lifted his nose to sample what the air was bringing to him. Many of the scents were new, but most greeted him like old friends. Stomach-tickling whiffs of hot food entwined with the equally appetizing odours of garbage and rotting fish, and the tang of horse sweat and urine fought with the dull stink of unwashed Humanity for the his attention. From beyond the town, the dark and moist perfumes of earth and vegetation wafted through the ship's timbers.

New sounds also made their way down into the dark recesses of the warship. The cries of merchants hawking their wares, the shrieking laughter of children at play, and the clop of horse's hooves on cobble-stones were all underscored by the rhythmic wash of waves against the stone seawalls. These noises settled on Wainscot's ears with almost-forgotten familiarity. The calls of the exotic birds that danced and flitted like Mardi-Gras revellers through the forests of the island's interior were refreshingly different from the raucous screeches of the seabirds that followed the ship on the open sea. Even the wind in the tree branches sang a song vastly more cheerful than the mournful wail it uttered when cutting through the rigging of the ship.

To the rats born of the ship these sounds and smells brought the promise of fresh food as new supplies were loaded aboard.

Although their arrival in port lifted Wainscot's spirits, it was also a painful reminder of the life he had lost. He was a Lander, and he ached to walk again on stable, unmoving ground, to breathe air free of the stink of the bilge, and to taste food that was not stale or half-rotten. He could almost hear Scuffle calling to him to run with her through the ratways of this new place. He knew that she had died in another town, on another shore far from this strange land, but this did not prevent him from imagining her on the quay, beckoning him to join her.

However, he would not be going ashore. His life was now inextricably entwined with that of his new clan. Even if the opportunity to escape the *Heloise* were to present itself, he knew that he would never abandon Moon.

Deep in the bowels of the ship, far from Wainscot's awareness, other rats had different plans—ones that would take them into the port town that night.

Spitkid assessed the small group of rats assembled before him. He concluded that they would do for the business that Dayrunner had assigned them. They would be going ashore on a raid, and he was confident that they would be successful.

The odours of the town, so overpowering during the day, diminished markedly with the cool breezes of night. The diverse sounds that piled upon each other in a bewildering cacophony during daylight hours were also gone, replaced by the somnolent buzz of insects and the soft intermittent calls of night creatures. Little moved in the streets during the small hours before dawn—just a few sailors trusted enough to have been granted shore-leave, who staggered back to their ships, alone or supporting each other in groups of two or three. Wobbly from the smoky pleasures of the town's many gin-palaces, these last remnants of the night's revelry would have drawn a scowl of disapproval from any decent town-dweller. Kingston's honest citizens, however, had long since sought their beds, and even the most industrious of thieves and night-agents had quit their shady endeavours for the night.

Moonlight angled through gaps between the ramshackle buildings leaning drunkenly over the street, painting irregular patches of silver over the uneven cobblestone. Decades of hard use by horse-drawn carts had worn the stones smooth and shiny along four shallow ruts running the length of the road.

A shadow detached itself from the darkness at the base of one of the buildings and moved across the cobblestones. Low to the ground and flowing like dark water, the shadow followed the path of one of the ruts for some distance up the street before angling off to merge with the gloom on the opposite side. During its crossing, the shadow briefly crossed a patch of moonlight, revealing itself to be a large group of rats moving silently and purposefully.

Afties.

There were some twenty of them, with Spitkid at their vanguard. His group was one of five that Dayrunner had ordered ashore that night. They had left the ship by way of one of the heavy hemp mooring lines, which, unlike the one which had so nearly cost Wainscot his life, was not blocked by a tin disk.

Although they had never been in Kingston before, Spitkid's party made their way unerringly toward the poorest part of town. The scents that drew them on were as clear to them as signposts; the smell of poverty is always the same, no matter where in the world it is. They knew that where they found that particular mixture of odours, they would also find rats.

The party slipped through a hole in the exterior wall of a dilapidated wooden building—once possibly a chandler's shop, but now just a dust-laden shell—and moved across the litter-strewn floor. The room was dark, but the moonlight leaking through gaps in the boarded-over windows provided more than enough light for them to navigate. With a whispered command, Spitkid ordered the group to a stop. He cocked his head and listened for what the building could tell him. And there it was: the telltale chittering, chewing and scurrying.

Spitkid spied a hole in the baseboards. Signalling his party to follow, he entered the ratways of the store.

They found their first Landers in the narrow spaces behind the wall. Two adult males and one young female slept curled together in a cosy nest of chewed wood and cloth fibre, unaware of the danger creeping up on silent feet. They woke, squealing with surprise, when Spitkid and two of his companions dragged them, none too gently, out onto the dusty floor of what had once been the store's office. Spitkid had the largest of the three by the scruff of the neck, and with a skilful lift of his head flipped the Lander onto his back. He placed both front feet on the stranger's chest and leaned down to speak directly into the creature's frightened face.

"Now listen to me, you rank, ugly Lander," he said, his voice pitched loudly enough that the other prisoners could also hear him clearly. "I could have your throat easily, but I'm not going to kill you. I'm going to let you live, but remember this: my generosity only goes so far. If you don't do exactly as I say I'll split you from tongue to tail. Got that?"

The Lander nodded agreement, but not quickly enough to avoid a painful cuff to the snout.

"Very good," said Spitkid. "We'll get on just fine. So now you're going to come with me, and I'm going to put you and your two friends here under guard. I'll leave you for a bit, and when I come back, we're all going on a little trip. You will not say anything, you will not ask any questions, and if you try to escape you will be killed immediately. There will be no second chances. Do you understand?"

Again the rat nodded, this time without hesitation.

Spitkid left the Landers under the guard of three of his largest rats, and, with his remaining sixteen raiders trailing behind him, made his way further into the abandoned building. The next rats that they encountered were not asleep. They were in the middle of a large room, busily chewing their way into the side of a wooden crate that smelled as though it might contain the rotting remains of something edible. There were eight of them, all fully-grown. Although thin and rangy, they had the look of experienced fighters.

Spitkid paused for a moment before commanding the attack. Although surprise was on their side, Spitkid's rats were at a disadvantage because they were hampered by the need not to kill or cripple their opponents. The Landers, however, were not aware of this constraint, and would be fighting for their lives. Still, the Afties outnumbered the land rats two to one. Spitkid ordered his party forward with a hiss.

The Landers turned, squealing their fury, as Spitkid's party drove into them. Spitkid's opponent—a tough-looking female—spun about with an agility that almost made him check his rush. As he bore in on her, she bared her teeth and reared up on her hind legs, sidestepping his charge and moving to drop down on his back.

Reacting quickly, Spitkid changed the angle of his attack and ducked under the stabbing teeth. He felt a flash of heat along his shoulder as he rammed the top of his head into the Lander's soft stomach. She bounced away from him with a cough of expelled air, and he was on her before she could scramble back to her feet. He took her throat between his teeth and resisted a lifetime's battle experience that urged him to bite down. He spoke calmly but firmly through a mouthful of skin and fur, "You have one chance. Do exactly as I say, and don't fight any more. Do you want to live?"

In a trembling, strangely-accented voice, the Lander said, "I want to live. I'll do as you say." She went limp in his grip.

Just as suddenly as it had begun, the scrap was over. It left Spitkid with a shallow but painful slash across his shoulder and two of the Landers dead. Spitkid was annoyed—their orders had been not to kill under any circumstances—but for now he let the matter lie. He was pleased with the haul, but the raid was still far from over.

His group herded the six new captives back to join the first three, and he increased the number of guards to five. He was not concerned that there were fewer guards than captives, as he was confident that the Landers were too disheartened to attempt an escape. Also, he needed his fighters with him if he were to take any more of the land rats. With a growled warning to the captives about what would happen to them if they showed any sign of resistance, Spitkid took his reduced party and headed back into the ratways in search of more Landers.

D ayrunner was satisfied with the results of the raid. More than satisfied—his press gangs had performed well beyond his most optimistic expectations. He had sent a little under a hundred of them into the streets of the port; they had brought back no fewer than fifty-three land rats, at a cost of only two of their number. The raiders had also carried out their mission without being discovered by the Men, which was quite an accomplishment. Group after group had scurried up the mooring rope, herding their prisoners before them, and not one had been spotted. Had the press gangs, hampered by their need to control their bewildered prisoners, been seen by Men while trying slip aboard, the slaughter would have been terrible. It had been a gamble, he knew, but one that his Afties had won. He would be sending more parties out into the streets on the next night, and for as many nights as the *Heloise* remained in port.

Granted, the shanghaied rats were a mixed bunch. Most of them were sorry specimens—weak and dispirited—and would not go very far toward reinforcing his ranks, but even the most useless of them could still serve a purpose. An army, after all, always needs its expend-ables to throw away when it does not make sense to risk more valuable warriors. Some of the stronger Landers, however, would do very well indeed. With training, the best of them might be crafted into reason-ably capable fighters.

Of course, the fact that the press gangs had taken them so easily did not speak well of their abilities, but Dayrunner set great store in his training methods. He knew that he could mould them into some-thing usable.

The captives were now huddled in a group before him, surrounded by a ring of guarding C'law. All eyes were on him.

"You are more fortunate than you realise," he said. He spoke calmly, his voice level, but lacking its usual gravelly menace. "You have been brought aboard this ship to join us in a great enterprise. I don't know who you were in your old lives, and I don't care. Those lives are over. You are now part of the Aft Clan—my clan."

This brought a stirring and a low murmur from the guarding C'law, but Dayrunner had expected as much. The fierce Aftey animosity towards strangers—especially Landers—was deeply ingrained; in the past any land rat unfortunate enough to find himself aboard the *Heloise* had been killed without ceremony. He could see by the agitated shifting in the ranks of the C'law that they were struggling to keep their instincts in check. However, it was vital that he bolster his army with new recruits, so he would deal with any dissent the way he always did: by the strength of his will and the sharpness of his claws.

"I was once as you are now," he continued. "I too came aboard this ship a stranger. I was a land rat, accustomed to land ways, and everything aboard the *Heloise* was foreign to me. I didn't know a sheet from a halyard, but I learned. I learned to understand the language of my new clan, the language of the sea, and even that of the *Heloise* herself, and now her ways are my ways. They'll soon be yours too."

He knew that the Landers were bewildered, disoriented, and too frightened to fully understand what he was saying, and that many of the words he used were unfamiliar to them. However, he trusted them to follow the thrust of his message.

"The Aft Clan is about to embark upon a grand adventure, and you have been *invited*—" the word drew a low chuckle from several of the C'law, "—to join us in our glory. You are Afties now, and you have been lucky enough to be chosen to share in the fortunes of your new clan. However, you will have to prove yourselves before you can be trusted fully by your clanmates. To earn your place you will be required to play an important role in the struggle to come."

He surveyed the ranks of Landers before him, searching for some sign that they understood what he was saying. They merely stared back at him, eyes wide and unblinking. It would take some time for the meaning of his words to filter through their paralysing fear.

Dayrunner continued, "If you shirk your duties or prove yourselves unworthy, you will not be permitted a place in the clan. You will be considered outsiders, and I warn you that the Aft Clan deals very harshly with outsiders. Until you are given the opportunity to join us fully, you will be kept under guard. You will soon come to realise that there is no escape from the *Heloise*. There is simply nowhere for you to go. If you attempt to escape, you will be killed. If you talk to any ship's rats other than your guards, you will be killed. If you fail to obey any of your orders, you will be killed."

Looking out over the captives' terrified faces, Dayrunner realised that it was important that he plant a seed of hope. He did not want them too demoralised to be of any use, but he needed them to understand that although they had some reason for hope, theirs was still a very precarious situation. It was a fine balance to maintain, but he was up to the task.

"If, however, you do your part, you will soon join us. You could not hope for anything better than to be part of my clan. We are on the move to greatness, and once rolling, we will be unstoppable. There is no rat on the ship who can stand before us. Soon the *Heloise* will belong to us alone."

With that he turned away from the assembled Landers and walked away through the ring of C'law guards. As he passed Spitkid, he said, too low for anyone else to hear, "Of course, they'll all likely be dead long before any of that comes to pass."

CHAPTER 20

THE RAID

The waves slapped rhythmically against the sides of the *Heloise* as she sliced cleanly through grey-green water. She was making good headway with the strong Atlantic wind angling across her port quarter. The growing gale that pushed her along whipped frothy spindrift from the tops of waves and howled mournfully as it blew through her rigging. Viewed from far above by an albatross searching for a much-needed resting perch, she appeared tiny and insignificant. From such a height, and in the feeble light that tried to burn its way through the low cloud cover, the great creamy billow of her sails was nothing but a chalk-smudge on the slate of the sea.

With a flex of feathers, the bird spilled air from beneath its wings and slipped sideways through the buffeting wind to investigate. As it approached, the details of the ship took shape. Heeled over to starboard, the *Heloise* clipped along swiftly under a vast spread of canvas. Sailors bustled about her windswept decks and scaled the hazardous heights of her thrumming rigging like monkeys. The Captain, hands behind his back and a frown on his face, paced the quarterdeck. His blue coat was dark with wet, and droplets of water beaded the brass of his sword hilt and shoe buckles.

Apparently judging that the *Heloise* would provide a suitable resting place on which to ride out the storm, the albatross dropped down low over the water and swept along the length the ship. Just before the bird climbed again to find a roost, its small stony eyes fixed for a moment on something odd on the side of the *Heloise*. Six rats were making their dangerous way along a narrow ledge running the length of her hull, clinging to the wood with fierce strength against a wind that plucked and pummelled, trying to toss them into the frothing sea. With a ragged squawk, the albatross angled up into the rigging, leaving the rats to their hazardous journey.

At the head of his group of five Afties, Dayrunner was beginning to question the wisdom of mounting a foray on such a rough sea. Back in the heart of Aftey territory, it had seemed a stroke of brilliance to take advantage of the fact that the Bowsers would be safe in their nests on such a day. He had reasoned that if he and his C'law were to make their way along the outside of the hull, they would be able to penetrate deep into Bowser territory without discovery. Now, however, as he dug his claws even deeper into the water-softened wood and hunched down against another gust of wind, he wondered whether he should have paid more heed to the warnings that Spitkid had tried to give him.

His lieutenant had been aghast at the idea of braving the elements when a gale was brewing. All of the Afties had learned that it was never wise to argue against Dayrunner's wishes, so Spitkid had not pressed his point too vigorously. When Dayrunner had said, in a tone that brooked no argument, that they *would* be going, the lieutenant had volunteered to join the raid.

Shivering with the cold, and eyes half-closed against the wind, Dayrunner wondered if Spitkid had any inkling that his Captain was as close to being afraid as he could ever remember being. *If we manage to get back to our nest*, he thought with a mental nod toward his lieutenant, *perhaps I'll listen more closely to Spitkid's advice.*

They continued to cling for their lives to the side of the ship as the storm raged about them. For a moment Dayrunner considered turning around and ordering the patrol back to the safety of Aftey territory. But only for a brief moment. He would not follow a leader who allowed fear to dictate his actions, and could see little reason why any other rat would do so either.

Besides, he was not even sure that going back was an option. The sloping hull above them was too slick to climb, and the ledge was too narrow for them to turn around.

They pushed forward, length by perilous length, until they eventually dragged themselves through a hawsehole into the forward manger. They crouched, shivering, on the straw-strewn floor, amazed that they had not lost a single member of their party.

When Dayrunner had told Spitkid of his intention to visit the heart of Bowser territory, the lieutenant had said, "Where exactly do you want to go?" Dayrunner suspected that his lieutenant had really wanted to ask, "Why would you want to do that?".

Had Dayrunner been the kind of rat to answer unasked questions, he would have said, "I know so little of my enemy, and even less of their territory, and I want to learn more. You've all lived with them for countless generations, and even the youngest pup in the clan knows more about them than I do."

However, even this would have been only part of the truth. He had another, darker purpose, but it was one that he could hardly admit—even to himself.

So he had answered only Spitkid's spoken question. "As near to their Council as possible," he had said.

He knew he was taking a significant risk in penetrating enemy territory so deeply with so few rats, but he had weighed the size of his party carefully. If it came to a fight they would be seriously outnumbered, but stealth was the key to achieving his objective—to have brought a larger group would have invited discovery. As it was, even such a small party would be hard-pressed to slip unnoticed through the unfamiliar Bowser ratways.

When they had recovered enough to move on, the patrol silently crossed the manger. Slipping through a hole in the deck, they entered the maze of dark passages below. Although they did not know where the Bowser Council chamber was, they knew that they could rely on their noses to lead them. The scents of the generations of rats who had used the passages before them left countless clues that pointed the way.

None of them doubted that they would reach their destination; however, they were less certain that they could do so without encountering any Bowsers. They stopped several times to allow unseen rats ahead of them to move on. Each time they crouched silently waiting in the gloom, they were aware that the longer they stayed in enemy territory the greater the risk that they would be discovered by a Bowser patrol. Despite their best efforts to be invisible, they left a telltale scent trail. Any Bowser happening across their path would instantly know that Afties had penetrated their territory, and the cry would go up.

Only Dayrunner seemed unworried by the danger all around them. He was calm and cool, and although the others were becoming increasingly anxious, they knew better than to voice their concerns to him.

They pushed on.

The Bowser Council retired to their chamber. When they were not dealing directly with other rats in the administration of the clan, they gathered together in their shared nest to sleep or discuss the welfare of their clanmates.

The Council's chamber was located on the orlop deck—the second lowest in the ship and one up from the holds. Cosy and secure, the nest was tucked into the open space behind and beneath a multi-drawer cabinet that housed the various tools, bolts, and nails used by the ship's carpenter. This huge, heavy cabinet was a floor-to-ceiling construction bolted to both the deck and bulkhead; the Bowsers entered the cavity in its base by a hole they had chewed through from the cable storage-room beyond. When the Council were in their chamber, two C'law guards always stood watch just outside.

Drogue was in a foul mood. He generally was, these days.

Until recently, the atmosphere in the nest had been companionable. The councilrats had no social interaction with any other members of their clan, and they used their time in the nest to relax. Even when they disagreed with each other about some aspect of the clan's rule, as they often did, they remained friendly. Lately, however, discord had crept into the nest, poisoning every word they spoke.

There was now a division within the Council, and Drogue fumed every time his control over his fellow councilrats wavered. Ever since his unexpected resistance over the matter of Moon's death-sentence, the old councilrat Currach had become a persistently irritating thorn in Drogue's side. When Drogue had rebuilt the Council, he had done so carefully, filling it with rats he knew to be mean-spirited enough to share his crueler instincts, but malleable enough that they would not resist him. He had thought that Currach would be nothing more than a silent witness to his increasingly draconian reign, but he was wrong. The old rat's surprising new resolve had come as a nasty shock to him. Prior to the cat attack, Currach had been the least outspoken of the councilrats, siding with the majority in every dispute. Now, however, he had found his voice.

Currach had assumed the role of sole defender of reason within Drogue's paw-picked Council. By stubborn resistance, he had managed to keep the cruelty of the Council in check. What surprised Drogue the most was not that Currach had grown a spine, but that some of the other councilrats had actually begun to side with him.

Drogue discovered that the problem with rats that he could bend to his will was that they were also bendable by others.

Spume was at the heart of the unrest that now plagued the Council. Since he had managed to worm his way into their business, he had developed a friendship with Drogue that baffled the other councilrats. In truth, Drogue himself was sometimes a little surprised that he had allowed the rat into his confidence. He recognised him for what he was—a nasty, backbiting sneak who was loathed by almost every rat in the clan—but there was something about Spume that spoke to him.

"Like is drawn to like," the other councilrats whispered to each other when they thought Drogue was out of earshot. If he were more inclined to be honest with himself, he might have agreed. It was obvious that Spume's toxic influence was fuel to the fires of hatred that burned in his withered old chest, but he welcomed it. As a result of this partnership, Spume was now virtually a seventh member of the Council—always lurking about in the shadows with his snout at Drogue's ear, whispering foul lies and staining the Council with his malevolence.

On this particular day, the councilrats were discussing food distribution. As usual, Drogue and Currach were at loggerheads. Unusually, Spume was not present.

"The Aftey attacks have been very effective lately," said Currach. "Our stores have been raided, and we're being chased back from the holds by Aftey patrols. Less and less food is making it back to the nests."

"My point exactly," said Drogue. "We need to increase the effectiveness of our fighters, and the only way to do that is to divert all the food to the strongest amongst us. The patrols must be well fed if they are to fight back the enemy incursions. We need to turn the tide against the Afties. If we push them back, we'll have more food. In the meantime, all the food will go to the rats of fighting age—and to the Council, of course."

"It must not," argued Currach. "The nursing mothers, the young. We can't divert—"

He was interrupted by a noise at the entrance to the nest—a squeal of alarm and the thump, hiss, and scratch of rats in combat.

Before any of the councilrats could move, three strangers burst into the nest. They were led by one of the largest rats Drogue had ever seen. It was obvious by his size and colour that the intruder was a Lander. His eyes were cold and hard as he leapt at Drogue with a hiss.

Drogue shrank back with a squeal of terror, certain that death had come for him.

CHAPTER 21

COUNCIL TOPPED

Something was wrong with the Bowser Clan. A buzz filtered through the ship like smoke from a fire unseen. The clan was afraid.

Even Wainscot and his companions were aware of the fear that held Moon's old clan in its grip. The air was so thick with it that they could almost smell it. In fact, at times they *could* smell it—the odour of the Bowser's urine and droppings was tainted by it.

The three attempted to discover what had happened by covertly listening and watching, but hardly any of the Bowsers were out and about. The usually busy thoroughfares of Bowser territory were abandoned. The few rats who ventured out to gather food hurried to and from their destinations and did not linger for conversation. At one point Mizzen crept close to a nesting area, but he could hear only furtive whispering, low and indistinct. It was as though the entire Bowser Clan were too frightened to speak.

Curled close together in their nest, Wainscot and his nestmates discussed the mystery. They spoke in low voices barely above a whisper, as if in sympathy with the rattled Bowsers.

"It must have something to do with your dream," said Moon.

"Dream?" asked Wainscot. He dreamt every time he slept. What was she talking about?

"The dream that you had about the Afties covered in cloth, like Men. The flying fish dream."

"Do you see any giant Afties about?" challenged Wainscot. "It was just a dream. It meant nothing."

"Dreams always mean something, Laddie," said Mizzen. "Yours foretold change, and something has definitely changed—for the Bowsers, if not for all of us."

"Nonsense," said Wainscot. "Something's up, I'll grant you, but it has nothing to do with my dream." Still, he was worried.

"Have to find out what's happened," said Mizzen. "Have to find out from a Bowser."

"How?" asked Moon. "We can't very well just walk up to one and ask."

Mizzen laughed. "You might not, but I certainly can. Wait here."

Before either Wainscot or Moon could react, Mizzen slipped out of the nest. They looked at each other in surprise, but did not follow.

It was some time before they heard the patter of feet, and Mizzen re-appeared through the entrance. He smelled of Bowser and blood.

"Had a lovely little chat with one of them," he said.

"Chat?" said Moon. "Are you hurt? I smell blood."

"Not mine. Chap I had my talk with was a little shy. Came 'round eventually, though."

Moon was shocked. "You didn't kill him, did you?"

"No. Wasn't necessary. Couple of well-placed bites was all it took. Soft, these Bowsers are. If he'd been an Aftey, one of mine, he'd have made a better show of it. Gave in without a fight, he did. Shameful, really. If it was my—"

"Never mind that," said Wainscot, impatience giving his voice an edge, "Did you learn anything?"

"What? Ah, yes. You see, the thing is, someone's gone and topped their Council."

"Topped? You mean killed?" Moon asked in disbelief.

"Exactly," said Mizzen.

"What, all of them?"

"All of them."

There was a moment of stunned silence. It was a tragedy of almost inconceivable consequence for a clan to lose its Council. Without one the clan was like a rudderless ship drifting aimlessly on a storm-tossed sea. It was particularly catastrophic for a clan that was under constant threat. Wainscot knew that unless the Bowsers could somehow find new leadership they would be at the mercy of the Afties. No defence was possible without some sort of overriding control, some authority that would ensure that guards were on station, patrols went out, food rationing was enforced, and all the other myriad activities required to keep a clan alive were carried out. Rats are not naturally disciplined, and will think only of their own immediate needs if left to themselves. When the cats had all but destroyed the Bowser Council, it had taken a rat with considerable strength of will—Drogue—to prevent the clan from succumbing to chaos and disintegrating. If the entire Council were now truly dead, then the Bowsers were in very real danger of being crushed by the Afties.

"How?" asked Moon. "Cats or Men?"

"Neither," said Mizzen. He dropped his eyes, and lowered his voice, as if ashamed of what he had to say. "Afties."

Moon's eyes widened, reflecting her disbelief. "No, it can't have been. There must be some mistake. No rat would do that. Not even an Aftey."

"Nevertheless, that is apparently exactly what happened."

Rats, even rats at war, did not deliberately destroy each other's

Councils. It was forbidden by both tradition and law. The proscription was so deeply ingrained in the fabric of the culture of the nest that even the concept of the destruction of an entire Council was almost unthinkable. Not as a tactic of war, and not as a means to a political end. Individual Council members might be—and often were—killed by their fellow councilrats, or ambitious outsiders hoping to usurp their position, but the integrity of the Council as a body was never jeopardised.

"Who would do such a thing?" asked Moon.

"As I said," said Mizzen, "It was Afties. Ashamed to admit it, but it was my old clan. Can't imagine what would lead them to do such a thing... No, that's not true: afraid I know exactly what, or rather who, it was."

"It was Dayrunner," Wainscot said with certainty.

"Aye, Lad," said Mizzen, "it was Dayrunner."

"He's aboard because of me."

Moon's and Mizzen's ears pricked up at this.

Wainscot hesitated. He had still not shared the story of his arrival aboard the *Heloise* with Mizzen, and he had never told Moon that Dayrunner had been one of the pursuing C'law. They looked at him, waiting for an explanation.

"He followed me onto the *Heloise*," said Wainscot. He was still felt uncomfortable about telling them of his ties to Dayrunner, and he was still not sure why. Perhaps it was because he was ashamed that he had been instrumental in bringing trouble to the ship, and did not want them to judge him harshly. Maybe he was just embarrassed that he not told them earlier. However, it was past time for them to know. "He was C'law in my old nest," Wainscot continued, "and he was one of the party that chased me on board. I didn't know he was on the ship until you told your tale, Mizzen."

"That *is* interesting," said Mizzen. "What do you know of him?"

"Very little. Nothing, really. Only that he had a reputation as a hard rat. I was too insignificant for him to have been aware of me. I would have been beneath his notice if I hadn't..." Wainscot's voice trailed off. He had no intention of telling Mizzen the story of his flight —at least not yet.

"Yes, well, you and I will have to have a little talk soon enough," said Mizzen. "For now though, let's hope Dayrunner no longer cares about our little friend here. If he does, we'll likely have a problem in the very near future."

Wainscot lay awake. Moon and Mizzen slept soundly, curled next to him. Their soft breathing rose and fell gently, keeping time with the rhythms of the ship. Wainscot doubted that Mizzen was very far from wakefulness. The old rat never seemed to fall into as deep a sleep as other rats did, and he always came awake instantly if there was a need.

Wainscot considered Mizzen. He wondered if he had been unfair to the old warrior. It had been many days since the ex-Aftey had joined them, and he had never once shown any sign that he meant them anything but good. He had been trustworthy and dependable, and had demonstrated his mettle on several occasions. *He's made a better showing of it than I have*, admitted Wainscot. *Look at the way he took care of finding out about the Bowsers. He just marched out, grabbed one, and made him talk. Simple, really, but I would have bungled it— if I even had the courage to try.* Mizzen might be pompous and irritating, but he was exactly the sort of rat that Wainscot and Moon needed.

Wainscot suddenly recognised the true reason for his continuing distrust of the older rat. He had thought himself jealous of the easy relationship between his two nestmates, but it was closer to the truth that Mizzen's impressive abilities were what irritated him so much.

Moon is fond of me: I know that, he thought, *but what can I give her? I can tell a good story, and I can cheer her up if she needs it, but I can't actually do anything heroic—or even useful. I certainly couldn't help her when we were taken by Spume.*

As he cast his mind back over the events of his life, Wainscot realised that he had always run. He had run from the bullies in the Nest and had left Scuffle to fight for him. When Scuffle had finally met her match on that horrible night, and he had faced the choice of fighting for her or fleeing, he had fled. It was true that if he had fought, he would have accomplished nothing more than to die beside her, but he knew that if their positions had been switched, Scuffle would have gone back for him. She would not have run. Neither would Moon, he knew—and although he hated to admit it, neither would Mizzen.

Wainscot felt that he was the only one who was not capable of standing up for his friends. He did not deserve the love he was so inexplicably offered, and he was ashamed.

I'm a burden, he thought. *All I do is drag them down. It would be best if I just left Moon in Mizzen's capable paws. I should just slip out of here and try to survive on my own, but I'm too cowardly to do even that.*

He lay quietly in the darkness, thinking and worrying. Sleep would not come.

Chapter 22

Justification

Spitkid had not spoken to anyone since arriving back in Aftey territory after the raid, and neither had any of the other C'law from the party. Too stunned by the enormity of what the Captain had done, they had not even discussed the events with each other. They were afraid of not only Dayrunner's displeasure, but also of the reaction of their clanmates, should word of the obscenity ever leak out.

Spitkid could still not fully accept the truth of what he had seen.

When he had set out with Dayrunner he had assumed that they were embarking on nothing more than a scouting mission. The shock of what had actually happened had shaken him to his core. He understood the Captain's need to know more about their enemy; he had expected that they would just slip quietly through Bowser territory, listening and observing, and then leave without confrontation.

He wondered how he would have reacted if Dayrunner had told him the real purpose of the raid before they set out. His fear of the Captain was too great for him to have refused to participate, but he would like to think that he would have made some effort to dissuade him and argue for sanity. Upon further consideration, he reluctantly admitted to himself that he would not have risked the Captain's anger. He would have gone along, doing nothing more than silently hoping that Dayrunner would rethink his plan as the expedition progressed.

Now that it was done, there was no undoing it.

Even when the raiding party had arrived at the entrance to the Bowser Council chamber, Spitkid had no inkling of the outrage to come. It was only when the Captain had ordered them to attack the guards that he had felt a flutter of unease. Then he had witnessed Dayrunner enter the chamber and had kill without hesitation. Spitkid and the others had not participated—they had merely watched, open-mouthed in shock.

There had been six rats in the chamber, and it was obvious to Spitkid that they were the Bowser Council. They were old, in a couple of cases quite frail, and they had about them that air of authority exclusive to councilrats. Dayrunner had attacked with a frightening efficiency, and all the Bowsers had died before any of the watching Afties could even consider uttering a protest.

They had left the chamber immediately after the killings, and quickly made their way back home by the same outboard path they had used previously, all still in utter disbelief. Spitkid had been surprised at the ease with which they had made their escape. They had not encountered any Bowsers on their retreat, although it was obvious from the sounds growing behind them that the alarm had been raised.

He supposed that the Bowser Clan, now decapitated, had lacked the ability to mount a pursuit.

Once back in their own territory, Dayrunner had dismissed the raiding party with a curt order to return to their nests until called for. He had not instructed them to keep silent about what had happened, but even so, Spitkid was certain that none of them would say anything; if fear of Dayrunner did not ensure their silence, uncertainty about the reaction of the rest of the clan would.

Arranged in their customary half-circle, the Aftey Council waited patiently for their Captain to explain himself. Calm and self-possessed, Dayrunner stood before them, the five rats who had accompanied him on the raid arrayed behind him. No others were present.

Dayrunner did not speak for some moments. He looked from councilrat to councilrat, holding each pair of eyes for several heartbeats before moving on. He waited, assessing the mood of his audience before he proceeded.

Now we'll see if they really belong to me, he thought.

When he spoke, his words were measured and his tone reasonable. "When I first came before you many days ago," he said, "I spoke of the potential of this clan. I also made promises. I told you that the Aft Clan could dominate this ship; should dominate it; *will* dominate it. I told you that I knew how we could overcome those enemies that stand between us and our rightful place. With organization and discipline, I told you, we will be unstoppable—and with your support, I've provided it. Then I told you that we needed to bolster our numbers by taking Landers to fill our ranks and, again with your support, I've provided those. I've delivered everything I promised, and now we're ready for the next step along the ratway to our destiny. In fact, today I took that step."

He paused, as if to emphasise the importance of what he was about to say, but it was not necessary. His next words struck the Council like a claw to the face.

"Today I led a raid into enemy territory and personally killed every member of the Bowser Council."

The councilrats gasped in unison. Two of them actually recoiled, taking a step back and breaking the curve of the half-circle.

Before any of them could recover enough to say anything, Dayrunner continued, "I'm well aware of the seriousness of this action, and I did not undertake it lightly, but the time for squeamishness has passed. We're embarking on a journey, the likes of which no rat has ever attempted, and we can't let the traditions of the past stand in our way. We're going to make the ship our own. To do so we will have to destroy the Bowsers completely. Old rules and conventions no longer apply, and we must cast aside everything that doesn't lead to victory, including fair play. There will be plenty of time to re-establish the niceties when we've defeated the Bowsers."

One of the councilrats found his voice.

"But the Council? We can't kill the Council, it's... it's unacceptable."

"It's already done," said Dayrunner, his voice iron hard. "A drastic step, possibly even unacceptable as you say, but necessary nonetheless. You knew we were going to destroy the Bowsers to the last rat. Did you think we were going to spare their Council? Did you think we were just going to let them live so they could hide away in some hole somewhere and plot against us? No, you all knew that they would have to be killed before we'd finished this thing, even if you hadn't admitted it to yourselves. I set out to take care of the problem, and I have—the Bowsers are leaderless."

He allowed his voice to soften, trickling honey on the iron, "And when all is said and done, I think you'll find that I haven't really killed a Council. Not a true one, anyway. It's *your* destiny, *your* right, to guide the whole ship—not just half of it. All I did was remove a false Council to clear the way for the true one. It's time for the rightful Council of the Heloise to assume its proper place."

The councilrat who had spoken previously had recovered some of his air of authority. "If such an unprecedented action was truly necessary, then it should have been us that made the decision, not you. It was not your place to act without consulting us," he said gravely.

Dayrunner unclenched his shoulder muscles, just a little. He had them. He had taken a risky gamble, and he had won. They had accepted the killing of the Bowser Council as necessary. He had shattered a long-standing taboo and laid the groundwork for the eventual destruction of the other Council on the *Heloise*.

CHAPTER 23

MADNESS

Dayrunner had not been to visit his rat-king for many days, and he was amazed at the difference that time had wrought in the pathetic thing. It was no longer just a collection of miserable young rats bound at the tail, but had, by some mysterious process, developed into a single creature. When the guards pulled away the pieces of wood blocking the entrance to the cell, six heads swung toward him in unison, twelve eyes followed his movements, and six throats uttered a low moan. Although they had not been exposed to light for many days, the eyes did not blink—they only stared at him, wide, red-rimmed and hot.

The rat-king had developed a level of coordination that it had previously lacked. When the C'law had first escorted it from the well, the six linked rats had found it difficult to move. They had become entangled with each other, and their progress had been a noisy, bumbling affair. Now, it moved as one animal. It was no longer clumsy, and although it was thin to the point of emaciation, its newfound agility lent it an air of vitality.

And there was a wildness to its eyes that had not been there before —Dayrunner was certain of it. As the creature stared at him, hatred, madness and something else—hunger, or longing for something half-forgotten—shifted and squirmed like living things behind its eyes.

It had also undergone a less obvious transformation. Dayrunner could now sense in it the presence of an intangible something that had previously been missing. That mysterious something had been absent when the rat-king was merely six separate rats, but he could feel it now. It was power, he knew, and although it was not nearly as strong as it had been in the rat-king of his old nest, it was there—and it was growing. It would only increase in intensity with time.

The rat-king required nurturing. Its power was buried deep within, and it could only be brought to the surface slowly, and with great care. For the component rats to truly become a rat-king, they had to be broken, battered, and crushed until they were no longer truly rats. Then the power could awaken, free to rise from the shattered remains of the six individuals. It would push their minds, already rendered fragile by the regimen of cruelty and deprivation, over the brink and into madness. The strange power of the rat-king fed on that madness, and as the creature spiralled down into lunacy, it grew in strength; as its strength grew, so did its value to Dayrunner and the clan.

Dayrunner held the rat-king's many-eyed gaze, saying nothing. Its roiling rage was palpable, billowing out like waves of heat. He did not fear a physical attack, but the intensity of its emotion made him uneasy. He had created this thing, but it was useless to him unless he could tame it. It had to recognise its master.

From the entrance of the cell, Spitkid watched the silent interplay. The guards were gone: sent away with instructions not to return until summoned, and he was the first rat other than Dayrunner to set eyes on the rat-king since the day of its imprisonment. He too was startled by the changes that he saw, but, unlike Dayrunner, he did not feel any pleasure at the sight. He was disturbed by the simmering madness. It was wrong to treat other rats—and fellow clan members at that—in such a way. He had not questioned Dayrunner's purpose at first, but as the Captain's interest in the poor creatures deepened into obsession, he had begun to harbour doubts.

Now, he examined Dayrunner sitting in the half-light, face-to-faces with the rat-king. For a moment he thought he saw the madness in the rat-king's eyes reflected in Dayrunner's own. It was only there for a breath and then gone, but he was sure that he had not imagined it. Could madness jump, like a spark from a fire, from one rat to another? He did not think so, but the six rats who made up the rat-king had certainly shared their lunacy with each other, and he could think of no reason why it should not spread to Dayrunner if he spent too much time with them.

Spitkid continued his vigil until hunger drove him to the clan's stores in search of food. When he returned, the Captain and the creature still faced each other, and, as far as he could tell, neither had moved or looked away. For a day and a half they remained that way, locked in some internal struggle, and although Spitkid continued to worry about the Captain, he did not dare interrupt whatever was taking place in the cell. He brought food and left it by the opening in case Dayrunner should require it, but it remained uneaten.

He slept occasionally, and each time he awoke, the tableaux before him was the same as when he had fallen asleep. Until, eventually, he was startled awake by Dayrunner's voice.

"Tell me."

With a shake of his head, Spitkid banished his drowsiness and looked into the cell. Dayrunner and the rat-king still faced each other, but their attitudes had changed. The Captain held his head high, looking down at the rat-king. The creature no longer held Dayrunner's gaze, staring instead at the floor.

Some balance, some equilibrium between the two that had held for a day and a half, had shifted, and Spitkid wished that he had not slept so that he might have seen what had happened.

"Tell me," Dayrunner said again.

The rat-king, its heads still bowed, raised its eyes to stare up at its interrogator. Then it began to speak, the voice coming from all six throats at once. Thin ropes of spittle snaked from its muzzles as it forced the words past clenched teeth. The sound was chilling.

"Pull back the night and twice the pups will chew through the water," it said. "I know of none that darkness will feed, and all quietly step along a dog's paw. If you look up into the sea, another dog will pull the pups that pull the night, and still the darkness will not feed them..."

Spitkid shook his head. The voice rambled on. It was nonsense. Worse than nonsense, it was a grotesque mess spewed from a fractured mind. Part of him harboured a suspicion that there might be some meaning buried deep within the blather, but if so, he did not want to understand it. He was disgusted and frightened by the bilge gushing from those drooling, unnatural mouths. He was not afraid of any physical threat from the emaciated rat-king, but he grew increasingly anxious with every baffling word the obscene creature uttered. He looked to see if Dayrunner shared his feelings, and was startled to see the Captain listening with rapt attention. His head was cocked to one side, silently mouthing words, perhaps the same words that were tumbling from the rat-king.

This was too much for Spitkid. He left his post and headed back toward his nest. He would let the Captain punish him if he chose, but he would not, could not, stay and listen to that horrible babble any longer. As he left, he wondered which he found more disturbing: the hogwash spewing from the rat-king's mouths, or the fact that Dayrunner seemed to be enthralled by it.

I understand it, thought Dayrunner with a thrill that surged the length of his body, making his fur stand on end. *There's no sense to the words, but I understand it.*

The rat-king spoke on, the words tripping over each other as they spilled from its mouths in an untidy tangle.

"...Bite the tall one: bite it and sniff the colour of death. Sniff and snuff: snuff and sniff. Dung will be the chaser of beetles. I have never tried to count the splinters in the cheese, but if we talk to the tall one, it will bite us..."

He could see patterns in the disjointed, disconnected images of the speech. Certain words and phrases became stable in the tumultuous torrent, and these arranged and rearranged themselves in Dayrunner's mind until ordered, coherent concepts made themselves evident.

The rat-king was telling him, with pictures and ideas and images, what would happen; what *must* happen. It was not a forecast, but a grand picture of the way that things would be if he could properly interpret what he was hearing and translate it into action. He briefly wondered if Spitkid could also understand what the Rat-king was saying, but he could not pull himself away to ask.

It was not simply that he could now pull sense from the stream of words that filled Dayrunner with wonder: it was also the meaning of what he was hearing. At the core of the jumble of ideas and concepts was a nugget of such savage beauty that he was almost humbled to contemplate it. He wished that he had conjured it up himself, but although the notion was staggeringly simple, he would never have arrived at it himself. It was not that the idea itself was difficult or complicated in any way, but it was so audacious, so outrageous, that it would simply never have occurred to him. Few rats would even dare to think such a thought, let alone consider acting on it, but he was nothing if not bold. He was just the rat to put such an idea to the test.

CHAPTER 24

TAKEN AGAIN

Marlinspike was not leading the group of C'law who came for Moon this time. There were about twenty of them, and even though Mizzen heard them before they came into sight, there was no avoiding a confrontation.

Wainscot and his two nestmates were foraging for clean bedding material in the dry stores near the magazine. He was side-by-side with Moon on a stack of folded cloth, and Mizzen was a few lengths away on his own stack. There was only one rat-entrance into the storeroom —a small triangular hole at the bottom of the door.

Each of the three had a mouth full of sweet-smelling linen, and they were heading for the hole when Mizzen stiffened, dropped his load, and cocked his head to listen. After a quick sniff of the air, he gestured to his companions with a swing of his head.

"Drop those and follow me," he said. Wainscot heard the urgency in his voice. It was possible that they had not been seen, and might still avoid detection. They made their way back to the tallest of the stacks and, urged on by Mizzen, quickly burrowed into the folds of material. They were on the opposite side of the room from the door, and stared past the piled stores at the hole at its base.

"What is it?" asked Moon.

"Rats," said Mizzen. "Large party of Bowsers. Just outside the door. Sniffing around the entrance."

"I didn't hear anything," said Wainscot.

"Not much of a surprise there," said Mizzen. "Good thing I'm here, with you and your Lander's ears. I heard them well enough. Noisy buggers. Not like my Aftey raiders. Wouldn't have heard my lads coming. Doubt we'll avoid this bunch though—our scent's too fresh for them to miss. I think we're in for a fight. Our only chance'll be if they're not looking for us and don't bother to search. Knew better than to come into a room with only one entrance, but I really wanted some new bedding. Can't be helped now."

It was the closest Wainscot had ever heard Mizzen come to admitting that he had made a mistake.

From their hiding place the three saw a pointed snout with twitching whiskers poke through the hole. A fair-sized rat followed the nose, and it, in turn, was followed by a large group of others. They milled about for a moment, testing the air with their noses, and then, picking up the scent, moved forward at a run straight toward the stack of linens.

"Right," said Mizzen, "that's it then. I'll take as many of them as I can. Try to slip away in the confusion. Rejoin you at the nest if I'm able."

Before either of the others could protest, he launched himself from the shelter with a shrill squeal and threw himself at the leading Bowser. The impact of his charge knocked the rat sprawling, and he was onto a second in an instant, teeth snapping for the other's throat.

Wainscot could not see what happened next, for the mass of Bowsers swarmed over Mizzen and his opponent and bore them out of sight behind a stack of wooden crates. He could hear the piercing squeals and frantic scrabbling of a desperate fight but could see nothing.

Before Moon and Wainscot could decide whether to join Mizzen in the attack or obey his order and risk a dash for the door, half of the Bowser party came surging back around the corner. They made straight for the hiding place in the linens.

Calling for Moon to follow, Wainscot twisted around and burrowed deeper into the cloth, hoping to tunnel through and escape to the other side, but before he could make any headway, strong teeth clamped down on his tail and dragged him squealing out to the open floor. He found himself beside Moon, pinned securely to the deck by several large, strong rats.

"Do we really have to drag them all the way back to the chamber?" asked one of their captors. "It'd be much easier just to do them here."

"You heard Captain Spume," said another. "She's not to be harmed. He has plans for her."

Captain Spume? Wainscot felt cold fingers close around his stomach. He looked at Moon and saw his fear staring back at him.

"Her, yes, but no one said nothing about him."

"Better bring him along, just to be on the safe side."

"What about the other one?"

"The boys'll take care of him. You just worry about getting these two back in one piece."

Teeth grasped the back of Wainscot's neck, and he and Moon were dragged away.

There was no Lieutenant Marlinspike to speak for her this time, and no Currach to balance reason against cruelty. In fact there were no voices speaking for her at all. This was no trial, no application of justice under the auspices of clan law—this was something else entirely.

The only witnesses were Keckle, Gorp, and five brutish-looking C'law who seemed to be strangers to Moon.

Spume had changed since they had last seen him. He still looked more or less the same—pinch-faced and twitchy—but there was now something about his eyes and the way that he carried himself that marked him as different. Although he was still a bundle of nervous energy, he now controlled it, and his habitual sneer was tempered and bent into something more dignified. He had evidently learned to disguise some of the more obvious outward signs of his nastiness. Perhaps some newly attained authority had given him the strength of will to suppress the most unpleasant aspects of his personality.

Despite these changes, Wainscot doubted that he and Moon would fare any better at the paws of this new version of their enemy. He was sure that Spume's thin veneer of respectability would crack soon enough, and the old monster would claw its way out to leave them face to face with the malevolent creature they knew so well.

Their captors had taken them to the Bowser Council chamber and dumped them unceremoniously at the feet of the waiting Spume. Despite his fear, Wainscot still had the clarity of mind to wonder why Spume had been allowed into the inner sanctum of the Council, and why the others insisted on referring to him as 'Captain'. From what Moon had told him of her clan, the title was ridiculous. The Bowser Clan had no Captain. It had a Council and lieutenants, but no single rat in a supreme position of authority. It was one of the traditions to which the Bowsers proudly adhered, especially because it distinguished them from the Aft Clan. Even if the Bowsers had bucked tradition and chosen a Captain, he could not imagine that they would have fallen so low as to select the loathsome Spume as their leader.

Spume paced back and forth before the two captives. The hulking Gorp stood behind him, and further back, partially obscured by shadow, lurked the silent Keckle. When Spume spoke, it was with the same thin voice and carefully spoken words that Wainscot remembered: that much had not changed.

"Ah, Pretty," he said. "Every time we meet these days, I seem to have you at a disadvantage. Never mind. I do not think we will be seeing much more of each other in future. Still, it is so pleasant to talk to you again. Keeping the same company, I see."

Spume stopped in front of Wainscot. He looked at him slowly from snout to tail before continuing, "I am not sure that I approve of your choice of friends, Scraps, but I suppose you have to settle for what you can get. There was another one, I am told. Quite a fighter, apparently."

Wainscot crouched with his head bowed, and while he made every effort not to catch the eye of any of their captors, Moon held hers high and looked straight at Spume.

"Mizzen," she said. "Where's Mizzen? Have you hurt him?"

"Mizzen is it?" said Spume. "Such a nasty Aftey-ish name. Oh well, we will not have to worry about him anymore."

Wainscot felt something cold squeeze his stomach. Moon made a small sobbing sound.

With an exaggerated, theatrical back-and-forth swing of his head, Spume cast his eyes about the Council chamber, as though searching for someone who was not there.

"But where is the heroic Lieutenant Marlinspike, Pretty?" he asked. "Is he not here to come to your rescue again? Oh, but then I had almost forgotten: he was not actually there the last time either, was he? Before we... well... conclude our business here, you will have to explain to me how you managed to conjure him up like that. It was rather neatly done, and I must admit it has piqued my curiosity."

"You still like to take chances, don't you," said Moon. "If Marlinspike or the Council find out that you've—"

"You tried to use the Council to frighten me last time we met. I was not impressed then. What makes you think I will be now?"

"Spume—"

"*Captain* Spume," he corrected.

Moon laughed. "Captain Spume, then," she said. "Better watch your step. If anyone else hears you calling yourself that, you'll be in for it."

"Ah, then you haven't heard. How delightful. Gorp, tell our little friend here about the changes that have taken place, and about our elevated new status."

"He's Captain now," said Gorp.

"Succinctly put, Gorp," said Spume. "I will elaborate. After the tragic demise of our esteemed Council—you must have heard about that, even off in your remote corner of the ship—there was something of a void. Someone had to step in to establish order. I had been quite close to the Council, as you know—advising them, letting them know how things stood with the common rat, that sort of thing. In any case, I had made some friends in the C'law—friends such as Eagre here—" He gestured to a sullen, brutish-looking rat. "—and they were supportive of my offer to do my part for the clan in its time of trouble. In fact, they insisted on my assuming the title of 'Captain'. Naturally, modesty made me hesitate, but they were quite persuasive, and as it was for the good of the clan, I agreed. There were some who questioned my right to rule, but they were soon persuaded that I was the rat for the job."

Looking at Gorp and Eagre, Wainscot had little doubt as to the method of persuasion employed.

"Marlinspike would never have stood for it," said Moon.

"Marlinspike again? You seem to place great store in that particular rat's abilities. Still, you are correct: he might have caused some trouble. For reasons I cannot quite explain, he has never been particularly fond of me. Fortunately, he was not present when I accepted the great burden of the Captaincy. He was off on a raid into Aftey territory at the time and did not return until my loyal supporters had already persuaded me to do my bit. I will grant that he was none too pleased about it when he found out. He has been something of a thorn in my side, but what is a leader without his detractors?"

Everything about Spume's story struck Wainscot as false. Spume might have had the ability to attract a motley following of bully-boys and like-minded clan pariahs, but he lacked the strength of character to assume the leadership of a clan. Even if he had managed, through luck and timing, to worm his way into a position of authority, what sensible rat would willingly follow such a leader? According to Moon, Spume had been unpopular for his entire life, and there was little reason to think that anything had changed. It was more likely that he had set himself up with a few followers, and the rest of the clan were simply too shattered by the death of their Council to do anything about him. From what Moon had told him of Marlinspike, Wainscot was sure it would not be long before Spume found himself violently ejected from his so-called Captaincy. Unfortunately, that happy event would come too late to do Moon and him any good.

"But we are not here to talk about Marlinspike," said Spume. "I have been looking forward to this day for quite some time now. I was beginning to despair that it might never come, but here you are. I have sent patrol after patrol out to find you, but you have proved remarkably elusive. The influence of your tough old Aftey friend, I suppose. I can hardly imagine that this striped Lander here has been much help. But still, I have you now, and I do not think we will be interrupted by any meddlers this time."

He turned his head toward Eagre. "Lieutenant, dismiss the guard. The four of us should be more than up to the task of taking care of these two."

With a barked command, Eagre ordered the C'law to leave the chamber. The remaining Bowsers shifted around to encircle Wainscot and Moon.

"You know," said Spume, "I really have nothing against this Lander. We will be quick with him, and then settle down to the serious work."

The circle began to close.

"This *will* be fun," said Spume.

CHAPTER 25

TWIN BATTLES

R e-provisioned, and with a full compliment of sailors—most of
whom had been escorted unwillingly aboard by the press
gangs—the *Heloise* left Jamaica and resumed her cruise back up the
east coast of the United States. She was now unencumbered by
prizes, which she had sent on ahead to the Vice Admiralty courts in
Halifax.

Her own journey was uneventful; she came across no enemy
merchant vessels, and the ships of the American Navy were wisely

hiding in the safety of their harbours, covered by the guns of their shore batteries.

Or rather, she came across no enemy vessels until she hove into the roads off New London, Connecticut. There, she was surprised to see an American frigate running out from the harbour at full sail. It was the *Mustang*, a remarkably capable ship, almost a twin to the *Heloise*. This American ship had been languishing in the harbour, leery of facing the larger British flotillas that patrolled the coast. However, she was eager for a fight and leapt at the chance to sail out to meet the *Heloise*.

The sailors of the *Heloise* cleared her decks and ran out her guns. Her masters-at-arms issued cutlasses and boarding pikes, and her seamen stacked rolled hammocks in netting along the edges of her upper decks to create breastworks. Her gun crews stood to their charges and her powder-monkeys scurried about, ferrying the volatile cartridges to her great cannons. Across the waves, the Men of the of the *Mustang* busied themselves doing the same. Marines—red-coated on the *Heloise* and blue on the *Mustang*—assembled on the decks or climbed to the fighting tops to assume firing positions. Carpenters readied the tools, patches and plugs they would need to repair the ships, and surgeons laid out their instruments to do the same for the Men.

The *Heloise* swung about the open sea, manoeuvring to gain the advantage of position and wind. Shortly before noon, she closed with the *Mustang*. They slid past each other, mere yards apart. Forty gun-captains pulled forty lanyards and forty flintlocks sparked on forty long-guns and carronades. The broadsides rippled along the ships from bow to stern, each gun belching fire and smoke a split-second after its neighbour.

The two ships erupted in billowing clouds of yellow-white smoke as tongues of flame stabbed out across the water. A great thundering roar flattened the chop of the sea between the combatants, and the *Heloise* shuddered from keel to masthead as a storm of iron raged into her.

Belowdecks, the Afties were on the move. All adults of fighting age—male and female, young and old—were sweeping through the holds like a black tide. They rolled over everything in their path, a living, breathing carpet that crested over barrel and box as they flowed through the ship's stores toward Bowser territory.

Dayrunner had planned well. The Men usually practiced their gunnery every day or two, and when they did, they abandoned the holds for the fighting decks. These drills were always preceded by the removal of all partitions on the gun decks and a sudden flurry of activity around the gunpowder room. Thinking ahead, Dayrunner had placed rats in hiding places near the guns and the magazine to watch for these signs two days after his destruction of the Bowser Council. The time to act was right. Confusion and fear would have spread through the entire Bowser Clan, but they would not yet have organised themselves sufficiently to assemble a new Council. The defences of their territory would be in disarray. Ready for a swift victory, the Aftey troops had been assembled and waiting, ready to move as soon as they were given the word.

When a watch-rat, breathless from his dash down from the gun-deck, had arrived to tell Dayrunner that the sailors had begun their preparation for gun practice, the Captain had issued the order and the army of the Aft Clan had advanced.

Dayrunner expected a few casualties before they left Aftey territory. There were always some Men in the holds, even during gun practice, and they would not fail to notice hundreds upon hundreds of rats on the move. Some of his troops would fall to clubs and stamping shoes, but his ranks were reinforced with pressed land rats, which meant that he could afford some early losses.

However, he did not have to pay for his progress with any expendables. When he led his Afties over the border into Bowser territory, they did not encounter a single Man. Then, just as Dayrunner was thinking how perfectly his plan was unfolding, the *Heloise* loosed the first of her broadsides, and everything changed.

The curved surface of the barrel beneath Dayrunner's feet jumped and shuddered as though the ship had been struck a tremendous blow. The stack of barrels over which he was running shifted and rolled, and it was all he could do to retain his footing. Some of his rats were not so fortunate; their squeals of terror rose above the roar of the guns as they fell to be crushed by the rolling barrels.

Something crashed into the ship in the dark space overhead, and the air was suddenly filled with a gale of flying splinters: wicked, spinning claws of wood that raked the ranks of Afties. Many of them were plucked from atop the barrels by the wooden daggers and either killed outright or dropped down to be mashed by the shifting stores. A rush of seawater followed the splinters, washing more rats away to their deaths.

The entire army stopped in its tracks and crouched down, frozen in place by terror. Dayrunner looked up and saw with shock that daylight was visible through a hole in the ship's hull. Then, the ragged circle of light disappeared, to be replaced by another gout of green water as the ship rolled and the hole plunged below the waterline.

For the first time in his life, Dayrunner was at a loss as to what to do. He did not know what was happening. None of the other gun practices had been like this. For precious heartbeats he sat motionless and uncertain, not knowing whether to advance or retreat. All around him, his army was similarly paralysed.

Suddenly, Spitkid appeared at his side.

The lieutenant spoke urgently in his ear, "We have to move, sir. We'll drown if we stay here. The barrels are already starting to float, and Men will be here soon to patch that hole. We can't be here when they arrive."

"What's happening?" asked Dayrunner. He was appalled at the quaver in his own voice. If he did not gain control of himself immediately, he ran the risk of showing weakness to his lieutenant.

"It's a battle, sir. It's not just practice," said Spitkid. "There's another ship out there. We must move."

With immense effort, Dayrunner roused himself and cast off his fear. "This changes nothing," he said, his voice steady again. "We move forward. The Bowsers will be even more disordered with this going on." He raised his voice to be heard above the cacophony and yelled, "Forward! On to the Bowsers!"

Leaping from barrel to shifting barrel without looking back, he bounded toward the enemy that lay ahead. For a moment nothing happened, then several rats moved to follow him. In a few heartbeats, like a wave running through their ranks, the paralysis shattered and the army surged forward.

They met almost no resistance. Since the death of their Council, the Bowsers had lacked the will to patrol their own territory, or even to post guards at the border. All order had disintegrated and most did nothing but hide, creeping out only when hunger drove them into the ratways to find food. As the invaders swept deeper into enemy territory, they found Bowsers hiding in nests, Bowsers crawling fearfully through ratruns, Bowsers alone and Bowsers in groups, Bowsers young and Bowsers old.

They killed every single one of them.

Some put up a good fight, but it was always a few against many. No matter how brave the resistance, the Bowsers fell, crushed by the overwhelming number of the disciplined Afties.

As the army advanced, the battle between the ships continued to rock the *Heloise*. Ball after ball smashed into the timbers of her hull, and she twitched and shuddered at each impact. Water rose in the holds and many Bowsers drowned in their nests, sparing themselves a bloodier death at the teeth of the Afties. Even over the sounds of their own battle, the rats could hear the cries of wounded Men and the rattle of musketfire overhead, all underscored by the roar of cannons as the *Heloise* sent death across the water to her enemy.

Soon, Dayrunner and his troops approached the heart of the Bowser domain: the Council chambers. They had carved a bloody path through the ship, the nests and ratways behind them clogged with Bowser dead.

Dayrunner called Spitkid to his side. The fur about the lieutenant's muzzle was matted with blood, his teeth stained pink. There was a fierce wildness in his eyes that Dayrunner knew was mirrored in his own.

"We're near their Council chamber now," said Dayrunner. "We'll have to go up to the orlop deck. I'll take ten patrol groups with me and go there now. You continue on through the holds with the main part of the army. I don't expect I'll find anything of interest—they won't have a new Council yet—but I want to make sure. I'll come down to rejoin you when I'm finished."

"Aye-aye, sir," said Spitkid.

"And kill everything you see, whether it resists or not. I don't want a single Bowser left alive by the end of this day."

Dayrunner took his party and scrambled up the rail of a ladder to the deck above, leaving Spitkid to continue the cleansing of the hold.

There had been no serious resistance by the Bowsers, so Dayrunner did not feel the need for caution, even with his reduced force. Speed was of the essence—in order to keep his losses as light as possible, it was vital that he utterly destroy the Bowsers before they had the chance to organise any effective defence. He doubted they would have the ability to co-ordinate any serious resistance without the leadership of a Council, but he did not intend to slow down long enough to find out.

At the head of his group of one hundred warriors, Dayrunner entered the cable storage room. The sailors had extinguished all lanterns before the battle as a precaution against fire, making the surroundings very dim. The thick anchor cables looped in great heaps, winding back and forth across the room like giant snakes lurking in the gloom. The massive cables, made of multiple hempen ropes bound together, were greater in diameter than three rats laid side by side.

The floor slats of the cable room were laid in an open pattern, leaving wide spaces to allow water to drain through to the holds below, and from there into the bilges, making the path across the room perilous for the quickly moving group. There was more than enough space between the slats for a clumsy rat to misstep and fall through.

Dayrunner clambered up onto a loop of cable and began to make his way across the room toward the entrance to the Bowser Council chamber. He was halfway when he heard a squeal of alarm from behind. Turning, he saw that the rear of his party had engaged a group of Bowsers who must have emerged from the hollows between the great coils of cable. It was an ambush, and he cursed his careless-ness even while consoling himself that this momentary lapse would not result in much harm. The attacking Bowsers were few—they looked to be only about a quarter of his own number—and he and his well-trained fighters would make short work of them.

As he scurried back along the cable toward the fray, he saw that several rats were already down. Looking closer, he was shocked to realise that all of them were Afties. The ambushers were apparently making a good showing of it. He threw himself at the closest of the Bowsers in retaliation. He took the rat, a fair-sized female, by the back of the neck and bit down savagely. She squealed and tried to turn, but his grip was too secure. He shook her vigorously until she ceased struggling, then dropped her and was onto the next Bowser in a bound.

He killed two more in quick succession, then, looking around for his next foe, spied a large battle-scarred male beyond the tangle of fighting rats. He identified the rat as their leader, seeing the four or five dead Afties scattered about the cables where the Bowser fought. Dayrunner pushed his way through the squirming mass toward his target.

The large Bowser, concentrating on dispatching yet another Aftey, did not see Dayrunner approaching. Fast and silent, the Captain came in low, his head down and incisors bared. He respected the skills of the Bowser enough that he did not expect to kill with the first blow. Instead of aiming for his enemy's throat, he went for a crippling wound that would allow him to finish him at leisure. He thrust for a thigh, but was surprised when his teeth closed on air.

The Bowser had sensed danger at the last instant and reared onto his hind legs, sidestepping with a startling nimbleness and dropping down onto Dayrunner's back. Dayrunner found himself beneath his foe, and winced at a sharp flash of pain as the Bowser's teeth split the skin on his back. Rather than punching into vulnerable muscle, however, the Bowser's teeth glanced off the hard knobs of Dayrunner's spine. The long shallow wound hurt fiercely, but Dayrunner was used to pain, and hardly noticed..

The force of the strike threw the Bowser off-balance, and Dayrunner managed to scramble out from under the other rat.

Breathing hard, the two adversaries faced each other, but neither attacked.

"Well, well," said Dayrunner. "You're quick, I'll give you that." It was an indication of his surprise at the Bowser's speed that he spoke at all. He never said anything to an opponent during a fight. He considered it a sign of weakness, so he always got straight to the business of killing. This time however, he took a moment to appraise the Bowser, which allowed him to look for vulnerability.

The Bowser said nothing. He too seemed to be assessing his opponent's abilities.

"I'm Dayrunner. Thought you might like to know the name of the rat who's going to kill you."

"Marlinspike," growled the Bowser.

"Very well, Marlinspike. Let's finish this, shall we?"

Dayrunner shot forward with a sudden thrust of his hind legs. He feinted low, then adjusted his strike upward, aiming for Marlinspike's shoulder. However, the Bowser was too seasoned a fighter to fall for the trick. He turned slightly to his right and thrust forward to meet the charge. The two rats crashed into each other, chest to chest, head to head, the jarring force of the impact bouncing them sideways from the top of the cables. They grappled as they fell, rolling down the hairy slope of the stacked ropes, each trying with snapping jaws to tear the throat from the other.

They struck the floor near one of the spaces between the slats. Although they had not fallen far, their momentum was enough to carry them over the edge. Feeling themselves topple, the two combatants released their grips on each other and scrambled for a clawhold. Dayrunner, who happened to be on top, kicked off from Marlinspike with his back legs, grunting with satisfaction as his nails bit into soft flesh. With a frantic scrabble of claws he pulled himself back up onto the slat and turned, ready to resume the fight.

However, Marlinspike was gone.

Dayrunner peered down into the gloom below the floor for any sign of the Bowser, but the darkness was complete. He could see nothing. The distance of the drop was likely not enough to have killed

Marlinspike, but at least he was rid of the troublesome rat for the time being.

Dayrunner climbed to the top of the cables and threw himself back into the struggle. By the time he could find no more Bowsers to fight, he had killed seven more of them. The surviving Afties, scattered across the tops of the cables and the deck below, stood or lay panting amid the bodies of the fallen.

Surveying the aftermath of the battle, Dayrunner realised with a shock that he had lost a good half of his party. The Bowsers, though beaten in the end, had accounted for more than twice their own number. *It was that Marlinspike*, he thought bitterly. A good leader can make all the difference. Marlinspike must have attracted the best rats in the Bowser Clan to his side, and then forged them into a highly effective fighting unit.

Marlinspike had proved that he was an enemy to respect, and Dayrunner was annoyed that he had been denied the chance to eliminate him. The Bowser had fought surprisingly well: he had stood against the Captain's attack, which was something no rat had ever done before.

He'll be back to bother me again, he thought. *However, he won't be more than an irritant if he does. His fighters made a good showing of it, but they're all dead now—by the end of this day there'll be no Bowsers left. Marlinspike will be a leader with no one to lead.*

Dayrunner called for his rats to regroup and join him. They were tired and wounded, but they still managed to come and cluster around him. Ordering the six nearest to follow, he crossed the remaining distance to the Bowser's Council chamber and crawled inside. The chamber was empty, but it had recently been occupied. The scent of Bowser was still fresh.

Dayrunner left the chamber and looked about. There was only one way—other than the dangerous drop through the floor slats—by which the Bowsers could have escaped: through the gap at the base of the main door to the cable-room. Marshalling his remaining troops, he set off in pursuit.

CHAPTER 26

ESCAPES

One of the guards burst into the chamber. Spume turned on him, furious. "You were told to remain outside," he growled. "Eagre, can you not control your rats?"

"Captain sir," said the guard, "It's Afties. They're outside the chamber."

Wainscot watched the play of emotions flicker across Spume's face. He could almost hear the conflicting thoughts tumbling through the Bowser's mind.

When the ship had first staggered under the impact of enemy fire, Wainscot had been amazed that Spume had not abandoned his plan to amuse himself with his prisoners. Wainscot was not exactly sure what was happening, but whatever it was, it was terrifying. Spume, it seemed, would not allow the affairs of Men to deprive him of his pleasure. However, an Aftey raid was another matter entirely, and one not so easily ignored.

Spume turned to Eagre. "Take your C'law and stop them," he said. "They must not be allowed to enter these chambers."

"Your pardon, sir," said the guard who had entered, "but there are too many of them. Hundreds I think. They're already in the cables. They'd be here now if it wasn't for Lieutenant Marlinspike."

At the mention of Marlinspike's name, Wainscot saw Spume's fear blossom into panic.

Spume leapt to the entrance of the chamber and peered out, clearly fighting the urge to flee. Wainscot could see past him and into the cable room beyond. He could could hear the din of rats in combat just on the other side of the nearest loop of cables. The faint smell of blood reached him, but there was no sign of Afties yet. Other than the four guards waiting uneasily just outside the chamber, there were no rats to be seen. It was not too late to escape.

Wainscot saw Spume's shoulders tense as he leaned forward, and wondered if he was going to slip away and leave the rest of his party to take their chances without him. Then Spume turned back into the chamber. Evidently he was not yet completely in the grip of his rising panic, and had calculated that he would be safer in the company of the others. Maybe he thought that, if nothing else, his guards would slow and distract any Aftey pursuers while he made his escape.

He turned to Eagre, Gorp, and Keckle. "Quickly," he said, "It is clear. We can get away before they arrive."

"What about them?" asked Gorp, gesturing at Wainscot and Moon.

"Kill them," said Spume, then quickly changed his mind. "No, wait... Take them with us. We'll find time for them later."

Wainscot was amazed that Spume's hatred for Moon was so deep that he still clung to it even when his world was coming apart about him. He would not give her a quick death and deny himself a long-anticipated pleasure.

Without waiting to see that his order was obeyed, Spume ran from the chamber and along the base of the bulkhead toward the gap at the bottom of the Man-door. Gorp, Keckle, Eagre, and the guards followed him, dragging Moon and Wainscot with them.

As soon as they squeezed beneath the door, sounds of pursuit rose in the cable room behind them. It was plain that the Afties were coming for them. Wainscot and Moon ran as quickly as they could, not offering any resistance, even though they knew they were running toward a fate much more unpleasant than they would face if caught by their pursuers. The Afties would just kill them, but Spume had something much worse in store for them.

Still, they ran because they were alive—while they were alive they had hope.

They were not far from the cable room door when they caught a first glimpse of their pursuers. Running up the centre of a wide passageway, they heard the scrabble of claws on wood behind. They glanced back to see a huge rat, bloody and terrifying, pushing out from beneath the door. It was Dayrunner, so transformed by his battle fury that Wainscot did not even recognise him.

The fugitives came to a side passage and turned into it. As soon as they had turned, Spume stopped and addressed the guards.

"Eagre," he said, "Leave these two with us. Take your rats and stop those Afties." His voice was shaking.

For a moment it looked as though Eagre would protest, but after a brief hesitation he nodded his head. Then he turned back toward the main passageway, taking his four C'law with him.

The rest continued at a run along the side passage. Glancing back, Wainscot saw that Eagre and his C'law did not turn toward the pursuing Afties as ordered, but instead ran in the opposite direction up the main passageway to escape.

He's smarter than he looks, he thought. Spume did not notice the dereliction of duty.

The rats were unfamiliar with the passage up which they were running. It was a Manway that they would not normally have used, so they were taken by surprise when it came to an abrupt end at a door only fifteen or twenty rat-lengths from the corner. The gap beneath the door was too narrow to allow them through.

They were trapped.

Spume scratched and bit desperately at the bottom of the door, but it was futile: their pursuers would be on them long before he could chew a large enough hole. Pressing themselves against the wood of the door, they stared back down the passageway, waiting for the Afties.

Moon laughed quietly. "At least Wainscot and I won't be the only ones dying today, Spume," she said. "I don't think things are going quite as you planned."

She laughed again, slightly louder. Wainscot would not have been surprised to hear a note of hysteria in the sound, but she seemed calm —almost happy, as though she were enjoying a quiet time in her nest, swapping stories with friends.

But death did not find them: not then at least.

The pursuing Afties reached the junction of hallways and continued on up the main passage in pursuit of Eagre and his small party of guards. Only one of them stopped to peer into the side passage. She took several steps into it. The gloom was too deep for her to see the cowering rats, but she lifted her head to sniff the air. She must have smelled them as they crouched motionless in the darkness, but she just stared blindly for a few breaths, then spun away and scurried off to rejoin her group.

The hiders waited until they were sure the Afties were gone, and then crept cautiously back to the main Manway. There were no rats to be seen in either direction.

"What were you saying, Pretty?" asked Spume in a whisper. He had regained a measure of his self-possession, though his voice still trembled. "It looks as though we will have a chance to finish our business after all." He turned his head toward Gorp and Keckle. "Watch them closely. I do not want them slipping away. We will just nip back to the Council chamber and pick up where we left off."

"Are you mad?" cried Moon. "That wasn't just a raiding party. The Afties are attacking the clan. They'll be back—if not them, then another group just like them. Everything's changing. Can't you feel it? Can't you smell it? There's death in the air: death for all of us. We've got to get away."

Spume crept along the passage back the way they had come. He kept close to the wall, looking around nervously. Keckle and Gorp pushed the two captives along behind him. Gorp cast his eyes about uneasily, but Keckle was as unperturbed as ever.

As he walked, Spume spoke over his shoulder. "You will not escape that easily." He stopped and hunched down as the ship quivered at the impact of an enemy broadside, then continued. "I have been looking forward to this for too long."

"Listen to me, Spume," said Moon. "What about the clan? If you really are the Captain, it's your duty to do something."

"It is sweet of you to think about the welfare of the clan, Scraps, but we are no longer your concern. Leave what is best for the Bowsers to me. You have other things to worry about at the moment."

Moon stopped and turned to face her guards. "Gorp," she said, "Keckle, surely you must see that this is madness. Use your minds. You can't be playing Spume's petty games right now. He's crazy—surely you can see that."

Something—a spark of reason, perhaps—flickered for a moment in Gorp's eyes and Wainscot felt a glimmer of hope, but then it was gone. Moon retreated a step as the huge rat bared his teeth. There was no change of expression from Keckle, nothing to indicate that she had even heard what Moon had said.

"You will have to do better than that." Spume laughed.

They reached the door to the cable room. Spume hesitated, sniffing the air that wafted out from beneath the door. The odours of blood and Aftey welling out from the cable room could have done little to ease his disquiet, but he could hardly have expected anything else, given the battle that had just taken place. He squeezed through the gap, and the rest followed.

"Almost there, Pretty," said Spume. "Then we will—"

He did not finish his sentence. A rat, hissing with fury, leaped from a stack of cables and landed squarely on Spume's back.

Dayrunner sniffed at the bodies. They had put up a reasonable fight. Nothing compared to what Marlinspike's bunch had done but respectable enough.

"There were more of them," he said to the rat nearest him. "Where are the others?"

"I don't know sir."

"Sir," said a voice farther back in the ranks, "I think I smelled someone in one of the side passages we passed."

Dayrunner shouldered his way through the press to the speaker. "You did, did you?" he said.

"Yes sir."

"And it never occurred to you to investigate?" he asked, angrily. "Don't you know my orders? No Bowsers are to survive."

The rat quailed, waiting for the blow. "No sir... Yes sir..." she stammered.

Dayrunner considered killing her immediately, but he had already lost enough of his party.

"Show me," he said instead.

Spume was knocked flat by the assault. He squealed and tried to wriggle free, but the strange rat was too strong for him. Sharp teeth closed around one of his forelegs. Before he could resist, the attacker flipped him onto his back. Belly exposed, he was at the mercy of the newcomer, who stood with his forelegs on Spume's chest, long yellow incisors poised just above the soft fur of the fallen rat's throat.

Moon took a step forward, hissing at Wainscot to follow. Gorp and Keckle did not move.

It took several breaths for Wainscot to realise that the rat standing over Spume was Mizzen. He was almost unrecognizable, but it was him. His coat was matted with blood, some of it obviously his own. Several long wounds were visible against the dark fur of his flank and part of his left ear was missing. His eyes glared from the spiky hair of his face, black beads rimmed with white, as he grinned with toothy menace, nothing less than fury incarnate. Gorp and Keckle must have been impressed as well, for neither moved to help the fallen Spume. Even the usually unflappable Keckle seemed taken aback. It was the first indication that Wainscot had seen that she was capable of feeling any emotion at all.

"Can't think of any reason why I shouldn't kill this piece of dung right now," said Mizzen.

Wainscot found it odd to hear Mizzen's genial, somewhat stuffy voice coming from this terrifying apparition. It made the warrior rat seem slightly less formidable.

Gorp and Keckle took a step forward.

"Wouldn't if I were you," said Mizzen. "Frankly I'm looking for a reason to do some damage to your loathsome friend here."

"Don't do anything to make him angry," squealed Spume. Gorp and Keckle took another step.

"That's how it's to be then, is it?" said Mizzen, and with a hiss of rage he threw himself at Gorp. His claws left long, angry wheals across Spume's chest as he pushed off.

Spume was left still on his back. Before he had a chance to right himself, Moon was on top of him. She was considerably smaller than he, but that did not matter to Spume. He kicked and squealed, but, surprisingly, made no attempt to fight her. Perhaps he was so frightened of Mizzen that he simply did not think to fight.

Wainscot stood to the rear, shifting from foot to foot, uncertain as to what to do. He did not run, but neither did he come to help Moon.

Mizzen struck Gorp at a run and the two rats tumbled in a clawing, spitting, biting tangle across the floor. Gorp managed to escape from Mizzen's grasp long enough to squeeze beneath the door, but just before he disappeared, Mizzen bit down onto the end of his tail and was dragged through the gap by the fleeing, larger rat.

It did not take Keckle so much as a heartbeat to determine where her loyalty lay. She wheeled about and scrambled under the door after Gorp and Mizzen.

Spume squealed even more loudly as he saw her leave. He stopped squirming and went slack. Moon stood over him, her front paws on his chest. Wainscot slipped quietly to his friend's side.

"I think we should leave," he said. His voice was low and subdued. He was ashamed of his inaction.

"We can't leave Spume, or he'll just be after us again," she said. "And what about Mizzen? He might need our help?"

"What can we do to help Mizzen? We're not fighters," said Wainscot, despising himself for his own cowardice. Mizzen had risked himself to come to their aid three times now, and he could not find the strength to even *try* to help the old warrior. "We have to leave," he added. "But first we should kill Spume. Of that I'm sure."

Spume said nothing, staring up at them with wide eyes. He seemed smaller now, more insignificant; he was no longer the cruel, sneering bully, but now merely a weak, frightened rat looking into the eyes of his own death, too crushed to resist. Wainscot would have felt sorry for him if not for his certainty that the vicious old Spume would return the moment Moon's fragile advantage evaporated.

"I don't think I can—" started Moon.

She was interrupted by a scuttling of claws at the base of the door. Side by side, Gorp and Keckle pushed through the gap. Wainscot retreated a step with a gasp, but the two did not attack. They ran past and climbed onto the cables.

A moment later, Mizzen came through beneath the door. He had a fresh cut over one eye. "Afties," he said. "Run."

"But Spume," said Moon. "We can't—"

"Run!"

He pushed Moon from atop Spume and nipped at her flank to start her running. Wainscot followed and so did Spume. There was the sound of many rats arriving on the other side of the door.

They kept ahead of the Afties, but only just. Their greater familiarity with the Bowser runs allowed them to evade their pursuers, but they could not shake them completely. At first, they made their way down into the holds, hoping to escape to the safety of their nest, but there they found only death. The bodies were everywhere, and it was soon evident that there would be no sanctuary anywhere in Bowser territory. The Bowser Clan had been wiped out.

Their only choice was to go up.

If they had had the luxury of time to consider their situation, Moon, Wainscot, and Mizzen would have been amazed to find themselves running in the company of Spume, Gorp, and Keckle. In this moment, they all shared a common need to escape; they were all driven along the same paths by the relentless pursuit. They were not so much together as merely all running in the same direction.

By default, Moon had become the leader of their flight. She was the only one who seemed to have any idea about where to go, and they followed her without question as she led them up through the ship. As they climbed higher, they left the world of the rat behind and entered the world of Man.

CHAPTER 27

ALOFT

In a slow, complicated dance of manoeuvre and counter-manoeuvre, the *Heloise* sailed back and forth across the sea, closing with and sheering away from the *Mustang*, trying to attain an advantage. She attempted to cross either bow or stern so that she could fire her guns down the length of her enemy and do maximum damage without receiving a broadside in return. Each time she closed in, her guns roared. She traded broadside for broadside with the American ship, and they battered each other mercilessly. The Heloise shuddered at each impact as if with pain, but she gave back as good as she received.

The carnage was horrifying. Ball after ball exploded through her hull timbers, spraying lethal splinters and carving bloody swaths through her guts. Grape and canister-shot swept her decks, reaping Men like a scythe through wheat.

Despite the slaughter and the massive pounding that she suffered, she did not receive a mortal blow. No damage was great enough to affect her ability to manoeuvre or fight. None of her masts were downed, her hull was not yet holed beyond repair, and only a few of her guns were disabled. Although the toll on her crew was horrifyingly high, she did not lose enough of them to render her incapable of continuing the fight. Across the battle-agitated expanse of water between the two combatants, the *Mustang* fought on, making plain that she had not been dealt a crippling blow either.

When her guns and marksmen had done their jobs sufficiently, the contest could be settled with cutlass and pistol. The *Heloise* slewed around and ran parallel with the *Mustang*, rapidly closing the gap between the two frigates. Her boarding parties stood to their weapons, their ropes and grapnels at the ready. Far above her decks, her spars smashed and broke with a ragged volley of gunshot cracks as she crashed against the *Mustang*, battered hull to battered hull. Rigging tangled, yards splintered, sails tore, and debris fell to her decks. Men fell too.

Grapnels snaked out from both ships and ensnared shrouds or hooked into wood. Muscular, tattooed arms drew the ropes taut and bound the ships together with a spider's web of crisscrossing lines.

With a shout of "*Heloise!*" and a waving of cutlasses, pikes, and axes, the *Heloise*'s sailors and marines vaulted across to the deck of the *Mustang*. The Americans rose to meet them, their own weapons raised and ready.

The fleeing group of rats bypassed the gundeck, scuttling up from level to level by secret ratways. The sailors had abandoned the lower decks, but the upper were crowded with Men. All was chaos. Yellow smoke, choking and sulphurous, drifted in thick ropes down into the ship through every crack and opening. The fugitives had encountered it before they had even reached the gundeck, and it thickened as they climbed.

Although it blinded them and denied them the use of their noses, Wainscot was grateful for it. *If we've lost our sense of smell,* he thought, *then so have the Afties, and it'll make it all that much harder for them to follow us.*

The noise was just as disorientating as the smell. The ship shook with the firing of the long guns, though the great rolling thunder of the broadsides had been replaced by sporadic single explosions now that the Men had brought the fight to each other with sword, pike, and pistol. The crackle of small-arms fire whipped through the air, accompanied by the clang of steel on steel. Even as loud as it was, the din could not bury the voices that rose through it. Shouts of rage or exultation, shrieks of fear, and screams of pain combined in a symphony of Human emotion that terrified and bewildered the fugitives.

The rats emerged from a drainage hole beneath one of the ship's boats, which was upturned on the main deck. The back half of the boat had been torn away by a cannonball, and they stared out through the opening in disbelief at a hellish shipscape that had been altered almost beyond recognition. A blanket of haze lay over everything, and the noon sunlight, blazing hot and fierce from directly overhead, could only pierce the gloom enough to paint the smoke a dull yellow. Men were everywhere. Many moved in and out of the fog, disappearing and reappearing like phantoms, but most within sight lay unmoving upon the deck or draped across the tangled wreckage. In some places upon the deck, the dead Men—or parts of them—were stacked several deep.

"They're still coming for us," said Wainscot. "I can hear them, even over this noise."

"Doubt you can, Laddie," said Mizzen. "Your fear's playing tricks on your ears. But I also doubt they've given up on us. They'll be here soon enough, and we should move on before they arrive." He glanced at Spume, Gorp, and Keckle, who were pressed back in the shadows as far away from the other rats as they could manage. "Company in here's unpleasant enough as it is."

Spume said nothing, but his loathing of Mizzen was written in every line of his body. At that moment it was possible that it rivalled his hatred for Moon.

"We'll have to go aloft," said Moon.

"Aloft?" said Mizzen. "Into the rigging, you mean? Can't agree with you there, Lass. Rigging's no place for rats."

"I've been up there countless times. Look around you. We can't continue across the decks. There are too many Men. We can't go back down, either. Look, even Wainscot has been aloft with me. He wasn't afraid—"

Oh yes I was, thought Wainscot, though he did not say it.

"—and he's a Lander."

Mizzen laughed. "You'll not shame me into going up there, Lass. I have no doubts about my own courage. It's the wisdom of the route I question. It's only death that waits for us up there, I'm sure."

"I'm not going up there," muttered Spume, just loudly enough for them to hear.

Mizzen turned on him with a hiss. "You weren't invited," he spat. "Half a mind to kill you now and be done with you. In any case, wherever we decide to go, you and your little gang won't be coming with us." Some of the fighting fury that had made him so frightening down in the cable-room surged back into him, and the Bowsers recoiled. He glared at them for a moment before turning back to Moon. He winked, careful not to let anyone but Moon and Wainscot see.

"I thought you'd gone mad when you attacked Spume back there," Moon whispered.

"Oh that," Mizzen whispered back. "Always get a little, er, worked up in a fight, but I never lose my head. Always know when to fight and when to run." He paused for a moment, cocking his head to one side to listen.

"They're here," he said. "Looks as though we'll have to do it your way. Lead on, Moon, and quickly."

Wainscot had heard nothing but knew better than to question

Mizzen's senses. Perhaps hoping for a moment when there would be no Men about, Moon waited for a while before moving. It quickly became obvious that none would be coming, so she dashed out across the open deck. The others followed.

They scuttled up onto the bulwark without incident, their feet red and sticky from the sheets of blood that ran across the deck and sluiced from the scuppers. Men were leaping from the *Heloise* to the enemy ship, and they stamped on the top of the bulwark as they launched themselves across the gap. The rats were almost crushed or kicked from their precarious perch several times before they made it to the bottom of the shrouds, the ropes that led up to the first of the ship's three masts. Then, they were onto the lines and climbing through the thick smoke to the dubious safety of the heights above.

The landscape of rope, spar, and sail that spread out above the *Heloise* was now only sparsely populated by Men. Wainscot paused in his climb to look down on the chaos below. The deck of the enemy ship roiled with knots of struggling Men. Even through the obscuring smoke he could see the glint of filtered sunlight on steel and the occasional flash of a pistol. With a shiver, he resumed his clamber up the lines.

The rats climbed high into the rigging, past splintered spars and shot-tattered sails and through drifting tendrils of smoke. They followed Moon, anxious to leave both the battle and the pursuing Afties as far below as possible. They put their trust in her to lead them to safety.

Finally, they reached the third yard, the long horizontal wooden spar that supported the fore upper topsail. The lightly damaged sail hung below it, flapping and rippling loosely in the wind. One end of the spar was entangled in the enemy ship's rigging.

Moon crawled out onto the yard, away from the bole of the mast. Wainscot pulled himself up beside her.

She said, "We could cross over the yards to the other ship. I don't know how things could be any worse for us there than they are on the *Heloise*."

Wainscot did not reply. He knew from his own experience the

challenges faced by a stranger aboard a ship, but he knew too little of the differences between one ship and another to offer an opinion.

Mizzen, who still clung to the shrouds, had no such uncertainty. He said, "Think about what you're suggesting here, Lass. The rats aboard that ship wouldn't be too keen to see us. If they're anything like us, they'd probably kill us as soon as they laid eyes on us."

"But all the rats aboard the Heloise want to kill us anyway," said Moon, "so we'd be no worse off than we are now. It might even be better."

"We'd be on a ship we don't know," said Mizzen. "We wouldn't know one end from the other. We'd be lost."

Moon considered for a moment. "You're probably right," she said. Her expression brightened. "Wait... Of course I know where we can go. Follow me."

She ran out along the yard, away from the rigging of the enemy ship. The group scurried after her. Among the confusion of ropes attached to the spar was a brace-line that ran across the gap to the next mast on the *Heloise*. The line was not drawn taut; it dipped down in the middle before rising again to meet the far mast. It swung alarmingly when Moon put her foot upon it, but she stepped out and began to run down its sweeping curve, her toes grasping the hairy surface with practised ease.

Wainscot hesitated for a moment before following. He felt unsteady; the deck looked to be a long way below him. He wound his tail around the line for additional support and started slowly along it. The rope bounced alarmingly as each of the other rats behind him stepped from the spar, and he had to will himself not to freeze in place. He was about halfway across the void when Moon reached the far side. She hopped onto the main upper yard and turned to watch the progress of her companions.

Wainscot saw movement above her. At first he thought it was a sailor shimmying down the mast toward her, but the shape was much too small to be a Man.

He called a warning, but was too late.

The creature—Man, and yet not Man—dropped onto the yard beside Moon and grabbed her in one hand. Then it swung down below the spar to hang by its free hand, and as it dangled above the dizzying drop, Wainscot could see it clearly for the first time.

Man-shaped, but less than half the size, it was decidedly not a Man. Covered from head to foot in a thick pelt of silver-grey fur, it grinned a grin full of very large, very un-Man-like teeth. Although Wainscot's experience of Men was limited, he was reasonably sure that they had no tails; this one's was long and nimble, snaking up and around the yard to help support the creature's weight. The thing uttered a screech that caused every hair on Wainscot's body to rise as it swung Moon back and forth through the air. She twisted and turned, trying to bite the long fingers wrapped around her middle, but she was unable to reach the hand.

"Out of the way, fool," came a voice from behind, and Wainscot was almost knocked from the line as Mizzen scrambled over him. The warrior rat was hissing with rage as he clawed his way along the rope toward Moon. In other circumstances, the sight of Mizzen charging the huge creature might have seemed ridiculous, but his anger was so great that he seemed to swell to be a match for the hairy Man-thing. The creature shrieked again as the furious Mizzen hurtled toward it.

Grinning even wider and revealing more of its terrifyingly large yellow teeth, it swung back up onto the top of spar. Then, to Wainscot's horror, it cocked back its arm and threw Moon at Mizzen.

Tumbling end over end, she flew squealing and twisting through the smoke-shrouded air. She missed both Mizzen and Wainscot, the tip of her tail slapping the top of Wainscot's head as she passed. She sailed through the air and ploughed squarely into Spume's body. The impact drove the Bowser backward along the rope, straight into Gorp. Scrambling desperately to save himself, Spume clawed and scratched, grasping Gorp with all four paws and clamping his teeth into the larger rat's thigh. Gorp grunted in pain and, thrown off-balance by Spume's weight, swung sideways from the line. With twin squeals of terror, the two rats fell into the smoke below.

Moon, meanwhile, had managed to wrap one paw around the rope. She dangled below it, her tail drooping. Her grip was good; she might have pulled herself back up onto the rope if not for the line jumping when Spume and Gorp fell. Now, she had lost grip with all but one toe. Wainscot looked back over his shoulder, but could not turn around on the thin rope to come to her aid. Keckle, still on the line and several lengths from Moon, sat silently staring, making no effort to help.

Moon looked at Wainscot with those strange, bulging eyes that he had grown to love. He saw sadness in them, but no fear.

"Be brave," she said. "You'll have to lead now. And trust Mizzen— he's one of us." Then, in a quieter voice, perhaps so that Keckle would not hear, she added, "Go to the breadroom for me."

With that she fell. She made no sound as she dropped to be swallowed up by the powdersmoke. Wainscot stared down into the drifting haze below. There was no sign of her. He could see that she must have fallen into the sea and his heart lifted at the thought. *She didn't land on the deck,* he thought. *She might have survived the fall.*

Then he remembered what Moon had told him about rats who went overboard when a ship is at sea:

They do not come back again. Ever.

He felt a sob welling up from deep within himself. He closed his eyes and swayed on the rope. Moon could not be gone. He could not, would not, accept it. For the briefest of moments he considered releasing his grip on the rope to fall down into the sea after her, but his ratty nature would not allow it. So he stood, frozen in place by his grief.

"Come along, Laddie. There's nothing we can do for her now."

Wainscot raised his eyes, giving his head a shake to break his paralysis. He saw that Mizzen had spoken to him from the yard at the far end of the rope. There was no sign of the Man-thing. Wainscot searched up and down the mast and scanned all about the nearby rigging, but he could not see it. It was as though he had imagined the whole episode, except that Moon was gone and his life was once again in tatters. He scuttled along the remaining distance to the mast in a daze, finally joining Mizzen on the yard. Keckle was close behind him, but before she could climb onto the spar, Mizzen blocked her way.

"You'll not be coming with us," he said sternly.

She blinked at him but said nothing.

"A far better rat than you just died," he continued, "and you did nothing to help her. You'd have killed her yourself, given half a chance, so listen well." He leaned down from the spar and brought his face close to Keckle's. "If I see you again, I'll kill you."

He turned and used his nose to push Wainscot along the yard. They made their way along the spar to the end where another brace-line ran across to the rearmost of the ship's three masts—the mizzen. Given what had just happened, Wainscot found it difficult to take the first step out onto the rope.

"Have to do it, Laddie," said Mizzen. There was a kindness, a solicitude in his voice that Wainscot had not heard before. "Monkey's far enough off that we should be able to make it across without further trouble. Can see it lurking down there behind the mainsail." He chuckled. "Sometimes I surprise even me: chasing away the monkey—who'd have thought it?"

Monkey? thought Wainscot. *So that's what it was.* Moon had warned him that the monkey was dangerous and unpredictable, but in reality it was much stranger than he could have imagined. *What sort of animal would bother with such mischief when the ship's being torn apart by battle?* he wondered. It frightened him.

"One step at a time," encouraged Mizzen. He gave Wainscot's rump a gentle push.

Wainscot shakily ventured out onto the brace. He gained a small amount of confidence after a couple of steps and scurried across to the far mast without incident. Mizzen was soon crouched safely beside him on the highest yard of mast.

"Best keep moving," said Mizzen. "I don't think Dayrunner will follow us up here, but I'd rather not wait for him. If he were to catch us here, that'd be an end to it."

"Dayrunner?" said Wainscot, still dazed. "Was that Dayrunner?"

"Thought you said you knew him."

"I do... I did... He's changed."

"Changed or not, I'd rather keep out of his way if it's all the same to you." Mizzen dropped his voice as if afraid they might be overheard, though there were no rats anywhere near. "Moon told you to go to the breadroom. You know a way into it?"

Wainscot was ashamed now that they had not shared this one last secret with Mizzen. "Yes," he said. "I'll show you."

"So Spume was right—you do know a secret way in. Well, well. Thought he was just using it as an excuse to torment you. Lead on, Laddie."

Wainscot looked back toward the mainmast, "What about Keckle?" he asked.

"Hasn't moved a muscle," Mizzen said. "Still sitting where we left her. Likely weighing going back down and risking running into the Afties against following us and having to deal with me. She'll choose to come after us in the end—at least I would. I may have given her something to think about, but Dayrunner's a different animal altogether. She'll be following us soon enough, so let's get as much of a lead as we can. Don't want her following us into the breadroom."

Wainscot was surprised that he no longer felt the need to keep the location of the breadroom from Mizzen. It had only taken two words from Moon—*trust Mizzen*—for his suspicion of the old rat to evaporate completely. *Perhaps it's just that I now have no one else to trust,* he thought, but knew that this last lingering morsel of doubt was just his jealousy making one last attempt to make itself heard before it disappeared forever. Mizzen had proven himself a good friend—*a better friend to Moon than I ever was,* he admitted to himself. *He risked his life for her, and for me, more than once, which was more than I could do. I'm lucky to have Mizzen. Why he stays with me, I'm not sure.*

Picking his way carefully through the tangle of the battle-ravaged rigging, Wainscot led Mizzen down the shrouds to the deck. The Human battle still raged; it was no easy task to scurry across the littered deck, but to his surprise, Wainscot managed to guide Mizzen to the hole through which Moon had previously taken him down into Aftey territory.

As Wainscot remembered the first time he had made this trip, his sadness at losing Moon came close to paralysing him again. However, something that he had never felt before drove him on. Deep inside, a tiny flame had kindled, and a part of him that had lain dormant had begun to stir into reluctant life. It was a feeling of responsibility. He was responsible for someone other than himself. Throughout his entire life others had always taken care of him: first his mother, then Scuffle, and finally Moon and Mizzen—but now, unless he could lead them to the sanctuary of the breadroom, not only he but also Mizzen would almost certainly die. It was a strange new sensation, but one that he welcomed, hoping perhaps that this new duty might help to fill the hole in his life left by Moon's loss.

Goaded on by his need to keep Mizzen safe, he rushed across the deck and, after a brief pause to sniff the air at the opening for telltale signs of danger, slipped cautiously down into Aftey territory.

CHAPTER 28

AFTERMATH

The *Heloise* rocked in the swell, cloaked in a ragged cloud of powder smoke and bound to her enemy by a spiderweb of lines. The fight still raged on, with pistols cracking, cutlasses clashing, and pikes thrusting in the haze. Then, one of the *Heloise*'s marine sharp-shooters fired a musket ball that passed through the chest of the American Captain and, just like that, the battle was over.

The clangs, rattles, and shouts faltered and died as the *Mustang*'s first lieutenant, himself severely wounded, judged that the last chance for victory had passed. He ordered the Stars and Stripes, fluttering tattered but proud at the stern of his ship, hauled down, signalling surrender. In the near silence that followed, the two ships creaked and groaned, as though moaning at the pain of their injuries.

Time would reveal the extent of the damage to both vessels, but it was quickly evident that although severely wounded, neither was permanently crippled. The battle had taken a terrible toll in both wood and blood; while the *Heloise* and her foe could be repaired, many of their Men could not.

For two days after those final shots, the battle-ravaged *Heloise* lay unmoving on the calm sea, licking her wounds as her carpenters effected repairs. But soon enough, both ships, captor and captive, were hale enough to make sail, limping and battered, for Halifax harbour.

Belowdecks, a peace had also settled on the rats, for their battle had ended at almost the same instant as the ships'.

Eventually, when the Men of the *Heloise* discovered the rat bodies that littered her lower reaches, they would wonder what had happened in her dark recesses. For the present, however, they were was too busy dealing with their own injuries to think much about ratty stowaways. Perhaps when they did they would worry about disease— any sickness that could wipe out a rat population might also pose a threat to the Men—but they would likely determine soon enough that they were in no danger, and would quickly lose interest in the hidden world of the ship's rodents.

For the rats of the *Heloise*, however, nothing would ever be the same again.

The Bowsers were no more.

Spitkid thought that there might still be a few stragglers hidden away in the darkest depths of the ship, but they were now clanless, and therefore would soon be rooted out. The Afties had carried out their sweep through Bowser territory with cold efficiency and had made very few mistakes. Except in the skirmish with Marlinspike's group in the cable-room, they had suffered almost no casualties. Even Dayrunner had seemed pleased, though he had not said as much to his rats.

After his troops had cleaned the last of the Bowsers from their hidey-holes and returned triumphant to Aftey territory, Dayrunner allowed them half a day's rest. Then he called for the patrol leaders to assemble near the Council chambers. He also asked the Council—more so ordered them—to attend. The councilrats might have protested this peremptory summons, but they were still reeling from the enormity of Dayrunner's victory, so they meekly complied.

Dayrunner's speech to the assembled rats was short and, Spitkid thought, very effective. He spoke of the greatness of the victory and commended them on their valour. The Aft Clan was now the only clan aboard the *Heloise*, he said, and was therefore no longer merely the Aft Clan, but had risen to become the *Heloise* Clan. He mentioned the part that the newest clan members—those rats brought aboard the ship by the press gangs in Kingston—had played in the battle, and said that these might soon be considered full members of the newly-named clan.

There was an uneasy stirring amongst the patrol leaders at this. Before the battle, Dayrunner had assured them that the land rats in their groups would be full clan members at the successful conclusion of the invasion, and they had passed this message on to their troops. They did not relish having to tell the Landers under their command that this was not to be; at least not for the present. None of them said anything, however. They knew better than to question the Captain.

Dayrunner concluded by saying that it was important for them all to rest for the next few days, for they would need their strength for the final great struggle. Then he retired, leaving Spitkid wondering, *What final great struggle? They had destroyed the Bowsers—what was there left to fight?* Looking around, he saw the same questions reflected in the bemused expressions on the other rats' faces.

He appealed to the Council, but the councilrats had no answers to give. They had questions of their own, but Dayrunner was not there to answer them.

The Captain went straight to the rat-king's cell with orders that no one was to disturb him. No one but Spitkid saw him for three days. The first lieutenant brought food to him and questions from the Council and the clan, but Dayrunner would not speak to him. The clan drifted leaderless, triumphant in their newfound dominance of the ship, but uneasy about what was still to come. They needed Dayrunner, but he was not there for them.

Dayrunner crouched at the opening to the rat-king's cell, rolling the events of the battle over in his mind. It had been a staggering success, but he could not shake himself free of the failures. Marlinspike had escaped him and so had Mizzen. He had crushed the Bowsers utterly, and it had been a victory on a scale never before seen in the rat world, yet the escape of two individuals was eating away at him. No, he corrected himself, there were three. There was still that first one, that Wainscot, who had eluded him all the way from his old Nest.

Dayrunner shook his head to clear it. He had larger issues to consider than three rats who no longer posed any threat. There were plans to be made, tactics to devise.

He forced his attention back to the rat-king. It squatted in the half-light, a great misshapen lump whose twelve eyes glittered as it watched him. It was talking. It was always talking, and the words that came spilling out of it would still have been gibberish to anyone but Dayrunner. Since that day of revelation when the thing's words had ordered themselves in Dayrunner's mind, he had become more adept at translating the fractured torrent of images. It was still difficult, but he could now understand almost all that the rat-king said, and he was also much better at getting it to understand him. He could now crack through the shell of madness that isolated the rat-king from the rest of the rat community. As he listened, untangling images from the mess of words, he felt a growing elation. What the rat-king had to say was thrilling—dangerous, yes, but thrilling—and he cocked his head to one side as he listened, concentrating on wresting every nugget of wisdom from the creature.

O utside the rat-king's cell, Spitkid listened to the same spew of words. He felt nothing but fear. Dayrunner was unaware of it, but Spitkid and the other lieutenants were concerned that these forays into the splintered mind of the rat-king were taking their toll on their Captain's own mind. In the days before the great attack on the Bowsers, his behaviour had become increasingly erratic and unpredictable. This latest disappearance at a time when his leadership was so badly needed by his clan was only the latest instance of Dayrunner's growing strangeness.

And there was something wrong about his eyes.

Spitkid had not seen the rat-king since he had fled from it many days before, but he remembered it well enough to see that Dayrunner's eyes now had the same hot, unfocused look. It was obvious that he had taken the first steps onto a steep, slippery slope and was sliding down toward the madness that had already claimed the rat-king.

When Dayrunner finally emerged from the cell, Spitkid met him with messages of concern from the Council. "Sir," he said, "you must meet with them. They've been calling for you for days."

"Must?" repeated Dayrunner.

"They request your presence. The clan needs direction."

"Then they shall have my presence. Go and tell them to assemble in the Council chamber. I'll join them shortly."

" W hy did you bring *that* here?" the oldest councilrat asked the Captain.

Spitkid had been wondering the same thing.

Bewildered and frightened, the rat-king cowered in the shadows just inside the Council chamber. It had been alone and in the dark for so long that it was overwhelmed by its new surroundings. Bone thin and smelling of madness and ill health, it kept its eyes downcast and muttered a string of quiet nonsense to itself.

The councilrats eyed the rat-king, disgust written on every one of their faces. Spitkid could see no hint of pity in their hard, black eyes despite the sad condition of the creature cowering before them. They had heard of it, of course, but none of them had seen it. He knew that they were concerned that their Captain spent so much time in the company of such an aberration, but as Dayrunner's power had grown, the Council had found themselves unable to do anything about it. They had tried to speak to him, but he had only responded with anger.

They knew the stories, of course—everyone did. The old tales about rat-kings and their unnatural powers were told to all the young rats, but few adult rats really believed any of it. Still, it was difficult not to view the creature with anything but suspicion and fear. Since Dayrunner had first taken the rat-king under his care, the councilrats had made it clear that they did not want to have anything to do with it and, in unspoken accord, had not even acknowledged its existence. But now it was here hulking in their chamber, drooling and muttering to itself.

"That... thing... has no place in this chamber," said the oldest councilrat. "You've gone too far, Dayrunner. We've reached the limit of our patience."

"It's funny you should say that," said Dayrunner, "because this is the very place that it does belong." He turned to Spitkid and said, "Leave us and take the guard with you."

Spitkid hesitated.

Dayrunner snapped, "Leave us, I said. The *rat-king*'s no threat to the Council."

Spitkid wondered at the odd emphasis Dayrunner had given the word 'rat-king'—was there something else that *was* a threat to the Council?—but he left as ordered. He told the guards to return to their nests until called for, but he remained just outside the chamber so that he could hear what happened within.

"I have a question for you," he heard Dayrunner say. "What purpose do you think a Council serves? It doesn't gather food; it doesn't give birth to pups; it doesn't defend the nest. When the time comes to fight, where do you find a Council? Back in its chambers, as far from danger as possible."

Spitkid could hear the councilrats shifting their feet nervously.

"Oh, don't look so worried," Dayrunner continued. "I know a Council's necessary for a clan. It may not gather food, raise young, or fight, but it plays an even more important role. Captains come and go, but a Council is constant. Its members may change, but it is always there—always thinking—always planning, and every rat sleeps better knowing that the wisest of the clan are looking after him. A Council guides a clan through the twists and turns of the tunnels it must travel. A Captain leads, but a Council guides."

The sound of shuffling feet ceased at this. Spitkid suspected that the Council was somewhat comforted by these words.

However, Dayrunner was far from finished. "We Afties have been finding ourselves in strange ratways recently. I've led us to places that no one on this ship could have expected, and our glorious journey is only just beginning. We have stranger paths still to tread, and this has led me to consider a problem. I've led, but have you, our Council, guided?"

The oldest councilrat started, "We have done as we—"

"Quiet!" snapped Dayrunner and the councilrat said no more, likely shocked into silence by the ferocity in the Captain's voice.

Spitkid fought the urge to re-enter the chamber.

"I'll answer the question for you," said Dayrunner, resuming a conversational tone. "No, you have not guided us. In fact, you've done little but resist my efforts to lead the clan. There *has* been a guiding voice behind our recent great achievements, but it hasn't been yours."

He paused. Spitkid could picture his eyes blazing feverishly, belying the calmness of his voice.

"Whose, then?" asked the oldest councilrat reluctantly after a moment.

"The rat-king's."

"That?" said another of the councilrats. "That thing has been giving you advice? It's mad—we can all see that."

"Yes, it is," said Dayrunner. "Completely mad, but that's what gives it the power to see the way of things. I've taken us down some strange ratways since I arrived, and I wouldn't have been able to do so without the guidance of the rat-king. I need it, and therefore so does the clan. Which leads me to why I brought it here—I wanted to show it its new quarters."

"New...?" said the spokesrat. "You can't seriously be suggesting that... that thing is going to be the clan's new Council?"

"I most certainly can," said Dayrunner, "but I'm left with a problem. What am I going to do with the old Council?"

There was a pause, then a rustle of movement followed by a squeal, and a shout of "Guards!" suddenly cut off. Spitkid rushed into the chamber.

He was greeted by a sight that, for an instant, his mind refused to accept. In a flash he was taken back to that awful moment when he had seen Dayrunner slaughter the Bowser Council, but as horrible as that had been, this was immeasurably worse. The Bowsers had at least been enemies. These were *Afties*. The Captain was killing Afties—and not just any Afties, but councilrats.

Without thinking, Spitkid threw himself at Dayrunner, every instinct driving him to protect his Council. He was no match for the larger rat, and soon found himself lying dazed and winded against the chamber wall. By the time he roused himself and dragged himself unsteadily to his feet, it was over. The unmoving bodies of the councilrats lay scattered about the chamber. The rat-king still hunched near the entrance, carrying on its impenetrable monologue and staring at the floor. It had not reacted at all to the events that had unfolded before its many eyes.

Dayrunner approached Spitkid, blood dripping from his muzzle. Spitkid tensed, waiting for the blow, but Dayrunner did not attack.

"Not since I was a pup have I allowed a rat to raise a paw against me and live," said Dayrunner, "but I'm going to make an exception for you because I understand why you did it. They were your Council." He gestured around the chamber with his snout, "A good rat fights for his Council"

"You killed them," said Spitkid. Relief that he was still alive gave him the courage to speak, but his voice trembled.

"That I did."

"But they were our Council. You can't kill our Council. How can we survive without them?"

"We have a new one," said Dayrunner.

Spitkid blinked, not understanding. The Captain's gaze travelled across the chamber and Spitkid's eyes followed. They settled on the rat-king.

"That?" said Spitkid in an unconscious echo of the now-dead councilrat. "You must be jok—"

He did not finish the sentence. Dayrunner lunged and snapped his head sideways, his teeth carving twin red lines across Spitkid's shoulder. Spitkid squealed with surprise and pain, falling onto his side. Dayrunner stood over him, teeth bared and a fierce, crazed expression on his face.

"I let you live," hissed the Captain, "but it would be a mistake for you to think that that gives you license to forget your position." He glanced at the wounds oozing on Spitkid's shoulder. "Not deep enough to cripple you, but perhaps the scars will remind you that even though I decided not to kill you now, I might change my mind at another time."

Spitkid looked up into his Captain's eyes. The fires of madness were burning fiercely.

CHAPTER 29

COMING TOGETHER

W ainscot and Mizzen were still alive.

They were alive when so many were dead. Hiding and alone in a ship that no longer had a place for them, they were safe for the moment, but Wainscot did not know how long they could remain that way.

They had travelled through Aftey territory to the breadroom without encountering a single rat, but he knew that their enemies would be back once they had finished their business with the Bowsers.

It would be too perilous for the two to venture out into the Aftey ratways, but it was also becoming increasingly dangerous to stay in the breadroom. Men had visited the room four times since their arrival, taking sacks or barrels of biscuits with them when they left. Each time the rats had managed to find a place to hide, but the hiding places became scarcer with every barrel removed. They would eventually be forced to make their way back out into the ship.

For a full day after their arrival in the sanctuary, neither rat had spoken to the other. Even the usually voluble Mizzen was silent, lost in his own ruminations. They ate and slept side by side, but neither felt ready to share his thoughts. Wainscot finally decided to break the silence; he felt that he owed something to Mizzen. He had been unfairly suspicious of the old rat from the moment they had met, and he knew that it would go some way toward apologizing if he were to bridge the gap he had created between them.

He settled himself down beside the older rat, who was gnawing on a sliver of barrel stave. Before he could say a word, Mizzen spoke.

"I loved her, you know," he said.

Surprised, Wainscot said, "I know. And she loved you."

"I think she did. I've had friends before, many of them, but none who cared for me the way she did. She loved you too. She was such a strange little creature. Would have died for her." Mizzen was silent for a moment, then he said, "I'd die for you too, Wainscot."

Once again Wainscot was ashamed of his own uncharitable thoughts. He knew it was the truth—the old fighter had risked his life for them on more than one occasion. He thought for a moment about how Moon had felt about her two new clanmates. "She would have died for you as well," he said, and then added, "And so would I." With a shock, he realised that it was true. "We're a clan. You're family."

Mizzen laughed. "Full of surprises, aren't you, Laddie," he said. "What happened to the suspicious little rat I ambushed in his nest all those days ago?"

"I think I may have left him up there in the rigging," said Wainscot.

They fell into silence again, but now there was a warmth between them. After a while, Wainscot spoke again.

"So, that was a monkey."

"Yes," said Mizzen.

"Is it a Man? A sort of Man?"

"Don't think so, but don't know for sure. Heard that the Men keep them and feed them, but don't know if they're related in some way. Maybe they're like mice to the Men's rats."

"Would it have eaten her?" asked Wainscot. He did not know if he wanted to know the answer.

Mizzen thought for a moment before replying, "Doubt it. Never heard of it at any rate."

"Then what did it want with her?"

"If I could answer that, I'd be a much wiser rat than I am," confessed Mizzen. "Don't understand the monkey. It does what it does, and there's no sense to it. All that smoke and noise: any animal in its right mind would've been cowering in a hole somewhere, and yet there it was, up in the rigging and looking for mischief. Always thought it was mad."

"You've met it before?"

"Never so close, but many's the time I've seen it leaping about the ship, acting the fool."

They were quiet again for many heartbeats, then Wainscot said, "Is there any chance she could have survived?"

Mizzen sighed. "Don't do it to yourself, Laddie. She's gone and that's the end of it."

"But she fell into water," Wainscot protested. "I'm sure I've heard of rats living after falling into water."

"Wasn't the fall. We were moving. She would have been left behind. A rat can't swim fast enough to catch a ship under sail."

Wainscot was not convinced. He still harboured hope that Moon might have managed to climb back aboard the ship.

Seeing this, Mizzen's voice hardened. "Listen well, Wainscot. I've been on the *Heloise* for a very long time, and seen just about anything that can happen aboard a ship. Known of many a rat who've fallen overboard when the ship was at sea and none of them were ever seen again. The sooner you accept that, the sooner you'll be able to get on with the business of keeping yourself alive. She's gone, and she's not coming back."

"Moon herself told me as much," said Wainscot.

"Smart rat," said Mizzen. "I'll miss her."

"So will I."

Mizzen climbed to his feet and stretched. He yawned, revealing a set of long, curved teeth, and a surprisingly delicate pink tongue that curled up at the end. "Well, Laddie," he said, "What do we do next?"

"I don't know. I was hoping you might have a suggestion."

"Not my place to say," said Mizzen.

This surprised Wainscot. "What do you mean?" he asked.

"Moon left you in charge. You're the leader. Said so just before she fell."

"She certainly did not."

"Heard her, Laddie," insisted Mizzen, "and so did you."

"That's ridiculous," Wainscot responded. "Even if she did, why was it her place to decide who's in charge?"

Mizzen looked at Wainscot appraisingly for several long heartbeats. Wainscot grew uncomfortable.

Mizzen spoke before he could say anything. "Sometimes I'm not sure if you're having me on, Laddie," he said. "She was the head of our clan, so it only seems right that we take her at her word when she picks a successor."

Head of our clan? thought Wainscot. He had not thought in such terms before, but he supposed that Mizzen was correct. They were a clan and every clan had a leader, whether a Council or a Captain. It had certainly not been he, and Mizzen—despite Wainscot's suspicions—had never made any effort to take control. They had left the making of decisions to Moon; she had been their leader all along, and Wainscot had not realised it.

As for his taking over her responsibilities now that she was gone, however, he thought that ridiculous. He did not feel that he was anywhere near up to the task.

"I think it would be better if we left the important decisions to you," Wainscot said. "You always know what to do. I'm not very good at anything."

"Always been a doer, not a thinker," said Mizzen. "Talk a good talk, but I don't really have anything to back it up."

Wainscot knew that this was not true, but said nothing.

Mizzen continued, "I'm not a leader. Even if I were, it wouldn't amount to much—she chose you."

Wainscot considered what Mizzen had said. He knew that he was not qualified to lead anything—he was young, inexperienced and, he felt, foolish. Despite this, Mizzen seemed determined to saddle him with the responsibility. Also, although he had tried to deny it, Moon *had* told him to lead. He took a deep breath.

"Very well," he said. "I'll do my best, but I'm going to need your help. The only thing I can do well is tell stories, and they won't be much use in the days to come."

"You'd be surprised how much good a well-told tale can do," said

Mizzen. "But there's more to you than just stories. Moon could see it, and so can I. Perhaps some day you'll see it too."

Wainscot wondered why other rats insisted in having faith in him. First Scuffle, then Moon, and now Mizzen. As far as he could remember he had never done anything to earn the friendship or respect of any rat. He had never hurt anyone, but surely that fact was not enough. The best thing that he could say about himself was that he was harmless, which was not the best thing to be in times such as these.

"I hope you're right," he said. "When Moon returns, we'll go back to the way things were. She'll be in charge again, agreed?"

Mizzen gave a sad sigh. "Look Laddie, I told you—"

"I know what you told me, but I'll never give up hope. My first order to you is that you'll not either."

"Aye-aye, sir," said Mizzen. There might have been a dusting of mockery on the words, but Wainscot did not think so.

"You know, Laddie, I really should box your ears," said Mizzen. "S'pose I can't since you're the boss. Respect for the position, and all."

"Why would you want to?" asked Wainscot, taken aback.

"Keeping all of this lovely food to yourselves the way you did. You and Moon should've been ashamed of yourselves."

Wainscot felt guilt well up inside him. "I can explain, Mizzen."

"No need, Laddie," said Mizzen with a laugh. "Just pulling your leg. Would've done the same thing in your place. Just don't do it again. No more secrets, all right?"

"No, sir," said Wainscot, hanging his head.

Mizzen laughed again, giving Wainscot's ear a light, playful boxing. "Fine leader you're shaping up to be."

CHAPTER 30

KECKLE SPEAKS

The cleaning-up operations were going well. There were still pockets of Bowsers scattered about the ship, but the Aftey forces were rooting more of them out daily. Spitkid doubted that there was more than a pawful still alive. There had been some skirmishes, which had surprised him because he had not thought any of the surviving Bowsers would still have the will to fight. He had actually lost some of his rats, which had surprised him even more. His fighters were the best the ship had ever seen, and no ragtag parcel of Bowsers should have been able to put a tooth into them.

Neither Mizzen nor Marlinspike had been found, which Spitkid knew was a matter of great concern to Dayrunner. Spitkid was also worried, but not about the missing rats. He was worried about his Captain.

After killing the Council, Dayrunner had closeted himself away in the Council chamber with the hideous rat-king. He had not set foot out of it since, and he had not seen anyone other than Spitkid since he began his sequestering. This was probably for the best, as the Captain's appearance and manner would have alarmed any rat who laid eyes on him. He looked haggard and worn, having lost much of his formidable bulk, and his lank fur hung on him as though his skin no longer fit properly. The fire that Spitkid had seen in his eyes at moments of anger was now ever-present, as though he were always on the verge of erupting into violent rage.

He looked, Spitkid thought, just like the rat-king.

He acted like the rat-king too. Occupying himself entirely with his unintelligible conversations with the thing—if conversations they were—he ignored everything else around him. Spitkid had overheard some of it on occasion, and none of it had made any sense. Often the Captain and the Rat-king would speak at the same time, seemingly oblivious to what the other was saying.

Although Spitkid knew the words they used, they seemed to be strung together in random order. On those rare occasions when Dayrunner actually spoke directly to Spitkid, it was always some nonsense about Marlinspike, Mizzen, or another rat named Wainscot, of whom Spitkid had never heard. On even rarer occasions, the babble was about some grand plan that would ensure Aftey mastery of the ship. Dayrunner never revealed the nature of this scheme, and Spitkid was afraid to ask.

Since the Captain no longer showed any interest in the running of the clan, Spitkid was forced to assume the duty himself. He told the C'law and patrol leaders that Dayrunner was busy with matters of vital importance to the clan, and that he would be passing the Captain's commands along to them for the time being. It took some effort to convince them that all was well, but they eventually accepted the new arrangement. He suspected that they were secretly relieved that they would be seeing less of their volatile leader.

He did not tell them that Dayrunner had murdered their Council and replaced it with a tail-bound collection of gibbering mad rats. There were limits to what they might accept, and at least the Captain's self-imposed confinement allowed him to keep that one great secret from them. Spitkid had told them that the Council was locked away in the chamber in consultation with the Captain. He suspected that even the clan's fear of Dayrunner would not stop them from rebelling if they knew what he had done.

Spitkid was asleep when the scuffling of rat feet roused him. He instantly snapped alert, catching a whiff of something he had not smelled for many days—a Bowser. He crawled warily from his nest, tense and ready for a fight, but relaxed when he saw four of his C'law waiting for him. They were escorting a prisoner.

"Sir," said the lead C'law, "we brought this cur to see you."

"Why didn't you just kill him—or her," Spitkid corrected himself as his nose brought him new information about the prisoner. "You know the Captain's orders."

"We didn't find this one, sir. She found us."

Spitkid waited.

"She turned herself over to one of our patrols," said the C'law, flustered. "They would have done her in there and then, but she said she knew something about the breadroom—about how to get in. The Captain might want to know."

"And?"

"She hasn't said anything since," the C'law responded, "even when we got a little rough with her. She's a tough one."

Spitkid shouldered past the C'law to stand face-to-face with the captive. There was something about her that made him uneasy. She was too confident, too coldly calm and sure of herself, considering her current situation. She reminded him of Dayrunner on that day, so long ago, when he had stood defiant before old Captain Plank.

"Tell me," he said.

She stared back at him, her chin lifted, but said nothing.

Spitkid turned away. "Kill her," he said.

"Mizzen," she said.

He turned back, now interested.

"Mizzen," she said again, "In the breadroom." Her voice was harsh and rasping, as though she seldom used it and it had rusted. "Mizzen and Wainscot."

"Wainscot?" he repeated. It was the unfamiliar rat in the trilogy of enemies that the Captain obsessed over. "What do you know of Wainscot?"

She would say nothing more.

Low voices bubbled from the opening to the chamber. Spitkid could hear both Dayrunner and the rat-king, and he was reluctant to enter. He did not want to be anywhere near the horrible creature, much less see the Captain engaged in his disturbing, incomprehensible conversation with it. Taking a deep breath, he slipped through the entrance.

Dayrunner and the rat-king were facing each other in the gloom, their positions and attitudes exactly as they had been when he had last seen them many days before. He wondered if they moved at all when he was not there. A small part of his mind also wondered what had happened to the bodies of the slain councilrats; they had disappeared, but that was all that he could gather from the scene before him.

"Captain, sir," Spitkid said.

Neither Dayrunner nor the rat-king acknowledged him. They continued talking as if they were alone in the chamber.

"I've brought a rat to see you, sir," he said, a little louder this time. "She knows something about the breadroom."

The strange conversation continued unabated.

"She knows about Mizzen and Wainscot."

The voices stopped with an audible pop as seven mouths snapped shut at the same time. Spitkid stifled the urge to flee. Dayrunner, who was facing away from the chamber's entrance, slowly turned. It took the Captain's eyes far too long to focus on him.

"Wainscot?" Dayrunner repeated. He dwelled on the name.

"Yes, sir."

"And Mizzen?"

"Yes, sir."

"What about Marlinspike?"

"She made no mention of Marlinspike. Should I bring her in?"

"No!" Dayrunner lunged forward. Spitkid retreated a step. The Captain brought his mouth close to Spitkid's ear and whispered, "No one must see the rat-king."

"I'll take her away," said Spitkid, starting to turn. He wanted nothing more than to be as far away from the chamber as possible.

"No," said Dayrunner. He stood motionless for a moment, and Spitkid could see that he was gripped by conflicting needs.

Is he afraid to leave the chamber? he wondered. *No, that's not possible. He's changed, but not that much.*

"I'll come out to see her," said Dayrunner. "Are there any other rats with her?"

"Four C'law guards," responded Spitkid.

"Send them away."

"But sir, she struck me as dangerous."

"So am I," said Dayrunner coldly.

Spitkid realised that, reduced though he was, the Captain was no less formidable than he had been before his obsession had carved away at his huge frame. He still frightened Spitkid as much as ever.

After Spitkid had dismissed the guard, Dayrunner emerged from the chamber. "Well, rat," he said to the captive, "what do you have to say for yourself?"

She stood silent.

"We'll start with your name, then," the Captain pressed.

"Keckle," the Bowser's voice sounded like a stiff door being forced open.

"So, Keckle, you know about Wainscot? He's alive? He's aboard the ship?"

"A trade," she said, more of a demand than an offer.

"I don't trade," said Dayrunner, "I take." He moved toward her, looming over her. She hunched down, but did not retreat.

"A trade," she said again.

Dayrunner swelled as his muscles tensed. For a moment it looked as though he would tear Keckle to pieces, but he mastered himself.

The old Dayrunner would not have shown his anger so readily, thought Spitkid, concerned. *He would have been calm right up until the moment he struck.*

"A trade," said Dayrunner. "And what do we have that you might want in trade?"

"My life," said Keckle.

"I'm not sure your life is worth all that much, although I suppose it is to you."

Keckle did not respond.

"Very well, you'll have your life," the Captain agreed. "If what you have to tell me is interesting enough, I might even allow you to join the clan. I'll admit, you impress me." He stepped back from Keckle and crouched, assuming a less threatening posture. "Tell me about Wainscot. Have you seen him?"

"Met him," said Keckle.

"Is he still alive?"

"Alive. With Mizzen."

"With Mizzen," said Dayrunner. "That is good news. Makes my job a little easier. Do you know Marlinspike?"

"Yes."

"Is he with them?"

"Don't know," Keckle admitted.

"But you do know where they are." Dayrunner leaned forward in evident eagerness.

"Breadroom."

Dayrunner rose to his feet. Spitkid could see the anger rising in him again. He wondered if Keckle knew how close she was to death.

"If you lie to me," he said, "I'll do much worse than kill you. It's not possible to enter the breadroom. Everyone knows that."

"Way in," said Keckle.

"You know a way in?"

"Yes."

"How?"

"Followed them. Didn't see me."

"And you'll tell me?" Dayrunner asked.

"No," Keckle said. "I'll show you."

Chapter 31

Survivors

M oving silently, placing their paws carefully to avoid the telltale click of claws, the line of rats filed slowly down the foot-polished rungs of the ladder. An enemy patrol lurked below them in the hold, half seen in the guttering lantern light.

The sea was rough and choppy, and thanks to the mauling she had received, the *Heloise* was not sailing well. Her hull was patched in many places and she was running with a makeshift rudder, her old one having been shot away. She was also low in the water because, patched though she was, she still leaked, and the seawater sat heavily in her holds. The sailors manned the pumps night and day and she was in no danger of sinking, but she ran sluggishly and no longer danced gracefully with the chop and swell. Every blow from the unruly sea jostled her, making it difficult for the rats to creep nimbly because they could not move to the rhythm of the ship.

One of the Afties hiding in the shadows looked in their direction. Marlinspike saw the glitter of eyes and hissed for his group to stop. The Aftey's gaze passed over them and the guard yawned. Exposed as they were by the glare of the lanterns swinging overhead, Marlinspike was surprised that the Aftey had not seen them. The bouncing of the ship, which made stealthy movement so difficult, also concealed his group because the lanterns swung wildly and his rats were lost in the crazily dancing shadows.

There were twelve of them in their motley bunch. Only four, including Marlinspike, were of any use in a fight. The rest were a collection of the too old, the too young, and in one case, the too pregnant. They were survivors of the massacre. Frightened, bewildered, and bedraggled, they had each somehow managed to live through the initial slaughter, and then avoid the enemy long enough for Marlinspike to find them. They were the smart and the lucky.

Marlinspike had gathered them together and now did his best to keep them alive. Since becoming the shepherd of this forlorn flock he had lost three of them to Aftey patrols. He had vowed to lose no more.

Stealth, craft, and vigilance kept them alive and one step ahead of the patrols. They survived by constantly moving; they never slept in the same place twice and always found new sources of food. They also only fought as a last resort—fighting slowed them down and they could not afford any more losses to their meagre number.

When he was sure that none of Afties were looking in their direction, Marlinspike signalled his group to move. They dropped down the rungs of the ladder to the deck and darted behind a stack of tubs containing carpenter's nails. Marlinspike waited until the last of them was out of sight of the Afties before whispering an order for them to follow him. He led them through the maze of stores on silent feet, thankful that they had not been forced to fight. The Aftey patrol had been small—only four rats—and Marlinspike knew he could have taken them without loss to his own group, but it was far better to avoid conflict.

He was leading them toward the powder magazine, confident that it would provide them with a hiding place for a day or two. They had spent too long on the orlop deck and risked leaving too many signs for the Aftey patrols, but he hated moving down into the lower reaches of the ship where the sailors ventured less frequently. Men were easier to avoid than Afties, and since the patrols tended to stay away from those areas with the heaviest Human traffic, he tried to keep his little party to the upper decks. It was vital, however, that they not establish any patterns of activity or frequent any one area of the ship for too long. They would return to the orlop in a few days.

Marlinspike wondered how much longer they could live this way. Hunted, hiding, and clanless, they managed to survive from day to day, but he knew that they were merely postponing the inevitable. A rat without a nest was a rat without a future.

We're not built to be nomads, he thought. *Sooner or later we'll make a mistake. Maybe we'll linger too long in one place, or let our guard down when we're crossing an open space, and they'll find us. And that will be the end of the Bowser Clan.*

In his weaker moments Marlinspike thought that it might be for the best if the Afties did find them. At least then, it would mean an end to the running. He was tired, bone tired, and besides, he had always enjoyed a good scrap. Perhaps he would have another go at Dayrunner. The Aftey Captain's strength and quickness had been astonishing, but Marlinspike knew that he himself was no pup when it came to a fight.

If we meet again, he thought, *I'll give that Dayrunner a good run of it. I might lose—probably will—but at least the brute will have a few new scars to remember me by.*

These moments of weariness of mind did not last, however, and the rat in him always roused itself. It whispered "survive" in his ear, and urged him to get on with the business of keeping his group alive.

Chapter 32

Moon's Clan

Wainscot showed Mizzen how to get out of the breadroom.

"Moon thought of that?" Mizzen asked after they had dropped from the door-rope and skittered off to find a hiding place. "Clever lass."

"Yes, she is," said Wainscot.

Mizzen cast him a worried glance. "Was," he corrected softly.

Wainscot did not respond.

"Not fond of having to wait 'til a Man arrives to get out, though," said Mizzen. "Like to find another way. If any enemy got in with us, we'd be trapped. It just doesn't sit well with me."

"I'm happy to listen to suggestions," offered Wainscot, "but I can't think of anything."

"Can't either, but I'm still not pleased. Though, I suppose the chances of a cat or an Aftey finding the way in are pretty slim."

Wainscot thought about being trapped in the breadroom with Dayrunner or one of the cats and shivered.

He urged Mizzen to follow him, and they began their first cautious exploration of the newly Aftey ship in search of a better hiding place than the breadroom.

They did not venture far. Fear of Aftey patrols kept them close to their sanctuary, and they knew that the farther afield they went, the greater the chance that they would stumble across a patrol. Also, the more they moved about the ship, the more evidence of their existence they left for questing Aftey noses.

Their first foray yielded no likely new hiding places, and although Wainscot was reluctant to return to the breadroom, he grudgingly led them back when it was time to sleep. While he lay waiting for sleep to take him, he wondered at the strange relationship that had developed between his sole clanmate and himself. Mizzen might have said that Wainscot was the leader of their two-rat clan, but this did not change the fact that the older rat often treated his young companion like a pup. But, Wainscot had to admit, although Mizzen frequently chastised him and listened to much of what he said with that patient, amused air that adults reserve for the very young or the very silly, he never questioned Wainscot's decisions. He would offer advice if asked, but his adherence to the younger rat's leadership was unfailing and unquestioning.

They set out again after sleep and some food, but they had no better luck on their second venture out. They did not find a suitable new refuge—but then again, they did not encounter any Aftey patrols either, so their luck was not entirely bad. They came across plenty of fresh Aftey droppings, and on one frightening occasion, had heard the scuttling of a large group of rats moving past them just out of sight, but they did not see any enemies or have to hide from them. Any hope they still harboured that the Afties might have been unsuccessful in their attack on the Bowsers was dashed when they discovered that there were no guards posted at the border. There was no need.

"Got a feeling you're the last of them, Laddie," said Mizzen when they returned to the breadroom.

"Them?" asked Wainscot.

"Bowsers."

"I'm not a Bowser. I'm a Lander, remember."

"You're the closest thing to a Bowser aboard the *Heloise* now, I'll wager."

"What about you? Surely you don't think of yourself as an Aftey anymore?" Wainscot asked.

He considered pointing out that Moon might still be alive and was more of a Bowser than he would ever be, but he was tiring of the argument. As the days passed he became less hopeful that she had survived.

Mizzen breathed a heavy sigh and said, "Stopped being an Aftey the day I ran from Dayrunner."

"You had to run. It's nothing to be ashamed of."

With a shake of his head, Mizzen said, "You misunderstand me, Laddie. Course I had to run. Be dead now if I hadn't. Not foolish enough to think that fighting's the solution to every problem. Retreat's a perfectly good, honourable tactic in some circumstances. No, I stopped being an Aftey not because of anything *I* did, but because the Afties themselves changed on that day. They're Dayrunner's clan now. They're not the Afties I knew."

"So you're just as much a Bowser as I am."

Mizzen shook his head again. "No," he said. "Never was a Bowser either. Rat can't change his fur. Wasn't born a Bowser, so I could never become one."

Wainscot was confused. "But you said I—"

"You're a Lander. That's different. Landers were never proper rats to begin with, so they can change into whatever they want."

Wainscot bridled. "Now that's just..." he began, and then saw the expression on Mizzen's face. "I don't know why I bother talking to you," he said, suppressing a laugh.

They shared some more comparable conversation, then curled up for a sleep before their next venture out.

When they woke, they reviewed their options for the next foray.

"Gun deck?"

Wainscot shuddered, remembering his previous adventures under one of the great guns as it went off.

"Not the gun deck, then," said Mizzen, seeing the look on Wainscot's face. "How 'bout the cable locker?"

Wainscot shook his head. "Too close to the old Bowser Council chamber," he said. "Dayrunner's bunch might be using it as their chamber now."

Mizzen closed his eyes as he pondered.

"Got it," he said after a moment. "Near the magazine."

"Nasty, smelly place," said Wainscot. "No rat goes anywhere near it, if they have a choice—it's perfect."

After refuelling on some of their stored food, they set out again. They made their way toward the middle of the ship, toward the magazine, travelling farther than they had on either of their other exploratory outings.

M arlinspike checked that his rats were still in close formation behind him. He had managed to instil in them the need to stay silent and to minimise the traces they left behind. He had successfully taught them where and when to pass droppings and urine, to recognise which surfaces held scents the longest, and that protuberances in a ratway might catch tufts of fur and leave them for a searching patrol. However, for some reason, he could not get them to grasp the importance of keeping a tight formation. They had a tendency to spread out behind him, stringing themselves loosely for easy discovery by an Aftey patrol. Today, however, they seemed to be keeping together fairly well, and he hustled them along without having to chastise any of them.

As they crept their way across the floor of the magazine, Marlinspike signalled a halt. He had heard the tiny but unmistakable sound of a rat moving stealthily through the darkness ahead of them. On further listening he determined that it was two rats rather than one—the second was so quiet, so skilful, that its movement was almost undetectable.

Marlinspike eased forward, listening and sniffing. They were actually inside the magazine, and the pungent smell of the powder masked the scent of the strangers. But for an instant, a teasing rat-odour tickled his nose. It was only there for a fleeting heartbeat and then gone, but it was enough to tell him that the rats ahead were Bowsers—though not entirely. Something was not quite right, but Marlinspike had taken it upon himself to gather any Bowsers that he was able to find. He crept forward, hoping to catch a glimpse of the rats before he had to decide whether to approach them or slip away undetected.

The strangers had stopped moving and were now motionless and silent. He could imagine them sitting in the shadows, cocking their heads to listen and sniffing the air in unintentional mimicry of his own actions. Marlinspike had enough faith in his own abilities to know that if they had heard him, then at least one of them was unusually alert—and therefore, probably a fighter.

He stopped his slow approach, thinking. Another fighter would be a welcome addition to his party, but something about the brief wisp of scent he had picked up bothered him. There had been a suggestion of Aftey about it. Perhaps it might be wise to exercise a little caution and withdraw.

But before he could reach a decision, a voice came from the shadows ahead. "If you want something of us, Laddie, then let's be about it. Haven't got all day to be sitting here waiting for you to make up your mind."

Marlinspike sighed. The speaker sounded to be seven or eight lengths away. He moved carefully forward, tense and ready for a fight. The voice had been amiable enough, but Marlinspike was too experienced to be taken in by a friendly manner. The light in the

252

magazine was very dim, and he was almost on top of the strangers before he could see them clearly. He smelled them before he saw them, however, and knew them to be two males: one young and the other older. He had been correct about their odour. It was partly Bowser, but the young rat had once been a Lander and the other had a strange combination of scents that said both Bowser and Aftey.

There's a story here, he thought.

"That's it, Laddie," said the older rat. He was a tough-looking fellow, all hard muscle and scar. Although his tone was friendly he was balanced and poised, ready to shift quickly in whatever direction this encounter took him. There was something familiar about him, and Marlinspike guessed that they might have faced each other in a scuffle at some time in the past. The other rat—a youngster with an odd streak of white running along his side—seemed frightened and uncertain, but Marlinspike sensed that if it came to a fight he would be up against both of them. The seasoned rat stood before the younger, as if protecting him.

There's a hard core to the little fellow, he thought, *though I don't think he knows it yet.*

"What's your clan?" asked Marlinspike.

"Now that's an interesting question," said the older rat. "Not sure I have an answer for you." He paused for a moment, obviously thinking, but his eyes never left Marlinspike's. "Moon Clan, I suppose."

The young rat opened his mouth as if to say something, but closed it without uttering a sound.

"Not Afties then?" said Marlinspike.

"No, nor Bowsers either."

"Neither are we anymore, I suppose," said Marlinspike. "Things have changed. Moon Clan, you said?"

"I did, Laddie."

Marlinspike brightened at the familiar name. "Wouldn't have anything to do with an odd-looking little rat by the name of Moonpatch, by any chance?"

"That it would," replied the older rat. "You knew her then?"

"Yes. Is she with you?

"No," said the stranger. There was a slight catch in his voice. "She's gone now."

Again the young rat shifted and seemed about to speak, but again he said nothing.

"I'm sorry to hear it," said Marlinspike sombrely. "She was a good rat, and life had not been kind to her." He made a quick decision. "You'll be joining us, then?"

"Us?"

"What's left of the Bowser Clan," Marlinspike explained. "I've gathered all I could find. We're not much, but we've managed to stay alive. I'm doing my best to see that we continue to do so. We could do with another set of sharp teeth." He looked at the smaller rat. "Your friend is welcome as well."

"Would you be Marlinspike?" asked the older stranger.

"I am."

"Heard of you. Name's Mizzen. This is Wainscot."

"I've heard of you as well," said Marlinspike, "though not of your little friend. You were first lieutenant of the Afties, yet here you are in the company of a Lander and smelling like a Bowser. You and I will have to have a long talk when there's an opportunity. So will you join us?"

"Not my decision to make," said Mizzen. "You'd best ask Wainscot."

Marlinspike thought it odd that Mizzen would defer to the young rat, but he asked, "Will you be coming with us, Wainscot?"

Wainscot stepped forward from behind Mizzen. He studied Marlinspike from head to tail, as if assessing him. "Moon told me about you. You're her friend?" he asked.

Marlinspike chose his words carefully. "For my part, yes, though the circumstances of our meetings were never the best."

"Then we'll join you."

"Good," said Marlinspike. For the first time since becoming aware of the two strangers he relaxed, and lowered his guard. He could see that Mizzen did the same.

"So, where are we going?" asked Wainscot.

The nest that Marlinspike had selected was in a neatly stacked store of firewood in a remote corner of the hold. The many gaps between the cords would provide ample hiding spaces for his party. He had gone ahead of the group to find the new nest the day before he had encountered Mizzen and Wainscot, and now he led them to it. He had considered staying in the magazine, but decided that it was too risky. The Men had not held a gun practice for some time, but when they did the magazine would become too busy for the rats to remain safely hidden.

Mizzen sensed the danger before Marlinspike. He nudged the lieutenant with his nose as they crept toward the stacked wood. "Are you taking us into that pile?" he asked.

"I am," said Marlinspike.

"Well you might want to be thinking about that a little. There're Afties in there."

None of Marlinspike's acute senses had warned him, but he trusted Mizzen. "We'll have a look then," he said.

Leaving the rest of the group hidden in the shadows, he and Mizzen crept toward the stacked firewood. The floor of the hold was uneven with piles of loose shingle ballast, and they stayed low, keeping to depressions in the shingle to shield their movement. When they were as close to the woodpile as Marlinspike dared, he lifted his head above the ballast for a look. He could see no rats, but his nose confirmed what Mizzen had said. There were Afties in the woodpile. Many of them.

Marlinspike and Mizzen carefully picked their way back to the waiting party.

"They must have come across my scent after I found the firewood yesterday," Marlinspike told the assembled rats. "They're waiting in ambush. We'll have to return to the magazine. I don't like it, but we need to find shelter."

"I have a suggestion," Wainscot piped up. "We know of a place."

He looked at Mizzen, as if asking permission, and Mizzen nodded.

Wainscot continued, "I don't much like going back there, but it's kept us safe since the battle."

"Lead on then," said Marlinspike.

Wainscot was very uneasy at the thought of sharing Moon's most precious secret with this strange group of rats. It was as though by showing them the way into the breadroom he would be giving up a part of her that he had hidden away in his heart; it had been a supreme act of trust for her to share the secret with him, and he treasured it. It was something that had belonged only to the two of them, and he felt as though he were betraying her. It had been difficult enough to give the secret to Mizzen, even knowing that the old rat loved Moon as much as he did. However, their need for shelter outweighed his sentimental conceit, so he grudgingly led them through the hidden ratways that Moon had shown him.

The fourteen rats moved slowly along the top of the beam toward the tin-clad wall of the breadroom. Wainscot had explained about the leap and although some of them were obviously frightened, they had all said that they would jump. Wainscot was at the front of the group, followed by Mizzen and Marlinspike, and the rest stretched out behind them along the beam like the knobs of a spine.

They reached the end of the beam, and Wainscot gathered himself for the jump. Before he could throw himself through the air, however, he felt a paw press down on the base of his tail, keeping him in place.

"Hold on a moment," said Mizzen. The old warrior had his nose up and was sniffing deeply. "Hate to always be the bearer of bad news," he said, "but we'll be needing to find ourselves another place to nest."

Behind Mizzen, Marlinspike said, "I smell them too. They covered their tracks well, but there's no mistaking it."

"Afties?" asked Wainscot. "In the breadroom?" He was horrified at the thought of interlopers in Moon's sanctum. It was bad enough that his newfound friends were about to enter, but this was intolerable.

"It's worse than that, Laddie," said Mizzen. "Dayrunner's with them. Keckle too. And..." he sniffed again, as if to confirm a suspicion. "Well, club me if that isn't a surprise."

Wainscot tested the air, searching for lingering evidence of the rats who had passed along the beam before them. It was faint, but he could just detect Aftey, and fainter still, the shadow of a familiar scent that sent a thrill of joy surging through him.

CHAPTER 33

A RETURN

The breadroom was empty.

There was no Mizzen, no Wainscot, and no Marlinspike. Spitkid, Dayrunner, Keckle, and two C'law were the only rats in the room. Dayrunner came very close to killing Keckle then and there. Spitkid watched him take a deep breath, evidently summoning up a colossal effort of will to wrestle down his swelling rage.

Dayrunner turned on Keckle with a hiss and raked his claws across her face. Squealing in surprise and pain, she tumbled back from him and sat staring as he advanced on her. He growled low in his throat. "Where are they?"

Spitkid was baffled. They were actually in the breadroom. *The breadroom*, where no Aftey had set foot in living memory. Here they were, surrounded by almost unimaginable riches—the air was so thick with the smell of biscuit that his legs were weak with the desire to eat —yet the Captain seemed blind to the place. He cared only that the objects of his hunt were not to be found.

Despite the fugitives' absence, Spitkid uncovered plenty of evidence that they had only recently vacated the room. Though they had been careful, they had left fresh droppings scattered here and there, and there was the distinct odour of two rats in the air. He recognised one scent as belonging to Mizzen, and he assumed that the other was Wainscot. Surely Dayrunner could read the signs.

"You said they were here," said Dayrunner. "I'll kill you for lying to me." His eyes bulged with the pressure of his fury. He raised a paw over Keckle's head.

He's mad, thought Spitkid.

Keckle made no effort to defend herself. She lowered her head and looked up at Dayrunner, waiting for the next blow to fall. Spitkid wondered why she did not say anything in her defence. Her silence was unsettling.

"Sir," said Spitkid, drawing the Captain's attention away from Keckle. "They *have* been here. Look around. Smell the air. She wasn't lying."

Slowly Dayrunner lowered his paw. He turned to face Spitkid, his eyes still blazing. For a moment, Spitkid was afraid that the Captain would attack him, but, with visible effort, he regained control of himself. He stood breathing heavily, and eventually some of the burning anger left his eyes.

"Yes, they were here," said Dayrunner, "and they'll be back. We'll wait for them." He stalked away and began to explore the room, leaving Spitkid and Keckle to stare bemusedly at each other.

259

M en visited the breadroom twice while the Afties waited. Each time the rats scurried to hide in the stores and crept cautiously out when the Men had left. It occurred to Spitkid that they had no way out of the room. After the Men had departed the second time, he mustered the courage to talk to Dayrunner. He found him on top of a barrel, eating a biscuit.

"Sir," he said, hoping that his voice was steady.

Dayrunner ignored him, intent on his gnawing. Keckle was somewhere at the other side of the room. She had not said a word to any of the Afties since entering the breadroom.

"Sir," said Spitkid again. Dayrunner glanced at him and then returned his attention to the biscuit. Spitkid bulled ahead. "Sir, we have no way out of here. Have you thought about how we're going to get out once we've finished with our business?"

Dayrunner laughed. Spitkid had never heard him laugh before, and it made him uneasy. It was not a happy sound.

"We'll kill them," said Dayrunner. His voice was too high and too loud.

"Kill who, sir?"

"The Men. When they come in here. We'll kill them and then leave through the door."

Kill the Men? Spitkid was appalled. The Captain might just as well have said that they would sprout wings and fly out, for all the sense it made.

"Sir—" he began, but before he could finish there was the scrabbling of claw on metal from above, and a rat dropped onto the barrel beside them.

Dayrunner reacted instantly. He was onto the newcomer with teeth bared before Spitkid had even started to move. Dayrunner did not kill the rat. Spitkid assumed that he stopped himself because he realised that the stranger was not Mizzen, Wainscot, or Marlinspike. It was a female, and a remarkably ugly one.

The Captain pulled his teeth away from her throat, but kept her pinned down beneath his forefeet. She squirmed under him, but was not strong enough to escape. Spitkid was surprised to see that she seemed more angry than frightened. That would change soon enough.

"Now this is a treat," Dayrunner said, examining her closely. "Spitkid, have a look at this one. Never seen anything quite like her." After another long look he corrected himself, "No, that's not true. I have seen her."

Spitkid moved to his side. After a moment, Keckle joined them. They looked down at the pinned newcomer.

"Bowser," said Spitkid. He spat the word as though it tasted bad

"What's your name?" demanded Dayrunner.

She was silent, so Keckle spoke for her, "Moonpatch."

CHAPTER 34

OVERBOARD

When Moon had fallen from the rigging, thrown in fury by the incomprehensible monkey, she had been horribly aware that it was all over for her. Or should have been.

She knew that she was dead the moment she hit the sea. No rat who fell overboard came back. Ever. She had told Wainscot herself.

The impact punched the breath out of her, and she sank beneath the surface. She hung in the water, half-stunned, for several heartbeats before the cold shocked her into action. Sputtering, she clawed her way to the surface and looked up to see the vast bulk of the Heloise gliding relentlessly past. She had fallen on the side of the ship away from the enemy vessel, but even over the splash of the sea, she could hear the sounds of the battle and feel the vibrations through the water as the two ships, bound together by grappling rope and tangled rigging, ground against each other.

She did not look around for Spume and Gorp.

The hull was close enough that she could swim to it, but it was too smooth to climb and there were no footholds within reach. It was moving fast—too quickly to keep up with—and was soon past her. As the great wall of the stern swept by, she slid down the side of a smooth green trough of water and was forced under by the turbulence of the wake. When she struggled to the surface again she could only watch helplessly as the only world she had ever known moved inexorably away from her. For a moment she wondered how long it would take her to drown, then put aside the thought as foolish. The sharks would find her long before that.

She knew full well that no one ever regained the ship if they fell overboard, but she was a rat and rats always try to survive, no matter the odds. She began to swim after the looming stern of the *Heloise*.

Then something struck her a stunning blow to the back, forcing her under the water yet again as a heavy mass moved over her.

Shark! screamed a voice in her mind.

Rendered almost insensible by the blow, she hung onto whatever it was that had attacked her out of instinct. She clung to it with every ounce of her strength as she was dragged through the water. As her rattled mind began to clear, she realised with a shock of recognition that she was clinging to a length of heavy rope.

Not a shark after all, she thought with relief.

With immense effort, she pulled herself up the rope until she was clear of the water. The rope led to what could only be a piece of spar, and she clambered onto it gratefully. She lay for many heartbeats while her head cleared and strength seeped back into her limbs. When she felt strong enough, she climbed unsteadily to her feet and looked around.

She was on a length of shattered spar poking from a great tangled mass of wood, rope, and canvas that moved through the sea with an uneven bobbing motion. The heavy line that she had climbed trailed behind like a tail.

It took a moment for her to understand. She had not been attacked; she had merely been in the way of a piece of wreckage that was being dragged behind the ship. Several long lines, twisted and knotted, ran in a dipping arc up from the debris and over the stern of the *Heloise*. She did not understand how a part of the ship could be in the sea behind it, but the mess was clearly broken pieces of spar and rigging, now all tangled together. Whether these had originally come from her own ship or the enemy's, she did not know.

What she did know was that she would be able to climb the ropes back onto the ship. For the first time in her knowledge, a rat who had fallen overboard when the ship was underway would be returning.

She was looking for a good route through the snarl of rope and wood when she realised with a start that she was not alone. There, on another fragment of spar not ten lengths from her, sat Spume, watching her. The warmth that had been seeping back into her body bled away in an instant.

Spume began to pick his way through the web of ropes toward her. She backed along her spar until she was out over the water at the rear of the tangle of rigging. The wood bounced and jigged with the movement of the wreckage.

At least Spume was alone. There was no sign of Gorp: he must not have been lucky enough to climb aboard the raft. She was surprised at the stab of sympathy she felt at the thought of Gorp alone in the vast sea, as the ship swept away from him and out of sight. Her own plight should have been enough to occupy her, for even without Gorp, Spume was more than her match in a fight. He had submitted to her back in the cable room only because he was afraid of Mizzen, but they both knew that there was no one to interrupt them this time.

He stepped onto her spar.

"How glad I am to see you, Scraps," he said.

She felt behind for more room to retreat, but her questing foot found only air.

"Careful, Pretty," said Spume. We do not want you falling, now do we? That would take all of the fun out of it."

"Spume," she said, "we can get back on board the ship. There's a rope."

"*I* can get back," he said, "but I am afraid that you will not be going anywhere."

"Don't be stupid, Spume. There are so few of us left. We need each other. Why do this?"

"I do not need you, and neither does the clan. You are a Jonah, and it is time we were rid of you."

He advanced until he was only a length from her.

"Please," she said.

Spume laughed. "Begging," he said. "How lovely. Thank you for making this—"

Without warning, and with the loudest hiss she could muster, Moon thrust her hind legs against the spar and threw herself at Spume, teeth bared and claws splayed.

Surprise threw him off balance. He reared back onto his haunches, eyes wide and front paws waving ineffectually. He uttered a squeal of distress as Moon crashed into him, her teeth closing on the loose skin under his neck. She bit down hard and pushed at the spar beneath her feet, her claws sinking deep into the water-softened wood as she forced her body into Spume's. She was much smaller and lighter, and had they been on solid deck it would have been but a moment's work for him to overpower her; however, they were not on solid deck, and the impact made him slide sideways from the top of the spar. He tried desperately to find a purchase with his feet, but Moon was beneath him and he could not see what he was doing. He fell, and as he did so, Moon—still gripping fiercely onto the skin of his neck—thrust as hard as she could against the spar. The two rats sailed out over the water.

Moon released her grip and they fell into the sea with twin splashes. She was closer than he to the trailing rope and quickly swam toward it. Spume, either not seeing the rope or too panicked to think clearly, began to paddle directly toward the bulk of the wreckage, which was moving rapidly away from him. Moon reached the rope before it swept past her, and clambered up it. Spume, realizing his mistake, changed direction, but it was too late. The frayed end of the rope snaked past him just out of reach. He watched helplessly as his only hope of salvation whipped away, and he was left alone in the great emptiness of the sea.

Halfway up the rope, Moon turned to look over her shoulder. She watched as Spume rose on a swell and disappeared over its crest only to reappear on the face of the next wave. She waited until his dark shape, ever diminishing with distance, was too far away to be seen and then clambered back onto the raft of debris.

After climbing up from the wreckage and back aboard the *Heloise*, Moon found the war still raging—both above decks and below. She quickly moved down into the depths of the ship, trying to make her way to the breadroom where she hoped to find

Wainscot and Mizzen, but again and again she encountered Aftey patrols and was forced to retreat. They had finished their grisly business in Bowser territory and had now moved to the rear of the ship to sweep for refugees who might have fled there in a vain attempt to escape. Finding herself continually frustrated, Moon was forced to make her way back toward the stern.

Eventually she decided to lay low. She found a hiding place in a crevice beneath a large octagonal wooden box. She had no way of knowing, but this was the rudder head cover, which covered the shaft of the rudder where it poked through the floor of the officer's wardroom. The Men often used it as a dining table. Exhausted, she fell into a deep sleep beneath it.

When she awoke, she had no idea how long she had lain insensible, but it was obvious that the battle between the Men was now over. The sailors seemed to be returning to their normal activities. Peering out from beneath the head cover, she could see their feet as they moved about the wardroom. She soon discovered that because this room was almost always occupied, she was safe from patrolling Afties, but she had to use all of her skills to remain undetected by the Men. She stayed in her hiding place as much as possible, creeping out only to find food and water, sometimes actually snatching crumbs from between the feet of sailors seated at the table.

Several times, when there were only a few Men in the wardroom, she slipped out into the ratways, cautiously checking to see whether she could now travel without being caught. However, she always encountered patrols and had to retreat back to her temporary nest.

While she waited in her enforced isolation, Moon thought almost continuously about Wainscot and Mizzen. Had they survived? Did they think she was dead? Were they looking for her? Her mind insisted that there was very little chance that they were still alive, but her heart clung to the hope that she would find them hiding in the breadroom. That hope, that slender hope, was all that she had to keep herself from descending into despair.

Occasionally, she thought about Spume. It was difficult to believe that he, who had been a source of misery throughout her entire short life, was now gone for good. She tried to muster up some feeling of satisfaction or pleasure at the thought, but try as she might, she could not. There was too much uncertainty, too much sadness, for her to rejoice in anything. Although Spume had hated her and would have killed her, she could not think of him floating away into the distance without a pang of pity. It was not a good way for any rat to die—even Spume. She wondered if he had drowned or if the sharks had found him first and was glad that she would never know.

Moon remained in her hiding place for several days, fearing for her life, before she finally managed to slip through the Aftey patrols. She then worked her way down through the ship, hoping against reason that Wainscot and Mizzen had made it safely to sanctuary. However, when she dropped into the breadroom she found a startled and irrational Dayrunner instead of her friends.

CHAPTER 35

HUNTING THE HUNTER

"Moon's in there with them," said Mizzen, his voice conveying a mixture of elation and trepidation.

"I believe she is," said Marlinspike.

"With Dayrunner." Mizzen spat the name.

"Yes."

"She must have come searching for us," added Wainscot.

There was silence for a few heartbeats as each rat considered the situation.

Wainscot waited, then said what he knew needed to be said. "We must go in after her." His voice was quiet but firm.

"We'd be trapped in there, youngster," said Marlinspike. "You might not know Dayrunner, but I've gone claw to claw with him and I don't relish doing it again—particularly in a place with no exit. To make matters worse, he's not alone. As much as I'd like to, I can't risk any of us for the sake of a single rat."

Wainscot did not argue. He knew that Marlinspike was right, but he also knew what he had to do. He had no choice. He moved back to the edge of the beam and settled into readiness for the jump. Mizzen placed a paw on his tail again.

"I have to try, Mizzen," said Wainscot. "Please don't stop me. If I don't go now, I'll lose my nerve."

"Not stopping you Laddie," said Mizzen, "but let me go first. There's going to be a fight and it'll be better if it's me in the lead. No offence, but you're not much of a scrapper."

Marlinspike spoke quietly to Mizzen, "This doesn't make sense. They've probably already killed her. You'll be risking yourself for nothing."

"Possibly," said Mizzen, "but if Wainscot's going, then so am I. Where my leader goes, I follow. Even if he weren't, I'd still give it a try. Moon might already be dead, but she might not."

Marlinspike looked back at the line of rats strung out along the beam behind them. He shook his head. "Very well," he said. "I can't afford to lose you, Mizzen, so I suppose I'll have to join you. There'll be a slightly better chance of our coming out of this with our skins in one piece if there are three of us. Give me a moment and then we'll get this foolishness underway."

He turned to the rat immediately behind him on the beam—a sturdy, unimaginative female named Scuttlerun. "Take the group back to our last nest in the magazine. We'll join you there later today. If we don't return, then you and Codline look after the rest. Keep them moving."

If Scuttlerun was surprised, she did not show it. "Yes sir," she said, and turned back on the beam to speak to the others.

"Right," said Marlinspike. "Let's get this over with."

W ainscot landed badly, half on and half off the barrel. The edge caught him across the ribs and knocked the breath from his lungs. He fell with a grunt to the deck below, landing on his feet. He cursed his luck and braced for the expected attack, but there was no rushing clatter of claws, and no biting, scratching bodies piled into him. He whirled about, searching the darkness for danger, but saw nothing.

There was a thump of rat on wood above him, and in a moment Marlinspike poked his pointed snout over the edge of the barrel and looked down at him. Mizzen's face, fierce eyed and looking for a fight, appeared beside Marlinspike's.

"They don't seem to be here," said Mizzen.

"No," said Marlinspike, sniffing. "But they were, and quite recently. Let's have a look around before we decide what to do next."

There was a small noise from Wainscot—half sigh and half sob.

"Are you hurt?" asked Marlinspike.

"No," said Wainscot. "It's just that I got myself all worked up, and now there's no one to fight. I'm almost disappointed. I think I just used up every last drop of my courage. I'll never be able to do anything like that again."

Both Marlinspike and Mizzen laughed.

"I think you might be wrong there," said Marlinspike. "There seems to be more to you than meets the eye. I'm sure you'll be the first to go for Dayrunner when we catch him up."

They searched the breadroom thoroughly. There were no Afties hiding in ambush, no signs of a fight, and, most encouragingly, no bodies or traces of blood. If Moon had not somehow managed to escape, then Dayrunner and his companions had her.

"Why would they take her with them?" asked Mizzen aloud. "To them she's a Bowser, and they're bent on destroying every last rat of the clan. Why didn't they just kill her here?" Before either of the others could speak, he answered his own question. "Dayrunner's a clever rat. He won't want the Men to know that we've found a way into the breadroom. If they know, they'll find the hole and block it. A rat's body'd be a dead giveaway."

"No," said Wainscot, "he's after me. I'm the reason he came aboard the *Heloise* in the first place. He's a C'law from my old clan, and he'll never rest until he's completed his mission. He must have thought I was dead, but once he learned otherwise, he came for me. He saw Moon with me and thinks she'll know where to find me."

"What's he talking about?" asked Marlinspike.

"It's a long tale, and I know only part of it," said Mizzen, "but he might be right."

"I slipped through his claws twice now," said Wainscot. "I imagine he'll do everything in his power to make sure it doesn't happen again,"

"I got away from him as well," said Marlinspike.

"And so did I," said Mizzen. "Looks like all our tails are caught in the same trap. If he knows we're together he's likely to become even more annoying. Suppose we'll have to go and ask him to stop bothering us."

"His trail is still fresh," said Marlinspike. "Although it probably isn't necessary to track him. I expect he'll return to the Aftey Council chamber."

"We're going after Moon?" asked Wainscot. He could not bear the thought of her in Aftey paws, but knew that there was nothing he could do about it on his own. Even with Mizzen and Marlinspike's help he was sure that there was little he could do for her, but he had to try.

His newfound resolve almost faltered at the thought of the dangers ahead, but his need to rescue Moon had taken on a life of its own, and it was dragging him along like a pup in a mother's mouth. It was almost as though he were a spectator of his own life, watching his actions with amazement. Rats like Mizzen and Marlinspike were capable of acts of courage, and supposedly, he was not—and yet he kept willingly risking his life for Moon.

"That we are," said Marlinspike. "It's been a day for stupid decisions, so I suppose one more won't hurt." He glanced about the breadroom. "I have one question, though. How do we get out of here?"

"He's completely mad, you know," said Moon.

Spitkid snapped at her to keep quiet. He was not quite sure how to deal with her, and his uncertainty made him edgy.

He was keeping guard over her just outside the Council chamber. Dayrunner had retired to commune with the rat-king, telling them to wait until he came out. He had muttered something about needing to see whether the signs were right for "the final battle". Spitkid could hear the low murmur of voices drifting from the chamber, and did his best not to listen.

"Mad and dangerous," said Moon. "He's going to get you all killed. You know it—I can see it in your eyes."

Spitkid pushed her against the wall with his chest and spoke into her face, low and menacing, "He won't let me kill you, but if you say another word, I'll hurt you. He won't mind that, but you will."

He stepped away from her and moved back. Keckle crept out of the shadows from which she had been silently watching the exchange. She crouched near Moonpatch, who did not seem pleased at her proximity. Keckle had not said a single word since she had identified Moon in the breadroom.

Of course Spitkid knew that Dayrunner was mad. Somehow the rat-king had managed to drag the Captain down into the stinking bilge of its own lunacy. Any doubt that he still had, protected and nurtured against the evidence of his own senses, had evaporated the moment the Captain suggested that they kill the Men in order to escape the breadroom. The enormity of the suggestion had stunned him so much that he had had trouble understanding Dayrunner's meaning.

After Moon had dropped in on them Dayrunner had decided that instead of killing her, they would keep her alive so that she might lead them to Mizzen and Wainscot, if the two did not arrive in the breadroom soon. Then Dayrunner had said again that they would attack the sailors. Only an argument from Spitkid—that Moonpatch might escape in the confusion—had convinced the Captain to reconsider the plan.

This had left them with the problem of how to leave the room. Spitkid knew that Moonpatch had the answer, but she would not speak, and no threat would sway her. Nor would she tell them when or whether Mizzen and Wainscot would be returning to the breadroom. Dayrunner would have forced the information from her eventually, but he had been distracted and had shown no interest in questioning her. He had become agitated and jumpy, and Spitkid could only think that it was because he wanted to get back to the rat-king.

At first, Dayrunner had said that they would continue to wait in the breadroom until their quarry returned, but as time passed he had become more and more unsettled and had eventually announced that they would be leaving as soon as an opportunity presented itself.

That opportunity had come soon enough.

There had been the sound of approaching Human feet, and the door had rattled open. As a Man carrying a lantern had appeared in the opening, Dayrunner had shouted, "With me!" and dashed between the Man's legs and out the door. The other rats, taken by surprise, had been slower to act. Keckle and Spitkid, driving Moon before them, had been through the door before the startled sailor could react, but the following C'law had not been so lucky. The Man brought a heavy shoe crashing down on the second of them.

Now safely back at the Council chamber, Spitkid marvelled that they had lost only one of their number in that ill-considered rush from the breadroom. It was further evidence of the Captain's deteriorating connection with reality.

Spitkid agreed with Moonpatch. Dayrunner was mad and dangerous, but he had no idea what to do about it.

"Spume and Gorp. Alive?"

The question startled Moon. She was certain she had never heard Keckle speak prior to that one word in the breadroom. In all her dealings with Spume and his gang, the strange rat had been silent—standing cold and menacing off to the side in the shadows, almost a shadow herself. She wondered what was behind the question. Did Keckle harbour any fondness for her old companions? Did she miss them and ask after them out of concern? Moon honestly did not know. Keckle had not demonstrated any concern when Mizzen had threatened to kill Spume, and she had shown no emotion when Spume and Gorp had tumbled from the rope into the sea; yet she had gone after Gorp, presumably to help him, when Mizzen had attacked in the cable room. Moon did not know what to think: Keckle was utterly inscrutable.

Regardless of the reasons for the question, Moon had no intention of answering. It was not just Spitkid's threat that kept her silent: Keckle frightened her badly, and she had no desire to talk to her.

Moon turned away from the odd rat, and considered her own situation. She could hope that Wainscot and Mizzen had survived - Mizzen was tough and resourceful, and Wainscot had demonstrated a remarkable ability to stay alive - but she had little reason to think that she would ever see them again. Deep in Aftey territory, under the watchful eye of Spitkid and his C'law guard, and at the mercy of the clearly irrational Dayrunner, her chances of living through the day, let alone escaping, were slim.

She settled down and closed her eyes, trying to rest. She would need her strength for whatever might come.

Chapter 36

Final Battle

When Dayrunner emerged from the Council chamber, Spitkid thought that he might have reverted to his old self—the rat that he had been before the rat-king had twisted him into something else. His eyes were clear, and he stood straighter. He even seemed to have regained some of his bulk.

"Call in the patrols and gather the C'law," said Dayrunner. "It is time."

Time for what? Spitkid wondered, but he did not ask. Instead he asked, "And the prisoners?"

"Leave them with me."

W ainscot shifted to keep his footing as the wood beneath him moved back and forth. He felt very exposed and very vulnerable.

"That's the third one we've seen," whispered Mizzen as the six-rat patrol passed close by their hiding place.

Wainscot, Mizzen, and Marlinspike were sitting on top of the tiller, the massive beam of wood that linked the ship's wheel to its rudder. Connected to the wheel by cables running through a succession of pulleys, the tiller shifted back and forth as the helmsman, two decks above, steered the ship. The three rats swung from side to side with the movement. They were partially hidden by shadow, but if the patrols had been vigilant, they would easily have spotted them.

"Told you they weren't looking for us," said Mizzen.

"It still seems like a foolish way to prove your point," said Marlinspike, "sitting out in the open like this."

"They're all heading to the same place we are—their Council chamber. Something's amiss."

"I'd wager my whiskers that Dayrunner's summoned them," said Marlinspike. "He's likely waiting for them to gather somewhere near the chamber. I'd love to hear what he has to say to them."

"Do you think Moon's still with him?" asked Wainscot.

"No way to know, Laddie," said Mizzen. "Still, it's the best guess we have right now, so it's to the Council chamber we're bound."

"Not that we'll be able to get near it," said Marlinspike. "They'll be thick as fleas around it."

"That they will," said Mizzen, "so we'll have to be particularly careful."

The Afties were going to war. Again.

Running behind Dayrunner, Spitkid could scarcely believe that he had been swept up in this lunatic scheme. He also could not believe that the clan would be following the Captain into such monumental folly.

He had listened with growing incredulity as Dayrunner had unveiled his grand plan to the C'law and the patrol leaders. He had looked about as the Captain had spoken, hoping to see his own shock reflected in the faces of the listening rats, but Spitkid had been dismayed to see their initial stunned disbelief gradually change into greedy enthusiasm.

Dayrunner had exercised all of his considerable skill when he had spoken to the gathered rats, and every sentence he had said had been utterly ludicrous—appallingly, laughably, painfully, tragically ludicrous. Nevertheless, they had listened, and worse, they had believed. He had told them that they were no longer the Aft Clan; that their old clan had ceased to exist in the same glorious battle that had destroyed the Bowsers. They were now the *Heloise* Clan, he had said, because the entire ship was now theirs. Or would be—and here he had paused as if to emphasise that what he was about to say was the crux of why he had gathered them together—if not for the Men. They had won their great victory, but even so they were still not the masters of their world. Despite their valour, they were not free to nest where they chose, to walk openly on the decks, or to eat the choicest foods in the galley, as should be their right.

The attentive rats had nodded their agreement, muttering to each other, while Spitkid had listened with growing unease as Dayrunner wove a glorious picture of life as it *should* be for the rats of the *Heloise* Clan; of the softest bedding material, of great stacks of ripe cheese, theirs for the taking, and of lives lived without the looming threat of sudden death. It was wonderful, and all that stood between them and this life of ease and plenty were the Men.

"So we must destroy them," he had declared at last. "We must destroy the Men."

Even the most fervent of the listeners had fallen silent at this. Spitkid had almost heard their unspoken questions. *How could they possibly destroy the Men? What use were their teeth and claws against clubs and boots?*

Dayrunner had seemingly been prepared for these questions, and had provided answers.

Alone, an individual rat was no match for a Man, but they were many and the Men were few. They would overwhelm them one at a time. And they would start as they had started with the Bowsers—by removing their enemy's head. They had destroyed the Bowser Council and the Bowsers had been helpless. If they killed the ship's Captain, the rest of the Men would go down too.

"By the rising of the tomorrow's sun," Dayrunner had concluded, "the *Heloise* Clan will be absolute masters of the ship. And when the sun sets you'll all be feasting on cheese and biscuit. Follow me, and I'll lead you to glory."

They had cheered him, thought Spitkid as he ran. *They had actually cheered him*. And now they were following him as he led them to their destruction. He looked at the rats around him. They were so used to following the Captain's orders that they had not even questioned the sanity of what he had said. Nor had they asked if the Council—the strangely absent Council—agreed. There was no need. If Dayrunner said it, it must be true.

Spitkid had argued, of course. His duty to his clan had required him to try to talk some sense into the Captain. It had been dangerous, but he had tried.

After the patrol leaders had left to assemble their troops and Spitkid was alone with Dayrunner, with only Moonpatch and Keckle as witnesses, he had said, "Surely you're not serious." He had not meant to be so blunt, but he was still reeling from what he had heard. Diplomacy was beyond him.

As soon as he had spoken he had tensed, expecting violence, but the Captain's response had been surprisingly mild.

"I'm disappointed in you, Spitkid," he had said, "but not surprised. I've known for some while now that you and I see things very differently. When this is over, I'm afraid I may have to rethink the command structure of the clan."

That such a rethinking would involve the death of the first lieutenant, Spitkid had little doubt, but he pressed on. He ignored the cautious, sensible part of himself that told him to keep his snout shut, and said, "Sir, we mustn't do this thing. We'll be slaughtered. It will be the end of the clan."

"We will prevail," said Dayrunner. "The rat-king has seen it."

"The rat-king—?" Spitkid shook his head. "The rat-king has seen it? Did the rat-king tell you what will happen if the Men are gone? Did it explain how the ship will sail? Did it tell you where the food will come from? Everything we have comes from Men. How will we survive without them?"

The flame of madness, which had been absent during the speech, flared again behind Dayrunner's eyes. "We are rats," he said, "we need no one. All that Man can do, we can do."

So now, Spitkid found himself running with the *Heloise* Clan as it raced toward its own end.

Although Dayrunner had deferred Spitkid's punishment, his fall from grace was already under way.

"Take that one and keep her close to me," Dayrunner had said, indicating Moonpatch. He seemed to have lost interest in Keckle. "Do not let her escape." And just like that, Spitkid was demoted from trusted lieutenant to jailor. He wondered why Dayrunner was so concerned with keeping the prisoner near him, but he was too heavy of heart to ask.

The rats of the *Heloise* Clan coursed through the holds in a furred wave as they made their way toward the Human Captain's spacious dayroom at the very rear of the ship. Dayrunner ran before them, and close behind him came the reluctant Spitkid and Moon.

"There she is," said Wainscot. "I see her."

They sat on the top step of a companionway watching the Afties stream through the hold beneath them. Once again, they were not well hidden, but the Afties were too preoccupied to pay them any attention.

"Come with me," said Wainscot, and before either Mizzen or

Marlinspike could protest, he dropped from the stairs onto a pile of stacked jute bags, and from there down into the mass of rats. Mizzen and Marlinspike followed.

If any of the Afties noticed the interlopers, they gave no sign. They were going to war and were too intent on the impending battle to concern themselves with the presence of a few wrong-smelling rats. Some of them might have recognised Mizzen, but likely thought it only fitting that their old first lieutenant should rejoin them in this day's glorious undertaking.

Wainscot worked his way up through the ranks toward the front of the pack where he had seen Moon. Mizzen and Marlinspike pressed forward behind him, wondering at finding themselves in the heart of the enemy. However, they trusted that Wainscot had some idea of what they would do when they caught up with their quarry.

The rolling horde of rats encountered sailors as they flowed through the holds, and each time they did, a few patrol groups peeled off from the main body to swarm up the legs of the horrified Man. The resulting writhing column of Man and rat would loom high above the seething mass of the army like promontories over a storm-chopped sea. The Men would flail and shriek, beating at the rats that clung to them and sending small broken bodies flying through the air. Dayrunner felt the thrill of battle lust course through his body every time he saw his troops surge up the body of a sailor, but he did not join in on any of these lesser fights. He would not be distracted from his purpose.

Up and up the army surged. Up ladder and stair, up from deck to deck. They raced from hold to orlop to gundeck, cresting and crashing over obstacles, never slowing as they hurtled toward the Captain's quarters. Down the last short hall they ran, only to be checked as they came to the closed door of the cabin. Like water they broke against the wood, but also like water they found the gap at the bottom of the door and squeezed through, squirming and worming, like liquid seeping into a leaky vessel. They boiled into the cabin in twos and threes, Dayrunner at their vanguard. He slid to a halt on the polished oaken floor and stared up silently at the Human Captain.

The Man, evidently having heard the cries of the sailors beyond the bulkheads, was halfway to the door from his desk at the rear of the cabin, fastening his sword belt about his waist as he moved.

His steps faltered as he saw the rats. After a moment's shocked hesitation, he yelled his astonishment, and swept his sword from its scabbard. The belt, still not buckled, fell at his feet with a clatter.

Dayrunner hissed, but did not move. The group of Afties around him swelled as more and more rats squeezed beneath the door and lined up, row upon row, along the inside face of the bulkhead. The Human Captain backed away until he stood with the backs of his thighs braced against the edge of his desk, his sword at the ready.

The rats held back, gathered and ready to charge on Dayrunner's command. Before they could do so the Man roared and rushed toward them. He swung his sword in a low sweeping arc that scythed through their ranks, scoring a long yellow groove in the wooden deck.

"Kill him," yelled Dayrunner, and crossed the floor to the Human Captain's legs in two bounds. With a rising squeal, the rats surged forward.

Wainscot was the first under the door, but Mizzen and Marlinspike pushed through just behind him. There were Afties all about them, jostling and pushing to move forward. Wainscot looked out across their backs and saw a large Man silhouetted against the huge bank of windows that made up most of the rear wall of the cabin. Dozens of rats clung to him, biting and clawing, and hundreds more milled about his feet, trying to leap onto his legs as he stamped and kicked. Bodies lay scattered about the floor where he had trampled or thrown them. The Man plucked rats from his body and flung them aside with one hand while slashing at the throng at his feet with the sword in the other. Relatively undamaged, he had kept most of the attackers away from his head and neck, and his heavy blue coat protected his body, but his white stockings were in shreds and his legs were streaked with crimson.

Wainscot saw Dayrunner halfway up the Man's coat, a brown body amongst a sea of black. He was climbing up the Man's chest, making his way toward the exposed throat that gleamed pale and inviting above the high, stiff collar.

The whole sight was so bizarre, so wrong, that if he had happened across it only the day before, Wainscot would have been transfixed. As it was, he had seen its like many times during the breathless rush up from the holds when the rat-tide had flowed over sailors, and he was able to turn his head away. He looked about and caught a glimpse of Moon's ugly, beautiful, goggle-eyed face through a gap in the shifting throng of rat-bodies. The sight of her, lovely to his eyes, caused a swell of pure pleasure to rise in his chest. Against all expectations, against all hopes, she was alive and only a few lengths away.

Without waiting to see if Mizzen and Marlinspike followed, Wainscot forced his way through the crowd toward her. He shouldered past a last rat and stepped out of the mass of surging Afties onto a stretch of empty floor. There, on the other side of the open space, stood Moon. She was not alone, however. A large and formidable rat stood beside her, obviously positioned there to keep her from escaping.

To Wainscot's own amazement, he hesitated for only a heartbeat before rushing across the floor toward Moon and her captor. He was not at all sure what he was going to do when he got there, but the need to rescue her was too strong for him to resist. That small part of his mind that still concerned itself with keeping him from being torn to pieces hoped against hope that Mizzen and Marlinspike were close behind.

Moon looked up and met his eyes as he raced toward her. "Wainscot!" she shouted. "No, he'll kill you!"

Which means, thought Wainscot fleetingly, *that Mizzen and Marlinspike aren't right behind me.*

He ploughed headfirst into the large rat. Before he could so much as land a blow, he found himself flipped onto his back and pinned to the floor by the substantial weight of the Aftey. Regretting only that he would not have the chance to say goodbye to Moon, he closed his eyes and waited for the pain. It did not come. Instead, a voice, soft and low, said, "I have no quarrel with you. Get up."

The weight lifted from him. He opened his eyes and scrambled to his feet.

The Aftey took a step back. He looked at Moon for several breaths, then sighed heavily and said, "Guarding you was the last order that I'll ever be given, and I'm disobeying it. What kind of soldier does that make me?" He shook his head slowly and glanced across the room at the colossal struggle taking place at the back of the cabin.

"It's all madness," he said, "but he is my Captain."

"Spitkid..." started Moon.

"You're free to go," said Spitkid. "Though what there will be left to go to after this, I can't say."

With that he left them and ran across the room toward the battle. Moon and Wainscot watched him disappear into the mass of rats, and then turned to each other.

"They said you were dead," said Wainscot quietly. He felt strangely shy.

"I was—or, I should have been," said Moon.

"You said that no rat ever comes back."

"No rat ever does."

"Yet here you are. I never gave up hope."

"I know," said Moon.

Wainscot was almost overwhelmed by the intensity of his emotions at standing muzzle to muzzle with Moon again. His earlier glimpses of her from a distance had not prepared him for the surge of warmth that washed over him as he stared into her eyes. He could tell that she was feeling the same way, and they were silent for some time, secure in their bubble of happiness while all around them chaos roiled.

There was a scrabble of claw on wood, and both Mizzen and Marlinspike came sliding to a halt beside them.

"Next time you decide to run off like that, Laddie, do us a favour and let us know," said Mizzen. "Oh, Moon, there you are."

Wainscot reluctantly pulled his eyes away from Moon's, and

looked at Mizzen. He was not fooled by the casual greeting—he knew that Mizzen was also deeply moved by the reunion.

"Here I am," said Moon back. There was a twinkle in her eye. Wainscot knew that she could see past the old rat's facade too.

"Wainscot never gave up hope," Mizzen echoed.

Moon nodded. "I know."

"Moonpatch," said Marlinspike, nodding his head to her. He did not have the same relationship with Moon as the other two, but the way he said her name eloquently expressed his pleasure at seeing her.

Marlinspike looked back toward the swarm of rats still squeezing beneath the door. "I think we'd best be moving along. I don't think this is the safest place to tarry. We can't go back the way we came, though: too crowded."

"Up there," said Wainscot pointing with his nose toward the bank of windows at the back of the cabin. Several of them were open to allow fresh sea-air into the room. They were hinged at the sides and swung out over the water. "We can leave by those windows and climb along the outside of the ship." There were some boxes stacked at the back of the cabin that would give them a path up to the windowsill. He had no idea if there was anything outside but a long drop to the sea, but the others, who knew considerably more about the landscape of the ship, did not argue, so he pressed on. "From there we can climb up to the deck and then find our way back to the others."

"Lead on then, Laddie," said Mizzen.

Dayrunner lost his grip on the Human Captain's coat and slipped down his body. The Man was shaking and twisting so violently that it was extremely difficult for the attacking rats to avoid being thrown from him. It was only their numbers that prevented him from freeing himself of them entirely. For every two that he threw to the floor, six more took their places. Dayrunner stopped his fall by hooking his claws into the top of a pocket flap, and resumed his climb up toward the Man's throat. Reaching the Captain's bucking right shoulder, he clung precariously to a gold-corded epaulet while steadying himself for the final assault. He was not sure how much damage he could inflict on such a massive enemy, but he was determined that he would not be plucked away before the Man had fallen.

An instant before he threw himself at the Man's throat, however, a movement to his left caught his eye. He glanced to the side and what he saw almost made him lose his grip on the epaulet. There, on the sill of the great windows at the back of the cabin, just beyond the desk and not more than three bounds away, was Wainscot. It was the first time he had clearly seen the criminal since that night when he had watched the scrawny rat dangle beneath a rope over the mist-shrouded water. There was no mistaking him—there could be no other rat, on sea or on land, with that streak of white running down his flank. Then, with a shock, he saw that the other two objects of his obsession —Marlinspike and Mizzen—were lined up neatly on the sill behind Wainscot. The fact that Moon had escaped and was also with them hardly registered.

Shrieking a squeal of pure rage, Dayrunner leapt from the Human's shoulder and landed on the top of the desk, scattering paper and upending an inkwell. A gout of thick black ink spattered across him. All thought of Men and conquest was banished from his mind; he saw only Wainscot, Mizzen, and Marlinspike, and he knew only the need to tear them apart. He was not even aware that the door behind him had burst open, and that Men were pouring into the cabin.

Watching from the sill, Wainscot saw the swing of the door clear an arc through the rats on the floor, sending bodies tumbling through the air. Six burly sailors, armed with clubs and belaying pins, rushed into the cabin and began to lay about them with mighty blows. The hallway behind them was carpeted with the bodies of dead or dying rats.

The Human Captain, seeing the reinforcements, redoubled his efforts to rid himself of his writhing coat of rats. Plucking, crushing, and punching, he threw the squealing creatures away, and was soon unencumbered enough to set to work with his sword.

The tide turned. The swarm that had been climbing over themselves in their driving desire to get to the Man suddenly began to move in the opposite direction. Almost simultaneously, they all turned to flee. Their squeals shifted from bloodlust to terror as they scrambled over their fallen comrades to escape the clubs that rose and fell in terrible, relentless rhythm.

Wainscot turned his face away from the carnage below and moved along the sill, leading his line of companions toward the nearest open section of window. A hiss and a thump from behind made him swivel his head back to see Dayrunner landing on the windowsill in a spray of ink. The great rat slid to a halt a length behind Marlinspike, the last of the line of four, leaving a smear of black on the white-painted surface. Wainscot squealed in terror.

The apparition was truly horrifying; huge and bristling with fury and madness. Dayrunner's great incisors gleamed yellow and wicked in the afternoon light. His fur, all matted and shiny with ink, stood in glistening points. Worst of all were his eyes—they were wide and glaring, seeming to glow with an inner light that had nothing to do with the sunlight glinting off of them in golden points. This was indeed the Dayrunner that Wainscot knew, but he could see little of the C'law from his old nest in the monster before them.

"Run," said Marlinspike. "I'll hold him."

Mizzen did not run. The windowsill was wide enough for two rats to stand side by side, and he stepped forward to take his place beside Marlinspike.

Wainscot and Moon did not run either. Wainscot's mind skittered and jumped with fear as he tried to think of something, anything, that might save them from the death that was about to descend upon them. Even the formidable Mizzen and Marlinspike seemed to him to be utterly insignificant before the black and glittering thing that even now was leaning forward in readiness to charge.

"Wait," said Wainscot over the backs of the two larger rats, "let's talk. We—"

Dayrunner did not pause to hear what Wainscot might have to say. He was well beyond the ability to listen, and launched himself at Marlinspike and Mizzen with an inarticulate cry of rage. Seasoned fighters though they were, and even outnumbering him as they did, the two rats were no match for him in his berserk rage.

Dayrunner's teeth closed on one of Mizzen's forelegs with a hideous crunch, and the old warrior squealed in pain. With a vicious twist of his head, Dayrunner tossed the wounded rat sideways over the outside edge of the sill. Mizzen dropped out of sight.

Marlinspike tried to fasten his own teeth into Dayrunner's neck, but he was not quick enough. Dayrunner swung back and down, and came up under Marlinspike's chin with the top of his head. The blow was hard enough to knock Marlinspike from his feet, and he landed on his side, partially dazed. Before he could regain his feet he toppled over the inside edge of the sill, missing the desk and falling to the deck below.

In the moments that had passed while Dayrunner was dealing with Mizzen and Marlinspike, Wainscot had moved to Moon's side. "Go," he said. "It's me that he wants. I won't give him much of a fight, but I might slow him down." He was startled to hear that his voice was steady considering that it was all that he could do to remain upright on his quivering legs.

Moon did not say anything, but neither did she move. The two small rats stood side by side, trembling, and waiting for the end that was only a heartbeat away.

Dayrunner paused for an instant to watch Marlinspike fall, and then advanced toward Moon and Wainscot. He did not hurry. Some of the raging fury that had driven him through Marlinspike and Mizzen must have burned off and left a scrap of reason behind. He ignored Moon and focused on Wainscot.

"So, you'll not be the one that got away from me after all," he said. Then he laughed. It was not a pleasant sound.

Still laughing and with teeth bared and claws spread to strike, he reared up on his hind legs, towering over Moon and Wainscot. Wainscot hissed and drew back his lips, showing his own teeth. It was an empty gesture of defiance, but he was determined to die like a rat. At the last instant before Dayrunner struck, however, his nerve failed him,. He closed his eyes and waited.

A flash of light burned red through his eyelids, and the sill jumped beneath his feet. The searing stab of pain he was expecting did not come. Surprised, he opened his eyes.

Where Dayrunner had been a moment before, the blade of the Human Captain's sword now quivered, its sharp edge imbedded deeply in the wood of the sill. Sunlight flashed again, reflected in the weapon's highly polished surface. There was no sign of Dayrunner except for a splash of bright blood on both the blade and the weathered oak of the sill.

The sword writhed as the Human Captain struggled to pull it from the grip of the wood, but for a moment it remained fast. Then it flew free with a spray of splinters.

"Quick," shouted Moon, "jump!"

Wainscot did not have to ask which way—out the window and down into the sea below. Better a death by drowning than to be cut in two by that awful blade.

He rolled sideways over the edge and fell upside down with his feet above him. Just as he cleared the sill, the sword struck again. He saw its point silhouetted against the sky, jutting out from the sill's edge where he had been but a heartbeat before.

Expecting a long fall to the cold waters below, Wainscot was surprised when he landed hard after dropping only a length or two. He scrambled to his feet, and found that he was on a ledge that ran the width of the stern just beneath the windows. Painted a rich gold, that was now badly dulled and pitted by the elements, the ledge was the top edge of a section of the decorative scrollwork that adorned the rear of the Heloise.

There was a thump on the ledge behind him. He turned to see that Moon had also dropped down from the sill. Behind her, awkwardly holding a badly mangled foreleg, sat Mizzen.

"Don't stand there gawping, Laddie," said Mizzen. "We should be getting a move on."

Chapter 37

New Beginnings

The *Heloise* limped into Halifax harbour, closely followed by the captive *Mustang*. She had suffered a terrible mauling and was in need of rest and repair. Despite her damage, she had enjoyed an extremely successful cruise, and her crew was looking forward to the substantial prize money that the captured ships would soon be providing them. She would be brought back to full strength and would set sail again, her crew confident in the qualities of both the ship and her Captain.

The two battles, however, had also taken their toll on the Men of the *Heloise*. The one with the *Mustang* had killed many sailors and marines, but that was only to be expected on a ship of war. The other battle—the one with the rats—was another thing entirely. Even though her crew had not suffered a single death during the second battle, the entire ship was unsettled, simply because what had happened was so inexplicable.

Why had the rats attacked? they wondered. *Were they diseased? Would sickness spread to the crew through the many bites they had suffered? Was there something wrong with the Heloise? Was she unlucky?*

Some answers came with time—no disease raged through the crew, and none of them succumbed to madness—but the ship could not shake its superstitious fear of the essential wrongness of the episode. In the end, by unspoken consent, her crew put the memory of the attack behind them, and after that day, none spoke of the unfathomable events again. Her Captain did not even record it in the ship's log, and none of her officers mentioned it in their journals or letters.

The number of rat bodies that her crew threw overboard was staggering, and it seemed as though every single rat on the *Heloise* must have been clubbed, stabbed, or crushed. Still, her Men conducted a bow to stern search and killed many more, including one very strange group of six that were bound together at the tail, like the spokes of a wheel. The sailors had never seen anything like it before, and its destruction brought to the *Heloise* a general feeling of relief, as though a curse might have been lifted.

After the hunt, the ship's younger sailors and the landsmen might have believed that the *Heloise* was now completely free of rats. However, her seasoned hands knew that it was virtually impossible to rid her of all of her rodent passengers. Still, they set traps and sent the ship's cats—all three had survived the battle—to the holds to practice their ratting arts, but even they had little success.

Some of her rats had survived, of course, but only a few. Slowly, in the days that followed the slaughter, they crept from their hiding places in her deepest, darkest places to gather in small groups. They began to rebuild their clan, quietly and cautiously, aware that their lives would continue to be hard and fraught with danger, but confident at least that their dark days of fighting rat against rat, clan against clan, were behind them.

T he choice of Marlinspike as first lieutenant of the new clan was easy.

Wainscot could certainly not think of another suitable choice. There were simply no other rats alive with the experience or character to assume the role. Mizzen might have been a candidate, but Dayrunner had crippled him.

After Dayrunner had fallen, Wainscot, Moon, and Mizzen had rejected the breadroom as a suitable sanctuary in which to lick their wounds. The thought of being trapped in a place from which there was only one exit made them nervous, so they had made their careful way to the old Bowser Council chamber beneath the huge carpentry tool chest. It had seemed to them to be the best place to survive whatever might come next for the shredded remains of the rat population of the *Heloise*.

When Marlinspike had found them in their hidey-hole, he had brought with him a few other rats to plant the seeds of the fledgling new clan. After escaping from the carnage in the Captain's cabin—and Wainscot knew that there was a story there that he would one day like to hear—Marlinspike had sought out the ragged band of Bowsers that he had left with Scuttlerun, and led them to where he suspected he would find the others.

They hid at the heart of the now extinct Bowser clan until the Men had completed their scouring of the ship. Only when they were sure that the Men were finished searching did they set out on a search of their own. Mizzen, too badly injured to join them, remained in the chamber.

Over the course of the next few days, they gathered together the beginnings of a new clan. Wainscot had thought that after the twin slaughters by the Afties and the Men they might find no more rats at all; it was true that they found no more Bowsers, but they did come across surviving Afties. Surprisingly, they also discovered that a number of the shanghaied land rats had slipped away from the army when it had become clear that Dayrunner was leading the clan to bloody disaster. Remarkably, these Landers had lived through both the battle and the subsequent rat-hunt by the Men. Even the older ship rats began to see the newcomers in a more favourable light.

The searchers turned up scattered survivors for three more days, until they had gathered some fifty of them, and then they found no more. They saw no sign of either Spitkid or Keckle. Wainscot suspected that they might have died in the Captain's cabin.

The gathered rats were really nothing more than a disorganised collection of individuals struggling to survive from day to day, but it was a start. "It only takes two rats to make a clan," Scuffle had once told Wainscot when he was feeling particularly bullied and alone, and although he had thought it nothing but empty comfort at the time, he now saw the sense in it. Even though there were not many of them in their new group, they made up for their lack of numbers with an abundance of good ratty grit. "Rats will do what rats will do," Scuffle had said to him. He could not now remember why she had said it— likely trying to cheer him up when he had suffered some indignity at the paws of his clanmates—but he knew that he and his fellow survivors would do what rats do and rebuild their clan. It would take time and effort, and likely take more than a few lives, but what else could a rat expect?

They started the reconstruction of the clan with a small Council, for which Wainscot, Moon, and Mizzen were the only nominees.

Wainscot enthusiastically supported the selection of Moon and Mizzen, but doubted the wisdom of his own nomination. The courage and strength of will he had demonstrated when leading the charge to save Moon had done little to change his ability to underesti-mate himself.

"I'm a storyteller," he argued. "That's all I ever wanted to be."

"We need storytellers," said Mizzen, "almost as much as we need councilrats—"

"Maybe more," interrupted Moon.

"Maybe more," agreed Mizzen. "So I propose that you become a councilrat *and* the clan storyteller."

"Here, here," said Moon.

Wainscot bowed his head and accepted the inevitable. It was worth the price of being a council rat to be able to tell stories to a whole clan. His heart soared at the thought.

When Mizzen suggested that Moon should be given additional authority as the new clan's Captain, Wainscot was relieved, but not surprised, that she rejected the idea.

"We've seen enough of Captains to last us for the rest of their lives," she said.

There was some discussion over the name of the clan. Because of their histories, both Bowser and Aft were unacceptable to all three of the new councilrats. They also rejected *Heloise*, as Dayrunner had led the *Heloise* Clan to destruction. Finally Mizzen said, "Well, we were the Moon Clan for a spell. It's as good a name as any, and better than most."

"Moon Clan?" asked Moon. "When were we ever the Moon Clan?"

"You weren't there," said Wainscot. "All in favour?"

And so they became the Moon Clan, much to the embarrassment of their namesake.

Wainscot was the only one of the three to hold two positions in the new clan. He had no doubts as to which role was more important.

"D o you think he survived?"

It was Wainscot who posed the question. None of them had to ask who 'he' was. They were settled in their nest; Mizzen and Marlinspike sat side-by-side gnawing at either end of the same piece of wood, and Moon was curled close to Wainscot, her head resting on his flank. She was half asleep but her eyes opened at the question.

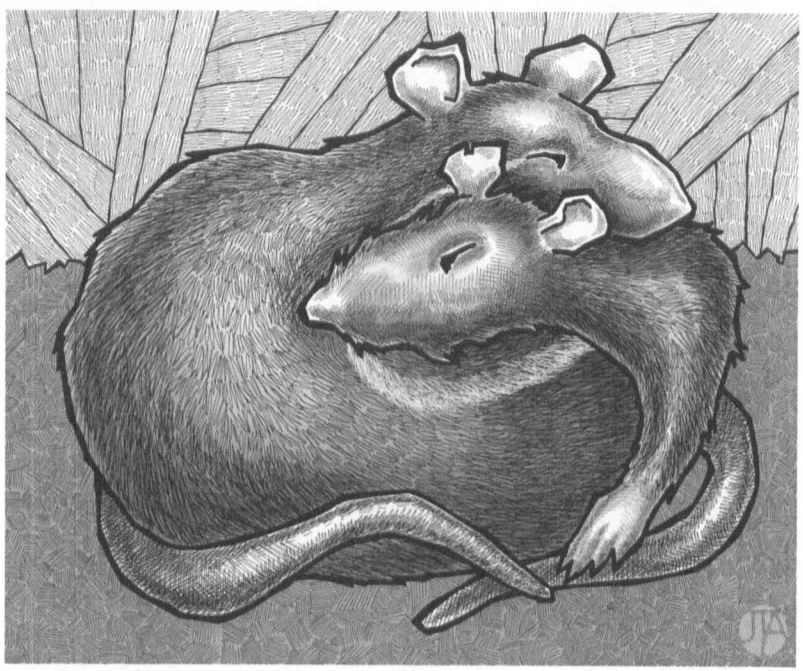

They had not talked about Dayrunner in the many days that had passed since the battle. It was almost as though they were afraid that by saying his name they might somehow bring him back. It had taken a great effort of will for Wainscot to ask the question, but he overcame his reticence because he felt that they needed to talk about the old Captain if they were to ever be truly rid of him.

There was silence for a moment as they all reluctantly allowed Dayrunner to emerge from the shadow of their thoughts. He had not been completely out of any of their minds for a moment since his fall, but they had all been hesitant to confront their memories of him.

Finally, Mizzen said, "No, he didn't survive, Laddie."

"No, he didn't," agreed Marlinspike.

"But how do you know?" asked Wainscot.

"I saw him fall," said Mizzen.

"Moon fell," Wainscot pointed out. "She survived."

"He was in two pieces. He isn't coming back."

Those few words, spoken at last, were all that they needed to put Dayrunner behind them.

Suddenly, Wainscot lifted his head and sniffed the air. An errant wisp of odour tickled his nose. It was maddeningly familiar but it was a moment before he could place it. Then he knew it. Home.

Even as deep as they were in the holds, a teasing tendril of fresh air from the breezes that washed across the ship had wound its way down to them. It brought with it the scent of land, but as Wainscot's nose confirmed, not just any land. The *Heloise* had returned to his home, to the city of the Nest.

"Home," he said, rising to his feet.

Now Moon smelled it too, and she stood beside him. "Not home," she said. "Your home is here on the *Heloise*. Here with us." She lowered her eyes. "With me."

Even as he thought with longing of his now half-forgotten life with Scuffle, Wainscot knew that Moon was right. There was no longer anything for him in the Nest. Everything that he loved was now aboard the ship.

"Yes," he said, turning to look into Moon's eyes. "You're right. I am home." He stood up and stretched. Moon watched him.

He *was* home. The *Heloise* was where he belonged, and where he would belong until the day he died, but still he could not help thinking of Scuffle. She was dead—he was almost certain of it—but Moon had been dead too, yet here she was, back with him. Perhaps Scuffle...

He shook his head, crushing the hope that was trying to take root in his mind. The *Heloise* was home, and Moon, Mizzen, Marlinspike, and the others were family. They were his world now, and all that he could allow to matter to him.

He turned to his new family. "Right now I'm so hungry I can't think straight," he said. "Who's for a trip to the breadroom?"

"Sounds good," said Moon, "But first, how about a story?"

THE END

ENDNOTES

4. AN INNOCENT ABOARD

1. See Appendix 1 for the story of Chewtooth and the Vixen

14. SKIRMISH

1. See Appendix 2 for the full story of The Rat Who Wanted To Fly

Appendix 1 - Chewtooth and the Vixen

As told by Wainscot

Chewtooth and Barge were wanderers. A clan of two, they rejected the safety, security, and companionship of the nest for the pleasures offered by the ratways of the wider world. As Chewtooth had done when he was on his own, they let their paws make their decisions for them. They were always on the move: drifting from place to place, stopping to eat when there was food, and walking with empty bellies when there was not.

Everywhere they went, they met rats. Town rats and country rats, welcoming rats and suspicious rats, and the two loved to hear the tales the strangers had to tell. Most of them talked about food—was there ever a rat who didn't love to talk about food?—but they also told the stories of their clans and ancestors, of great battles fought, of hardships suffered.

As the two companions wandered, a character called the Fox began to appear in more and more of the rat's stories. "Have you met the Fox?" the strangers would ask, and when the two said no, would tell tales of the cleverness of the Fox. "He's a trickster, you know," they would say. "None cleverer."

Sorry? What's a fox? You've never heard of a fox? Well... it's a dog, I suppose, but it doesn't run with Men the way a dog usually does. Thinks for itself too, which a dog never does. It eats rats, if it can catch them, although I've heard that it prefers rabbits.

This particular fox, however, was said to be a friend to the rats of the area—I expect there's another story there, but I've never heard it. What I do know is that the rats considered it quite the most cunning creature in the whole world, and apparently the Fox shared their opinion.

Now, as you probably know, Chewtooth himself was no slouch when it came to cleverness, and he listened to the stories about the fox with skepticism. As he and Barge wandered on, meeting more rats, and hearing more tales about the Fox, he decided that he very much wanted to meet this paragon of cunning.

Not wanting to sing his own praises, he always left it to Barge to speak for him when they met new rats.

"This fox, then," Barge said to the next rat who told them about the trickster, "he's a clever one?'

"The cleverest," said the stranger.

"Clever as a rat?"

"Without a doubt."

"Clever as my friend, Chewtooth, here?" Barge pressed.

The stranger looked Chewtooth up and down. "What's so special about him?" he asked.

"He's *the* Chewtooth. Chewtooth the Liar."

"Never heard of him."

"I'm not surprised—I just made up that Liar bit, but whether you've heard of him or not, Chewtooth is the cunningest rat you'll ever meet."

The stranger snorted. "So you say," he said.

"You'll see. Where's this fox, then?"

The stranger just laughed and scuttled away.

The next two rats they met reacted the same way, but the one after that appraised them for several breaths before saying, "You want to meet the Fox, do you?"

"Yes," said Barge.

"But will he want to meet you? He might just decide to eat you."

"I guess we'll have to see."

"Right then. What you want to do is walk in that direction," said the stranger, gesturing with her nose, "until you smell the river ahead of you. It will probably take the better part of the day."

"And then?" asked Barge.

"And then you'll be far enough away from me that I won't be bothered by your nonsense any more. Meet the Fox, indeed."

Barge took a step toward the stranger. "You might have noticed that I'm considerably larger than you," he said, "and that I'm beginning to get annoyed."

"All right, all right. Don't get your tail in a knot. Do as I say and walk in that direction, all the way into the trees on the other side of the valley. That's where the Fox generally hunts. His burrow is on the banks of the stream that runs through the wood. I'd wait until dark, if I were you. He sleeps during the day, and you don't want to wake him up." With that, the stranger turned away. "I don't expect we'll be seeing you two again," she said over her shoulder.

It was fully dark by the time Chewtooth and Barge came to the stream. Exploring its banks, they found the mouth of something that looked very much like a fox's den. They hesitated before entering.

"Is this a good idea?" asked Barge.

"When have we ever worried about whether something was a good idea before we did it?" asked Chewtooth. He walked into the opening. Barge followed.

The tunnel, wide enough for the two rats to walk side by side, sloped down at a gentle angle. They could easily see by the glow of moonlight from the opening behind them, and were some twenty lengths into the burrow when it widened into a sleeping chamber. The smell of fox hung heavily in the air.

"Looks like no one's home," said Barge.

Something large then moved into the mouth of the burrow behind them, blocking the moonlight, and casting the two rats in darkness. A cloud of musky odour washed over them.

"Wrong," said a voice in a low half-growl. "I do hope you have a good reason for being in my den. Most rats show better judgement."

Chewtooth turned, and settled his rump to the floor of the tunnel. He didn't say a word.

"In fact," said the voice, "I'm having trouble thinking of anything more stupid than a rat entering my home. And here are two of them. What makes you think you'll be getting out of here?"

"What makes you think I want to?" asked Chewtooth. His eyes

were adjusting to the gloom, and he could just make out the glint of the fox's eyes. "I came to see the Fox, and unless I miss my bet, here you are."

"Interesting, little rat. But it's the Vixen, not the Fox."

"Vixen, is it?" said Chewtooth.

"Then why do they call you the Fox?" asked Barge.

"Who?"

"The rats around here," said Barge.

"They're rats," said the Vixen with a contemptuous sniff. "What do they know?"

"So," said Chewtooth, "I'm thinking that if they're wrong about that, then they're likely also wrong about what else they say about you."

"And what else do they say about me?"

"That you're the cleverest," said Chewtooth.

"Oh, they aren't wrong about that," the Vixen said smugly.

"And that you're a friend to the rats," Barge added. "They say you don't eat them."

"Well, we'll see about that."

"So, they're wrong about your gender, they're wrong about you not eating them," said Chewtooth, "and I know for a fact that they're wrong about you being the cleverest. It seems to me that the rats around here aren't the most reliable sources of information."

"Probably not," said the Vixen, "but why do you say that I'm not the cleverest? Don't I outwit the dogs every time they're on my trail? Don't I think my way past every trap the farmer sets to keep me out of his chicken coops? Most tellingly, isn't it me who tricks the sun into rising every morning?"

Chewtooth laughed. "You'll have to tell me how you do that some time. No, I'm sure you're clever—maybe *very* clever— but as for being the clever*est,* how can you be, when I am?"

"And what have you done that's so impressive?" asked the Vixen.

Chewtooth rattled off a litany of his accomplishments, starting with his adventure with the ginger cats, and following with a series of other exploits that may or may not have happened. He was called the Liar, after all, or soon would be.

"So you can see why I wanted to meet you," he concluded. "We can't both be the cleverest."

"I could just eat you," said the Vixen. "Then, there'd be no question."

"You could, but then you'd always wonder if I was right. I think this calls for a contest of some sort."

"Riddles," said the Vixen. "I've always been fond of those. We could give each other riddles, and whoever can't guess the solutions loses."

"Riddles?" scoffed Chewtooth. "Where's the danger in riddles? We need something with higher stakes."

"I could eat you if you lose, if that would help."

"Well, that would be a danger for me, but what about you? You need to have something at stake too."

"You could eat me if I lose."

"Tempting, but I suspect that you might have second thoughts if it came to it. No, we'll just have to come up with something else."

He lowered his head, closed his eyes, and began to think. The Vixen did the same.

"Got it," said Chewtooth, after the passing of a dozen breaths. "You claim that you trick the Sun into coming up every morning, yes?"

"Yes," said the Vixen.

"So tomorrow, trick it into coming up in the middle of the night."

"That would confirm my cleverness, but would do nothing to establish yours. Anyway, I thought you wanted higher stakes. There's no risk in your challenge."

"Dogs, then," said Chewtooth. "Something with dogs. They're your enemies, right?"

"Yes they are. As cats are yours."

"As cats are mine," agreed Chewtooth. "So something with both dogs and cats." He thought for a moment. "I have it," he said.

"Yes?" said the Vixen.

"There's a farm, correct? With a dog and a cat?"

"Yes."

"Then it's easy. I'll convince the dog to bring you a chicken from the farm and lay it at your feet. You'll do the same for me with the cat and some nice fresh cheese. Whoever is suc-cessful is the cleverest."

"And if we both succeed?" asked the Vixen.

"We won't."

"All right. I agree," said the Vixen. A look of cunning flitted across her face. "Who goes first?"

Chewtooth looked up at the roof of the den, considering. "I'm the challenger," he said. "It's only fair that I go first."

The Vixen grinned. "Agreed."

"So, show me where this farm is."

After some discussion, they worked out the details of the challenge. The Vixen would wait in a small meadow near the farm at dawn the next morning. She would sit beside the large yew tree that grew at its centre and wait for Chewtooth, the dog, and the dog's gift. The follow-ing morning, Chewtooth would sit in the same place, and wait for the cat and the cheese. The whole time that they discussed these arrangements, the Vixen grinned her wide foxy grin.

A little while later, when the Vixen had left them for a night's hunting, Chewtooth and Barge huddled together in the safety of a bramble hedge.

"And you think this is a good idea?" asked Barge.

"I think it's an excellent idea," said Chewtooth.

"It's going to get you killed."

Chewtooth shrugged. "Likely."

"How are you going to talk the dog into doing this for you?"

"Leave that to me."

Barge sighed. "All right," he said. What do you want me to do?"

"I'll show you."

The sun was just beginning to rise above the roofs of the farm, its rays painting the tops of the trees at the edge of the meadow a warm red. The fox sat in the allotted spot beside the yew tree, looking in the direction of the low hedge that delineated the edge of the meadow, beyond which lay the farm. She was still grinning.

Barge sat beside her.

"You know" she said. "I don't think your Chewtooth is quite as clever as he thinks he is."

"No?" asked Barge. "What makes you say that?"

"Well, if he'd taken the time to look into it, he'd have found that the dog on that farm is more of a ratter than a fox hunter. He'll gobble up your little friend the moment he sees him."

"We shall see."

"Yes we shall."

They didn't have long to wait.

Chewtooth's arrival was heralded by a rustling in the hedgerow. A moment later, the rat burst from the shrubbery at a full run. He bore straight at the Vixen. The moment Chewtooth appeared, Barge was on the move too. He skittered in front of the startled Vixen and dove into the undergrowth at the base of the yew tree.

"What are you—?" said the Vixen, turning her head to watch Barge. She swivelled back to face the oncoming Chewtooth. "Where's the dog?"

As if in answer, the dog hurtled from the hedge in a shower of twigs and leaves. Black fur bristling in fury, it tore into the meadow in pursuit of the fleeing Chewtooth. Chewtooth changed the direction of his flight and angled toward the yew tree. In a flash, he disappeared into the hole that Barge had dug during the night. Barge waited for him in the darkness.

The Vixen had no such refuge, however; just as she was turning to flee, the dog drove into her. It may have been a ratter, not a fox hunter, but it was big enough for the job. It bowled the Vixen over, and they tumbled through the low grass in a snarling ball of black and orange fur.

In the hole, Chewtooth and Barge heard the thump of impact and a shriek of vulpine terror, followed by the rapid patter of running feet.

Chewtooth poked his head out and saw the Vixen's tail disappearing into the undergrowth on the far side of the meadow, the dog only a couple of strides behind.

"Who's cleverer now? He called after the pair as the dog vanished into the woods.

Later, as they were moving on, leaving the area to seek adventure elsewhere, Chewtooth and Barge happened to meet the rat who had told them where to find the Vixen.

"You're still alive, then, are you?" she said, genuinely surprised.

"So it would seem," said Chewtooth.

"The Fox didn't eat you."

Barge laughed.

"Vixen," corrected Chewtooth.

"What?" asked the rat.

"Never mind. No, the Fox didn't eat me."

"And did you find out who is the cleverest?"

"He certainly did," said Barge.

"And it's you?"

Barge laughed again.

"I don't believe you," said the rat. "What proof do you have?"

"That's the thing about cleverness," said Chewtooth. "It doesn't need to be proven. It just is."

With that, the two turned and ambled away. The other rat watched them go, shaking her head.

Appendix 2

The Rat Who Wanted to Fly
As told by Wainscot

Now there are many things that rats were never meant to do. We were never meant to climb trees like squirrels, or swim in the water like fish, or hunt the night like cats, or do any of the ridiculous things that Men do. Oh, we *can* climb, and we *can* swim, and there isn't a cat alive that can teach us anything about cunning—but these are not our ways. And as for the things that Men do... Well, almost everything about them is completely incomprehensible, so of course their ways were never meant for us. We were meant to do what rats were meant to do, and nothing more.

We were certainly never meant to fly.

Most rats don't want to, don't even dream of it, but Crunchbeetle did. He very much wanted to fly.

To look at him, you wouldn't have thought that there was anything very unusual about Crunchbeetle. He had only just reached the full weight of adulthood, but had yet to mate and had not established his position in the clan. He was restless, which is typical for a young rat looking to find his place in the world; he lacked confidence, but that was only to be expected of a youngster who still didn't know himself very well. While you might not have thought that there was anything unusual about him, just as you might not have thought that there was anything unusual about his clan, you would have been wrong in both cases, as you'll see in a moment.

Because he was still finding his way, Crunchbeetle spent most of his time by himself. He was born during the off-season, so there were few rats of his own age in the clan and he had grown up out of step with the other youngsters. He did not often join the pups in play any more—he considered himself a little too old for that now—but he wasn't yet comfortable with the older rats. The adults, for their part, didn't make any effort to spend time with him, but they didn't deliberately avoid him either. They didn't think badly of him, they just didn't think of him at all. He was just there: one of the many young rats who might or might not make a name for themselves if given enough time. I suppose you shiprats would say he was 'hull down beyond the horizon'.

Crunchbeetle did have one friend, though—a fellow named Orn. Orn was several seasons older and also a loner. Now, most of the clan thought Orn very dull, perhaps even a little backwards. He spoke slowly and moved only when necessary. While he was not truly stupid, he always appeared to be a little off because he never actually seemed to do anything, except hunt for a certain mushroom of which he was particularly fond. I suppose it was just that he seldom saw a reason to hurry, and he preferred to imagine his adventures than to live them. He was happy in his dreamy solitude, and saw a kindred spirit in Crunchbeetle. They were united by their relative invisibility, and although the two were not always in each other's company, they were always available should either feel the need for companionship.

However, there was one significant difference between them. While Orn was perfectly happy to live out his life on the fringes of the clan's society, Crunchbeetle was not. You see, Crunchbeetle was a rat with ambition—he knew that he wanted to be *someone*. He wanted future storytellers to thrill the young rats of the clan with tales of 'Crunchbeetle the Brave' or 'Crunchbeetle the Wise'. He wanted cries of "tell us the tale of Crunchbeetle and the Long-nosed Newt" or "It's been a long time since I've heard the one about Crunchbeetle and the Hanging Cheese" to echo around the nest long after he was gone from the world. In truth, he wanted to be the legendary Chewtooth.

Unfortunately there was little opportunity for adventure in Crunchbeetle's world. His ability to play the hero was limited to the landscape of his imagination.

And this is where we get to what was unusual about Crunchbeetle's clan.

The clan lived in a large shed on a sprawling farm, and life was very good for them. The farm was flourishing, and there was always plenty to eat because the rats had come to an understanding with the farmer. They didn't take any more of his food than they needed, didn't despoil what they didn't eat, and didn't damage his property. In fact, they had gone so far as to establish laws that governed how they behaved. It was forbidden, for example, for them to eat any crops that were still on the stem, to expand their nest beyond the limits of the shed, or to leave droppings or pass water in certain parts of the farm.

Now this may sound like a very odd way for rats to behave, and it was. We rats don't change our ways just to please Men, as you know, and we often go out of our way to torment them. We need them, it's true, but we take what we want, and we never ask permission.

But Crunchbeetle's clan had a good reason for doing what they did. I'm not saying I agree with them—in fact I think they lost far more than they gained in giving up a part of their essential 'ratness'— but my feelings are irrelevant to this tale. They did what they did, and they thought that what they got back from the farmer was well worth the price. You see, what he gave them was nothing. That is, in exchange for their respecting his crops and property, the farmer left the clan completely alone. He didn't set traps, didn't allow cats on the farm, and kept only large, stupid dogs that had as much chance of catching a rat as a rat has of, well, flying.

This made life in the nest safe and quiet, but more than a little dull. There was no adventure to be had. Adventure was something that happened only in stories, and never intruded into the clan's quiet existence, which left Crunchbeetle with something of a problem. He needed adventure. He needed it to achieve the fame he desired, but how could he find it within the restrictive confines of the clan's rules? He couldn't, so he would have to break a law. If he wanted to be remembered, truly remembered, it would have to be a really important law.

Luckily for him there was one law that was more important than all the others. It was so important that if a rat were to break it, he would be a hero—or be banished from the clan, which to Crunchbeetle's mind was just as good, because in either case his fame would be assured.

This law, this most important law—the one that every rat in the clan knew from the day they were weaned—was that they were never to touch the farmer's honey.

The farmer kept honeybees, you see, and for reasons beyond the understanding of the clan, he valued their honey beyond anything else in the world. He had row upon row of white wooden hives in which his bees lived and toiled, and around these gleaming treasure boxes he had erected a wall of sheetmetal so high and smooth that no rat could ever hope to scale it. Beneath the wall, he had buried heavy wire mesh so that no rat could tunnel under it. He had even gone so far as to chop down all the nearby trees so that no rat could drop down onto the hives from above. He had taken every conceivable precaution to keep the rats away from his honey, but they were all unnecessary, for the clan had the law, and it was unthinkable that any of them would break it.

There was not a rat among them who had experienced the pleasure of honey's delectable sweetness, and none of them ever expected to. They all dreamed of it, and every one of them secretly devised plans by which they might steal a honeycomb or two, but none did more than dream and plan. The fine balance of their compact with the farmer hinged upon honey; while other rules might be broken, honey was sacrosanct, and every rat knew it.

Crunchbeetle knew it too, but he was young, daring, and if truth be known, not very bright. He decided to steal some honey. *That* would get his clan to notice him. Crunchbeetle the Honeythief—it had a heroic ring to it. Or better still, Crunchbeetle, Conqueror of Bees. Yes, they'd remember him for sure.

He decided to time the theft so that he could march into the next Council meeting with his prize between his teeth and lay it at the feet of the councilrats. Let them try to ignore him after that.

The problem—and this was the only flaw in his plan, as far as he could see—was that he had no idea of how to go about stealing the honey.

For two days he pondered the problem, looking at it from every angle. He even banged his head against the ground in an attempt to shake loose some ideas, but all that he got from the exercise was a headache. The task was obviously beyond him. He would have to ask Orn.

He found his friend lying on his back in a patch of sun beside the small stream that ran through the farmyard. The older rat was gazing vacantly at the leaves of the trees as they swayed gently in the breeze above him. He was completely exposed, and if a predator had happened on him, it would have gone very badly indeed, but that wasn't the sort of thing that worried Orn. How he managed to survive from day to day was a mystery to most of the clan, but Crunchbeetle wasn't baffled by Orn's apparent stupidity; instead, he was impressed. He knew that his friend, as a serious thinker, didn't waste valuable pondering time on such trivialities as personal safety.

But Crunchbeetle did worry about being eaten, so he looked around carefully, assuring himself that the area was free of foxes, weasels, or cats, before dropping down onto the warm turf beside Orn.

He rolled onto his back and stared up, wondering what it was about the leaves that his friend found so fascinating. They were pretty enough—their shiny undersides reflecting back the points of light that sparkled off the surface of the stream—but their rhythmic swaying made him dizzy. No doubt this mesmerizing effect was leading Orn to great and profound thought.

Crunchbeetle turned on his side, and said, "Orn?"

"Huh?" replied Orn, after several heartbeats. Apparently all the deep thinking was making him drowsy. He sounded half asleep.

"Orn, I need your thoughts about something."

"Huh?" said Orn again.

"I need to know how to get into the hive enclosure. I need to get to the honey."

Orn said nothing. Crunchbeetle waited patiently. He knew that his friend was applying his fine brain to the problem.

Orn began to snore.

"Orn," said Crunchbeetle loudly, nudging him with the point of his snout.

"Huh?" said Orn, starting awake.

"The hive enclosure. Do you think there's a way into the enclosure?"

With a soft sigh, Orn rolled onto his side and looked at Crunchbeetle. His eyes were pointing in different directions, and it was a moment before they focused.

"Oh, good morning Crunchbeetle," he said.

"Orn, please think for me. How is it possible to get into the hive enclosure?"

Orn stared at Crunchbeetle. He licked his lips and yawned. "You want to get into the hive enclosure?"

"Yes"

"Isn't that forbidden?"

"Yes"

"Wouldn't there be trouble if you broke the law?"

"Yes."

"Oh." This did not bother Orn—very little did. "Does anyone get into the enclosure?" he asked.

"The farmer does, I suppose. And the bees." Crunchbeetle was not entirely satisfied with the way the conversation was going.

"Then go in the same way the bees do," said Orn, rolling back to resume his contemplation of the trees.

"But they fly in," said Crunchbeetle.

"Then you'll have to fly in too."

"How?"

Orn began to snore again.

Two days later, Crunchbeetle returned to the stream. He found Orn, still on his back and still gazing heavy-lidded at the leaves. Crunchbeetle wondered whether his friend had moved from the spot. *Surely he must eat*, he thought, and might have asked about it, but he had more important things on his mind.

"Orn," he said, "how can I fly?"

"Huh?" said Orn.

Eventually, after several attempts, Crunchbeetle managed to get Orn to focus on the question.

"Why do you want to fly?" asked Orn.

"To get into the hive enclosure."

"Isn't that forbidden?"

"Never mind that," said Crunchbeetle. "Just tell me how I can fly."

Orn was quiet for some time. Crunchbeetle considered the absence of snoring promising, since it probably meant that his friend was pondering the problem.

Eventually, Orn said, "Bees can fly, can't they?"

"Yes."

"Then you must swallow bees. Many bees. With all of those bees inside you, you'll be able to fly."

"Swallow bees?" Crunchbeetle was sceptical. "But surely if I swallow bees, they'll sting me from the inside?"

"Flies then. I don't care," said Orn. He closed his eyes and began to snore again.

Swallow flies. Of course. It was brilliant, yet simple. Crunchbeetle resolved to put the plan into action the very next day.

Finding flies on a farm is never difficult, and early the next morning Crunchbeetle set out for the barn where the farmer kept his dairy cows. Where there are cows, there is dung, and where there is dung, there are flies.

He settled next to a particularly steamy pile and snapped at one of the three flies buzzing about it. He missed. He tried again, and then again, but kept missing. After countless attempts, he discovered that the trick was not to snap at where the flies were, but at where they would be.

Once he had made this discovery it was only a moment's work for him to swallow all three flies. The temptation to chew was almost overwhelming, but he resisted, and was gratified to feel all three flies buzzing angrily in his stomach.

He made a couple of small, tentative hops, but if he were any lighter, it was not enough to notice.

More flies, he thought, and settled down to wait for them to arrive at the pile of dung. Before the day was half over, he had swallowed some thirty or forty flies. There was a buzzing, shifting, squirming ball of the things inside him, and he doubted if there was room for any more.

If these aren't enough, he thought, *I'll have to try something else.*

Taking a deep breath, he bent his legs and made a mighty leap straight up into the air. He started to drop back to earth, but just before his feet made contact, he stopped. Wobbling slightly, he floated a tail's width above the straw-scattered floor of the barn.

Great rattraps, it works, he thought. *That Orn is a genius. Now, it's off to the hives for me.*

Then he discovered the second flaw in his plan. He had no idea of how to make the flies fly in the direction he wanted. In fact he had no idea of how to make them fly at all. At present, they were just hovering.

The thing to do, he knew, was to go to Orn and present him with this new problem, but he wasn't quite sure how to do that. His feet dangled uselessly, with the tips of his claws not quite touching the floor. He was trapped.

He began to move his legs rapidly, running in place, but that only made him rock from side to side. Panicking, he swung his tail about wildly. It struck the ground a resounding thump, and the impact jarred his body. The shock must have startled the flies, because the buzzing in his stomach suddenly increased, and he found himself hurtling toward the roof of the barn. He bounced off a beam, fetching himself a stinging crack on the head in the process, and then changed direction, angling away to ricochet off a startled cow.

Now I don't know how long Crunchbeetle spent bouncing about the inside of the barn, but by the time his haphazardly hurtling body happened upon an open window and sailed out into the sun-drenched yard, he was only partially conscious.

The flies, feeling the heat of the morning sun through his body, stopped. Once again Crunchbeetle hung motionless in the air. He shook his head, trying to regain his senses, and eventually the fog in his mind dissipated. He was many rat-lengths above the ground, and he gazed in wonder at the farm laid out below him. Everything looked different from this new perspective, and it took a moment for him to orient himself.

There it was, below and to the right; the object of his mission, the hive enclosure.

"Right, you stupid flies," he said out loud. Perhaps they would respond to direct orders. "Turn right and go down closer to the ground."

Nothing happened.

As he was hanging suspended, one of his clanmates wandered across the yard and happened to look up. The newcomer stared in open-mouthed disbelief for a few breaths. He then scurried off to summon some of his fellows, probably to see if they too could see a rat floating in the air above the farm.

When the rat returned with a small group of clanmates, Crunchbeetle was still hanging in place, helpless and frustrated.

"Help!" he cried.

At the sound the flies began to move again. Crunchbeetle soared across the yard away from the barn. The watching rats trotted after him, chattering excitedly.

For an instant, Crunchbeetle was heartened to see that he was heading in the right direction. His flight was taking him directly toward the centre of the hive enclosure. Then his trajectory changed, and suddenly he was arrowing toward the ground. He struck in a cloud of dust, and the impact whacked a loud squeak out of him. Scrabbling frantically at the earth, he tried to hold himself down, but was soon airborne again with nothing to show for his efforts but four pawfuls of dirt.

He hurtled toward the hives, soaring across the sheetmetal wall with scant clearance to spare. He was halfway across the enclosure when he smashed into the side of one of the hive boxes. With a bone-rattling thump he knocked the hive from its supporting table, and he and it fell to the ground together. The box shattered when it struck, and Crunchbeetle found himself lying half-stunned in a sticky mass of honey, splinters, and very angry bees.

The flies recovered swiftly, and with a rising buzz began to pull Crunchbeetle skyward. Leaving dirt and honey footprints smeared across the white surface of the flattened hive, he clawed desperately to remain earthbound, but to no avail. He lofted into the air again.

Now not too far from the farm, on the other side of a small river, lay a fair-sized village, and just beyond that was a large midden-heap. Even deep in Crunchbeetle's stomach, the flies could feel the allure of the rotting garbage and made their way eagerly toward it.

On the ground, the watching rats stared dumbfounded as Crunchbeetle, dripping honey and trailing a cloud of angry bees, dwindled into the distance.

"Wasn't that Crunchbottle?" asked one of them.

"Who?" asked another.

Crunchbeetle never returned to his clan. Orn hardly noticed that he was gone. There were, after all, leaves to study.

Of course, things were never the same again after Crunchbeetle's spectacular departure. The farmer discovered the shattered hive, saw the dirty pawprints, and promptly left to get some cats.

The clan stayed on at the farm, but were forced to slip back into the old ways of stealth, cunning, and theft. It was difficult for them at first, for over the generations they had lost many of the skills that they needed to survive. Many died in those hard first days, but in time they learned to be rats again; I venture to say that in the end they were happier this way. After all, everyone knows that food tastes better when it's stolen.

As for Crunchbeetle, he was never seen by his clan again, but he was remembered in their stories. He was known as either 'Crunchbeetle of the Air', or 'that Idiot Crunchbeetle' depending upon the teller of the tale. I suppose that either would have satisfied him.

ABOUT THE AUTHOR

Terry Addington lives in the quaint village of Unionville, Canada, with his wife, Tobey, and their two Dalmatians. When he's not writing about rodents, Terry loves to draw, revisit favourite vintage movies, and read about anything and everything. And drink tea, of course.

Website: jterryaddington.com
Instagram: instagram.com/jterryaddington
Facebook: facebook.com/terry.addington.12/

www.ingramcontent.com/pod-product-compliance
Lightning Source LLC
Chambersburg PA
CBHW060523030726
47498CB00004B/1056